MURDER ON THE AIR

MURDER ON THE AIR

Ric Meyers

THE MYSTERIOUS PRESS

New York • London • Tokyo • Sweden

Mysterious Press books are published in association with Warner Books, Inc.

The Mysterious Press, 129 West 56th Street, New York, N.Y. 10019

Printed in the United States of America
First Trade Printing: April 1989

10 9 8 7 6 5 4 3 2 1

Library of Congress Cataloging-in-Publication Data

Meyers, Richard, 1953–
Murder on the air / Ric Meyers.
304 pp.
ISBN 0-89296-977-6
I. Title.
PS3563.E96M87 1989 88-31311
813'.54—dc19 CIP

DEDICATION

For Stuart Stewart

Every family's got its black sheep . . . this one's mine.

ACKNOWLEDGMENTS

On the left coast:
William Guest
Virginia Aalko
Craig Strete
Philip DeGuere
Bill Connolly
Jerry Neeley

On the right coast:
Chris Steinbrunner
Art Bourgeau
Patricia J. MacDonald
William L. DeAndrea
Orania Papazoglou

Somewhere in between:
Max Allan Collins
Francis M. Nevins

Hard- and software:
Michelle M. Terriault
William B. Chaplinsky
The gang at TRW

The Head Office:
Dominick Abel
Mike Seidman
Otto Penzler

My incredible, ultimate sponsor, Bill Malloy.
Let's take lunch and not give it back.

CONTENTS

FOREWORD

WHY DO PEOPLE HAVE TO DIE?

It's the ultimate question, and one reason for *Murder on the Air*.

Mortality. And fear. We are born knowing it's a dead-end trip. And if we don't know then, then we know soon afterward. Of all the creatures on earth, we are the only ones who are aware of our own mortality. It's what sets us apart and gives us an excuse for the extraordinary things we do. It goes a long way toward explaining the fascinating and tragic aspects of our lives—why we smoke and drink and eat and drive things we know are dangerous.

If this theory is followed far enough, it leads to another: all entertainment exists to deal with this fear of mortality. On one hand, some entertainment makes us forget. People have even studied laughter, attempting to understand its cause and basis. I have a modest proposal. Laughter is our only real escape from fear of mortality. In the moment it takes us to laugh, death is forgotten.

That, however, does not explain the tragedy, or, more specifically, the murder mystery. If entertainment is a shield, why is a genre which exploits fear so popular? An immediate response is that in confronting the fear, we conquer it. Another is that our own pain is lessened by watching another's greater pain. The "somebody else" theorem is an explanation in which there is no solace. That can't be the best reason this genre is so successful.

My first memory of television was witnessing a pretty blonde nurse attacked and dragged into a car. Hardly an auspicious beginning. Fleeting memories of blazing guns and people falling crowd my mind as I write this. I played cowboys and Indians, then cops and robbers, then spy and counter-spy as I grew up. I cherish these memories. I love those television shows. I wrote an entire book glorifying them.

Not once did I think why . . . until now.

So, this is another book glorifying those shows. But while *TV Detectives* showed who, what, when, and where, this work says how. And it asks why. This volume examines the most successful and influential crime shows in the history of the medium. But this time, that influence doesn't stop at other television programs. It extends to the audience.

Don't worry. I don't dwell on the dying bodies. They're so much wood, fodder for the flashing guns and flying bullets. As a kid, I only had eyes for the men clutching those fire-spitting weapons. Yes, *men*. White men with set expressions, eyes glittering with stage light and righteousness. They attracted me because they knew what they were doing, took care of business, were never wrong, and never missed.

These heroes made me forget mortality. They righted wrongs. They seemed to embody justice and a certain cosmic truth: if you work hard enough and your cause is just, then you can win, no matter what the odds.

What did I know? I was a child.

What I know now is that television is a hungry medium. It eats everything . . . and an hour later it's hungry again. People slave their entire lives to keep the starving monster fed—and a day later, most of that work is forgotten. The set yells "feed me" and the process begins again. It is little wonder that television devours some of its most distinctive contributors, turns them into satires of themselves, then kills them—often at an early age. Rod Serling. Jack Webb.

I was left with misleading, but comfortable, memories of my favorites. My perception was fuzzy; indistinct; out of focus. I didn't really remember the plots. Maybe I could recall a few stories, a handful of scenes; but upon research, I found even those recollections inaccurate. But I did remember the characters—those heroes who saved my life when I was a lonely, imaginative child. I remember their passionate goals and compassionate desires.

It is important to know that good triumphs, even if it's only in fantasy. That's the significance of *Murder on the Air*. Television is so pervasive and encompassing, it's easy to forget it is also an art form. It is the most forgettable art form, which makes the marking of its greatest accomplishments so necessary.

My deepest thanks go out to everyone who granted me interviews: Ralph Bellamy, Roy Huggins, Craig Stevens, Harold Gast, Buddy Ebsen, Mike Connors, Harvey Frand, Robert Shayne, Donald Bellisario, Peter Fischer, and William Link. I also want to mark the passing of two other greats of the medium who died before this book was published: Richard Levinson and Howard Rodman. Their kindness and cooperation was heartfelt and appreciated.

I tried to make the result a book for the television fan, so we can share fond memories; for the innocent bystander, to see how television is shaped; and for the concerned critic, to explain why these murder mysteries succeed . . . and endure.

The television mystery, be it private eye or cop show, won't go away, no matter how artificial it seems or redundant it gets. It is sustained, nurtured, and perfected in this medium, while it struggles on stage and in cinema. It is exciting, both on a superficial action level, and in that the greatest TV detectives are the last of a breed—the person who seeks the truth no matter what the odds.

Finally, like it or not, the television mystery is an important part of our folklore and a telling piece of American popular culture. We can all be the TV detective now, on an investigation into a beloved genre that's been in nearly everyone's home for forty years.

Turn the page. Maybe we can forget mortality for a while.

CHAPTER

The Visible Hand

"Come out here with your hands up!"

—Martin Kane

TELEVISION'S FIRST STAR WAS FELIX THE CAT. IN A 1928 EXPERIMENT, A three-dimensional model of the comic strip and cartoon character was placed on a turntable and its image was transmitted from New York to Kansas by the then infant National Broadcasting Company. The fuzzy, heavily lined picture hardly seemed to place this invention in the same category as the light bulb or the telephone, but in two decades television had made great strides. Even then, however, TV was a joke.

The broadcasting schedule for 1948 gave new meaning to the term "mindless entertainment." It had yet to become even the visual equivalent of radio—the technology was too limited for that. Radio drama and comedy involved the listener's imagination. Doomsayers maintained that television could never equal the mind's eye. The audience's imagination would never be engaged the way radio veterans Fred Allen, Orson Welles, or Jack Webb could engage their audience.

So television had to do with the likes of pseudo-sports (wrestling and roller derby) and stagnant game shows until many saw the promise inherent in the new form. The first to pave the way were baggy-pants comedians with nowhere else to go once vaudeville died, and fading cowboy movie stars who channeled dozens of their grade-B, sixty-minute sagebrush sagas onto the tube.

In the beginning were three major networks—the National Broadcasting Company, the Columbia Broadcasting System, and the American

Broadcasting Companies—but the first to experiment with transposing radio detective dramas onto TV was the long forgotten DuMont Television Network, owned by the Allen B. DuMont Laboratories and Paramount Pictures. Their first step was tentative.

In 1948 they presented *They Stand Accused*, a combination dramatization and game show presided over by Illinois Assistant Attorney General William Wines. It featured real judges and lawyers in addition to actors and contestants. The professionals re-created the trial, and the amateurs tried to win prizes by guessing the outcome. Variations of this court show have prospered to this day—turning real-life suffering into entertainment.

But it was NBC who officially opened the floodgates with the unassuming *Barney Blake, Police Reporter*, the first official detective series, starring Gene O'Donnell as the intrepid interviewer of criminals and

Judy Parrish played the hero's girl, Gene O'Donnell played the hero, and Joan Arliss (*right*) played various parts on *Barney Blake: Police Reporter*.

victims. Although a fairly static and talky half hour, presented live, it was very important for a very curious reason. Its sponsor was the American Tobacco Company. And American tobacco companies loved television.

It's no secret that television exists for commercials. The more successful a series is, the more soap it sells. But in the days just after World War II, the sponsor was also the mightiest creative source. It had financed the technology and paid the series' bills, so all bowed before it. In the same way new continents were opened by exploring traders in the 1600's, television was opened by visionary cigarette peddlers. It was the cough heard round the world.

The U.S. Tobacco Company was so impressed by television's ability to reach into American homes with images as well as sound that they got behind the medium with millions. They saw the possibilities immediately. TV was the infant offspring of both radio and the movies. They wanted to sell a lot of product, so they needed a more commercial project to follow the American Tobacco Company's awkward fledgling *Barney Blake.*

At J. Walter Thompson and Co.'s Madison Avenue office, there was an executive named Martin Kane. The tobacco company liked the sound of that name as well as the concept of a hard-boiled dick—just like the ones so popular on radio. From these two sources came what was first known only as *Private Eye.*

It was simplicity itself. Martin Kane would be a classic rough-and-tumble gumshoe who stumbled over murder at every opportunity. Kane's only passion, besides crime, would be Sano cigarettes. As dictated by tradition—and the sponsor—a burning "bogart" would never be far from Kane's lips. And, in an engaging touch, Kane would not only frequent Happy McMann's tobacco shop, he would stop there in midcase every week to discuss the many pleasures to be found in the U.S. Tobacco Company's products.

To essay the leading role they hired William Gargan, a respected movie and stage actor who made a name for himself on Broadway in 1932's *The Animal Kindgom,* and garnered an Oscar nomination in 1940 for *They Knew What They Wanted* starring Carole Lombard. Between then and Kane, Gargan played detectives in several films, and even starred as "America's Master Crime Solver" Ellery Queen in three Columbia Pictures potboilers (*A Close Call for Ellery Queen, A Desperate Chance for Ellery Queen,* and *Enemy Agents Meet Ellery Queen,* all released in 1942).

But in 1948, nothing much was going on in his career. Gargan was a recognizable workhorse of the industry and U.S. Tobacco could get him cheap. He was the perfect sort of actor for the medium: familiar, but not so popular that he could make unreasonable demands.

Surprisingly, no one had commanded that television stars be hand-

William Gargan is stunned by Margaret Lindsay's phone in *A Desperate Chance for Ellery Queen*.

some rakes. This was still the era of Jimmy Cagney, Pat O'Brien, and, of course Humphrey Bogart, all of whom were neither classically handsome nor stereotypically romantic. Television sponsors were looking for engaging characters, the kind families would welcome into their homes. Gargan seemed perfect: a man the masses could look up to.

Television was still in its infancy. Only nine percent of U.S. homes had sets, less than four million in 1949. Still, four million people were a lot more than the U.S. Tobacco Company could reach through movies or plays, and in a lot less time. By September 1, 1949, *Private Eye* was on the air.

At first, the television industry didn't seem to know what to make of this new addition. They had sports, game shows, and variety programs, but this was the first action series. So, initially the series was not called a drama or a mystery. It was termed "sketches."

And actually that was pretty much what it was. Radio was the blueprint for the medium, so it was decided that the programs be telecast live, once weekly. The cameras were huge, bulky, heavy leviathans. The writing and rehearsal time was minimal, so what audiences saw was a rushed, claustrophobic play . . . with all the warts.

This rush soon gave rise to virtual ritual, wherein one show looked pretty much like the other, putting the bulk of the responsibility for its success directly on the star—who, in this case, had to sell the cigarettes as well as stereotypical stories. Commercials would eventually become their own insidious art form, but at this time the leading actor's charm was the primary ingredient for series success.

William Gargan was up to the challenge. Starring in a television drama held the same thrill as car racing or bronco busting. It was you out there, riding on the seat of your pants, holding on by the skin of your teeth, remaining calm and in control while chaos raged around you. It was the naked thrill many actors had gone into show business for.

Since the show was produced in Manhattan, the studio was filled with New York actors, toughened by years on the stage and street. Although they overacted at first, once they saw their embarrassing arm-waving and shouting—the kind of acting necessary to fill a theater—they rechanneled their energy. They had finally found a medium in which they could be subtle.

Some actors still couldn't adjust and played for cliché, feigning toughness, but most realized that less was more. Eyes could talk louder than lips or hands. It was stillness which made this new medium work, not extreme movement. Amidst the melodrama of these early perfor-

The original Kane, William Gargan.

mances was a raw, naked intensity the like of which would establish the "Golden Age of Television" within just a few years.

Gargan played in the twilight zone for two seasons, the black eye of the camera swallowing his image. There was very little feedback from the audience, since TV was still a curiosity. No one seemed to be taking it seriously except the sponsors. It was to them the actors increasingly turned.

The show improved slowly. The title was changed from *Private Eye* to *Martin Kane, Private Eye.* Its listing in the infant TV guides went from "sketches," to "drama," and then, finally, "mystery." A genre had been officially recognized. Those who could, watched with wonder and amusement. Television's initial effect was similar to the ancient storyteller's. As the fables became more fascinating, more and more people would gather around the fire to hear them.

The vision would not be denied. TV became the new hearth in the late forties. Many adults remember sneaking a peek at the neighborhood's one television through the owner's window. More and more parties were arranged for the evening of a favorite program. And, as in radio, the dramas and comedies with continuing characters who became friends as the weeks passed were the most habit-forming.

Martin Kane was one such friend. His mean streets were in a strange, flat Manhattan whose buildings wobbled whenever an actor got too close. It was an eerie, bleached-out city, populated by only one or two people at a time. Everyone would talk tough, and at least once every show, no matter if he was on the way to interrogate a chorus girl or nab a killer, Kane would stop by at Happy McMann's smoke shop and cheerfully discuss just how good Sano cigarettes were (Walter Kinsella played Happy McMann and while that was pretty much his only major claim to fame, *Martin Kane*'s initial announcer went on to better things in the news business. His name was Walter Cronkite).

In the two years that Gargan's version of the show was on the air, sales of TV sets nearly tripled, and the sponsor decided that Sano cigarettes had been in the limelight long enough. It was time to promote Encore cigarettes, a companion line. With dubious wisdom, they decided that a new cigarette demanded a new Martin Kane.

The logic was that Gargan had become identified with the character, and the character was identified with Sano. To temper fans' anguish, they replaced Gargan with a popular movie star. On June 30, 1951, it was announced that Lloyd Nolan had signed an unprecedented three-year contract which not only netted him $750,000, but also allowed him to make twelve guest appearances a year on any other show.

Such appeasements were necessary to collar Nolan, who was doing well elsewhere. He had graduated from being the heavy in 1930's westerns to appearing as the star in such hard-bitten flicks as *Undercover Doctor*

Reluctant Kane
Lloyd Nolan.

(1939) and *Johnny Apollo* (1940). He solidified his popularity in the forties by starring as private eye Michael Shayne in a series of seven 20th Century-Fox films. His most acclaimed film performances were in *Bataan, Guadalcanal Diary* (both 1943) and *A Tree Grows in Brooklyn* (1945).

The terse official explanation for Gargan's exit was that he wanted to put together his own detective show (which never materialized). No letter-writing campaigns or demonstrations were held to get him back. In those days, people took what they could get. Sadly, Lloyd Nolan's experience with the show (and early television in general) was not a happy one. On August 30, 1951, he officially replaced Gargan as Martin Kane. He lasted only one of the three contractual seasons. He was, after all, a movie star—not an industry workhorse. The drab, derivative storylines of the Nolan era, many culled and adapted from Gargan's tenure, could not compare to the breezy Shayne movies, and the audience's discontent grew. The sponsor could tell because Encore cigarettes weren't selling the way Sano had.

In later years, Nolan termed it an "unfortunate experience. It was done live and was no fun at all. Second-rate all the way." Probably the oddest part of his tenure was when he was cast as the lead of another short-lived live show and had to do both programs essentially at the same time, running from rehearsals and broadcasts of one to the other. It seemed the U.S. Tobacco Company was making him work for his three-quarters of a million dollars.

Nolan had continued the Martin Kane tradition as a tough-talking, hard-hitting private detective, a tradition the sponsor had no intention of stopping. But they learned their lesson. No more movie stars. His replacement was a character actor in the Gargan mold. On May 29, 1952, Lee Tracy took over. Kane became a pipe puffer and a very vocal proponent of Old Briar tobacco.

In retrospect, Tracy seemed to be made for television. He had already starred in one series on ABC, *The Amazing Mr. Malone*, playing Craig Rice's fictional criminal lawyer John J. Malone from September 1951 to March 1952. Perhaps the reason that program didn't fly longer was that the J.J. Malone of the books was short and dumpy, not like the tall and lanky Lee. And Tracy played him much the same way he had played Hildy Johnson in the original Broadway production of *The Front Page*, or the way he had played a whole group of fast-talking wiseacres in movies like *Dinner at Eight* (1933) and *The Lemon Drop Kid* (1934).

It's a lesson all the media are still hard pressed to learn. If a literary character is successful, changing him or her for television or movies might destroy the concept, no matter how popular the actor. That certainly was true of Lee Tracy's John J. Malone. He was better suited to the affable Kane.

Tracy had an engaging personality, part best buddy, part favorite uncle. He was always one step ahead and in control. Whether faced by his best friend or worst enemy, his wit never failed. Tracy approached his new role with the same energy the new Kane approached his cases.

"It's a trite thing to say," he explained to *TV Guide*, "but every show is an opening night. It's the closest thing we have today to the old stock theater. And for an actor, there just isn't anything like it."

His schedule was murder. They rehearsed from Monday to Wednesday. On Thursday, the day of the live broadcast, they worked for twelve hours with only a quick lunch break. At ten P.M., they played the show

This Kane is able—
Lee Tracy.

live for a half hour, including the commercial in Happy McMann's shop. For this murderous four-day week, Tracy was paid $3,000. Tough as it was, he professed to loving it.

The only problem was that his cases had changed. Instead of just solving murder mysteries, Kane found himself foiling scam after scam, uncovering racket after racket. This was due to the success of CBS' *Racket Squad*. It was being telecast at the same time, starting June 7, 1951, and the competition foolishly attempted to emulate it, rather than compete with it. That set a precedent which has not diminished, no matter how many times it has proved disastrous.

U.S. Tobacco wanted to reach as many people as possible and would do whatever it thought best to achieve greater sales. And if that meant riding *Racket Squad*'s coattails, it would do so unashamedly. They preferred making business decisions, rather than creative ones. This time it worked, in no small part due to Tracy's skill in keeping Kane believable. Besides, those coattails weren't so clean to start with. Series like *Rackets Are My Racket* had been appearing since 1948.

After a month of foiling loan sharks, the new Martin Kane got to smash a dope ring on Coney Island. It was another week before he stumbled across his first murder. From then on, the stories seemed to go in cycles. One week, Kane would uncover and foil a racketeer. The next week he'd solve a juicy murder. And the third week there would be some exotic crime, involving a foreign country or unusual occupation. Then the cycle would start over again.

In their effort to create a half-hour script, in time for the weekly live telecast, the writers turned increasingly toward subjects they knew intimately. It wasn't long before Kane was solving murders in game shows, for mystery authors, and in the realm of comic strips and comic books. In one of the more famous episodes, Kane tracks down the killer of a famous painter, corners him in a closet, and blasts him through the door. The door swings open, the body falls out, and everyone plainly sees that the door is unscathed. Perhaps this was the moment the idea for the neutron bomb took shape.

Another classic story concept which TV adopted because of its tight schedule was the animosity between cop and private peeper. In the case

Lee Tracy as Martin Kane thanks Walter Kinsella as Happy McMann for stocking all that Old Briar pipe tobacco in his smoke shop.

of William Gargan, Fred Hillebrand played Lieutenant Bender, Kane's cop connection. Nicholas Saunders played Sergeant Ross, Lloyd Nolan's friend on the force. But King Calder's Lieutenant Grey was a hapless police bumpkin Tracy's Kane constantly showed up. As the work load increased, the writers found it easier to create friction and trade insults than it was to maintain a cooperative relationship between the private sector and the force. Screenwriters would agree for years to come.

Through it all, Tracy's quick thinking and crooked smile came to the series' rescue. Although hardly a handsome loverboy, he was always clever and commanding. He seemed to love what he was doing and the audience perceived that. Unfortunately, Tracy was to come up against opposition he never dreamed of, in the person of television's first auteur—Jack Webb.

Webb had gone from radio work during wartime to radio fame in 1949 with the original *Dragnet*. When he could only get small roles in movies like *Sunset Boulevard* and *The Men* (both 1950), he brought *Dragnet* to television and with it a new kind of realism. Today, most people remember the series as an inadvertent satire, with its emotionless emoting and melodramatic music. But in 1950, Webb's series was amazing, riveting, and violent.

Dragnet essentially wrote television's Declaration of Independence. Although adapted from radio, it was free from radio and movie traditions. It stood on its own as a television experience—and was wildly successful. Along with Milton Berle and Lucille Ball, Jack Webb created the foundation upon which television's enormous popularity is based. *Dragnet*'s influence can be ridiculed but not overestimated.

Its immediate effect was to change *Martin Kane*'s direction and, ultimately, kill it. On July 2, 1953, it was announced that Martin Kane was to be replaced a third time. The president of U.S. Tobacco invited Lee Tracy to his house the previous April to break the news. The actor was told that the company was very pleased, but he had done too good a job. According to Tracy, they could no longer supply the demand for pipe tobacco so they thought it best to now push the king-size cigarette —even though the series' ratings had gone up twelve points.

The sponsor wanted a "higher-toned" show. When Tracy still couldn't understand why that necessitated his replacement, the president just laughed and said the actor didn't understand how radical the change was going to be. What U.S. Tobacco had in mind was changing Kane from a private eye to a police lieutenant and using actual police files as the basis for the stories. In other words, do a carbon (and tar and nicotine) copy of *Dragnet*.

Tracy had the last laugh, of sorts. When the company discovered that about a half a dozen new shows were planning to do the same thing, they hastily returned Kane's P.I. license. But that was just about all which

Kane on "Friday"—pseudo-auteur Mark Stevens.

remained. Tracy's portrayal of what he termed a "hard-boiled cynic with a thick streak of sentimentality" was out. The new sort of Webb realism was in. The sponsor looked to actor Mark Stevens to supply it.

Stevens was young, ambitious, and inspired by Jack Webb's example. His film career had stalled after promising roles in *Objective Burma* (1945) and *The Dark Corner* (1946), but he still had quite an effect on *Martin Kane* (he would later go on to do an auteur number on a subsequent series—writing, directing, producing, and starring in *Big Town* on NBC).

Professing to have seen the show only once, he demanded that the "Private Eye" in the title be changed to "Detective," that four additional writers be hired, that Kane not be called Marty, that integrated commercials be dropped, that Happy McMann's store be razed, and, most importantly, that the police not be portrayed as idiots.

"The legendary private eye is a myth," he declared, "and sometimes a laughable one."

Stevens and the sponsor seemed well suited to one another, as both seemed to want the same thing. Stevens called it authenticity. He also decreed that the show incorporate more long shots to differentiate it from *Dragnet*, which featured tight close-ups. All of this was just window dressing. It's the same sort of clarion call which is always heard when someone wants to pretend they're not doing a blatant rip-off.

Everyone but the audience seemed pleased by the change. Reviewers praised the show, *TV Guide* calling it "the most improved show of its kind." The sponsor felt that Stevens well embodied the younger man to whom king-size cigarette smoking was associated. But the show was no longer *Martin Kane, Private Eye.* As *Martin Kane, Detective,* it lost most of the charm Gargan and Tracy had brought to it. It may have been more realistic, better produced, and more sharply scripted, but it was an uncomfortable hybrid of a beloved and brand new show.

After dispensing with some leftover plot lines from the previous administration, concerning racketeers and backstage theater murders, Stevens instigated his own form of storytelling. The detective got involved with his own loved ones' problems when his ex-girlfriend's husband is murdered, a device which was to be used through the decades to make the lead more vulnerable and human. Stevens' Kane also became more high-brow, investigating deaths at a college, a country club, and other upscale settings.

His last case was an utter cliché. Kane is hired as a bodyguard for a beautiful model wearing a priceless necklace. Naturally the necklace is stolen and the model murdered, proving once again that detectives should detect, not guard. Any good detective would know that.

U.S. Tobacco finally had to pay for its pandering. They had started as a trailblazer and ended as an imitator. They had also sold a sinful amount of tobacco. After four actors and almost six years, *Martin Kane* broadcast its last original episode on June 17, 1954.

It didn't end there. To prove that "old TV ideas don't die, they simply rerun away," *The New Adventures of Martin Kane* appeared in 1957. This syndicated series made a mockery of the earlier version, especially since William Gargan returned in the role—now grown uncomfortable with age. He had been forty-four in 1949; he was now fifty-two and wearily playing a wisecracking dirty old man whose office was in London. It was a sad, uncomfortable mess.

Television had grown so much in the interim between Kane's demise and resurrection, however, that the market desperately needed product and even this pale plagiarism would do. Producer Harry Alan Towers made thirty-nine episodes (advertised with the phrase "Suspence in London, Action in Rome, Mystery in Paris!") and sold them as a single package to independent stations all over the country, to be used as filler wherever the station saw fit.

For one strange season the coarsened Gargan was everywhere. After that, Martin Kane was no more.

The actors who played him went on to greater fame, for the most part. Ironically, William Gargan is best remembered as a campaigner against smoking for the American Cancer Society and the author of the book *Why Me?*—his autobiographical account of his laryngectomy as a result of throat cancer and the subsequent efforts to learn to speak again. His connection with Sano cigarettes was well and truly severed. He died in 1979, after nearly twenty years of cancer fund-raising and teaching.

Lloyd Nolan was to regain his fair share of fame for his Broadway and television portrayal of Captain Queeg in *The Caine Mutiny Court Marital* (he lost the movie version to Humphrey Bogart). He appeared in films and television until his death in 1985. Fittingly, his last performance was in an episode of *Murder, She Wrote.*

Lee Tracy shared another role with William Gargan at the end of his own career. He was nominated for an Oscar for the film version of *The Best Man*, the stage version of which Gargan was appearing in when his cancer was diagnosed. Tracy died in 1968.

Mark Stevens continued a strong television career, then worked in both American and European films through the sixties. His name regained a certain mild prominence with the appearance of a Mark Stevens in X-rated films of the seventies. TV talk shows and news programs soon revealed it was not the same man.

No matter what the relative quality of each version of the show and no matter how mercenary the approach of the sponsor, *Martin Kane* left a legacy. He was the first. He established the format. It would be years before the creative crews could get the visible hand of the money men off the scripts.

CHAPTER

Watching the Accident

"These lenses are concave . . .
you are very nearsighted!"

—Mike Barnett

IMAGINING WHAT EARLY TELEVISION LOOKED LIKE IS HARD FOR THE MODERN viewer. Even watching current live telecasts cannot give new audiences the same feel or thrill. A detective show of the early fifties was like a high-wire act at a run-down circus. One never knew when the trapeze artist would fall or the line snap. On early television, both happened often.

Case in point: *Man Against Crime*. Although it is often reported as the first private eye show on television, it premiered October 7, 1949, putting it a good month behind *Martin Kane*. It was, however, the more consistent of the two shows simply because it had a single actor in the lead during its initial five-season run. It was also the more popular show, both critically and commercially. Although much of the credit belongs to the creator, Paul Klee, the majority of its success must be attributed to its star, Ralph Bellamy.

Bellamy is a devoted actor. He came into the business with a dedication that was enviable. Before approaching Broadway or Hollywood he worked in fifteen stock and traveling companies for ten years, acting in over four hundred performances. By the time he had garnered his greatest success in the mid-forties he had already appeared in over eighty movies, including essaying the most personable of the screen's Ellery Queens in four Columbia Pictures (before William Gargan took over).

He chose to do *Man Against Crime* when he was at the pinnacle

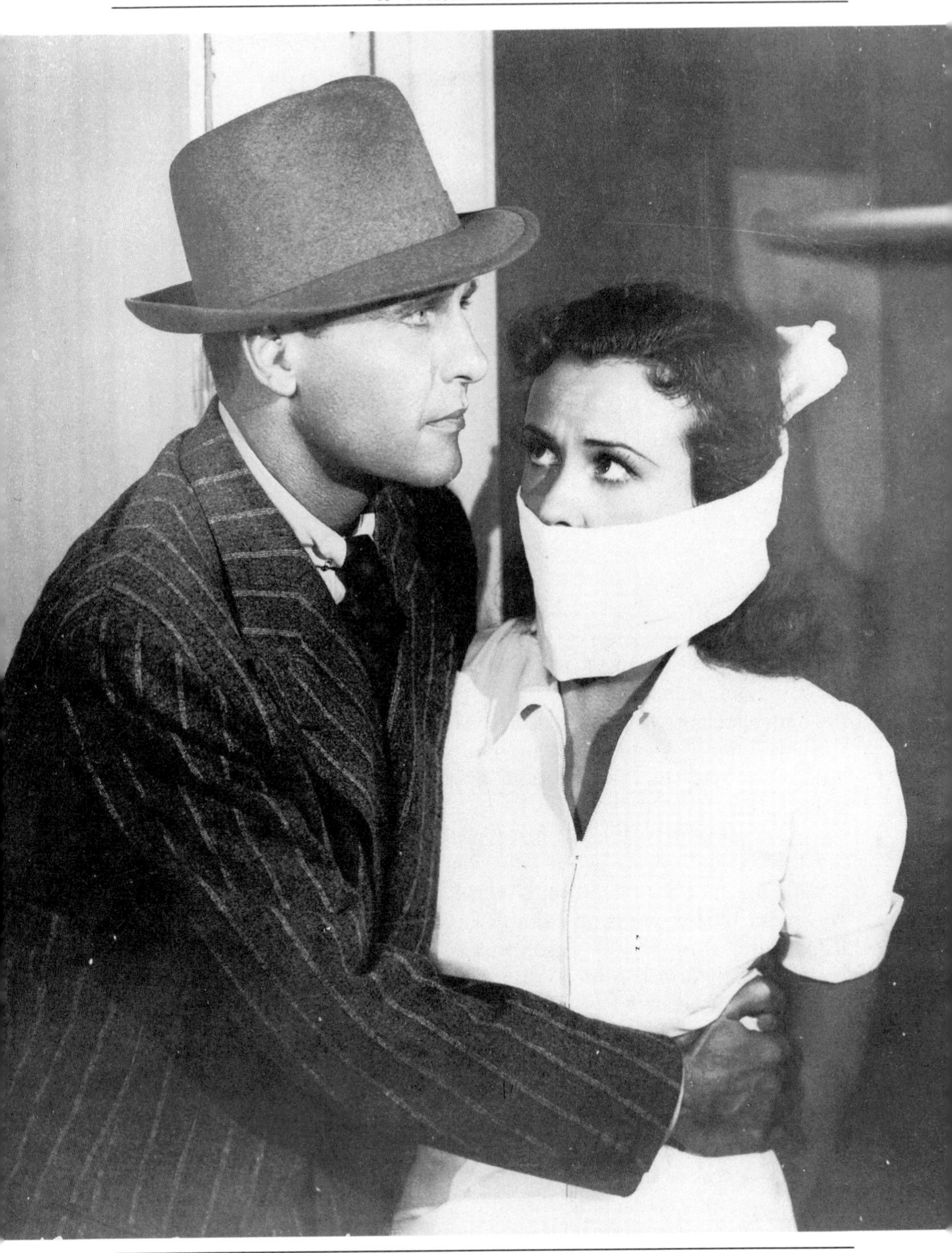

Ralph Bellamy enjoys Margaret Lindsay's big gag in *Ellery Queen and the Murder Ring*.

of his success. He had been nominated for an Oscar for *The Awful Truth* (1937), his return to Broadway in 1943 was a triumphant sixty-two-week run in *Tomorrow the World*, followed by the lead in the Pulitzer Prize-winning play, *State of the Union*. At the tender age of forty-nine, he started playing Jim McLeod in *Detective Story* on stage. Then, without leaving the play, accepted the role of Mike Barnett.

Bellamy's memories of the show still delighted him in 1986, at the age of seventy-five. It is through his eyes that we can understand the exhilarating chaos of those faltering, experimenting days. He had always been an actor who loved his work and the double duty from 1949 to 1951 was just the sort of challenge he relished.

"I would do the show every Friday," he told me, "and every Friday the curtain for *Detective Story* would go up late. They would hold the curtain and I would race to the Hudson Theater in a squad car. I had just enough time to get upstairs and get my makeup on before my cue was spoken." He would change clothes in the car.

The actor spoke as if it wasn't an uncommon situation. "I knew actors who went from the studio to the theater in ambulances," he contends. "When the traffic got heavy, they'd just turn on the siren."

Creator Klee conceived *Man Against Crime* as a ground-breaking series. First, Mike Barnett wouldn't carry a gun. There was no particular reason Bellamy could recall other than the character's intrinsic dislike of the weapon and his desire to take on the underworld with only his wits and fists.

Perhaps the real reason was that blank gun technology was wretched back then, necessitating the sound man to play recorded gunshots whenever the armed actor would shove his weapon forward. This led to constant mixups and mistakes. Guns would go off when the actor's hand was empty, or he'd pull the trigger . . . and nothing. "Silencer," Bellamy remembered another quick-thinking actor saying once to cover up this typical goof.

Better Barnett should swing his arm and the villain fall down.

Second, Klee wanted his new show to be more sophisticated than its few contemporaries, causing Bellamy to really be put through his paces. Mike wouldn't just hang around Manhattan, he would battle villains around the world. For that they needed a bigger studio space than was available.

"Grand Central Station was the only place we could film it at first," Bellamy recalled. They took a huge section, cordoned it off, and used it like a warehouse. These beginnings were fraught with risk. With the camera taking a killer's point of view, *Man Against Crime*'s very first scene wound through a hall and into a room where Mike Barnett stood near a corpse. As Bellamy was about to invite the audience to watch what happened next, an offscreen voice announced, "Get the hell off me, I'm dead."

The camera had run into the "corpse."

This sort of thing was par for the course at a time when all mystery series were telecast live and kinoscopes of the performance were mailed to stations across the country. Things were made even tougher by the sponsor's desire to be in control. The first episode of *Man Against Crime* was directed by a woman from the advertising agency for Camel cigarettes. "Nice woman," Bellamy said, "but she knew nothing."

Professional directors were then hastily brought in and Paul Klee began slaving on a half-hour script per week for the next two years, scripts which tried to take advantage of the new medium rather than fight it. These scripts showcased how much the Camel cigarette company trusted Klee and how much faith they had in their star.

There were murders aplenty that first year. The very first episode was "Night Club Murder," followed by killings most foul in Greenwich Village, New Orleans, Stockholm, and Vienna. The foreign deaths were accomplished with some exotic painted backdrops and actors who could do European accents. Once that was established, Mike went from fighting foreign agents in Lisbon to protecting a cat named Tybalt, who had inherited a hundred grand.

Bellamy remembers the broadcasts as a flurry of heavy equipment and pointing fingers. No writer could afford stylistic tricks, so the scripts were heavily regimented. Barnett was more than a detective; he was the drama's host. He led the viewer through the plot, as if the audience were another character.

Since Barnett was in every scene, Bellamy would run from set to set, following the silent directions of the stage manager or technicians. He would leap over the thick wires which were everywhere, avoiding the lights, stage walls, and cameras, hoping that he was about to emerge onto the correct set.

But accidents would happen. Often. In every imaginable way. Sound effects were mistimed. Technicians would be seen leaning casually in the shot. Any sequence set in anything but a room was asking for trouble. In those days, they created an ocean by rippling dark cotton sheets along the studio floor. And more often than not, the audience would see the ripplers' hands or spot a supposedly sunken body stretched out on the concrete.

"There was one show when I was supposed to interrogate this store owner to get the name of the killer," Bellamy related. "And the guy just wouldn't say anything. I would ask him a question, which he was supposed to answer, but he just kept his mouth shut. So I would answer the question myself.

"This goes on for the whole scene and finally I ask if this other guy is the one I'm looking for, and finally he says something. 'No.' He was supposed to say yes. So I say, 'Well, I think that's the guy I want anyway,' and run off to catch the murderer in his apartment. Only when I arrive, there's no one there! The actor had gone upstairs to take his makeup off. He thought we didn't need him anymore. Luckily there was an open window on the set so I played the whole scene to it, as if the guy was out on the fire escape."

Bellamy had to do this sort of thing every week, thirty-nine times a year. But that was really nothing. There were some shows which ran fifty-two weeks a year, no matter what. "Why not?" seemed to be the sponsors' position. "Radio does it." But radio didn't require makeup, costume, or choreography. No matter. There were cigarettes to sell.

They rehearsed every day, even on Wednesdays before matinee performances of *Dectective Story*. In order to give Bellamy a six-week vacation in the first season, they introduced Mike's brother Pat Barnett, played by Robert Preston with a rakish mustache.

"We shared a show to introduce him," Bellamy explained (in which Mike and Pat investigate murder among fashion models), "and at the first run-through, he does all his lines with a thick brogue. I went to the director and asked about this broad Irish accent, but he said it was okay, you know, the guy had just come off the boat. Turns out the whole thing was a gag."

The crew could afford to be mischievous. The hard work and murderous schedule had paid off. *Man Against Crime* had become one of television's most popular shows. After some communication confusion, which led to Mike Barnett being referred to as Nick Barnett in the press, the star became so valued that the series was listed in the TV Guides as *Ralph Bellamy Against Crime* in the early fifties.

In 1950, it was in the top ten. In 1951, it garnered *TV Guide*'s Best Mystery Show of the Year award. In a 1952 review, the same publication gave the series their highest rating, commending the writing and production, but especially the "personal magnetism and skill of its star."

Still, the endless repetition could get to even the most avid actor. In a cleverly conceived article, the editors of *TV Guide* brought together Bellamy, Lee Tracy (who was playing Martin Kane at the time), and Lee Bowman (who was playing Ellery Queen) as the stars of a hypothetical new show. For the "show," the trio agreed on three rules they'd love to see accepted as television gospel.

One, no more than one slugging a week. Two, give them the girl once in a while (she always went off at the end of the half hour with somebody else). And three, let them see the money (for all the danger, the TV private eye never got paid).

Once the kidding was over, the actors got down to some serious gripes. Bellamy complained of patterning. There were so many standard elements that were now considered sacrosanct that the stories were straitjacketed. Week in and week out, it was the same old thing. The camera would come upon Barnett at the beginning of a new case. It would follow him on interrogations. Midway through the half hour he'd be knocked unconscious by an unknown assailant so a commercial could run. Although Bellamy was not forced to do that commercial himself, the technique gave the impression that he was dreaming it. Then consciousness would return and he'd track down the villain, finally inviting the audience back next week for another exciting assignment. Still, it seemed as if the public couldn't get enough of it . . . or the sponsor's products.

Detective Story ended its run and Bellamy was free to concentrate on *Man Against Crime*, but Paul Klee had burned out. When he left, most of Barnett's globe-trotting went with him. The crew didn't need the extra headaches foreign "locations" required. For the remainder of *Man Against Crime*'s run, Mike handled most of the bad guys on this side of the Atlantic.

To fill Klee's position the company hired writers like Max Ehrlich, Vincent Bogart, and Burt Benjamin, all veterans of the medium. They also had the benefit of advancing technology, which allowed them to move out of the kinoscope age and into film—in this case, the original Thomas Edison studio in the Bronx, remodeled, enlarged, and renamed the Bedford Park Studios.

While Klee had concentrated on creating a classically engaging private eye with episodes titled "Duel for a Jewel," "Bigamy and Bullets," and "A Medium for Murder" (about a killer swami), the new team let more of their star's style through. Some of the stories which kept the series at the top were "Sic Transit Gloria," in which Mike goes undercover at a burlesque show; "Death Wears Lead Shoes," where a gangster doesn't want a sunken barge raised; "Murder in the Rough," which was about killing on a golf course; "Petite Larceny," concerning midget pickpockets; and "Holler Uncle," about a millionaire's murderous nephews.

It was business as usual. A particularly painful business, as it turned out. The plots would change ever so slightly, but the beginning, middle, and end were still the same. Every week, Mike Barnett would be hit on the head in the middle of every case. And every week, Ralph Bellamy would go down on the same knee. "That was the hardest concrete floor I've ever come across," he said. His right knee is still affected. Another on-screen result of the weekly clubbing was that Mike Barnett developed a personal method of entering a room, a technique which would become his trademark. He came in slowly, along the wall, arms out, always waiting for that club to swing.

Bellamy would do the hawking at the program's conclusion. Happily smoking a Camel cigarette, he would preview the next episode, always ending with the same farewell. "See the entire story from beginning to end . . . [long draw on the cigarette] . . . next week." He still remembers the time a fleck of tobacco lodged in his throat and he finished the program choking, tears pouring from his eyes.

Ralph Bellamy's fists were quick as the gunless Mike Barnett, *Man Against Crime*.

The agony and exhilaration of pioneering TV ended for Bellamy in the summer of 1954. The cast and crew were just too exhausted to continue. The second-to-last episode was called "Next to Closing," in which Mike trapped a bank robber in a roadside diner. His final case was "No Place to Hide," in which he solved the murder of a gorgeous dame. It was a brisk finale for the breezy, intelligent, tough Mike Barnett.

The cancellation of the show did not end its popularity, however. *Man Against Crime* had been the first series to be telecast on two networks at the same time, as well as the first private eye show to run on three networks. CBS broadcast the original episodes, while NBC and DuMont aired reruns on the same day and at the same time, Sundays at 10:30 P.M.

The collected filmed episodes of the last three seasons were retitled *Follow That Man,* and that's how they played until the summer of 1956 when NBC showed all-new live episodes of the series, now starring Frank Lovejoy as Mike Barnett. Lovejoy was a lantern-jawed actor who was used to good effect as a detective in *In a Lonely Place* (1950) starring Humphrey Bogart, and as a spy in *I Was a Communist for the F.B.I.* (1951).

His performance as Barnett was unexciting, a fact that seemed apparent even to him. After Bellamy and the filmed episodes, these staid live productions were hardly an acceptable substitute. They were a throwback to days the audience seemed ready to forget. Television was opening up their world. The new *Man Against Crime* was claustrophobic in comparison. The producers tried hard, quickly sending Barnett off on an ocean cruise, then to the Swiss Alps and the Casbah, but the same small, flat set walls greeted him wherever he roamed.

Lovejoy used the abortive series as an introduction to television audiences, and returned the following summer in *Meet McGraw,* also on NBC. Now he was his own man against crime, a no-first-name troubleshooter who'd take any job that piqued his sense of justice.

"Meet McGraw," the ads said, "a dynamic new tough guy caught by fate between cop and killer . . . with a trigger mind and a finger to match. McGraw, played by Frank Lovejoy, never ducks a date with a dame, danger . . . or destiny!" Heaven knows it is difficult to duck destiny. But *Meet McGraw,* later known as *The Adventures of McGraw,* was good for forty-two episodes over two seasons on both NBC and ABC.

Lovejoy went on to a long film and television career, finding his greatest fame in the original Broadway version of *The Best Man.* He died of a heart attack during the touring run of the same play, years before the movie version (for which Lee Tracy received an Oscar nomination).

Ralph Bellamy, meanwhile, climaxed his admirable career with his stage and film performance as Franklin Roosevelt in *Sunrise at Campobello* (1960). The last time I saw him was on the set of the new *Twilight*

This Barnett packed heat, but less of a wallop—Frank Lovejoy as another *Man Against Crime.*

Zone series in 1985, after he had co-starred in the Eddie Murphy and Dan Ackroyd hit *Trading Places* (1983), and he recalled his Barnett years with great fondness.

When playing Barnett he had been made honorary president of the Associated Licensed Detectives of New York State and was presented a badge giving him honorary membership in the New York Police Department. Cops had tipped their hats to him on the street. He had even popularized a form of judo he used on the series. "Mike was a pretty sophisticated guy," he considered across forty years, remembering the days when all an actor's skills were needed to keep a series afloat. "Pretty smart, but he made mistakes."

With a smile, he explained. "He got hit on the head a lot."

CHAPTER

Whodunit and Why?

"I give you . . . THE CHALLENGE. You have all the facts in your possession essential to a clear solution of the mystery. Everything is there; no essential clue or fact is missing. Can you put them together and—not make them spell 'mother' to be sure—by a process of logical reasoning arrive at the one and only possible solution?"

—Ellery Queen
The Chinese Orange Mystery (1934)

NO SURVEY OF THE DETECTIVE GENRE IN GENERAL, AND THE TV DETECTIVE in particular, would be complete without an examination of Ellery Queen. Not only did the character shape American mystery literature during his forty-two-year career, but he's also the longest-running television investigator, appearing time and again over a twenty-five-year period in no fewer than seven incarnations.

As the ultimate gentleman detective, he established the formula to be followed in the whodunit, or "closed," mystery format. His television record is extraordinary even though he has never had a single successful series. What brings producers back to the man (and his format) time and again?

It is a question of thought versus action. Ellery Queen represents the armchair detective, in contrast to his peers and contemporaries who

America's Master Crime Solver . . . artist's prerogative.

are more comfortable slugging or shooting a suspect. Ellery, on the other hand, thinks them to a pulp. Like the great Sherlock, he is renowned for his mental acuity, not his fast feet or fists. So just why was he such an honored character in a medium which required speed, not finesse?

Ellery Queen represents one of the very first questions in the mystery of television: what is so attractive about the classic "play fair" murder mystery? Why is the puzzle of finding the murderer so popular?

Agatha Christie is still the world's bestselling mystery author, even all these years after her death. Although her work was not always play fair, it is her murder puzzles (not her writing style or characterizations)

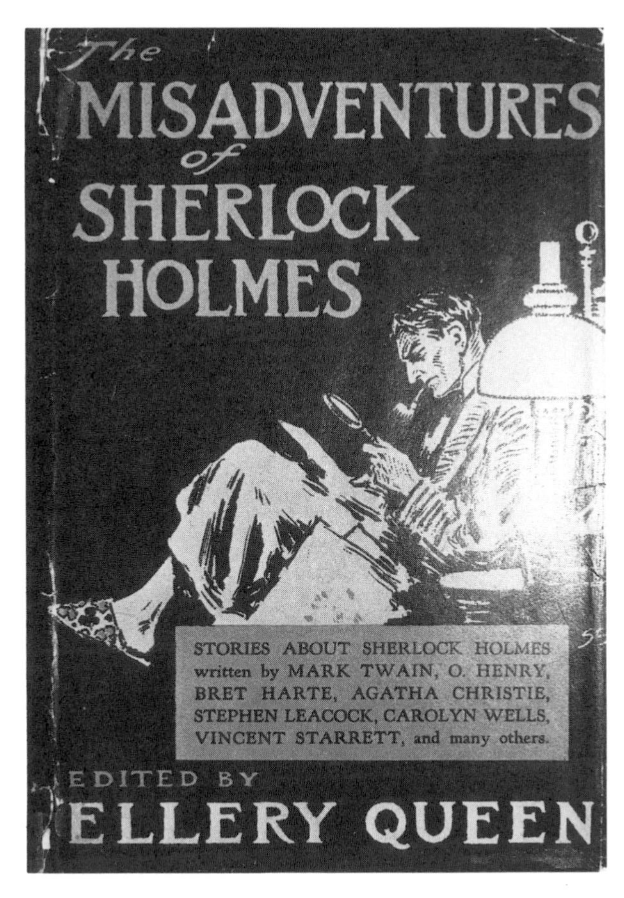

Two worthy sleuths together: EQ edits SH.

for which she is renowned. She is the queen of the whodunit, but it was not she, or her famous detectives Hercule Poirot and Miss Marple, upon whom Ellery was based.

As created by cousins Frederic Dannay and Manfred B. Lee in 1928, Ellery was essentially a knockoff of Philo Vance (the detective in S.S. Van Dine's novels), a supercilious, aloof young man who was too smart for his own good. A humanizing factor in Ellery's sometimes insufferable early behavior was the influence of his small, grizzled, widowed father, Richard, who also happened to be an N.Y.P.D. homicide inspector.

Curiously, there is almost no mention ever made of his mother—who may have been responsible for Ellery's occasionally frosty, usually indifferent, but nearly always detached attitude toward the shapely sex (EQ had fallen in love one or two times in his novels, but the romances seemed false and always soured quickly).

It was the authors' ability to create fascinating, sometimes agoniz-

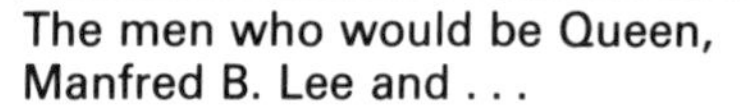

The men who would be Queen, Manfred B. Lee and . . .

. . . Frederic Dannay, the secret Ellery.

ingly intricate murder mysteries in the Christie tradition, and Ellery's uncanny ability to solve them, which attracted readers. Adding to the pleasure was an innovative gimmick: not only was Ellery a writer in the novels, but he was their author as well. His was the only name on the books' covers, and Lee and Dannay were unknown to Queen's many fans. In their eyes, Ellery Queen himself wrote the books in which he appeared.

Perhaps that is why the readers were not intimidated by Queen's almost ludicrous wealth of knowledge—knowledge he used to extend the unmasking of the murderer to dozens of pages. The slim, bespectacled detective turns over and unravels every possible clue to a stupefying degree. A number, letter, or a word was never just that in an Ellery Queen novel. Its allusions and implications could run the gamut from the ancient Egyptians to the latest Broadway hit. All this erudition was lost on film and television producers, however.

By the time of the first film adaptation of the character (*The Spanish Cape Mystery*, 1935, starring Donald Cook), Ellery Queen had gone through ten books and an unusual personality change. Whereas most authors don't fool around with anything that sells, Dannay and Lee started giving Queen a conscience. They gave him something that almost no detective could afford to have: guilt.

The full-blown neurosis of his later novels was forestalled by the call of Hollywood. Ellery started appearing regularly on film in the shape of Eddie Quinlan (*The Mandarin Mystery*, 1937, based on 1934's *The Chinese Orange Mystery*), Ralph Bellamy, and William Gargan—while his voice was heard regularly on radio starting in 1939. Therefore, the book character also moved to California, casually solving Hollywood murders in the company of his newly created secretary, Nikki Porter (a character originally devised for the radio dramas).

It was this laid-back Ellery, as personified by Bellamy, which caught on. So while Queen's character continued to deepen in novels subsequent to 1942, the visual image was frozen as that dapper, affable, fairly indifferent young man seen in the movies. No doubt the phrase used by most filmmakers when faced by Lee and Dannay's prickly genius and labyrinthine mysteries was "no one likes a know-it-all." So Ellery stayed just a nice, smart young man.

The film series ended in 1942 but the radio dramas continued till the late forties, when television was ready to take over. Lee worked with the justly famous critic and author Anthony Boucher on the radio series while Dannay occupied himself making *Ellery Queen's Mystery Magazine* into the premier genre periodical. In both cases, Queen's character continued to deepen. None of the writers were satisfied with mere mystery puzzles anymore. They wanted their murders to have deeper sociological meaning.

This guilt-ridden Ellery did not seem to be a perfect subject for live mystery telecasts. He was too clever, too unusual (and, at this point, too tortured), to be a welcome guest in millions of homes. But that didn't stop brothers Norman and Irving Pincus. What they fixed on was not the actual literary character, but his fame. What they saw was a star of every medium, with an undeniably memorable name (the "queen" connotation was not as prevalent then; when asked about it, Dannay always replied, "Who knew?").

Undaunted by the challenge of creating a whodunit for Ellery to solve within a half hour every week, the Pincus brothers brought Queen to television. They hired Eugene Burr as story editor, Donald Richardson as director, and an unassuming actor named Richard Hart to play the lead.

Hart had an unspectacular career highlighted by the role of the Witch Boy in the original Broadway production of *Dark of the Moon* (1945). He had appeared in four movies, but getting the lead in *The Adventures of Ellery Queen* was his big break.

For the important role of Inspector Richard Queen, they cast Florenz Ames, a well-respected character actor who was sixty-six when he took the part. Like Ralph Bellamy, he held down a Broadway role which he would race to every night after rehearsal or the weekly broadcast. When the 1950's TV Ellery Queen is remembered, it is usually Ames who is recalled. There were probably two reasons for this. One, the TV Ellery was unequivocably bland. And two, Ames remained while various Ellerys came and went.

The first departure was a tragic one. Hart made a likable enough

The doomed Queen, Richard Hart.

lead (even though he sported an incongruous pencil-thin mustache) but was heftier than any previous Ellery. He was also adept at ignoring the mistakes which afflicted almost every live broadcast of the time. During one episode's introduction, Ellery is supposed to stop typing his latest novel upon "noticing" the audience. Hart looked up from the machine just as he pushed the typewriter roll-carriage back—knocking a vase off the desk, out of shot, never to be seen or acknowledged again.

Hart did only eleven episodes (three of which were based on previously published Ellery Queen stories, and a fourth, "The Blind Bullet," which boasted a plot similar to the 1952 novel *The King Is Dead*), and was rehearsing the twelfth when he died of a heart attack. Ironically, that episode was titled "The Survivors' Club."

With less than twenty-four hours notice, Lee Bowman was brought in as replacement. Bowman was remarkably similar to Hart in looks—with the same pencil-thin mustache—and age, both men having been born in 1914.

Bowman was also similar in that his résumé was hardly spectacular at the time he was asked to play Ellery. After debuting on screen in 1937,

The resurrected Queen, Lee Bowman.

he co-starred in at least three movies a year up until 1945. He kept busy, but his work was less than inspiring. Among them were *Sophie Lang Goes West* (1937), *Dancing Co-ed* (1938), *Gold Rush Maisie* (1940), *Kid Glove Killer* (1942), and *Three Hearts for Julia* (1943). He's best remembered for starring opposite Susan Hayward in *Smash-up* (1947), but that didn't lead to bigger things. He did three more uninspiring films before the emergency rescue on Ellery Queen.

He was a nice enough fellow, and his Ellery was a trifle more assured than Hart's, but the producers had no intention of using the change to give the series more depth. They didn't have time. They had already learned that producing a valid whodunit every week was much tougher than having a hard-boiled dick spit lead.

The show was still a half hour, still live on the DuMont network, and still sponsored by the Kaiser-Frazer automobile company. In fact, in the episode in which Hart's Ellery knocks over the vase ("The Hanging Acrobat"), he's quick to mention that he, Ellery Queen, drives a Kaiser. But that sort of intrusion was a relief after what the show's original sponsor, the Bayuk Cigar Company, put the writers through.

They were not allowed to mention the word cigarette or have a cigarette anywhere on the set. They weren't even allowed to have crushed cigarettes in the ashtrays, or as clues. In fact, they weren't even allowed to smoke cigars on the set—it was decided they looked too ugly. Only unsmoked, whole Bayuk cigars could appear on *The Adventures of Ellery Queen*.

Looking back on the few episodes of the original series available today, the program seems feeble and dated, but at the time it was impressive enough to garner a 1950 *TV Guide* award as Best Mystery Show of the Year. "Here," they said, "one of the all-time greats among fictional detectives has been brought to video life with emphatic success in excellently produced and performed stories that feature the suspense, pace, and small, human touches that distinquish the Ellery Queen novels."

I can't help but wonder which novels they were referring to, since by that time the novelized Ellery was going through emotional hell. He all but had a nervous breakdown in *Ten Days' Wonder* (1948) and nearly gave up mystery solving in *Cat of Many Tails* (1949). From this time on, it was the unfortunate fate of the character's personality to be ignored just when he had developed psychological complexities worthy of a Sherlock Holmes. The performance possibilities were striking, but they were not allowed to intrude.

The sort of psychological shocks already on display in the live TV anthology drama programs were verboten on the continuing series. Weekly, continuing drama series (that is, shows which have the same character featured week after week) were already becoming a balancing act. Producers were intent on not upsetting any viewer, just in case it might affect the sales of the sponsor's product. The ongoing motto seemed to be: "Why take risks?"

So Lee Bowman's Ellery, with Florenz Ames still in tow, became more and more similar to the adventurers on other programs. Mixed in with the classic whodunits were plots which seemed to come right out of *Man Against Crime*. In episodes titled "Prescription for Treason," "The Fashion Story Murder," and "The Baseball Murder Case" Ellery handled "theme" killings. In "The Clay Pigeon," he's held hostage by a cop killer . . . hardly a framework in which to be brilliantly deductive.

As the TV EQ became blander, the EQ novels became more passionate.

Happily, however, most of the episodes still allowed Ellery to be clever. The best tales were quintessential whodunits—occasionally involving the Queen trademark of a "dying clue"—the telltale but cryptic message left by the dying victim. A good whodunit is always involving and, if the solution is clever and logical, the unmasking of the murderer can be satisfying at least, exhilarating at best.

The whodunit always seems fascinating to writers, saleable to the networks, and attractive to audiences. The question, as before, is why? The easiest answer is that life isn't easy. Modern survival is frustrating and complex, so it's comforting to sit down after a hard day and watch a likable fellow casually unravel the ultimate affront.

And while the whodunit does not answer the question "Why do people die?" it does make sure that no one gets away with murder. The great detective separates the innocent from the guilty and balances the scales of justice—without complications.

On a deeper level, however, the whodunit may be a bastion for the rational. That may be the reason so many writers and readers are attracted to it. It is not easy, because it requires complex thought. Only through scrupulous logic can it be made completely satisfying—as the producers and actors on the Ellery Queen shows were soon to discover.

It was this satisfaction which carried the original series until late 1952, establishing Bowman as the "suave, cynical, literate all-night prowler of the bachelor school of detectives," as one review put it. This was certainly a far cry from the Ellery of the books, who in his obsessive 1950's investigations into the very nature of evil itself had practically become a manic-depressive.

Although television had been growing by leaps and bounds, it was still far from being a sophisticated art form. Most of the mail Bowman got did not involve plot, character, or motivation. It involved the most niggling of mistakes. "Everybody is an expert," Bowman complained in a letter to *TV Guide*. "It's not the kibitzers in the studio who bother me, it's the bona fide experts at home. Show a shot of any kind of machine and letters pour in . . . citing minute improvements. . . . If a door is stiff, gets stuck, or slams, the [armchair] carpenters write. . . . Housewives are among our sharpest observers. If an extra pinch of salt goes in, we hear about it. I think viewers . . . develop a visual acuity that emphasizes even the most trivial error." He signed the letter both Lee Bowman and Ellery Queen.

Even if television producers were ignoring the performance possibilities inherent in the novels, almost all the actors who portrayed Queen found the part fascinating. It seemed so enjoyable to play the brilliant crime solver that more than one man had a hard time deciding where his portrayal stopped and his life started.

One of the radio actors became so enamored of the role that he

Lee Bowman strikes a likely pose on the EQ set.

charged a personal wardrobe to the show and had all his own clothes monogrammed "E.Q." Frederic Dannay had to explain to him that while he was just playing the part, the authors *were* Ellery Queen.

That actor was Hugh Marlowe, and he got to slip into Ellery's shirts once more when *The New Adventures of Ellery Queen* were produced in 1954. By then, television had become big business, with stars like Milton Berle and Jackie Gleason negotiating 5-million- and 11-million-dollar deals. Major playwrights like Robert E. Sherwood had warmed to the medium, fashioning teleplays with the belief that, as Sherwood put it, "You've got to clobber" the audience!

The New Adventures didn't clobber, they rehashed. At least half of the half-hour stories were adapted from the earlier series. Even Inspector Queen was the same—Florenz Ames. No network would have them, so Marlowe's familiar stories were syndicated (sold to individual, independent stations to be run, and repeatedly rerun when and where the channels wished). For instance, in the Philadelphia area, they were telecast at 2:30 on Sunday afternoons.

By then, the writers had discovered that creating plausible whodunits was not as simple as it appeared. The great ones, Christie and Queen among them, made it look easy—no matter how long the detectives droned on during the denouement. Meanwhile, actors like Bowman had discovered the hard way just how great the audience's "visual acuity" had become. It may have manifested itself in niggling letters to the star, but it no doubt extended to the meat of the mystery for non-letter-writing viewers.

The whodunit is a more elegant format than the hard-boiled caper. Books, movies, and radio had taught the audience that the gentleman detective was smarter than the two-fisted gumshoes, so they came to expect better things from the genre. No doubt seeing Bowman's and Marlowe's Ellery busting rackets in episodes like "One Week to Live" (about a life insurance scam), and breaking up narcotics rings ("Mr. Big") led to a certain dissatisfaction—even though the Pincus brothers would attempt something ambitious every two dozen episodes or so.

In 1951 they had "Adventure of the Twilight Zone," with Ellery behind the Iron Curtain (which inspired one critic to call the episode "particularly grim"). In 1952 they had "Men Without Faces," based on a radio script in which Ellery confronted masked neo-fascist vigilantes. Not all of the best early episodes were controversial. The week before Florenz Ames took center stage, solving four crimes while Ellery was on vacation (giving Bowman a much needed month-long rest), there was "Dead Secret," in which Ellery's life depended upon how well he recalled the details of a routine visit to the bank.

But for every decent episode, there were at least five that just tread water. The whodunit format consists of two important ingredients: an interesting detective and a perplexing mystery. These two parts are by no means equal, however. As important as the sleuths are, they can take the form of an incisive English genius, an egg-headed Belgian, a fat New Yorker, or a doddering old lady for all the difference it made. If the cases aren't good the detectives will not be remembered, no matter how eccentric they are. The mystery is the thing, and to be really effective, it has to be airtight . . . or at least water-resistant.

The truly brilliant practitioners of the form only came up with a few dozen such puzzles in their lifetimes. TV people have to come up with one every week. Is it any wonder that there have been only two really successful whodunit series out of the dozens tried? *Perry Mason* (1957–64, 1973–74) succeeded, as did *Murder, She Wrote* (1984–). Those two had exceptional writing staffs. The early Ellery Queen did not.

Hugh Marlowe's new/old cases disappeared by mid-1955 and it appeared that Ellery might hang up his typewriter and retire. Dannay and Lee were slowing down, seemingly having said everything that could be said in the mystery format. Then Albert McCleery, a driving force in television's live drama presentations, announced in 1957 that he would be doing *The Further Adventures of Ellery Queen* in Hollywood. But instead of using film cameras in a studio, he decided to telecast live from a theater stage.

The reasons for McCleery's choices are unfathomable. He openly admitted he had never read any of the Queen novels or short stories, and he didn't care that the character had been done so many times before. This was very odd indeed, since McCleery had also stated that the Queen canon would be the basis for the bulk of his teleplays. Furthermore, his weekly budget would be between $35,000 and $40,000—small change, even for then.

"We're going to spend the money on scripts and actors," he said testily, "not costly props and sets."

Then he cast George Nader, whose own career nadir was 1953's *Robot Monster*, one of the worst films ever made. Les Tremayne was cast as Inspector Queen. On the basis of reports made at the time, almost no one was eager to do the show. The result seemed to be that no one was eager to watch it, either. This initial version lasted until February 1959.

Then, in the space of a week, the series moved cross-country. McCleery was still having it telecast live, but from New York—with Lee Philips as Ellery Queen and Inspector Queen nowhere in sight. This change was good for only a few more months and the *Further Adventures* ended in the summer of 1959. The entire fiasco had the feel of a "contract breaker"—a way to fulfill a contractual obligation without working too hard.

Jaded audiences could only view the stage-bound, live performances

Live from Hollywood, George Nader as Ellery Queen.

as quaint throwbacks. By then they were watching the action-packed filmed adventures of such shows as *M Squad* (1957–60). *The Further Adventures of Ellery Queen* fell into the ocean of media without causing a ripple. Its single claim to enduring fame was that it was the only series whose foundation was the Queen novels.

Six of the first eight episodes were based on Ellery Queen books. And not just the lighter novels of the detective's Hollywood days, either. These were the angst-ridden efforts in which Ellery confronted his own responsibility in the deaths which raged around him. The very first episode was "The Glass Village," from an Ellery Queen novel in which Ellery did not appear as a character. Inspired by Senator Joseph McCarthy's communist witch hunts, this work concerned mass hysteria and bigotry.

Following that were "The King Is Dead" and "Ten Days' Wonder," two Queen books in which Ellery took on his concept of modern, ultimate evil. Coming shortly afterward was "Cat of Many Tails," which many consider the greatest Ellery Queen novel, in which the detective/writer nearly has a mental breakdown.

Live from New York, Lee Phillips as Ellery Queen.

When the aborted series wasn't trying to adapt the great Queen books, they were shoving Ellery into works by such great mystery writers as Hillary Waugh ("The Eighth Mrs. Bluebeard"), William P. McGivern ("Margin of Terror"), Harold Q. Masur ("Bury Me Deep"), and Edgar Box (the pseudonym for Gore Vidal—"Death Likes It Hot" and "Death Before Bedtime"). And when they couldn't find a good enough novel, they wedged Ellery into the "actual courthouse files" of a British case in which the foreman of a jury that acquits a murderer then discovers proof of his guilt (the "Body of the Crime" episode).

This could have been the stuff of great television, but it didn't work. The production values were chintzy and the performances lacked conviction. It had the body but not the heart. The plots were there but not the thematic or psychological underpinnings so important to an engrossing mystery. The message seemed clear: Ellery Queen had finally outgrown his television usefulness.

That seemed to finish the character for good. The fittingly titled 1958 Queen novel was *The Finishing Stroke*, which Lee and Dannay intended to be the final book in the series. The former member of the team was making noise about retiring, but the latter couldn't stop thinking of clever mysteries and audacious subjects.

Ellery returned in the 1963 novel *The Player on the Other Side*, rumored to have been plotted by Dannay, but written by science-fiction great Theodore Sturgeon. Meanwhile, the cousins were reportedly waving off any more attempts to buy the film or television rights to their character.

Manfred Bennington Lee died in 1971. No Queen novel was to follow 1971's *A Fine and Private Place*, a gimmicky but satisfactorily complex mystery which wrung out every last use of the number nine. Although many believe that Lee hadn't written any of the Queen novels since 1963, Dannay was not anxious to address that rumor. He was ready, however, to allow more media optioning. Unfortunately, Ellery's treatment at the hands of moviemakers realized his creators' deepest fears.

An expensive French film version of *Ten Days' Wonder* (1972) starring Orson Welles and Anthony Perkins was made, but Ellery Queen wasn't in it. A college professor played by Michel Piccoli solves the mystery, which was rendered stolid and uninvolving.

And then there was the 1971 television pilot. "For years, Universal Studios wanted to acquire the Ellery Queen stories," said Richard Levinson. "When they did, they came to us."

"Us" meant Levinson and William Link, partners in award-winning television writing and production. Although not related as Dannay and Lee were, they originally teamed in junior high school and were friends ever since. "We're neurotic in complementing ways," Levinson explained.

They were also great lovers of mystery, and became known for their complex, controversial, yet successful TV endeavors (usually the "two c's"—controversy and complexity—were considered death sentences by network and studio executives).

They both agreed that what Universal, and rewriter Leslie Stevens, did with their 1971 script adaptation of *Cat of Many Tails* was not good (they replaced their names on the credits with the pseudonym Ted Leighton). This was the pilot for a series which was ultimately rejected, then replaced by *McMillan and Wife* (1971–77). NBC must be credited for a good call. So as not to waste their production costs, they telecast the pilot film as a made-for-television movie.

What aired in November was the very odd *Ellery Queen: Don't Look Behind You*. It was not so much what was missing that killed this effort, but what was there. Gone was the novel's nerve-racking concept of a mass strangler loose in the hottest Manhattan summer on record, and gone was Ellery's guilt-ridden soul searching. Also gone was a solution so shattering it made the detective swear he would never solve another murder mystery.

Instead there was a near-winter killer hunted by Inspector Richard Queen, played by Harry Morgan (who found greater fame as Colonel Potter on the television version of *M*A*S*H*). Aiding and abetting him was his diffident playboy nephew Ellery, played by, of all people, Peter Lawford.

Casting Lawford as Queen was like casting Al Pacino as Sherlock Holmes. It simply did not work, and was a frightening example of what corporate and committee thinking can do to a project. Ellery Queen novels were undeniably successful, having been repeatedly reprinted for forty years. It is astonishing that television executives couldn't understand that they were successful, at least in part, because of the individual characteristics of the detective.

No matter. Television executives always manage to stay superior to their mistakes by pointing out the difference in audience size. "If every reader of Ellery Queen were to watch every episode," goes the thinking, "we'd still have a failure on our hands." Thus come changes which are designed to please the masses. And, at that time, at least, came NBC and Universal's idea of Ellery Queen—a mod, middle-aged Englishman.

But Universal was not giving up on the idea of reviving the character yet. Three years later Levinson and Link had won an Emmy for their TV movie *My Sweet Charlie* (1970) and had created *Columbo* (1971–77)—the first great "how-to-prove-whodunit." At that point they were given Ellery Queen and creative control.

"We were old enough to remember the Ellery Queen radio series," Levinson told me, "and the one thing we really liked about it was that before they revealed the solution they'd have some guest armchair detectives guess. We also remembered the great old mystery books we got as kids where they would seal the last chapter and you could get your money back if you didn't break the seal." The early Ellery Queen novels, too, had the "Challenge to the Reader" in which the author Ellery invited the audience to match wits with the fictional detective Ellery.

"So we decided to set it back in the forties," Levinson continued. "We didn't want to do serious, drug-related crime—we wanted to do exotic, bizarre crime. And, if we're going to do it in the forties, let's make it look like a forties movie; let's use all the forties' film stylisms."

Although very few period pieces have been successful (*The Untouchables*, 1959–63, being the exception), Levinson and Link were talented and powerful enough to get their vision through the network gantlet. The result was a two-hour made-for-television movie pilot set in the forties (but ironically adapted from the 1965 novel *The Fourth Side of the Triangle*) which aired March 25, 1975. When later sold to syndication, it had been given the title "Too Many Suspects." But at the time it was known only as *Ellery Queen*.

It did have the look of a forties melodrama, complete with an all-

The ludicrous Queen: casting Peter Lawford made as much sense as having Chevy Chase play Sherlock Holmes.

star cast featuring Ray Milland and Kim Hunter, and the famous challenge to the viewer in which Ellery steps out of character and speaks directly to the camera.

"Do you know who done it? If you've been watching closely, you should be able to figure out the murderer. Is it the estranged son? Could it be the jilted mistress . . . ?"

It was a ratings success, so a full-scale series was mounted for premiere September 11 of the same year. The main cast of the movie was back. David Wayne played Inspector Queen, Tom Reese was the hulking Sergeant Velie, and Jim Hutton, co-star of films like *Where the Boys Are* (1960), *Walk, Don't Run* (1966), and *The Green Berets* (1968), was Ellery Queen. Nikki Porter was not around but in her stead came another new character, created by Levinson and Link specifically for the show.

The apathetic Queen: Jim Hutton listens diffidently in the company of David Wayne as Inspector Queen, N.Y.P.D.

"We created Simon Brimmer [played by John Hillerman] to give Ellery an antagonist," explained Levinson. Brimmer was a smug radio personality who prided himself on solving the crimes before Ellery. "He was supposed to appear in every third or fourth show, but we realized we had trapped ourselves. Brimmer had to have a solution to the crimes which had to be logical but incorrect, so Ellery could say, 'That's wonderful, Simon. It's wrong, but it's very ingenious.' The way Holmes used to say, 'I admire you, Watson. The fact that you're totally wrong in no way detracts from your ingenuity.' " Coming up with two solutions every fourth show was too much for the staff, causing Brimmer to fade away.

Otherwise, the show had almost everything. Very clever stories—including the third and best adaptation of "The Mad Tea Party"—good production values, and a great co-producer in Peter Fischer.

"To test him, we gave him 'The Mad Tea Party' story," said Levinson, "and he wrote a script in five minutes. He said, 'I can do this, yes, I want to do this show.' "

That also set the gimmick of having every episode's title start with "The Adventure of . . . ," an affectation Dannay and Lee themselves had borrowed from the Sherlock Holmes canon. Some of the best were "The Adventure of the Comic Book Crusader," where a man dies while preparing an Ellery Queen comic book (placing the dying clue within the comic panel), "The Adventure of the Blunt Instrument," where another mystery writer is murdered while gloating on the phone to Ellery, and "The Adventure of the Sinister Scenario," in which an actor playing Ellery in an Ellery Queen movie is murdered . . . on film.

So why did the new series only last one season; a paltry twenty-three episodes? The casts were star-filled. The mysteries were valid, play-fair stumpers, and the production values were plush. What done it? Could it have been the period jinx, where most crime shows set in past fail? Could it have been the time slot problem, when a program is scheduled opposite a far more popular series?

Or could it have been the star syndrome?

The only thing the series seemed to be lacking was an involving leading man.

"We auditioned a lot of actors for the part," Levinson recalled. "But the network liked Jim [Hutton], and the head of television production at Universal liked Jim, and he was a very nice guy. It was a tough role to play because we made Ellery absentminded and kind of blundering. But," Levinson went on sadly, "it's true Jim didn't have the energy."

Jim Hutton was the most visually accurate of all the TV Ellerys, and the reworking of the character into a shambling, forgetful fellow was purposeful. "Who wants to watch a good-looking actor with those kind of brains?" Levinson wondered. "People would resent him." But no one could understand Hutton's increasingly apathetic portrayal.

Watching the show was an exercise in increasing frustration. The Ellery of the books cared more and more with each passing page, giving his investigations a driving momentum. But the television Ellery didn't seem to care about anything, not the murderer nor the victim nor even his father. He drifted through the crimes, diffidently asking questions and indifferently solving the murders as meaningless afterthoughts.

The whodunit is the genre of the rational person. In a way, it is also a genre for those who care. The irrational person could hardly care less for justice or truth—but it is these things which drive the detective.

Jim Hutton's EQ couldn't care less, so it was hard for the audience to.

The hard-boiled dick may be in it for the thrills, but the armchair detective seeks an orderly, logical world. Perhaps they get their thrill from the godlike position of putting everything in order, seeing to it that all is right.

The audience cannot help but perceive this. It just doesn't make sense that Ellery Queen would be an uncaring, unsympathetic man. At one time or another during his career he had been a cold, didactic scholar with an aversion to the sight of blood, a brilliant analyzer of modern crime, a guilt-ridden martyr, and a mere mortal battling darkest evil with just his intellect. What he had never been was spiritless.

"We now feel that Jim wasn't right for Ellery," Levinson admitted. "He looked great but had we known about him, the guy we probably should have hired was Edward Herrman [star of *Eleanor and Franklin,* 1976]."

Sadly, Hutton never had a chance to make his Ellery grow. Although popular with critics and building a cult audience, the new *Ellery Queen* was cancelled after one season. Hutton himself died of cancer in 1979.

"It probably would have continued," mused Levinson, "had Sonny and Cher not reunited. First NBC put us opposite *The Streets of San Francisco,* then moved us opposite the reunited *Sonny and Cher Show.* So we were two or three share [ratings] points from being renewed."

The last case was "The Adventure of the Disappearing Dagger," in which Ellery solves the murder of a private eye, as well as the case the P.I. was working on when he died. Since then, Ellery Queen has not reappeared. Thankfully there is room for more incarnations of the character, especially since he has never been accurately portrayed in the fifty years Hollywood has been trying.

CHAPTER

4

Enter the Auteur

"How's that?"

—Sergeant Joe Friday
Dragnet *1949, 1952, 1966, 1967*

"THIS IS THE CITY. LOS ANGELES, CALIFORNIA. I WORK HERE. I CARRY A badge."

Dum de dum dum.

It is hard to decide what is more famous: the format or the music. If Walter Schumann had done nothing else but write those four notes, his place in entertainment history would be secure. But the lyrics-less music went on, into the song "Danger Ahead," otherwise known as the "Dragnet March."

At one point there was a lawsuit declaring that the four-note theme highlight was stolen from the soundtrack of *The Killers* (1946), composed by Miklos Rosza, but nothing much came of that. The ominous, simple, heavy, threatening theme will always be synonymous with the basset-hound face and pond-frog voice of Jack Webb.

He began life as John Randolph Webb in 1920 and began acting in high school. He was not what anyone would call classically handsome, with a low forehead and elephant ears, but he was certainly memorable. Even in the beginning he had a way of quietly and intently taking the scene, building on a fast but even-tempered delivery. He considered art as a career, and was noted for cartooning in college, but took a job in a men's clothing store instead. He toiled there until World War II.

His family was poor, and broken. He supported his mother during the war, even after enlisting in the Army air corps in 1943. The military allowed him to pursue his interest in communications, and by the time VJ Day came in 1945 he was ready to try his luck as an actor. He started in San Francisco as a disc jockey, where he continued to develop his on-air style.

There he met Richard L. Breen and James E. Moser, two freelance radio writers, both fresh from the war. They met, listened to what was popular, and collaborated. First came *Johnny Modero, Pier 23*, with Webb essaying a tough San Francisco waterfront detective. That fledgling effort hardly flew, so then came *Jeff Regan, Investigator*, with Webb as a hard-boiled private eye. That too, sank into listeners' ears without a trace.

Learning from all their mistakes, they hit upon *Pat Novak for Hire* in 1947 with two outs, bases loaded, and a full count. This didn't exactly hit it out of the park, but it was good for a couple of runs. Pat Novak was similar to Modero and Regan, but the writers and the director/actor had streamlined their work, eliminating much of the previous efforts' chaff and pretension. This was tightly written and tightly performed, giving it an energy the others did not have.

The energy was duly noted. While Moser stayed on with the Novak radio show, Richard Breen went to Hollywood, where he beckoned to Webb. Breen was immediately in demand and saw three of his screenplays go into production (*A Foreign Affair*, *Isn't It Romantic?* and *Miss Tatlock's Millions*, all in 1948). He certain that his contacts could make the going easy for Webb as well.

One look at the already drooping face was enough to relegate Webb to cameo status, no matter how effective his deep voice was. His first movie was *Hollow Truimph* (1948), about a killer taking on the guise of a doctor. He then appeared in *He Walked by Night*, also in 1948. It was on that film, about a police manhunt, where the police consultant for the film suggested the need for a believable, realistic radio police drama, using actual police files as a basis.

Webb was suddenly blessed with momentary genius. Breen, Moser, and he had been flailing around, trying to find a formula that would work for them. Like so many others before and since, they tried to imitate, which ultimately led to creative dissatisfaction and failure. But this idea was so blindingly simple. Not only could a realistic police drama be done, but it could be done inexpensively. Life had already written the stories for them.

Webb returned to radio, carrying a thunderbolt. "I created it," he said, "because I was starving. NBC radio took it out of sheer need to fill time left vacant when their stars deserted en masse to CBS."

Webb used a term he heard on the set of *He Walked by Night* as a title. That movie was about a manhunt—otherwise known, in police terms, as a dragnet. It was the perfect combination of verisimilitude and evocative sound. It was dramatic and authentic at the same time. *Dragnet* was on the air—a 1948 summer replacement for *The Life of Riley*.

Portrait of the auteur as a young man.

"It didn't knock anyone out," Webb said. "After eighteen weeks, it even got a sponsor."

The radio series was not an immediate success. In fact, it was met with great skepticism. If not for the NBC radio stars' exit, it would have been cancelled.

"The cast played their familiar lines in competent style," said *Variety*. "It may have been factually accurate, but dramatically it was artificial."

They were unmoved by the framing devices of strong music and clipped narration. They had heard it all before. Perhaps not this flatly and plainly, but the consensus was that this new approach was just not new enough. One reviewer took the stance that it was the listener who would find it dull, not he.

The one dissenting voice was John Crosby, whose column was to radio what Louella Parsons' was to movies. He called *Dragnet* "astonishing because nothing astonishing happens." He agreed that radio veterans might find it dull, but he found it absorbing, pointing out that the show concentrated on detection rather than mystery. "In the place of the customary brilliance and derring-do," he wrote, "the attractive, intelligent, and very hard-working young men substitute thoroughness, a minute attention to detail, and enormous patience. Trouble is, most police work is so methodical, it's hard to make exciting. The alternative is to put crime detection in human terms, which *Dragnet* seems to be trying to do." He concluded by saying, "I greatly prefer the real McCoy to the malarkey that is usually served up."

Only one person seemed to understand what Webb, Breen, and Moser were up to, but in this case that was all it took. The ratings situation began to turn around. Just in time, too.

"They told us we'd never get away with it," Webb remembered of the radio executives. "So we decided to throw away all the old claptrap and play it straight for one summer before going back to all the private eye capers we'd been doing. It happened to come along at the right time. Our idea was to let the listener eavesdrop on the police detective as he goes through his daily routine, and hear him as he actually is—an average, working man with an above average amount of patience."

Using Sergeant Marty Wynn of the Los Angeles Police as consultant, Webb, Moser, and Breen created Joe Friday, and his partner, Sergeant Ben Romero—played by a radio actor of limited experience, Barton Yarborough. Together they spit out intrinsically riveting dialogue. What they were saying was passionate. How they were saying it was passionless.

"We didn't do it by underplaying," Webb said. "Because underplaying is still acting. We tried to make it as real as a guy pouring a cup of coffee." And just as exciting. Only this time, the drama was not undercut by the medium's limitations, it was made suspenseful by the medium limiting itself! As the events mounted, the case became frustrating, and lines of investigation ended abruptly, the tension couldn't help but build.

"We just read," said Webb, "and let Jim Moser, our writer, take care of the characterizations and the dramatic impact. He put a lot of punch into it by writing the dialogue against a situation. When Joe Friday came across a corpse, I reported it with about as much emotion as a man finding a penny on the sidewalk . . . and with the same amount of preparation. It seemed to work better than the big musical build-up, followed by a shriek, that you heard on some of the private eye shows." Including his own earlier work.

"We used the old-fashioned, plain way of reporting," Webb concluded, "where you don't know any more than the cops do. It makes the audience the cop and they unwind the story."

But it was more than that. Already Webb was undercutting himself by making less of his achievement, a tendency which would dog his career. Webb was also doing the unimaginable: he was treating his audience like intelligent human beings.

"We realize the man in Duluth may not understand the first time he hears it that an A.P.B. stands for an All Points Bulletin," Webb said at the time. "But we think he'd prefer the true ring of the dialogue to some pointed-up, stilted translation."

Part of *Dragnet*'s attraction was making the listener feel like he was on the inside. Webb had always been a stickler for police procedure, up to and including the numbered codes used to identify crimes. Pretty soon, 459's and 211's were the talk of playgrounds and office buildings alike. The authentic cop lingo became so prevalent that one of the first *Dragnet* satires was a magazine article entitled: "Impress Your Friends! Understand Jack Webb! Presenting the Dragnet-to-English Dictionary."

The producer/director/star certainly seemed to be right on all counts, because *Dragnet* became a full-fledged hit by the end of its first year. Its popularity was not mere happenstance, however. Beyond the hard work of writer Moser, director Webb was making his presence felt.

He commanded a crew of five sound effects men, when the usual number was two. He experimented with many technical methods to heighten the realism, including speaking some distance from the microphone and actually making a long distance call to record the conversation for a scene when Friday calls the East Coast. "The control room people thought we were nuts," he recalled. The height of his technical virtuosity came when a sequence was sustained for almost three minutes by sound effects alone—no dialogue at all.

The radio show was such a success that the writing was already on the NBC wall. "I am most anxious," Webb said at the time, "to find out what we 'can't get away with' in television."

Webb had tried to parlay the radio success of *Dragnet* into a movie acting career, but it had just led to only slightly less frustrating small roles in *The Men, Sunset Boulevard*, and *Dark City* in 1950. After *The Halls of Montezuma, You're in the Navy Now*, and *Appointment with Danger* in 1951, Webb got restless. He had vision and he had a vehicle. Movies were more prestigious, but television was the growing industry. More importantly, movies were already an art. Television was nothing.

The networks' schedules had exploded by 1950, but the dozens of half-hour shows were little more than filmed cabaret and vaudeville acts. Even the mysteries were hastily arranged, televised amateur plays. For the most part, it was visual radio. It had no identity of its own.

It was quaint, it was comforting, it was soothing, it was unchallenging. Up until Jack Webb, the staged murder mystery deaths had no real meaning. These weren't real people who were being killed. These were cardboard cutouts, devoid of humanity from the outset. They had entered the drama as the victim, fulfilled their roles, and disappeared from sight (to be run over by the camera or whatever).

Dragnet was going to change all that. It was going to drop the real world in the viewer's lap. They wouldn't telecast it live from New York. They would film it in Hollywood. They would not use several cameras to catch all the action, they would use one: lighting the scene first for Friday's dialogue, then for Romero's.

Webb teamed with producer Stanley Meyer for the initial series, and they went to town with the pilot film. The creative crew reveled in the righteousness of their effort, nonchalantly hacking away at the clichés which had already become commonplace in TV crime fiction. The mistakes and problems of television at that time were so readily apparent from Webb's point of view that his show was almost a vicious parody of them. He showed by example how limp and derivative the rest were.

The network supposedly suggested Lloyd Nolan for the part of Joe Friday. They didn't think the audience would accept Jack Webb as a leading man.

On January 3, 1952, actor Vernon Charney walked into a Los Angeles City Hall set with a bomb in his hands. For the next thirty minutes, the audience was thrust into the tensest situation they had yet witnessed on TV. Viewers were kept on the edge of their seats as one attempt after another failed to defuse the situation. Finally, at the last possible moment, Friday got his hands on the bomb and raced outside. He tripped before reaching the pail of water. The bomb tumbled down the City Hall steps. It did not go off. It was a dud.

The show was not. *Variety* called it "masterfully constructed."

Fred Rayfield's review in *The Daily Compass* was representative, saying the show "approaches Joseph Pulitzer's famous ideal: accurate, terse, accurate. *Dragnet* oozes realism—in fact, it's laid on with a trowel. No fuss, no gab, they just do their job. Even the psychotic doesn't ham it up. He just displays quiet, unobtrusive grimness. This is, I suppose, a kind of relief."

The highest accolade came from *The New York Times*. "It does not regard police officers as either boobs or glamour boys, but only as intelligent mortals. . . . Webb displays a complete disdain for the clichés of the conventional crime show." They concluded by saying, "Apparently the motion picture capital is beginning to get the hang of television."

This was not true. Hollywood was not getting the hang of television—Jack Webb was. He knew exactly what he was doing, and he was going to do all of it. The network left him alone, probably because they didn't have his understanding of his product or of the medium—

and they knew it. What's more, Jack Webb knew they knew it. He moved ahead with a creative passion which knew little bound.

The only thing which tripped him up was the sudden death of Barton Yarborough from a heart attack after three episodes. Webb had the character of Sergeant Ben Romero also die, of the same illness, on both the radio and television show (one of the few times Joe Friday showed any real emotion). There followed an awkward search for a replacement, one of the few times the first season *Dragnet* stumbled. Part of its success was its frills-less approach. Introducing and reintroducing new partners distracted from the strong stories' linear lines.

First there was Sergeant Ed Jacobs, played by Barney Phillips. Jacobs was supposed to be more laid-back than the dour Friday, but Phillips was very similar in looks to Webb—making the barrage of close-ups very confusing. He was soon replaced by Herb Ellis, playing Officer Frank Smith.

This first Frank Smith, finishing out the initial season, pointed up a vital ingredient in the original *Dragnet*. Contrary to popular opinion, just being a flat, monotonal actor was not enough to make the show work. Ellis' Smith was a nonentity who did not compare favorably with the seemingly calm Friday. In truth, Friday was practically humming with virtue. His patience just barely contained his passion for the law and his job.

The second season saw heavy-set Ben Alexander as the new Officer Frank Smith. There was hardly any press about it, since Webb wanted the show to be its own star, but it was immediately apparent that the chemistry was now right. Alexander looked like everyone's favorite uncle or friendly neighbor. He looked like someone you could trust. Frank Smith was not as absorbed as Joe Friday. He represented the Everyman policeman, while Friday, like it or not, was a super cop.

"We built the series on pure authenticity," Webb maintained. "As such we made every effort to hire good but unrecognizable actors, meaning no recognizable stars, who might detract our audience from the almost documentary realism we were trying to achieve."

The second season *Dragnet* seemed to buzz. With everything finally in place, the show itself shined, giving television its own context. It was clear in Webb's approach that his detectives made up for a lack of Sherlock Holmes–like brilliance with the assembly line method of crime busting.

His cops never caught criminals with clever deductions. Instead, it was the painstaking accumulation of evidence which brought the quarry down. And the slower Friday and Smith went, meticulously gathering "just the facts, ma'am," the more delicious it was to watch. Webb never allowed the human element to break through, but that only heightened the impact of every grimace.

Moser, then John Robinson, continued to turn out scripts based on

Jack Webb and Frank Alexander make sure the story they are about to enact is true and that the names have been changed to protect the innocent.

actual police files, which had the drama built in. Some of the season's most memorable episodes came in two real time programs: the first had Friday and Smith rescue a suicidal man from a ledge in thirty minutes. The second was a half-hour interrogation which was wonderfully sustained by the "alleged perpetrator," played by the then unknown Lee Marvin.

"In a half hour, the man showed toughness, malice, bravado, innocence, craftiness, stupidity, and ultimately dejection," one critic marveled. This was early television at its best. This was Jack Webb's contribution. While "The Golden Age of Television" consisted of filming great plays and enacting great plays written for the small screen, *Dragnet* almost single-handedly created the television series.

Then there was the "Accident Trilogy," wherein Webb exposed the full horror and heartbreak of everyday traffic fatalities. The first had a motorcycle policeman killed by a negligent woman driver, who was unrepentant until Friday made her aware of the slain cop's family. The following two episodes spun variations on the theme. All along, however, Friday's expression and tone hardly changed.

The human drama was heightened because it had to struggle to get out. The tension was also heightened by Webb's obvious internal energy. It became quite clear that if Friday hadn't been in love with the law, he would have beaten every crook to a pulp or mowed them down, Eliot Ness–style. But he never did. In fact, Webb was quite pleased that in the first season only fifteen shots were fired and there were only three fights.

"A cop's work is rarely violent," he said, "and if we put too much violent action into the episode, we wouldn't be realistic."

Because of Webb's techniques, the occasional gunplay and fisticuffs fairly exploded on the screen. They had a resonance and power the other shows couldn't touch.

All that work and no play made Jack a rich boy. On 1952 television, there were Milton Berle, Lucille Ball, Sid Caesar, Jackie Gleason, Ed Sullivan, Arthur Godfrey—and Jack Webb. He was the only star of a continuing dramatic series who carried any weight at all. He proved television mystery could be unique and wildly successful. That success could be gauged monetarily as well as in influence.

On top of everything else, *Dragnet* was eminently and immediately parodible. There were Daffy Duck cartoons making fun of the monotone voices, Stan Freberg's "St. George and the Dragonet" lampooning the narration, *Mad* magazine satires which concentrated on the booming music punctuations, and even Art Buchwald's "French" version in his syndicated newspaper column: "Drag Filet" in which Sergeant Vendredi (French for Friday) and partner Sergeant Samedi (Saturday) go after Noir Lundi (Black Monday) on orders from the Chief, Captain Dimanche (Sunday). All to the tune of "Ooh, la, la-la."

By 1953, Webb and *Dragnet* represented all television detectives. In a seminal *Look* magazine article of the time, he was already being referred to as "Orson Webb." The series had doubled its television audience from sixteen to thirty-two million viewers, and it still had over ten million listeners for the radio version.

Webb was still finding engrossing stories for both versions, but the format had already been perfected. Once this, the medium's greatest straitjacket, had been designed, all that was left to do was tighten it. Webb proudly announced to *Look* that he had mastered "the ditch-digging approach to art. If more entertainers did that and forgot artiness, the general quality on television would be higher."

He also informed them that he was no longer lavishing five working days on any episode. He had it down to two or three, but that didn't mean his cast or crew could rest. He was planning to film enough by December to supply the network with *Dragnet* until November of 1954.

The culmination of his slave driving came on Christmas Eve 1953, when "Dragnet's Christmas Story" was telecast in both black-and-white and color. Although many critics sniffed at both the quality of the color and the script, the story of a poor little boy who prayed for a red wagon from Santa touched viewers. The cops were called in after the child stole a statue of Jesus, only to discover that the boy had promised God that Christ would get the first ride in his wagon if he got it.

That was the last of Webb's best work. The *Dragnet* machine kept grinding out episodes, but the staff was getting restless. Jim Moser moved on to create and produce *Medic* (1954–56) from case histories supplied by the L.A. County Medical Association. Webb was given a chance to co-produce this similar show, which critics were soon calling "Drugnet," but he didn't think a "Dr. Joe Friday" would work. He was right. It lasted only two seasons.

Besides, Webb had other fish to fry. He had proven everything he had wanted to with *Dragnet*; the seams were already beginning to show. Friday's patience was wearing thin. While he used to be occasionally sardonic, now he was starting to pontificate. For the most part, the audience loved it. The network received fifteen thousand letters requesting a copy of the speech Friday made about a policeman's life. It was duly printed up, sent out, and titled "What Is a Cop?"

Webb tried different tacks to extend Friday's shelf life. He hired Dorothy Abbott to play Joe's long-suffering, equally patient girlfriend. She lasted less than a season. He should have known better than to try.

"Friday was actually a neutral character," he would later say. "He has no religion, no childhood, no educational background, no war record, no personal side at all."

More properly, Webb turned his concentration to the stories, which were the real stars of his show. The most extreme plot they had that year was about test rats escaping a lab after being infected with bubonic plague. Thankfully, by then, the audience couldn't care less whether the more outlandish stories were true or not. Just so long as it made for consistently interesting viewing.

"Of course we didn't go so far with realism to use terms which might offend," said Webb. "But otherwise we tried to tell the truth about police work. We even showed that although an individual cop might turn bad, the overwhelming majority were good, hard-working, sincere men. Our realism didn't go so far that we forgot we were supposed to entertain the audience."

Enough was enough. Webb was doing *Dragnet* on both television and radio, as well as producing and starring in the radio story of a Roaring Twenties jazz trumpeter, *Pete Kelly's Blues*. He was unarguably the king of TV detectives. Now was the time to conquer film. Webb made a deal with Warner Brothers for a *Dragnet* (1954) movie.

It is hard to say who demanded a Friday movie first. Although the studio knew the series was a presold commodity, television and film rarely mixed. No matter how sophisticated television became, it was always considered a poor cousin to the cinema. On the other hand, while Webb wanted to prove himself beyond the Friday persona, *Dragnet* was something he knew like the back of his hand. It was a good way to get his foot in the movie-theater door.

It is probably safe to say that Webb and Warners agreed to agree. They would strike while the iron was hot. Instead of the three-day television shooting schedule, he budgeted out twenty-four days at much less than a half-million dollars. It took him and police consultant Captain James Hamilton three months to decide on the 1944 case of an ex-convict's murder.

The reason for such a seemingly simple story becomes apparent upon viewing. The investigation allowed Friday and Smith to stalk through the underworld of Los Angeles' low-lifes, allowing sharper and more suggestive dialogue. There was even a scene in a talent agent's office which involved an exotic dancer whose motto was "Have maracas, will travel."

The story also had the kind of irony Webb liked. For one of the few times on record, the criminal slips through Friday's fingers. The slimy killer Max Troy, as played by Stacy Harris, dies of a cancerous ulcer before he can stand trial. Although several reviewers contended that the movie was not successful, the customary Dragnet atmosphere translated well to Technicolor, and the mood just managed to sustain the film's eighty-nine-minute running length.

The movie version made more than $5 million—plenty of profit, but just not enough to warrant a full-fledged Webb assault on an original screenplay. Instead, he made another interesting deal with Warners. He would make another film, this one based on *Pete Kelly's Blues*, which would serve as both a theatrical feature and as a pilot film for a possible television series. It was an offer the studio would be hard pressed to refuse.

"After Pete Kelly," he told *Look* magazine, "I just want to produce and direct. I want to branch out and find what I can do. It would be horrible to think I'd have to go on playing the same character for the rest of my life. If I thought so, I'd shoot myself."

Which is just what he figuratively did.

Pete Kelly's Blues came out in 1955 and, fairly naturally, did less business than the *Dragnet* movie. Rather than dwell on his failure to pin movies down, Webb plunged into other projects. He brought the radio *Dragnet* to an end in 1955, ended his partnership with Stanley Meyer, and signed a ten-year pact with NBC. He continued on television as Joe Friday while producing and directing *Noah's Ark*, a fairly obvious twist on *Medic*.

It premiered late in 1956, starring Paul Burke as Dr. Noah McCann, a warm, caring veterinarian working at an animal hospital. All the stories were based on actual Southern California Veterinary Medical Association and American Humane Society files. It was the first step down into unintentional self-parody that Webb would take. In an ironic twist that Joe Friday would appreciate, *Noah's Ark* lasted as long as *Medic*: two seasons. *Dragnet*, meanwhile, gave no hint of slowing down.

In 1956, Webb exploited his series' success with a book called *The Badge*, which was an anecdotal telling of stories which didn't make it to the show. It was a modest success, with two hardcover printings, but it hardly made up for his relative failures in the other media, failures which were becoming galling.

Webb's desires were beginning to run counter to his characteristics. He had the momentary genius but an inability to recognize where his brilliance lay. He had the talent, but was unwilling to let it loose. His creative soul was in constant conflict with his business mind. He told himself he was a good whore when he should have been saying that he was a great artist. Instead of moving forward, he began to retreat.

"I'm a limited actor and a limited director," he said to Joe Hyams in 1957. "I've made many mistakes in my work, in business, and in my private life. . . ." He had been married twice—"subdivided," he called it—but found himself unwilling to divide his time equally between office and home. "I regret them all but I've made a bridge from mistake to mistake and learned something. The point is I'm in the business of selling something creative and you know what that is. It's a handful of air."

Webb made fists of both hands and tried again. He directed and starred in another movie, *The D.I.*, which came out in 1957. Instead of a patient police detective, he was the ultimate impatient marine drill instructor—a role which made use of his passion and patter. When Webb started his mouth going, little could slow it down.

Frank Capra, director of such excellent movies as *Mr. Smith Goes to Washington* (1939) and *It's a Wonderful Life* (1946) was one of Webb's ardent supporters. In his book, *The Name Above the Title*, he reveals that one of his favorite techniques was having his actors talk quickly, which gave everything they did an urgency. The only other director who specialized in that technique, he maintained, was Jack Webb.

But Webb stumbled when it came to another film ingredient Capra excelled at, and everyone thought would be a natural for the man who gave them *Dragnet*. "No messages," Webb told Hyams, concerning his movies. "I'll just stick to entertainment and let more qualified people attend to the soul searching." What Webb couldn't seem to accept was that much of the greatest entertainment—much of his own greatest work—was all about messages.

The D.I. was popular, but not popular enough. There was little to it besides actor Webb's strong performance and director Webb's patriotic conviction. Although there was talk of other films—including *The Fifty Cent Soldiers*, a civil war tale; *Twenty-four Hour Alert*, about the air force; and *Purple Is the Color*, about the heroin trade—nothing came of it. It was back to *Dragnet* for another few years. Back to *Dragnet* and rationalization.

"When we started," he told *Newsweek* at the time, "I put in sixteen- to eighteen-hour days, and spent as much as five days on a half-hour show. Now we put the show out in two days and I've cut down to twelve hours." When asked about the series' ongoing success, this was Webb's answer: "The public dictates and you listen. You give them, not approximately, but exactly what they want."

Of course, all Webb knew was what the letter-writing public wanted, which probably made up less than five percent of his audience, and which was notoriously subjective. But at this point it would take a howitzer to dent *Dragnet*'s traditions, and Webb knew it. In fact, he celebrated it.

"For a regular half-hour show, stylization and a consistent format are desperately needed. Once you get them, they should be treasured. In thirty minutes you can't get a real story. You're lucky if you can stumble through a vignette." So it seemed Webb had stopped even trying. After almost a decade smashing up against the entertainment wall, he was ready to bury himself under the one thing that got through.

"I used to think every year was the end," he said to *Newsweek* about *Dragnet*. "I used to think I was getting too old to play Sergeant Friday. Now I'm convinced we can go on indefinitely—if that's what the public wants."

The critics weren't so sure. They started taking him to task for what he swore he wouldn't do in his movies. It now appeared as if Friday was carrying around a soap box on patrol. The height of his propaganda phase came with the production of two films for the government (*Red Nightmare* and *The U.S. Fighting Man's Code of Conduct*), and the 1957 "Constitution Address" episode of *Dragnet*, in which Friday rattles off the preamble to the Constitution to some commie lovers while a patriotic theme swelled on the soundtrack.

"It was more maudlin than stirring," said *Variety*. "In the future let's hope Webb sticks to gumshoeing and leaves the orations to politicians."

No chance. The series carried on, more and more of its dramatic weight resting on Friday's mouth. At the beginning of the seventh season, *Variety* had this to say. "It still boasts some of the solidest story construction and most flawless production in the business, but we could do without the indulgence of needless moralizing. The story speaks for itself without Webb having to spell it out."

In 1957, *Dragnet* was the eleventh-highest-rated series on the air—behind three comedies, two game shows, two anthology drama series, two variety programs, one western, and no other mysteries. By 1958, it wasn't even in the top twenty-five. It was still an industry, however. Both the first-run version and syndicated reruns under the title of *Badge 714* were playing. It just wasn't the runaway hit it had been.

Westerns were now the big thing. *Peter Gunn* and *Perry Mason* were on the air, adding new wrinkles to the mystery format. Webb found himself falling further and further behind.

"Let's be honest," he said to *TV Guide* in January of 1959. "*Dragnet* got a good running start. We had our radio reputation going for us and we hit television at a time when there was virtually no competition. If we were to start from scratch and got a time slot opposite *Gunsmoke*, I don't think we'd ever get off the ground."

Certainly not with the kind of show he was packaging at that time. Back in the early fifties, Webb was possessed with vision and energy. The first three seasons were timeless and original; the facts, just the facts, were all the program needed to touch hearts and minds. But as Friday's success grew and grew, the less satisfied Webb became. Instead of letting the character develop he stuck Joe on a treadmill, thinking that quantity was quality. And as he cranked the cast and crew faster, Friday had to work that much harder to give the program validity.

At first, the audience could identify with the show through Joe. But as Friday became more stern, more sarcastic, and more indignant, he was no longer a police conscience or an audience's alter ego. He was a scolding parent. He was a nag. The realism and authenticity with which the shows had started had become hollow. Webb had replaced the clichés of the other shows with his own; and he was unable to break or even recognize them.

The original *Dragnet* went off the air in September of 1959.

Jack Webb took advantage of the seeming setback by creating, producing, directing, and starring in other film and television projects. His output for 1959 was prodigious. Premiering January 3 on NBC was *The D.A.'s Man*, a half-hour detective drama starring John Compton as a private eye known only as Shannon.

The logic behind this effort appears simple. Webb was best known for his police television show, but it had just been cancelled. So the powers that were wanted something "just like it . . . but different." *The D.A.'s Man* had all the law and order, represented by First Assistant District Attorney Al Bonacorsi, played by Ralph Manza. But while he was a no-nonsense legal eagle in the Joe Friday mold, the investigator he used was anything but.

Shannon was a classic blood-and-guts type of tough guy; a throwback to Modero, Regan, and Pat Novak. His manners and approach were in sharp, violent contrast to Friday's and came as quite a shock to complacent newspaper and magazine reviewers. So, while actor Compton did speak in a fast, Fridayesque monotone, the reviewers were merciless on him, and the series. It was off the air in a matter of months.

Premiering April 4 of the same year, on the same network, was *Pete Kelly's Blues*, Webb's personal labor of love. He had been a jazz fan for years, and this story of a Kansas City trumpet player was close to his heart. Of course there was a lot of Roaring Twenties spice thrown in, with chanteuses and mobsters, and what-not. It made for a fairly successful radio series, starring Webb, a moderately successful movie starring Webb, and a bigger television failure than *The D.A's Man*, not starring Webb.

Thinking that the public had their fill of him (besides, he still wanted that movie career), he cast William Reynolds as the TV Kelly. He, and the series, lasted five months; a veritable summer replacement show, which was never renewed. Furthermore, the expensive film version pilot was fairly useless since Pete Kelly was played by a different man.

No matter. There was always—*30*—, Jack Webb's new starring and directing movie vehicle, this being the story of one night in the life of a major metropolitan newspaper. Webb played the reporter, and William Conrad played his editor in the ninety-six-minute Warner Brothers motion picture. The title was reporter lingo for "the end," and, true to form, this film almost killed Webb in the movie business.

It seemed a natural. Webb was always saying he was not really a director or actor, but a "frustrated reporter." Unfortunately, he was attacked as a director and an actor. The reviews ranged from perplexed disappointment to savagery. The film was called pretentious at best, and atrocious at worst. In the space of one year, Jack Webb had struck out three times, retiring the side.

The news stories about him had changed. He was no longer a genius; they now called him a jerk. Art Moser, a public relations man (and perhaps a relative of Jim Moser), went on record calling Webb the "most miserable, most temperamental, and most recalcitrant" man he had ever worked for. According to Moser, Webb was "ninety percent temper. Everything we did seemed to be a crisis." Moser also delighted in labeling Webb a skinflint—an attack not exactly uncorroborated by Webb's contemporaries.

But those peers were also quick to point out that Webb went out of his way to be one of the guys and that he never stayed mad long. That could be testified to by the dozens of actors and crew members who Webb constantly used and reused on all his projects. Anyone Webb liked could depend on a job whenever Webb worked—even including his ex-wife Julie London, her new husband Bobby Troup, and ex-Friday partners Barney Phillips and Herb Ellis.

Nothing could keep Webb down. It was a rough couple of years after the failures of 1959, but Webb's mug was back on movie screens in 1961 with *The Last Time I Saw Archie*, starring Robert Mitchum as the title character—a con man at an army air force base. Webb directed and co-starred, playing the screenwriter, William Bowers, whose recollections the film was based on. In fact, the real Archie, Archie Hall, sued for invasion of privacy.

Although not a huge success, the generally amiable film reminded audiences how much they missed Webb's presence. Most surprising was a 1962 article in *The Village Voice*, in which Martin Williams came both to praise and bury him.

"In the name of realism," he wrote of *Dragnet*, "no actor raises his voice or his temper above the impatient monotone of Sergeant Joe Friday. Everyone talks exactly like everyone else. That is, everyone follows the anti-acting of Jack Webb. And, in the name of realism, dramaturgy is made incredibly crude . . . parodies of *Dragnet* weren't even necessary, for the series provided its own."

But, he continued, "*Dragnet* was one of the first shows to attempt a television style. Sometimes that attempt led to the most pompously irrelevant sort of visual artiness, but . . . *Dragnet* was a real effort. The only shows I know which have gone beyond *Dragnet*'s crude but authentic revelations are *Huckleberry Hound* and *Bullwinkle*." He concluded by saying that anyone who had seen those two satiric cartoon shows knew what he meant.

Such an approving back of the hand from a counterculture publication could only mean one thing. Jack Webb was back in action. Indeed, when Warner Brothers Television Division needed someone to take over in a hurry, Webb was the one they turned to. In February of 1963 he became the head of that department, with total control of the studio's series and the promise of at least one movie production.

The movie never happened, but a new television series did. Jack Webb took over the hosting chores of General Electric's series from Ronald Reagan. In the changing of the guard, the program went from *General Electric Theater* (1953–62) to *General Electric's True*. Fittingly, all the dramatized stories in this CBS anthology series were based on nonfiction tales from the pages of *True* magazine.

The resurgence of Webb's popularity was short-lived. He was just as patriotic and intent as ever, but he still had the kiss of death. The

Jack Webb, dragnetted down in the sixties.

program died after the first season. Three months later, on December 18, 1963, Warner Brothers broke their three-year contract with Webb, ousting him as division boss after only ten months. Webb immediately sued. Ten months after that, the studio settled out of court by paying him $3,000 a week for the remainder of the broken contract.

Neither Webb nor the studio has ever gone on record as to why the split occurred. It is fairly evident, however, that Webb was up to his old tricks. He couldn't seem to understand that *Dragnet* had been a success because it broke with convention. Webb needed to continue to find the shortcomings of stereotypical shows and correct them. He never did. Instead, he clinged to the now hackneyed realism and authenticity of his greatest success.

At least he hung on to the wreckage. All around him, television continued to sink. By 1965, comedy was once again king. Lucille Ball was back, joined by Red Skelton, Andy Griffith, Jackie Gleason, and Dick Van Dyke. Also the spectre of camp had reared its ugly head. In addition to such rustic slapstick as *The Beverly Hillbillies* (1962–71), *Gomer Pyle, U.S.M.C.* (1964–70), *Petticoat Junction* (1963–70), and *Green Acres* (1965–71), campy shows like *Batman* (1966–68), *Get Smart* (1965–70), and *The Man From U.N.C.L.E.* (1964–68) were in the top twenty. Capping it off were such odd favorites as *Hogan's Heroes* (1965–71), a comedy set in a Nazi prisoner of war camp, and *Gilligan's Island* (1964–67).

That period of television was marked by a notable embarrassment on the part of network executives. In that light, they were looking everywhere for projects that had some sort of dramatic validity. It was Universal Studios which came up with the idea to make more mature movies specifically for television, not for theatrical distribution. This concept unleashed a wide variety of talents, intent on making harder-hitting product.

The first film set for telecasting, though, hit a little bit too hard. *The Killers* (1964) was loosely based on Ernest Hemingway's story (from which the 1946 Burt Lancaster film had been made). This new version showcased the assassins—most notably the tarnished antihero played by Lee Marvin, and Ronald Reagan in his last film role, as an especially nasty crime boss. Universal and NBC took one look at the brutal finished product and cried foul. The studio sent it to the theaters and the network looked for something a little less disturbing in its approach.

They found Jack Webb. He found a fairly well publicized case of a multiple murderer of attractive, inexperienced models. They sold him on the idea of a made-for-TV *Dragnet* movie and he sold them 278 episodes of the original series for a cool $5 million. Warner Brothers' loss was now Universal's gain. Whether they wanted it or not, they had Joe Friday.

They wanted him at first. Webb dove into the making of *Dragnet 1966* with an enthusiasm he hadn't felt for years. He scheduled twenty-one days of filming at $600,000. He supervised the writing of a 191-page script with sixty-two speaking roles. Once more he took on the role of Joe Friday and called Ben Alexander to get Frank Smith out of retirement.

It was too late. Alexander had taken the comeback role of Desk Sergeant Dan Briggs on the ABC series *Felony Squad* (1966–68). Ironically Barney Phillips was also on the show, playing the captain to two street detectives played by Howard Duff and Dennis Cole. Herb Ellis certainly wouldn't work, so Friday went looking for another partner.

He found him in Harry Morgan, born Henry Bratsburg (not to be confused with the acerbic radio and television comedian Henry Morgan). Harry was the short, blond acting workhorse who had co-starred in *The Ox-bow Incident* (1943), *A Bell for Adano (1945)*, *The Big Clock* (1948), *Madame Bovary* (1949), *High Noon* (1952), *The Teahouse of the August Moon* (1956), *Inherit the Wind* (1960), *How the West Was Won* (1962), and many, many others. He had starred in two previous television shows, *December Bride* (1954–59) and *Pete And Gladys* (1960–62). He had also co-starred in the *Dark City* movie with Jack Webb.

Morgan had the same sort of touch Alexander had, being a sort of Everyman, though shorter and thinner than the previous actor. Most importantly, he was a complete professional and not subject to the "soul-searching" Webb detested. He became Officer Bill Gannon, Joe Friday's new partner.

Webb had what fun he was capable of with Morgan's character, making him slightly irascible, mildly eccentric, extremely well meaning, and rapidly approaching retirement. The movie's running joke was the lousy dentures his son-in-law kept making him. The levity was necessary for such a grim plot, one of the grimmest *Dragnet* had ever presented.

While there were one or two subplots, or parallel cases Friday and Gannon worked on, the main story was about a sexual psychotic who kidnapped women, took photos and films of them in bondage, then murdered them. The detectives went after the killer with admirable relish, leading up to a very satisfying climax in which Friday is forced to climb a rocky cliff in a rainstorm to grab the suspect from behind. Although ugly in content, Webb was civilized in his filmmaking technique.

The suitably ironic finale had a tired and grimy Friday intent on discovering the murderer's motive. After being intimidated by the reporters, the killer revealed the truth—taken verbatim from the actual case.

FRIDAY: "Why did you kill them?"

KILLER: "Because they asked me to."

FRIDAY: "How's that?"

KILLER: "They said they'd rather die than be with me."

Webb whipped his cast and crew through the complex, technically challenging script in short order. Rather than waste time on rehearsals, he had teleprompters set up off camera to help the actors. He still felt that coming upon the dialogue (reading it spontaneously) was better than memorizing it.

The final product was surprisingly fresh and effective. Although it hardly leaped off the screen the way the original series pilot had, the joys of the format were much in evidence. It no longer seemed realistic or authentic, but it had a quiet strength which was agreeable amid the mid-sixties dross.

Most incredibly, however, it also shared something with the most

Joe Friday and his new partner Frank Gannon (Harry Morgan) just want the facts, ma'am . . . Ma'am?

popular shows of the period. It was camp. Despite the depraved subject matter and Webb's earnestness, *Dragnet* had stopped being hard-hitting. Friday's deadpan delivery and the show's trademark techniques were now the ultimate in kitsch.

Webb was without shame. When Universal came to him for a subsequent series, he readily agreed. He was game and was fighting on the side of the angels.

"We will continue to hit robberies, homicides, and murders, just as in the past," he told reporters. "But there will be some slight differences which will be detectable in sociological mores. Historically, the policeman's job has always been to enforce the law. It was not intended that he become involved with sociological problems. But the new cop is younger, better educated, and more sophisticated. He's also more technically knowledgeable. All of this will be taken into account in the new *Dragnet* episodes. Otherwise the basic approach will be the same. Hard-core cops after the facts and dedicated to enforcement of the law."

He revealed other intents and desires in the series' production notes. "The total disregard today for Constitutional authority is appalling," he wrote. That, too, would be integrated in the new *Dragnet*. Even so, Webb the producer still refused Webb the director any creative slack. While the 1952 series headquarters set was so authentic carpenters came to him when renovating the real building, the new sets were spartan in the extreme.

The same crew of actors, including Vic Perrin, Virginia Gregg, Stacy Harris, Vernon Charney, and Ann Morgan Guilbert, the same flat lighting, and the same teleprompters were used. So were all the traditions. The same theme, the same pre-credit "this is the city" narration, the same post-credit "we were working the day shift, my name's Friday" narration, the same ongoing time-keeping narration ("11:52 A.M.; Bill and I went to lunch"), and the same wrap-ups—including the trial results just before the closing credits.

Nothing had changed, except maybe Friday himself. He was older, he was heavier, and he was flatter—in every way. But he was unbowed, and he would not be denied. The very first episode of *Dragnet 1967* concerned Friday and Gannon on the day watch, working out of public relations. Friday was to be on a talk show otherwise consisting of pro-youth, pro-legalization drug advocates.

It was something to see. The next day, *Variety* didn't seem sure what to make of it. "A phlegmatic, offbeat non-drama," they said. "A sort of parody of late night talk [shows]." Elsewhere in the review they termed it a "soupy charade" of a "cartoon conception." The stage was set for the second coming of the series. From there, things didn't get much better.

As usual, Webb's heart was in the right place, and it wasn't hard to guess what he was thinking. The problem, as always, was that Webb the artist refused to treat the subject with the respect Webb the advocate gave it. While his desires were huge, his production was miserly. The new *Dragnet* existed in some sort of horrible, artificial motel hell where everything was flat, monochromatic, and nobody moved their arms when they ran.

Webb continued to interject ambitious stories amid the robbery, bunco, homicide, forgery, fraud, and accident cases, but he also continued to grind out the weekly half-hour episodes in three days or less. The stories of his skinflinting were now legend. Morgan remembered that he never had Friday or Gannon change clothes so wardrobe would be cheap and editing would always be easy.

He even had the process of story editing down to a well-worn science. Every police officer was invited to submit stories, all were routed to Webb's office, each was evaluated for dramatic context ("Can we do that on TV?") and production feasibility ("How much will it cost?"); then it was routed to the writing staff. The final script was sent to Webb, who sent it on to the police department for clearance and the assigning of a technical advisor—often the cop who suggested the story in the first place.

Dragnet 1967 was not a huge smash, but it was a satisfactory effort, more than worthy of renewal. Interestingly, another show based on actual law enforcement files was a bona fide hit that year. In yet another irony, it's probable that *The F.B.I.* (1965–74) would not have been the consistent favorite it was had it not been for the original *Dragnet*.

Things continued on their merry way the following year. Nothing changed: not Webb's delivery nor his approach. "I no longer have much 'spiz' left," he admitted to *TV Guide*, however. "Age has slowed me down." But the passage of time did not lessen his conviction or willingness to speak out. He just couldn't find the time to package his beliefs in a viable way.

What the new *Dragnet* will always be remembered for is its narcotics episodes. Webb went after the "turn on, tune in, drop out" generation with a cheesy vengeance. The episodes are both admirable and laughable in retrospect.

To his credit, Webb arrested the pushers, took pity on the users, and saved his greatest wrath for the dupes—the adult proponents of the acid generation, those college professors and self-styled gurus who should have known better. Friday always saved his best speeches for them, pity and dislike dripping from his angry, clipped monotone. His patience had given out long ago. He was only patient now in that he didn't kill them on the spot. Instead he tried to make them see the light, hammering at them with his delivery and diction. His politics may have been demented, but there was no mistaking his passion. Joe Friday talked hard, he talked long, and he talked fast.

"I've seen it, professor. So often my stomach turns every time I think of it. All the things you can't put in a test tube or analyze in a computer. Rich kids, middle class kids, and poor kids, all attaching themselves to something they can't find any other way except by blowing grass or dropping a pill or mainlining heroin. Now, if they get the chance they grow up. Maybe. But what do they become? Vegetables? Welfare cases? Husbands, wives, mothers, fathers, that don't have the maturity or emotional balance to handle their own lives much less influence others. They live in their own little world of rosy red paths and cloudy dreams. And when the dreams are over, what's left? They're sick, they're psycho, they're broken, or they're dead."

Dum de dum dum . . . !

To his debit, Webb could no longer escape from his own plastic, unconvincing world of preaching and proselytizing to make viewers believe what Friday said. In hindsight, everything Friday said on that show was right. More's the pity he no longer had the inclination to present it in a way that was credible. The momentary genius had fled, leaving him with only a money-making format.

Dragnet rolled on, getting stiffer with each episode. In 1970, its final year, *Variety* aptly dubbed it "The Fuzz Industrial" ("industrials" being the artificial, forced commercial films made by businesses to promote themselves to clients). "The hard close-up style and rapid editing is ludicrous when there's no action," they continued. "*Dragnet 1970* seems like a sorry parody of itself."

But Webb was secure in his righteousness, just as Friday had always been. "If *Dragnet 1970* can define a few of the problems the police face," he said, "maybe then we're a public service as well as an entertainment form. We're in the entertainment business, but if you feel you're pursuing a career that is on the side of right, then I think you're making a contribution."

As laughable as Friday's resurrection became, Jack Webb had the last laugh. *Dragnet* was crumbling away from under him, but he was back in the saddle again, possessed of a new, improved, slightly moderated vision. During the first year of the revived *Dragnet* he conceived of another cop show, which he produced, directed, and wrote the pilot for (under his first two real names, John Randolph).

"It'll be a thrill-a-minute," he promised, "when you get an unknown trouble call and hit a backyard at two in the morning, never knowing who you'll meet . . . a kid with a knife . . . a pillhead with a gun . . . or two ex-cons with nothing to lose."

The series was *Adam 12* (1968–75), police lingo for the name of a certain patrol car. In it was veteran Officer Pete Malloy, played by Martin Milner, and rookie Officer Jim Reed, played by Kent McCord. When both actors appeared on the Mike Douglas talk show, they recalled Webb's

Kent McCord and Martin Milner show more emotion than usual in this violent moment from Adam 12.

most repeated direction. "Just say the words," he would continually advise. "Just say the words."

Surprisingly, they said the words for seven seasons, with all the energy of reading the phone book. It was just the first success for the newly revitalized Jack Webb. The second was *Emergency* (1972–77), a spin-off of *Adam 12*. Both series were based on actual police and fire department paramedical files.

This was not to say that Webb suffered no more failures. He had more failures than successes even in this final phase (among them: *The D.A.*, starring Robert Conrad in 1971; *O'Hara, U.S. Treasury*, starring David Janssen in 1971; *Chase*, starring Mitchell Ryan in 1973; *Sierra*, starring James Richardson in 1974; *Mobile One*, starring Jackie Cooper in 1975; *Sam*—a howler using the files of the Canine Corps—starring Mark Harmon in 1978; and, finally, *Project U.F.O.*, starring William Jordan in 1978). But he had proven something. He had proven that *Dragnet* was not a complete fluke. He had proven he could have other successes.

At the end of his life, Webb had more plans. There was talk of taking his last made-for-TV movie, about women rookies (*The 25th Man/Ms.*), to series. He was developing an answer to all the latest realistic cop dramas, called *The Department*. And there were even plans to have Joe Friday trudge forward one more time.

"We've never had such a surge of rising criminal acts in our country," Webb said. "At one time there seemed to be a clear-cut motivation in crime. Now you can't be certain why an illegal act is committed. There are no longer distinct areas from which particular crimes habitually emanate. They're the same crimes, but someone is constantly adding a new twist to them."

Yeah, maybe it was about time for a toughened, exhausted, elderly Joe Friday to come forward again, and try to shame the bad guys into rehabilitation. Maybe this time there would be no speeches. Maybe this time he'd be toting a gun and Bill Gannon would be hauling a broom to sweep up the corpses.

No. No chance. Joe would still be having a passionate affair with the law. He'd always stray with his mouth, but never his mind. That was what went wrong with the 1987 movie lampoon of the house that Jack built. The new *Dragnet* film starring (and co-written by) Dan Aykroyd didn't understand what they were satirizing. Aykroyd did a good Joe Friday, but the movie had nothing to do with the law. Satire works upon an understanding of what it is joking about. The TV *Dragnet* wasn't all flat filming and fast talking. It was about the law.

Something funny could have been said about how the law is being mutated by too much liberalization. No doubt something serious would have been said about it had Joe Friday returned. But *Dragnet* the comedy

Satire without subject—Dan Aykroyd and Tom Hanks ignore the law, but do a mean Jack Webb impersonation during the flaccid comedy remake of *Dragnet.*

movie drooled about a corrupt evangelist and a girlie magazine publisher, while seemingly having no conception at all of the way law worked. I don't see any way Webb could have liked it. He was too much a structuralist to ignore the fact that the movie wasn't "about" anything—soul-searching aside.

Jack Webb died on December 23, 1982. The L.A.P.D. flags were flown at half staff. Joe Friday's badge, number 714, the one inscribed "to the best reel cop from the best real cops," was retired, buried in the Police Academy classroom building cornerstone. And no matter how much anyone, including me, dwells on his failures, his success gave television something it never had before. An identity.

The thirty years this TV auteur spent diluting his achievement doesn't take away what he achieved. *Dragnet*, when it started, was brilliant. It was powerful, meaningful, and it made people care. Perhaps it was the result of momentary, inadvertent genius, but that's irrelevant. There were almost a hundred episodes of effective, important, quasi-documentary work upon which almost all television mystery is based.

"The story you have just seen is true. The names were changed to protect the innocent."

CHAPTER

Good Is Good

"I killed a man tonight. That's bad for my reputation."

—Peter Gunn

WHATEVER BLAKE EDWARDS WANTED, BLAKE EDWARDS GOT. HIS WAS AN astonishing ascension into the ranks of the major writers, producers, and directors, mainly because he knew what he wanted; what he wanted was commercial and economically feasible; and he wouldn't settle for less. Oh yes, and everyone considered him a genius.

There was reason for that. Lee Marvin once said, "If you do your cliché well, you'll kill them. They will be dumbfounded with its greatness." Such was the case with Edwards. He simply provided what everyone wanted better than anyone else. He could write it, he could direct it, and he could produce it.

He had created the radio character Richard Diamond for Dick Powell, but Diamond's personality changed when he went to television. On the radio, he had been a bright, quipping, singing P.I. who occasionally crooned duets with his secretary. On TV, in the person of David Janssen, he was more serious, even dour. This moody charisma was at odds with stories designed for the original witty persona. The scripts and the television actor didn't jibe, so it's little wonder that *Richard Diamond, Private Detective* (1957–60) hardly made it through two seasons.

But it gave Blake Edwards an idea for a better series. The respected filmmaker had started his career by writing and acting in westerns like *Panhandle* (1948) and *Stampede* (1949) before partnering with director Richard Quine to script such films as *Rainbow 'Round My Shoulder*

(1952), *All Ashore* (1953), and *Drive a Crooked Road* (1954). He started directing his own films in 1955, adding *Bring Your Smile Along* and *Mister Cory* (1957), among others, to his résumé.

Then television beckoned. In 1957, the medium boasted Lucille Ball, Danny Thomas, Jack Benny, Steve Allen, Burns and Allen, Arthur Godfrey, Phil Silvers, Red Skelton, Ozzie and Harriet, Jackie Gleason, Perry Como, Sid Caesar, Walter Winchell, and Edward R. Murrow. There was *Kraft Television Theatre, Playhouse 90, Goodyear TV Playhouse, Omnibus, General Electric Theater, Studio One, DuPont Theater, Armstrong Circle Theater, Ford Theater, The U.S. Steel Hour, Climax, Lux Video Theatre,* and even the *Schlitz Playhouse.*

It was an incredibly exciting time for creators and the audience. TV was a treasure trove of honest laughter and heartfelt tears. It was television's "Golden Age," but just about the only voice of mystery, suspense, and murder was Jack Webb's. The new television frontier was the mystery, and it was ripe for exploration.

Producer Don Sharpe was the key. He had brought Blake Edwards and Dick Powell together before, and called the writer again just after Edwards had finished conceiving a new private eye. Sharpe was excited by it, and why not? What Edwards had done was tailor the series specifically to the limitations of television. It wasn't adapted from radio or books—it was the first detective designed just for the small screen. What others saw as problems, Edwards saw as technique.

Edwards found his character's name the same way he had found Richard Diamond. A common first name and a metaphorical last name. Only he wouldn't make the same mistake the producers of the previous series had. When their Richard didn't sparkle like a Diamond, their program failed. Edwards conceived his new man as a combination of sophistication and toughness. His first name gave the impression of both dependability and elegance. Peter. The last name spat lead. Gunn.

Peter Gunn was a soldier of fortune who had found a well-paying gimmick . . . trouble. People would hire him to take care of it. They could always find him at Mother's, a hip jazz joint where sultry Edie Hart was the singer. He lived in this city—Any City, U.S.A.—in a dank, deserted, dark, black-and-white world. This place was populated only by odd characters, eccentrics of all types and description. There seemed to be only two solid men in the entire place: Lieutenant Jacoby of the police—and Peter Gunn.

The program had everything. It was relevant but old-fashioned. It was modern but traditional. It was avant-garde but familiar. It was audacious but inexpensive. It had the solid scripting of a radio drama and a film noir look. Edwards had the talent. Sharpe had the money to make a pilot. Now all they needed was a Peter Gunn.

He was in Hawaii.

"I had just finished a play in Florida with my wife Alexis Smith," remembered Craig Stevens, "and had an invitation to go to Honolulu, so off we went. While we were there we got a call from Blake Edwards. I, of course, thought he wanted to speak to Alexis because she had done a picture with him about a year and a half before [*This Happy Feeling*, 1958]. He told her, 'It's always a pleasure to talk to you, but I'd like to speak to your old man, if I may.'

"So she put me on and he said, 'Craig, I've been preparing a property for some time now. Naturally we started with Clark Gable and Gary Cooper as one always does, but through a lot of discussions, we feel you might be right for this property. Will you do me the favor of reading it?' I said of course. Through Alexis I had read quite a bit of his work, which I respected very much. He said, 'I've taken the liberty of sending you the script, it's on its way.'

"I received it and was tremendously surprised. It had the exact flavor which eventually happened. So I wired him back saying how great I thought the idea was and signed the wire 'Peter Gunn.' So I was Peter Gunn from that point on."

By that time Stevens had done more than fifty films as a contract player at Warner Brothers, and as a freelance actor did some 400 television shows. But nothing would grace him the way *Peter Gunn* would. He attributes all the show's success directly to Blake Edwards.

"It was all Blake's conception," Stevens says. "He wanted it to look a certain way and be stylized a certain way. It wasn't just by chance. Peter Gunn was very tailored, very clean, and very neat. Even though he worked in very tacky surroundings, Gunn was always neat as a pin. Blake wanted that contrast. He wanted Gunn to look very Madison Avenue against all these raunchy, coarse characters. That was thought out and very purposeful."

Edwards was making Gunn in his own image, with a dash of Cary Grant thrown in. The writer-producer himself was very collegiate looking, always being described as Ivy League. He came from a family of filmmakers, with his grandfather, Jay Gordon Edwards a silent movie director, and his dad, Jack McEdwards (the original family name) a 20th Century-Fox staff assistant director. Jack McEdwards became his son's production manager and the family welcomed Craig Stevens into the fold.

"Blake went to the barber with me and said, 'You'll probably kill me if you don't get the role or we don't sell the series, but I want Gunn to have a crewcut with a part.' And that became known as the Peter Gunn Haircut. The clothes were all Blake's as well. He took me to his own tailor and everything had to be done through him. And we had to have a lot of clothes, too, because of all the action in the show. At one point I think I had over three hundred and eighty suits!"

The power of the executive producer has rarely been more obvious.

Sleuthing in the *noir* zone—Craig Stevens protects Erica Elliott.

Given TV's time limitations, it was often a pleasure for a sponsor or network to find someone who wanted what they wanted and knew exactly how to get it without costing an arm and a leg. Edwards saw what television lacked and filled the need in a way which made use of the medium. They made the pilot episode, "The Kill," co-starring Gavin (*Love Boat*) MacLeod as a gangster who needs Gunn's help after a quartet of his contemporaries are massacred.

"The popularity of it was amazing even before it got on the air," Stevens marveled. Don Sharpe saw the pilot at 11:30 one morning. By that afternoon he had sold it to the first sponsor who saw it, Bristol-Myers.

"And they owned nine o'clock Monday on NBC," Stevens continued. "NBC had nothing to do with it. Blake and Don Sharpe made up Spartan Productions and they owned the show. I think that was the last independent show done."

They had named their production company well. Spartan was the word for it. Part of *Peter Gunn*'s marvel was that it was done so economically as well as so well. "Blake got calls continually from other producers for about six months," Stevens says, "because it was an example of what you could do for that amount of money at that time."

Viewers were getting something that looked familiar. There was a smart, tough detective walking down gloomy, wet, mean streets (which didn't wobble). But these weren't the real streets of Jack Webb or the highly stylized streets of film noir. This was video noir and the studio's backlot, where no one took the time to make anything artistically exact. Blake Edwards opened up this world to the viewers by writing the lion's share of scripts and controlling the mood.

In the second episode, "The Vicious Dog," the solution to an ugly attack on a crusading newspaperman lies in the hobo jungle. Then there was the case of "The Blind Pianist" who witnessed a murder, followed by "The Chinese Hangman," where Gunn takes on a Chinatown cult. Then there was "Lynn's Blues," where Gunn protects a girl named Martel. All the while, you could hear cool jazz in the background. This was the first show you could call smoky.

Edwards' control went beyond the script and direction. It also extended to the vital post-production, and, most successfully, the soundtrack music.

"He had worked with Henry Mancini over at Universal," Stevens elaborated, "and wanted to give him a chance. Well, you know what happened as a result of that! The theme from *Peter Gunn* remained a bestseller on the charts for about three years: which amazed Hank because he originally wrote it as background music."

The style, the form, the music, all made *Peter Gunn* an immediate success with critics and viewers alike. I think everyone was surprised that

A dubious Gunn surveys the willing Millicent Deming.

something fresh could be found in the clogged schedules of the late fifties. Everyone then hunkered down to prepare for the long haul of TV success and the unavoidable decline in quality. The question in TV production, then as now, is not if the series will worsen, but when. Producer Edwards found a way around even that.

"Blake said, 'You will develop the characters with your own personality,' " Stevens recollected, "which was very true. He said, 'After you play the character for a while, you'll almost be able to write the dialogue yourself.' And that became true as well. I learned the style, form, and feeling of it. A lot of the character rubs off on you just as you rub off on it. Particularly if you're happy with it and it's successful."

Peter Gunn was successful and stayed that way for a simple reason —Edwards wasn't in it just for the money. He knew when to say when.

The first season kept the characters at Mother's, the jazz club, overseen by Mother herself, initially played by Hope Emerson. "A wonderful lady," Stevens said. "Again, an example of Blake's genius; here's this tall, tough woman, and he wrote love scenes for us. Gunn had great respect

Peter Gunn wears one of his 380 suits for mysterious Chana Eden.

for her and they had talks—suddenly you realize it was being played as a romantic scene. The thought of establishing their relationship like that was Blake again."

Hope Emerson died shortly after leaving the show, where she was replaced by Minerva Urecal, but the transition didn't quite take. "The character was so identified with Hope that we didn't use Mother as much after that," Stevens admitted. "It just didn't work out. It was very difficult. We just sort of feathered it out." The new Mother was introduced in the "Protection" episode of 1959, up against gangsters offering insurance, the same problem the original Mother had faced in the pilot. But it wasn't long before Mother was phased out and Gunn was trying to solve the mystery of a woman who refuses to name her assailant even though he keeps trying to kill her ("Edge of the Knife"), and trying to set the troubled son of a death-row denizen straight ("The Young Assassins").

That was also part of Blake Edwards' art. His task was to create engrossing half-hour adventures which didn't seem either rushed or truncated. Craig Stevens' art was making Gunn seem casual yet concerned, serious but stylish. A detective for all seasons. It worked because both men knew what they were doing. The producer-writer knew how to create tension in each scene and the actor knew how to play it.

In a way, it was fortunate that the actress who played Edie Hart, the torch singer, was campaigning for a bigger role. This allowed the producers to change Mother's to Edie's in the third year. Lola Albright, the actress, was finally fairly content. "Blake used to say that Lola was about two beats off center and that was very true," Stevens said. "She is an exceptional woman; not stock or normal. She's hard to describe . . . she's just that interesting and that different. Like her singing. Blake said he didn't want a professional singer. 'I want someone who would be singing at Mother's,' you know?"

If Gunn's scenes with Mother were a romance, his scenes with Edie were an affair. They were always sultry, just like her, with the singer's voice dripping allure and innuendo. In a word, it was an adult relationship, with an enormous helping of physical attraction. Edwards played with that. One of the more famous fade-outs occurred after Edie spent the entire show promising Gunn a great surprise if he returned to her after a case. He did and the surprise was that they played cards all night.

Seems the only person Gunn could really depend on was Lieutenant Jacoby, played by Herschel Bernardi (the voice of Charlie the Tuna and the Jolly Green Giant). "We got along great," recalls Stevens. "We complemented each other as actors and characters."

Blake Edwards deflated what was becoming a bad P.I. and cop cliché. Gunn and Jacoby cooperated logically instead of barking insults at each other. They were practically a team, even though there was the hint of friction arising from the occasional conflicting interest.

When Gunn was through watching all these women, he always came home to Edie Hart, played by Lola Albright.

"Some of the best scenes took place in Jacoby's office," Stevens recounts, "but in the script they were the dullest because they were usually pure exposition. So we came up with business to make them interesting. Gunn walked in one day and Jacoby was on his knees trying to level off his desk, going from one desk leg to the other. We played about eight pages of dialogue as he went from one corner to the next while Gunn just watched. Naturally the tag to the scene was that I took a matchbook and put it under one desk leg, corrected the problem, said, 'I'll see you,' and left. And dissolve on his look of 'Why me?' It may not sound like much, but it played."

The relationship between the hired Gunn and the cop deepened so much that when Bernardi fractured his thigh in a car accident, Edwards refused to fire him or even write him out (despite rumors of anti-Semitic pressure from outside sources). Instead the accident was written into the script as an attack on Jacoby, and the entire crew invaded the North Hollywood Emergency Hospital to film three episodes' worth of Gunn-Jacoby conversations ("Bullet for a Badge," "Kill from Nowhere," and "Vendetta").

Still, Peter Gunn walked alone, for the most part, down the empty video noir backlot streets, with Henry Mancini's jazz score wailing in the distance. The episodes hold up because Edwards made them seem almost dreamlike. Although he invented a wide mix of bizarre and interesting characters, they only seemed to converse with Gunn one at a time. During chase scenes, there always seemed to be just two men in empty alleys (or two cars on empty streets).

The height of that technique came in "The Hunt" episode in 1960, where Gunn goes one on one with a hit man. Once the plot is introduced, the bulk of the episode is sustained without dialogue. It was just the bleak black-and-white images, Stevens' acting, Mancini's music, and Edwards' control. Very impressionistic, very engaging, and very inexpensive.

Style aside, it all boiled down to Gunn's steady, rock-hard character. He was both a hard-boiled and a gentleman detective. Although wry, he was never a wiseacre. Gunn took what he was doing seriously and would never laugh off a corpse, a confrontation, or a client.

"Gunn was a very gentle man and a very decent man," Stevens judged. "For instance, he never cheated on Edie even though he was out with all sorts of different people. He was also loyal to Jacoby even though he was constantly barbing him. But when the chips were down they were like brothers."

But once the novelty of the series wore off, it came under fire for its atmosphere of violence. *Peter Gunn*'s action seemed more extreme because the mood was more extreme. Mike Hammer and Richard Diamond leveled guys in daylight and well-lit rooms. Peter Gunn's world was always dark.

"It wasn't a violent show," Stevens contended, "it was a strong show. We didn't feature gunplay as much as my physically taking care of myself. Shooting someone was a last resort. I don't think Gunn killed or was responsible for killing more than two or three people a season. Blake made a point of that: 'Gunn is not a superhero.' When the police could take care of something, they did."

Stevens' memory did not deceive him. Throughout, Gunn's character remained consistent. He never liked killing—"bad for my reputation." The idea of a detective who takes care of himself but doesn't seek violence will always be successful because it creates an immediate tension. It seems contrary to the character of a private eye, but Edwards built this series on such seeming contradictions.

The crew pounded out approximately thirty-five shows a season, all designed to fascinate from the very first scene (sometimes the very first image). There was "I Know It's Murder," where a clairvoyant foresees death, "A Kill and a Half," which starts with a masked trick-or-treater gunning down a home owner, and "The Deep End," which starts with a young girl drowning while her swimming instructor ignores her.

After 1961, the demands on Blake Edwards became too great. "He came to me at the end of the year," Stevens remembered, "and said, 'Craig, I've got so many film commitments that I just don't think I can stay with the show next season. But I don't want to trade off of the success we've had. I'd rather go out on top.' Well, I agreed with that. It could have gone on for eight or nine seasons if he had stayed with it, but film had become very important to him. It was never cancelled. He actually took it off the air."

The only problem with leaving them wanting more was that, in television, that's millions of people. There was something mesmerizing about the character—he didn't seem like much, but people reacted as if an old friend had disappeared. The clamor for more Gunn was constant.

"Almost every year for ten or fifteen years there was a move to bring him back," Stevens remembers. But Edwards was at the height of his film career, coming off successes with *Breakfast at Tiffany's* (1961), *Experiment in Terror* (1962), *Days of Wine and Roses* (1963), the first two Pink Panther movies (both 1964), and *The Great Race* (1965). After that, Edwards could pretty much get whatever he wanted. And what he wanted was a major motion picture Gunn.

So, instead of a new series of video noir, there was a 1967 movie called, simply, *Gunn* (1967). Surprisingly, it was not film noir but a shockingly bright, full-color effort starring Craig Stevens—but not co-starring Lola Albright or Herschel Bernardi.

"I was terribly upset when they couldn't do it," Stevens recalled. "Lola had just had an accident and Blake was afraid she might not be up to it, while Herschel was on Broadway in *Zorba*. Blake talked to Hal

Prince [*Zorba*'s director] I don't know how many times, but they just couldn't work out a suitable schedule."

So Stevens went it alone in an unfortunate attempt to pave new ground. William Peter Blatty (author of *The Exorcist*) and Edwards wrote a screenplay that borrowed far too much from Mickey Spillane, rather than updating the TV show's look. But the jarring change was totally purposeful.

"Blake went out of his way to be as bizarre and different as he could," Stevens explained. "He thought the film needed that. But the film was way ahead of its time, and Blake was unjustly crucified for it."

There was method to Edwards' madness, but it didn't work. Why dispel what Peter Gunn did best? Why trounce on pleasant memories? Edwards could have done an excellent film noir, a task to which he was well suited. To his credit, he sought to explore new territory. To his debit, he used Peter Gunn to do it. He jammed Gunn into a flashy, trashy world where the violent, bloody killer was a transvestite. It was as awkward and uncomfortable as the moody, tarnished Richard Diamond.

The film was contrary to everything the television series had been —except the contrast between a button-down gentleman gumshoe and a violent world. But without the balancing forces of loving Edie and dependable Jacoby, Peter Gunn was left to flounder in a shocking series of incidents which seemed to shake even him. It certainly shook his faithful audience, who came to see the old friend they remembered. They got their faces rubbed in sleaze instead.

According to the star, other moviemakers still can't understand why the film failed, in spite of the controversial alterations. "I think it had a lot to do with the change at Paramount [the distributor]," Stevens reasoned. "I'll never forget what happened when I returned to New York after making the picture. I was ready to go on a publicity tour and had a lot of ideas for promotion, so I called them. They said, 'Who is this? What picture are you talking about?' They had no idea who I was or what the film was about! This is no excuse, but this sort of thing happens. There's no support. Films get lost. They don't get launched properly."

The failure of the film—intended to be the first in a series—hasn't done that much to dampen the ongoing popularity of the original show, however. More attempts were made to get new episodes on television, the closest to being successful coming in 1977 when 20th Century Fox went so far as to order scripts. The rub came when Blake Edwards couldn't secure his usual creative control. Time had marched on. The artist who could do no wrong had stumbled with *Gunn* and the subsequent *Darling Lili* (1970), *Wild Rovers* (1971) *The Carey Treatment (1972), and The Tamarind Seed* (1974).

Even though he rebounded with new Pink Panther films in 1975 and 1976, Hollywood was unforgiving. They wouldn't let him shoot his new Gunn.

Jo Ann Pflug and Craig Stevens tried to fill Myrna Loy and William Powell's shoes for the 1975 television movie *Nick and Nora*.

The original series hit its syndication stride in the mid-eighties, appearing in all parts of the country, sometimes five days a week. And Craig Stevens isn't the only one who feels that it holds up.

"This is not a modest statement," he disclaims, "but it's better than many of the things I see today. I'll always be proud of it. In fact, when I finished it, I got all sorts of calls to do another private eye show. But if you can't get another one that good, what's the point? It's like everything: good is good. There's no substitute for that."

CHAPTER

The Greed Machine

"Sunset Strip is a body of County territory entirely surrounded by the city of Los Angeles, a mile and a half of relentlessly contemporary architecture housing restaurants, bistros, Hollywood agents, and shops where the sell is as soft as a snowflake and just as cold.

"There are also a few office buildings, and number 77 is one of them. I have an office there that I can't really afford, but I keep it anyway on the happy thought that the address is good for business and the view is good for my soul."

–Stuart Bailey
77 Sunset Strip (1958)

IT WAS 1958, AND FOR ABC THE LIVING WAS EASY. A SCANT FIVE YEARS before, the network was in danger of folding. They were rescued by a merger with United Paramount Theaters. Then the deals started and ABC's luck held. In 1954 they lent Walt Disney a half million dollars to help build Disneyland. The brilliant animator repaid the cash and then the favor by giving them popular TV shows, starting with *Disneyland* (1954–61), and the cult classic *The Mickey Mouse Club* (1955–59).

It was the DuMont network which folded in 1955, and ABC was

"As private-eye Stuart Bailey on *77 Sunset Strip*, Efrem Zimbalist, Jr. is always on the lookout for either crooks or women in trouble. To tell the truth, he prefers women." That's what the press caption says.

there to pick up the pieces—filling their coffers even more. But it was their exclusive pact with Warner Brothers which opened a gold mine. In the 1958–59 season, they owned Sunday with *Maverick* (1957–62), and Tuesday with *Cheyenne* (1955–63), *Sugarfoot* (1957–61), *The Life and Legend of Wyatt Earp* (1955–61), and *The Rifleman* (1958–63). Now they wanted something to follow the new *Walt Disney Presents* on Friday.

They turned to the man who had created several of their already established western series, Roy Huggins. "I went into television in 1955 for a very specific reason," he explained. "It was becoming clear that television was a producer's medium while movies were a director's. And while I wrote screenplays and directed films, I decided I didn't want to do that. I had flat feet and hated standing on my feet all day . . . which directors have to do.

"But I also felt that I could make more money in television and I would have freedom. And I was right. All of my assumptions about television turned out to be true. So I went in and started doing westerns, which were my first love. I did *Maverick*, which was a huge success and also changed attitudes toward westerns a great deal. And then I created *77 Sunset Strip*.

"It was just something I had to sell," he continued. "I said to the studio and network, 'There has never been a one-hour private eye show and there ought to be. It would work.' " He was right on both counts. Up until 1957, there were no hour-long detective series. There was *Perry Mason* (1957–64), but it was a legal whodunit. There were no cop or hard-boiled sixty-minute shows. There were hardly any mystery shows at all.

"They thought it over and decided, yes, I was probably right. Private eyes worked as a half hour, why the hell wouldn't it work as an hour? There had been no one-hour western series either until I did *Cheyenne*. So I said the next step is to do a private eye and they said go do it."

To do it, Huggins went back to his initial career as novelist. The first book he ever wrote was called *The Double Take* and featured a hero named Stuart Bailey—"the private eye with the Ivy-League look and the dock-walloper's punch." That work was popular enough to be bought by Columbia Pictures, where film director S. Sylvan Simon took over. He retitled the project *I Love Trouble* (1948), cast Franchot Tone as the P.I., and hired Huggins to write the script.

"I said, 'Sylvan, the essence of the hard-boiled private eye is that he doesn't love trouble. He wants life to be simple and easy. He isn't a romantic, but he doesn't love trouble. So you can't call it that.' He said, 'Oh, who knows from all that shit. We're calling it *I Love Trouble*. People will like that.' "

Bailey the trouble hater appeared twice in *The Saturday Evening Post* during 1946 ("Appointment with Fear" and "Now You See It"), and once in a 1952 *Esquire* ("Death and the Skylark"). From the latter novelette came a screenplay, "Anything for Money," which appeared as an episode of a Warner Brothers anthology series, *Conflict*, in 1956.

That registered well enough to lead to another proposal incorporating all the stories, this one originally titled *77 Sunset Boulevard*. "Bill Orr [executive producer William T. Orr] said, 'Why don't you call it *77 Sunset Strip*?' And I said, 'Jesus, that's much better.' So we did it."

The result was a script by Marion Hargrove for a ninety-minute movie (ultimately titled *Girl on the Run*) with Stuart Bailey protecting a beautiful girl from a very zealous young hit man named Kenneth Smiley. The finished product was an atmospheric, generally engaging effort produced by Huggins and directed by Richard L. Bare.

The order for a subsequent series featuring Stuart Bailey surprised no one. But the ultimate fate of the villainous Smiley surprised everyone. "Marion Hargrove had seen something happen in the world," Huggins relates. "He had seen the younger generation developing people who were probably very close to being sociopathic. Probably because they were raised on a 'do-anything-you-want' theory. So we made this kid, this hired killer, an absolute heavy—a repulsive human being.

This is the truth: the ABC publicity department actually carried around this 77 Sunset Strip awning and stuck it on almost any door for photo opportunities.

"The plan was to release the movie in theaters if it didn't sell as a television series, so we took it out and previewed it. Well, I was standing out in the lobby with Bill Orr waiting for the people to come out, and Edd Byrnes [the actor playing Smiley] came out with the audience right behind him. He saw us, was starting toward us, when he was mobbed. Edd Byrnes was literally mobbed. There were kids there that wanted to go down on him, right there, right now.

"Here he was, a sociopath, a psychopath, a killer—there were no mitigating circumstances, there were no redeeming virtues in his character. He was just rotten through and through. Absolutely rotten. And they loved him. We just stood there and watched it happen. There was no predicting it. We had no idea it was going to happen."

The moment of magic, besides Smiley's use of hip lingo, came right after the good guys threatened to drop the hit man off a cliff. His condescending manner finally broke and he confessed—but not before he took a moment to comb his hair. That was it: the essense of the character. Orr and Huggins knew that persona, and that phenomenon, had to be part of the new show.

From sociopathic killer to teen heartthrob: Edd Kookie Byrnes goes cheek to cheek with Laura Mitchell.

But certainly not as a heinous psychotic. And not alone with Stuart Bailey. When the word came through that Warner Brothers and ABC wanted it as a series, Huggins already knew that the demands on the actors' time would be debilitating.

"I discovered when I did *Maverick* that you couldn't do an hour series with one lead because you would run out of time. It took six days minimum to do an hour show, which was on the air every week. And the least number the networks would buy was twenty-six, and then they wouldn't preempt."

Preemption is a common thing today when news, sports, and specials take precedence over expensive, intricate series which have trouble finishing even twenty-two episodes a season. The modern solution is to rerun or replace with little concern. Huggins' 1950's answer was to revolve.

"Back then they thought a preemption would destroy a show. Besides they weren't prepared for them. They didn't have specials in those days. I figured it all out and realized there was no way, so after the seventh *Maverick*, I brought in a brother (so each could be featured biweekly). So it was implicit in the 77 *Sunset Strip* pilot that there would be a partner in the series."

The partner was named Jeff Spencer, described in Huggins' words as a "younger, better-looking, lighter" character than the classy, mature Bailey. They had a name for everyone but Edd Byrnes' character. They couldn't bring him back as Kenneth Smiley, the unrepentant murderer, so Huggins harked back to the editing phase of the pilot production.

"In cutting I would sit there saying, 'Look, when the kook comes in, cut immediately.' 'Extend the kook combing his hair,' I'd say. And Bill Orr and Hugh Benson [the associate producer] would be sitting in the back now and then, and they thought his name was Kook. So they started referring to him as Kookie."

Even after Huggins told them the character's real name, they said, "Oh, we like Kookie." So Kookie it was, developing into Gerald Lloyd Kookson III, the cool parking lot attendant at 79 Sunset Strip—Dino's restaurant (which actually existed at that address).

This was where Huggins and the other producers parted company. As always, Huggins wanted to do a serious, realistic treatment of the P.I.'s lot. The concept Orr harbored could be charitably termed "giddy."

The firm of Bailey and Spencer would be a swinging, finger-popping place next-door to Dino's—a groovy hangout for all sorts of daffy characters (most notably a comedy relief horseplayer named Roscoe, who had his fingers in more pies than Jack Horner). Instead of a secretary, the boys would use the lobby office of the Sunset Answering Service, manned by Suzanne Fabray—a French girl who had her own fractured Gallic form of the Queen's English.

Huggins stepped aside, but he asked for a creator's credit and all the money which went along with it. The studio had no intention of giving it to him. Every business seeks to excel as practically as it can, but the studio's desire to own everything at the expense of their hired talent could only be called cutthroat. They balked at Huggins' claim, setting in motion a lawsuit which they ultimately won, and from which Huggins is still smarting.

"It [*Girl on the Run*] was never shown in American theaters except for some little island in the Caribbean, so they were able to say, 'This is a movie he did and now we're adapting.' And they even pretended to do another pilot so that I would never be able to collect the royalties."

Roger Smith (*right*) tries not to laugh at Louis Quinn playing Roscoe the hapless horse tout.

The new pilot was *Lovely Lady, Pity Me,* the first episode of the first season, in which the concept shaped by Orr, Benson, and producer Howie Horwitz showed up. Everything was exaggerated to the point of effervescence. While Roscoe, played by Louis Quinn, talked handicaps, and Suzanne, played by real French import Jacqueline Beer, merely tried to be understood—Kookie was going out of his way not to be. Howie Horwitz had put together a new language for him, supposedly aided and abetted by his teenage daughter.

Kookie didn't get excited, he "blew his jets." He didn't forget, he had "smog in the noggin." He didn't get a cold, he got "buzzed by germsville." And of course, every man was "Daddy-O." He drove a souped-up Model T and, of course, the comb was never far away from his hand or hair.

In the realm of high comedy and serious drama, the series was clearly different and an immediate success. Kookie was an instant teen heartthrob. On the even weeks, Stuart Bailey would take cases, spotlighting star Efrem Zimbalist, Jr., who had played the detective through *Conflict*, the movie, and the ostensible pilot. And while it was initially gratifying to star in a successful show, the shooting schedule and the degenerating scripts soon got to him.

"The dialogue and characters don't change," he complained at the time. "Only the locations." He went on to say that he didn't even bother to memorize his lines anymore. "The show is utter boredom," he concluded. And he made no secret of how much he wanted out. Warner Brothers had refused to lighten his schedule or cancel his contract, which kept him from starring in *Butterfield 8* (1960) and *Portrait in Black* (1960). It has long been his contention that the series kept him from greater movie stardom.

The problem was just the opposite with Roger Smith, who played Jeff Spencer. Instead of his demanding to leave the show, there was some early talk of firing him. Roger Smith thought television was an inferior art form and the idea for the series stank. He came in angry and it showed very clearly in his early episodes (which alternated with Zimbalist's). He couldn't understand how a person as young as he could be a private eye. "I tried to look older," he said at the time. "I tried to copy Robert Mitchum. I never smiled."

It was only a chance meeting with his mentor, Jimmy Cagney, that set him right. Reportedly Smith marveled how Cagney always looked happy, no matter how tough things were. Cagney suggested he try it. That simple instruction and the fact that Smith's fan mail was almost negligible got his pearly whites showing. What was good enough for Jimmy Cagney was good enough for him. Smith turned on the charm and his position on the show became secure.

About the only thing to smile about was the success of the series. The actual production was murder, especially for Kookie. While Zimbalist and Smith appeared in every other episode, the word came down from on high that Byrnes had to appear in every one. So Byrnes had to run back and forth between the two crews simultaneously filming the Spencer and Bailey episodes, learning both scripts and fitting into both plots.

The situation was further complicated in that the actor was playing a part which was totally opposite his natural character. While Zimbalist and Smith were ultimately playing themselves, Byrnes was nothing like Kookie in real life. He was conservative while his screen persona was hopelessly hip.

No matter. Their iron-clad contracts kept them running through jaunty plotlines like "A Nice Social Evening," in which Stu protects a Central American playboy, "The Well Selected Frame," where Jeff gets

Roger Smith as the continually unsmiling Jeff Spencer protects Janet De Gore.

set up by a murderous bride, and "The Iron Curtain Caper" (the first of many "caper" titles), where Stu fights commies to get a reporter out of East Germany (commies were common adversaries in the late fifties, as psycho Vietnam vets would become in the seventies).

The first episode of 1959 was Kookie's first starring shot. "Hit and Run" sees the parking attendant framed for vehicular manslaughter with Stu's car. After that it was business as usual, the storytelling getting looser and looser. Stu goes after racketeers who blind a reporter in "Dark Vengeance." Jeff protects a coed from a college killer's "Conspiracy of Silence." And so on.

Danielle De Metz doesn't seem very interested in Kookie's comb.

It wasn't long before the strain began to reach the writing staff. To keep the wheels oiled, they started recycling scripts from other Warner shows. "Spark of Freedom," with Stu trying to save a scientist in Budapest, was taken from their anthology series *Conflict* (1956–57). The very next week saw "Perfect Setup," which was a frame first used on *Maverick*. The week after that came "Sierra," taken from *Cheyenne*, with Stu in the mountains being stalked by man and beast.

An unusually original script came the week after that, with "The Silent Caper," written by and starring Roger Smith. Jeff Spencer saves a kidnapped stripper so she can testify before a crime commission—all without the benefit of dialogue. Not a word was spoken in the entire hour. The dramatics were accomplished with music, sound effects, mood, and mime.

It was episodes like this which showed the promise of *77 Sunset Strip*. Within the framework of the "cool" program came opportunities to satirize and experiment. But this promise was one the studio seemed intent on wearing out.

The memory of *77 Sunset Strip* would have rested far easier had its own studio not supplied most of its competition. This was not competition in an opposing time slot or on any other network—this was competition for the loyalty of the audience supplied by its own creators. This was incestuous competition; ripoffs all in the family.

77 Sunset Strip was a huge success in 1958, so the powers that be saw no reason not to put into play the lessons they learned with *Cheyenne*. Get it started, keep it going, spin it off. *Cheyenne* begat *Bronco* which begat *Sugarfoot* which begat *Wyatt Earp* which begat *Colt .45* which begat *The Rifleman* which begat *Maverick*. At least all those were individual westerns with a common problem—Warners treated its actors the same no matter how successful their series became.

This led to walkouts and lawsuits, but the studio was willing to suffer the anger and frustration because the shows made them so much money. Warners was the last of the star system studios, trying to fill its movie, TV, and record departments as simply and successfully as possible. To them, the tightly contracted talent was just a cog in their machine.

So, it was time for *77 Sunset Strip* to beget something. *Bourbon Street Beat* (1959–60) was the first effort which shared the format. Like its predecessor, it was developed from an episode of the Warner anthology series, *Conflict*. "The Money" starred Andrew Duggan as a corrupt private eye named Michael Austin who had killed a New Orleans woman for her fortune. Writer Charles Hoffman eliminated that unsavory character and had Duggan play an ex–bayou village policeman named Cal Calhoun. Cal now co-owned a detective agency next to the Old Absinthe House in the French Quarter. Rex Randolph, a young Ivy-Leaguer from a rich Louisiana family played by Richard Long, was his partner in "Randolph and Calhoun Special Services."

Instead of a Kookie type, there was wealthy Texan Kenny Madison (played by Van Williams), who was a part-timer at the agency while studying for a Tulane University law degree. Instead of Suzanne, the dippy French answering service girl, there was Melody Lee Mercer (Arlene Howell), a normal secretary. Instead of Roscoe, there was jazzman Billy the Baron (Eddie Cole). Hoffman then added a new side to the equation—a singer with the unlikely name of Lusti Weather (how could they miss "Stormi"?), played by Nita Talbot.

Actually, this was refreshing. Randolph and Calhoun didn't have gimmicks as much as characteristics. Rex was a sophisticated gourmet. Cal was charming but messy. Hoffman's only concession to *77 Sunset Strip*'s hip lingo gimmick was a New Orleans greeting. Instead of shaking hands, Cal and Rex would put their shoes "sole to sole." *Bourbon Street*

Beat was not a carbon copy, the same way *Maverick* was not a copy of *Cheyenne*. If this new private eye show had succeeded, the format might have endured much longer. Unfortunately, it died after only a year.

Warner Brothers wasn't used to this, and they weren't happy. Bill Orr still thought the format had possibilities, he still liked the actors involved, and he knew that advertisers were waiting in line to back a show like *77 Sunset Strip*. He had known that the year before and had taken steps to cover his losses.

Just two days after *Bourbon Street Beat* went on the air, *Hawaiian Eye* (1959–63) premiered. The New Orleans series was revolutionary compared to the design of the island-based program. The new series was not so much a reworking as it was a remake. Instead of Zimbalist, there was Anthony Eisley as Tracy Steele. Instead of Smith, there was Robert Conrad as Tom Lopaka, who was suppossed to be half Hawaiian. And instead of a parking lot attendant, there was a taxi driver. There was a female singer here too.

Originally, Warner Brothers had asked for a series set in the Caribbean called *The Islander*. Neither Orr nor story editor Jack Emanuel was crazy about the idea. Coincidentally, Emanuel soon went on vacation

Robert Conrad displays the talents that piqued the producers of *Hawaiian Eye*.

Anthony Eisley goes cheesy-tropic for *Hawaiian Eye*.

in Honolulu where he (the story goes) was taxied to his hotel by a talkative cabbie wearing a goofy hat called a "pupule" ("wacky").

Emanuel visited the daughter of a Hollywood friend the next day. She was a free spirit named Cricket. The story editor returned to work with an outline for a show about two house detectives for the Hawaiian Village hotel. They are aided by a part-time photographer and full-time singer at the hotel named Chryseis "Cricket" Blake, and a pupule-hatted taxi driver named Kazuo Kim.

Orr himself had been working in the meantime, looking for an environment as bright and breezy as the Sunset Strip. He had mentally scrapped *The Islander* concept as well because he hated the Caribbean. He had decided on the Hawaiian locale at the same time Emanuel had. When the two got together, it was cause for celebration. They had their new show.

It had been a sunny sendoff, but they soon hit stormy seas. Emanuel's and Orr's visions of the show's style didn't match, so the story editor was forced out. Orr finished the casting himself, signing Poncie Ponce (who had been discovered as a singing waiter at an L.A. restaurant) and Connie Stevens, who had co-starred in Jerry Lewis' *Rock-A-Bye Baby* (1958).

At first the series was treated as a joke. The network didn't see why *Hawaiian Eye* would last any longer than *Bourbon Street Beat*. It was scheduled opposite the very popular *Perry Como Show* (1948–63), so most thought it didn't have a chance. But they hadn't taken into consideration how many years Como had been on the air, how strong the *77 Sunset Strip* formula was, nor how engaging the *Hawaiian Eye* stars were. By the end of the season, *Hawaiian Eye* was one ratings point away from *Perry Como*.

Warner was inspired by their accomplishment. Since *Bourbon Street Beat* was gone, ABC had an hour open on Monday nights. Even then, producers didn't work on the basis of the words "good" or "bad." They worked on the basis of "works" and "doesn't work." New Orleans didn't work. Hawaii did. New characters didn't work. Variations on established characters did. Unusual or normal-looking leads didn't work. Pretty girls and handsome boys did. Put it all together and it spells *Surfside Six* (1960–62).

Kenny Madison (Van Williams) had moved into a Florida houseboat with a Stuart Bailey type—former New York prosecutor Dave Thorne (Lee Patterson)—and a Gerald Lloyd Kookson III type—upper-crust beach boy Sandy Winfield II (Troy Donahue). Anchored next door was the houseboat of gorgeous socialite Daphne Dutton (Diane McBain), and right across the channel is the fabulous Fontainebleau hotel, where the Mexican-Irish spitfire Cha Cha O'Brien entertained (Margarita Sierra).

Signs of creative suicide were all over this show. *Hawaiian Eye* looked similar to *77 Sunset Strip*. *Surfside Six* was a dead ringer for

Connie Stevens sings for her *Hawaiian Eye* supper.

Hawaiian Eye. The studio's attitude toward the public was becoming all too clear. They were no longer borrowing, they were shoplifting. The attitude toward their actors was even worse. Previously, stars of *Cheyenne*, *Maverick*, and *Colt .45* had walked off their sets. The Sunset Strip stars' anguish was already well documented. But Warner still started their stars off with weekly salaries of approximately $250.

They compounded the actors' problem with overwork. Connie Stevens had a number-one radio hit with the "Kookie, Kookie, Lend Me

The cast of *Surfside Six* have a smoke and sing-along. From the left, Lee Patterson, Van Williams, Troy Donahue, and Margarita Sierra.

Your Comb" single, then co-starred in several money-making movies with Troy Donahue. Warners refused to let them do outside work for much better money, then put both on a hectic publicity schedule—all while insisting they regularly appear on their weekly shows. Even Orr admitted this schedule all but killed Donahue's movie career. It also led to Stevens' three physical collapses during 1962.

The actors weren't the only ones dissatisfied. There was also a Warner Brothers writers' strike. Since the producers had to fill 123 episode slots no matter what, old scripts for westerns suddenly became new scripts for private eye shows—and vice versa. Again, everyone suffered. About the only humorous aspect of the situation was the creation of "W. Hermanos," a new staff writer. It was he who supplied many of this period's scripts.

"Hermanos" means "brothers" in Spanish.

By their third year, most of the acting stable was getting $750 a week, but that was still hardly enough considering the amounts the programs brought in. Grant Williams, the star of *The Incredible Shrinking Man* (1958), was brought into *Hawaiian Eye* as Greg MacKenzie after a year of being tested in guest appearances. Then, in an attempt to further bolster the ratings, Troy Donahue was "traded" over during the last season to play Phil Barton, Cricket's boyfriend. Connie Stevens quit soon after.

Look . . . up in the sky . . . it's a clone . . . it's a copy . . . It's Lee Patterson, Troy Donahue, and Van Williams of *Surfside Six*.

Tina Cole was cast as Cricket's replacement, Sunny Day, for the last few episodes.

By that time, *Surfside Six* had been cancelled, and all the shows Warner Brothers had created from the *77 Sunset Strip* mold were in their death throes. It was not a pretty sight. Although most of the actors involved went on to better things, the potentially wonderful experience of starring in a breezy private eye series was not a particularly fruitful or productive one.

Meanwhile, all was not swell with the source of the format either.

The situation became even more extreme when Warners decided to film a whopping forty-three episodes of *77 Sunset Strip* in 1960. Not only did that continue to weaken the scripts, but the actors could no longer do it. The firm of Bailey and Spencer had to be expanded. No problem, thought William Orr. All he had to do was take a character from a failed Warner Brothers detective show and slot him into this one.

Orr moved Rex Randolph of *Bourbon Street Beat* from New Orleans to Hollywood. It was a clever combination of business and creative sense. If the audience accepted the lightheaded mood of the series, they would certainly accept some moonlighting. That set the stage for a flurry of travel by a whole bunch of fictional TV characters. When Warner Brothers hit upon a seemingly successful gimmick, they hammered it into the ground.

In addition to Sam from *Richard Diamond* making a leggy appearance, other characters from *Bourbon Street Beat*, as well as *Hawaiian*

Eye and *Surfside Six*, showed up on the Sunset Strip. Occasionally the actors who played these parts also guest-starred as other characters. By this time the original, ground-breaking series had become a grinning, winking mess—its tongue practically rammed through its cheek.

"The Widescreen Caper" had all the detectives featured, each protecting a star at a trouble-plagued film festival. "Double Trouble" featured the ludicrous, but now well-worn, concept of Stu's evil hit man twin. "Tiger by the Tail" has Stu fighting assassins among a maharajah's entourage while Kookie saves the princess. Only the final episode of 1960 had any real panache. "Once Upon a Caper" was the second episode Roger Smith wrote; a twist on *Rashomon* in which Rex asks the others how the detective agency was created—and gets three, wildly divergent answers.

Most of the time, however, the cast was put through decreasingly interesting paces on the Warner backlot. Finally Edd Byrnes couldn't take it anymore. He had spent three seasons yukking it up in every episode; sometimes ludicrously and unbelievably appearing where the character could not have been (he magically appeared as a Chinese rickshaw driver in "The Hong Kong Caper"). He wanted more respect or he would take his comb and go home.

In fact, Byrnes did leave the show in a contract dispute, allowing Orr to replace him with Troy Donahue (playing Sandy Winfield II of *Surfside Six*) until they cast a more permanent replacement. That was Robert Logan, a college athlete spotted by a talent scout, supposedly while he was eating lunch. Orr and Horwitz created the character of J.R. Hale around him. Initially he was to be nicknamed Junior, but Logan put his muscular foot down. "No one calls me Junior!" Therefore "Jr." became "J.R." Get it?

Hale got it, complete with Kookie's old parking lot attendant job and speech defect. While Kookie spoke hip, J.R. spoke in initials. Nothing to it became N.T.I. Unknown at moment was U.A.M. And S.F. and S.O. It was annoyingly transparent that the producers were not actually replacing Kookie, but were trying to clone him.

Byrnes stayed away for fifteen episodes at the end of 1961, during which time the ratings dropped, so the studio was anxious to get him back. In his absence came six capers ("The Rival Eye," "The Iverness Cape," "The Desert Spa," "The Missing Daddy," "The Navy," and "The Cold Cash Caper"), some business-as-usual episodes, and one more classic. "Reserved for Mr. Bailey" was both the title and what was written on a note attached to a noose in a ghost town. This is considered Efrem Zimbalist, Jr.'s shining hour, since he was the only actor on screen throughout.

Edd Byrnes returned to the show in "The Unremembered," where he and Jeff go after a thief who disguises himself as famous film characters.

Kookie becomes a ranking private eye with suave, smoking Stu, and all the fun went out of his character.

Only this time Kookie was a private eye, despite the associate producer's contention he was only a detective on the side of his usual parking lot duties. Right. They didn't even fire J.R. Hale. It was moonlighting as usual on an already overcrowded show.

Kookie dropped most of his youthful braggadocio and wore suits from then on. He traded in his Model T for a Ford Falcon. Although Byrnes had gained some respect, Kookie's charm was all but gone. He was now just another private dick on a show that had too many private dicks as it was.

But by then the charm of the entire show was all but gone. The structure Warner Brothers and Orr had locked the series into gave little room for growing or even breathing. For every Roger Smith script or

Efrem Zimbalist, Jr. star turn, there were at least thirty-five grindingly familiar capers. The series which had revolutionized the television private eye was now strangling it—and introducing a dreadful concept to the genre: camp.

"I was pleased with the characters," Roy Huggins remembered, "but I thought the stories stunk. They were just typically bad. Television doesn't tell a good story; they don't believe in it. But it was the first hour private eye series, Efrem was wonderful, Roger was charming, and Kookie obviously had an audience, so it worked in spite of the fact that the execution of the show was truly awful."

The 1963 episodes scraped the bottom of the barrel. Rather than borrow from another series, "Target Island" recycled an earlier episode of the same series! Instead of Stu being trapped on an island set for destruction, as in 1959's "Secret Island," Jeff and J.R. are. The ratings took a nosedive. The network wasn't happy and fans were up in arms. Warner Brothers told William Orr, Howie Horwitz, and Hugh Benson to leave.

The studio brought in some heavy hitters to give *77 Sunset Strip* a facelift. The replacements had high batting averages indeed. Jack Webb was named Executive in Charge of Warner Brothers Television, and William Conrad was made producer of the series. They, in turn, asked Smith, Byrnes, Beer, Long, Logan, and the rest of the cast to scram. Jeff Spencer's last case was "The Left Field Caper," a full eight episodes away from the end of the season. Kookie's last case was "Never to Have Loved" where he falls for the actress he's protecting. The "real" Stuart Bailey's last case had him protecting a deaf librarian marked for murder ("Terror in Silence").

Then the new producers did something staggering—they moved Stuart Bailey to the Bradbury Building, way off the Sunset Strip. When the series premiered for its sixth and final season, gone was the catchy theme song by Mack David and Jerry Livingston. Gone was the jaunty tone. Gone was everything but the title and Stuart Bailey. The show was still called *77 Sunset Strip*, but no one could figure out why. Instead of improving the series, making it as good and clever as it could have been, they gutted it and hung it out to dry.

All the changes, Webb maintained, were supported by the network—but not by the studio, which ousted the man shortly after the program reappeared. That left Conrad to deal with the changing attitudes of both the studio and network. After seeing the first three, hard-hitting, controversial scripts Conrad prepared, both wanted a serious backslide. That led to an unprecedented five-part season opener, simply titled "5."

It was a star-studded, globe-trotting adventure in which Bailey tries to solve the hit and run murder of a New York art collector, which leads to a European chase for hidden treasure. From then on, each hour episode took the form of a flashback; Bailey would relate the case to his secretary (played by Joan Staley). By then, Conrad was gone too, replaced by Jim Lydon for the last gasping programs.

The only episode close to what Webb and Conrad had envisioned was "White Lie," in which a black passing for white refuses to acknowledge his heritage. But mostly there were safe, non-threatening shows like "Paper Chase," about blackmail in a stationery factory, and "Not Such a Simple Knot," where Stuart babysits a gambling genius in Las Vegas.

The series' final hour, episode number 204, was "The Target," where Stuart protects the author of a crime exposé, played by none other than William Conrad. The series was still winking at the audience to the bitter end.

In the final analysis, 77 *Sunset Strip* was a contradiction in television terms. It was innovative but derivative, original but repetitive, clever but pedantic, exhilarating and enervating—then died with both a bang and a whimper. The problem was that the public would see its like again. And again and again and again, almost immediately, thanks to the "mon-

Efrem Zimbalist, Jr. left the Strip behind, becoming Lewis Erskine, the government operative who could wound a suspect in the shoulder from any distance or angle, on *The F.B.I.*

key-see, monkey-do" money machine of 1950's and 1960's Warner Brothers Television.

It's Roy Huggins who has the last word on this particular chapter in television history. "When they ran out of things to imitate," he said, "they closed down."

CHAPTER

The Eternal Eye

"Before this all the private eye characters were cynical, à la Bogart. I think that's one of the reasons it didn't work well on television. Because, week in and week out, you want to like the person. You want to get to know him. You want to feel that he cares."

—Mike Connors

THAT WAS PART OF IT. THAT WAS ONE OF TWO KEYS TO THE RESURRECTION of the television private eye and the success of *Mannix*. While there were to be other private eyes smarter than he was, while others would be better detectives, no one was stronger than Joe Mannix—both in a physical and emotional sense.

After the fear and loathing of the fifties, where sponsors and networks struggled to control the studios' work while Senator Joseph McCarthy's communist witch hunts raged around them, the television industry settled into a comfortable, complacent groove. They manufactured escapist material to help soothe the masses in times of a worsening political situation and assassinations.

There was Gilligan, Batman, Jed Clampett, Marshal Dillon, Captain Kirk, Ben, Hoss, and Little Joe Cartwright, Maxwell Smart, Lawrence Welk, and many others whose motto seemed to be: "Forget your troubles, come on, get happy." But when they weren't marooned, cartooned, lost in space, or in the wild west, they were literally running for their lives. *The Fugitive* was the most successful drama on the air.

Into this came Bruce Geller. While some producers are lauded because of their prolific output, others disappear after only a few groundbreaking series. Television has a ferocious appetite and if one is not constantly in the public eye, one is forgotten. Sadly, many reporters like to marvel at junk rather than laud Geller's subtler accomplishments.

Mannix? Subtle? Not on the surface, of course. But while some create gaudy garbage which lasts forever in syndication, *Mannix* lasted eight years in first-run episodes. It also brought into focus the delicate synergy between a solid, workable concept and the importance of an attractive star. While it has already been said that the lead actors can make or break a series, this series shows that *Mannix* couldn't have made

He's got an attitude. He's got a gun. He's got a heavy wool jacket in L.A. He's Mike Connors as *Mannix*.

it without Mike Connors . . . but Connors couldn't have made it without the right Mannix. And neither of them would have survived without the producer's vision.

Everyone's name was changed to protect the innocent. Connors started life as Krekor Ohanian, an Armenian-American, in Fresno, California. When he became a high school basketball star, he was introduced to Henry Wilson of the Famous Artists Agency, the man who named Rock, Rory, Race, Tab, and Troy. He dubbed Krekor Touch Connors, in deference to the student's nickname on the basketball court.

"*Sudden Fear* (1952) was my first film," Connors reported, "which I still consider the best picture I've done to date. Not that I was so good in it, but it was still the best picture, overall, I've been associated with. Then came a whole slew of low-budget pictures; things like *Voodoo Woman* (1957), *The Oklahoma Woman* (1956), *Swamp Women* (1955), and a bunch of westerns."

Saving him from all those abysmal women were Russell Rouse and Clarence Green, who had planned a television series called *Tightrope* (1959–60). In it, the newly renamed Mike Connors played Nick Stone, an undercover government operative who had a unique way of both hiding his gun and drawing it. He developed the style by talking with the series' consultant, as well as an F.B.I. agent.

The F.B.I. man advised pulling your coat in the opposite direction as the drawn gun to distract your opponent. The consultant, a former vice cop, told the actor about putting the gun in the small of the back to avoid detection. Connors put both ideas together, had the prop man make a special slanted holster, and came up with Nick's flashy way of avoiding disarmament and getting the drop on the bad guys. A gimmick was born.

So was an actor. Mike Connors, in the lexicon of the business, was a natural. He avoided the stiffness of Robert Conrad, the smarm of Robert Wagner, and the moodiness of David Janssen. He was able to combine looking relaxed on screen with being ready for action. He had a casual energy which made him trustworthy and likable.

The abundant action and Connors' panache made *Tightrope* popular, but it was cancelled after one season. It was caught in the undeclared war between sponsors and networks. From Martin Kane to Peter Gunn, sponsors had their own slots of time and, as Craig Stevens has said, the networks had nothing to do with it. But the channels had been wresting control back, sometimes in nasty tugs-of-war. That, in itself, might not have been enough to kill *Tightrope*, but its fate was sealed by another source.

"Somebody at *TV Guide* wrote that in one season we had twenty-two buckets of blood," Connors said, "twenty-seven machine gunnings, so many switchblade killings . . . all false. But when that article hit, no

Artist's prerogative:
Tightrope.

matter how much we denied it, our goose was cooked. Because of that CBS probably wanted to move us to a later time slot.

"Our sponsor, Pharmaceuticals Incorporated, said, 'We've had this time of night for five years now and we finally have a successful show. And you want to take it away from us.' The network replied, 'If you don't accept the time we want you to go on, then we don't want your show.'

"The show was dropped. We immediately went to ABC and did an hour pilot, but the format was changed considerably. I already knew we were in trouble because the guy went from being a loner to having a government contact and a police associate. It took away all that larger-than-life adventure. It was a well-made pilot, Dina Merrill and Zachary Scott were in it, but the show never went on."

Connors consoled himself with better performances in higher-quality movies like *Good Neighbor Sam* (1964), *Harlow* (1965), the remake of *Stagecoach* (1966), and *Situation Hopeless—But Not Serious* (1965) with Robert Redford and Alec Guinness. Meanwhile, the TV private eye was taking it on the chin.

"It was in the dumper," as Connors aptly put it. Richard Levinson and William Link wanted to do something about that.

Levinson takes up the story: "Bill and I were freelance writers, and we brought our idea for a new private eye series to Desilu [the studio created by Desi Arnaz and Lucille Ball, which was also responsible for *The Untouchables* and *Star Trek*]. Herb Solo ran it then and he said, 'What's your idea?' We said, 'Humphrey Bogart at MCA.' "

MCA was the company which ran Universal Studios—known for its strict corporate structure. "That was the hook," Levinson continued, "the line that attracted them. What we meant was a large detective agency, like Pinkerton's, which we made an analogy with MCA. You know, the 'black tower' and the time clocks, everybody has to wear a dark suit, and each cubicle had its own TV camera.

"Into this we put the one humanist. He would hang his sport jacket over the camera and be in constant conflict with the guy who ran the place, Lou Wickersham—who was a homage to Lew Wasserman [head of MCA]. Our concept was to place the computerized, mechanistic firm against the free-swinging, independent maverick. And they bought it."

Levinson and Link's concept went deeper than that. By making the character a maverick, he would naturally take on cases for the underdog, making him immediately appealing. He would also be an outlaw among his peers, and audiences almost always cheer rebellion against authority.

What Desilu bought was a script called *Intertect*, named after the detective agency. The free-swinging maverick was named Joe Mannix. "We wrote down about thirty names before we hit on that," Levinson revealed. "We had names like Solitaire, Solo, you know, all those names. Then it turned out that there was an Eddie Mannix at MGM, and there was a fellow named Mannix we went to high school with. We liked the sharp sound of that."

So Mannix it was, and Desilu set about preparing the production. Originally Gene Roddenberry was to ride herd on it, but he was diverted by his creation of the Starship *Enterprise.* So Solo turned to the already successful producer of *Rawhide* (1959–66) and *Mission: Impossible* (1966–73), Bruce Geller. But it was not the producer or the creators who matched the actor and his character. (Levinson and Link had suggested Darren McGavin, the star of the first television *Mike Hammer*, 1957–59.) It was the owner of the studio.

"I ran into Gary Morton (Lucille Ball's second husband) one day on the Desilu lot," Connors recalled. The actor had just finished a cheap foreign James Bond knockoff called *Kiss the Girls and Make Them Die* (1967). "And he said, 'We just got a script across our desk you'd be fantastic for.' So I read it and fell in love with it. We talked and made a deal."

It wasn't long before *Mannix* was on the air. Success was not instantaneous, although the first season contained some of the highest energy and strongest interpersonal drama in the genre. The sparks came from the tense relationship between the free-spirited Mannix and the

Artist's prerogative: *Intertect,* the pilot film that launched *Mannix.*

button-downed Wickersham (played by Joseph Campanella). Geller sustained this tension for the entire season. Mannix constantly defied his employer by taking cases Wickersham swore Intertect would never touch.

From the very start, Geller demanded unusual plots and relevant themes. In one of the more haunting episodes, "Warning, Live Blueberries," Joe investigates a hippie commune where a boy was killed. The teenagers were portrayed as lost souls, not stereotypically drugged-out freaks as they were on every other series at this time (composer Lalo Schifrin wrote an especially effective theme for this episode).

Establishing another Mannix tradition was the episode in which a wounded Mannix is forced to run a makeshift obstacle course in a dirty, deserted town. Throughout the series came episodes designed to test both the P.I.'s intellect and stamina. Then there were the classic twists and turns of the traditional hard-boiled mystery, as in the episode where a seemingly innocent mother hires Mannix in a custody battle to create a cover for killing her ex-husband.

It was enough that Geller had original, involving stories with a tough but tender edge, but he didn't leave it at that. He built the friction between Mannix and Wickersham until it exploded in a two-part episode of anger, resentment, and violence ("Deadfall").

"Joe Campanella and I happened to like each other very much from the beginning," Connors said. "He was a terrific, warmhearted guy; a family man. We both had ethnic backgrounds, respected and understood each other. So we saw to it that the genuine care the characters had for each other showed through all the fighting. Underlying all the on-screen tension was that personal regard we had for each other."

Mannix and Wickersham were like brothers, and acted like it on screen. Lou was the elder, more set in his ways and resentful of Mannix's instincts. Joe was the younger man, who alternately respected and distrusted his superior's rigid authority. Other producers have let that kind of unnatural friction fester throughout their series' run. Geller had Levinson's and Link's characters confront their anger in the sixteenth episode. But once that happened, there was nowhere for the relationship to go.

"They discovered the writers couldn't sustain weekly stories in which man versus machine," said Levinson.

"Even though it was well produced, it was not doing well," Connors concurred. "It didn't make sense that I was in constant conflict with the company. At the end of the first year, it was really a marginal show."

"It looked like the series was going to be cancelled," Levinson agreed.

Geller had gambled and seemingly lost. He had let the drama take its natural course instead of milking it ad nauseum. Seeing the writing on the wall, he produced "You Can Get Killed Out There," the last episode of the first season, in which Joe Mannix quits Intertect.

It was time for the second team. CBS and Desilu knew the show had promise, but not in its present form. They brought in Ivan Goff and Ben Roberts, who did something small but spectacular.

"They got rid of the concept which sold the show," Levinson announced. "Our hook sold the series, but then again, two freelancers couldn't sell a show on their concept." In recounting how it happened, Levinson took on the roles of a writer pitching an idea and a sarcastic network executive.

" 'What have you got?'

" 'A private eye who solves cases.'

" 'Brilliant!' "

Levinson shrugged. "But on that concept it ran eight years."

Simple as that: Mannix was an ex-cop who left the police force to solve the killing of his partner, went to work for a big detective agency, then quit. He opened up his own private detective agency at 17 Paseo Verde, with the wife of his murdered partner as his secretary.

"We had started shooting the first show of the new season and we

"Humphrey Bogart at MCA"—Mike Connors and Joseph Campanella starred as clashing detectives in the first season.

still didn't have an actress to play the secretary," Connors related. "But Bruce Geller came down to the set and said, 'I want you to meet somebody we're considering to be your secretary . . . I'd like to know how you feel and hear what you think.' So I was introduced to Gail Fisher and we talked. She had a good personality and was very nice. When Bruce called later, I said she seems fine to me. So she became Peggy Fair."

It seemed like a big deal just to cast a secretary, but Gail Fisher was black in a decade when black co-stars were extremely uncommon. Bill Cosby had become the first black co-star of a series (*I Spy*, 1965–68) three seasons before, but television has always been slow coming around. Not to put too fine an edge on it, Hollywood was racist.

Of course the cover is that they don't want to do anything which would disturb the viewers, as *The Nat "King" Cole Show* (1956–57) had done (only to bigots, but, heavens, if executives started categorizing viewers by sin, where would they be?). But three years after *I Spy*, many were still running around saying that Cosby was the exception, not the rule.

"Geller, Goff, and Roberts decided that nothing would ever be made of the fact that I was white and she was black," Connors elaborates. "Color was never an issue or even acknowledged. It was a relationship between two people and that's how we played it." Of course that was the safe way to play it as well. And as Goff and Roberts were to say when Fisher voiced displeasure in later seasons (when she wasn't given much to do), this was a show about Mannix, not his secretary.

While the series concept was streamlined, the producers set to work enriching the man's character. "What Goff and Roberts brought to the show is something I didn't see for many years afterward," Connors maintained. "Vulnerability.

"I remembered discussing how far we dare go with the emotional scenes. They said, 'How do you feel about that?' I said I thought I'd go for it; all of it, the tears, the soft, emotional side of the man. I felt the character wouldn't be afraid of showing his emotion for fear of losing his machismo. And they said, 'Great. Because we think that's very important.' They brought a great deal of warmth and understanding to the series, which I think made the audience go with the character through thick and thin."

Joe Mannix became the distillation of every private eye who had ever been on television. Tough but tender. Aggressive but philosophic. He had Sam Spade's savvy but Philip Marlowe's sensitivity. He had a solid, consistent, serious, one-hour series. He represented the television detective. He was the eternal eye.

Also helping were Geller's precepts, which were held over from the first season. Never be afraid to try something different. The very first episode of the second season, "The Silent Cry," featured actors from the National Theater for the Deaf. The second episode, "To the Swiftest,

Joe Mannix tells his secretary, Peggy Fair (Gail Fisher), which letter to take.

Death," introduced Mannix's love of auto racing, and the third, "Pressure Point," showed that they could still do flat-out hard-boiled mysteries. In that, a victim's dying words, "kelly green frame" lead to a judge's daughter and her three mafia punk pals.

The ratings began to climb. "The audience really seemed to like him," Connors stated. "They thought he was a nice human being even though he could kick ass and raise hell. Things meant something to him . . . inside."

Mannix could certainly kick ass. Years later, Levinson thought of his and Link's creation as the archetypal violent detective show. It was held up to derision and satire for its violence, which many remember as pretty extreme. Which is not surprising, really, because it *was* pretty extreme. Mannix would rarely resist shooting his snub-nosed revolver and was never reluctant to punch someone out. Joe Mannix was always in motion.

No viewer could be mistaken about the show after seeing the opening credits. While Lalo Schifrin's lilting theme played, a checkerboard of images appeared: Joe running across a bridge from a driver's point of view . . . a race car flying off a cliff . . . Joe leaping from a dune buggy, rolling, and coming up shooting . . . and Joe burning himself taking toast from a toaster. This was a thriller controlled by an average, "real" man.

Mannix was a synthesis of everything which had preceded it, stripped of most of their artifice. He wasn't a tortured man; he was a good man. He wasn't an avenger; he was a do-gooder. He wasn't a bully; he was tough. He had the two ingredients which made a successful television hero, passion and compassion. But unlike the ones before and the ones after, he drew no attention to it. All the class went into the handsome production values. Geller saw to it that the writing, directing, and filming were top-notch.

While it is true that Mannix could take care of himself and did so very often, there was a special edge Geller, Goff, and Roberts brought to even the action. "Dick Ziker was my double and the stunt coordinator," Connors related. "He was terrific. He was literally ready to lay down his life to make the show look good." This was no exaggeration. Hollywood stuntmen are made that way.

"But we had one rule between us," Connors went on. "We would never do a stunt for a stunt's sake—just because it would look spectacular. We laid down the law in the second season. If it looked like a stunt, we won't do it. Dick fought that for a little while but he soon realized that's what gave the show its reality. I'll tell you, I'm so sick of that scene of a car going up a hidden ramp, turning over, exploding, and skidding in flames! It was the scarcity of that sort of thing which made people believe in our show, no matter how wild it got."

It also, probably unknowingly, helped the program succeed so resoundingly. Mannix's violence was the sort that attracted an audience, rather than repelling it. Because it was so immediate and physical, without the ludicrous aspects of many other television fight scenes, the action became more than exciting. It became interesting. On other shows, there is the impression that the heroes cannot be hurt. Here, thanks to Connors' vulnerability and the stunting edict, there's always a sense of real danger.

Ziker gave the action an energy the other shows didn't have. Although the fights were still larger than life, they had a weight never before achieved on TV. The camera angles would often be high when Mannix was thrown down, and low when he decked the villains. You could watch him fall from a godlike perspective, then watch the bad guys hit hard right before your eyes.

"I have to admit," Connors continued, "that for the sake of the story, Mannix had to be a little stupid sometimes. One thing you can

Mike Connors hits the mattress for the cameras, with real-life "French Connection-buster" Eddie Egan as guest star.

say for him, though, he was really hard-headed. And he didn't look behind doors for blackjacks often enough . . . ."

Mannix wasn't hard-hearted, however. That was something the entire staff worked on. The most fan mail was received after the episodes in which Mannix went home. He had grown up in Summer's Grove, California, and developed a tense relationship with his Armenian father, Stephen (played by Victor Jory). "Mannix's father always wanted him to be a rancher," explained Connors. "And they'd always end up arguing. It was a little like the Mannix-Wickersham relationship."

That dynamic was maintained throughout the series. When Joe wasn't arguing with his dad, he might be bantering with Lieutenant Adam Tobias, the most successful of four police associates Mannix had. "My relationship with Robert Reed [the actor who played Tobias] was also like Campanella in a way," Connors said. "Again, when Bob and I worked in a scene, it was like sign lanquage. It clicked, there was a spark. He was only going to do one episode originally, because he was starring in *The Brady Bunch* (1969–74), but we had such a good time and there was so much chemistry he wanted to come back."

Reed regularly substituted for the first cop character, Lieutenant Art Malcolm, played by Ward Wood. This was the same season which featured such relevant episodes as "Eagles Sometimes Can't Fly," about an American Indian on the run; such classic mysteries as "Tooth of the Serpent," in which everyone (including Mannix's client) is hiding something during his investigation into a two-year-old hospital scandal; such popular stamina episodes as "End Game," where a vengeful, court-martialed Korean war vet traps Joe in a booby-trapped building; and "The Sound of Darkness," which garnered Connors his first Emmy nomination for portraying the detective stricken with psychosomatic blindness.

As the many years progressed, antagonistic Lieutenant Dan Ives (Jack Ging) took over for Tobias, occasionally supplemented by sullen Lieutenant George Kramer (Larry Linville, who was to play Frank Burns on *M*A*S*H*, 1972–83). Throughout, Mannix defended his sympathetic, likable character against all odds and all comers.

"Both Goff and Roberts cared enough that they spent hours every week making sure all the scripts were consistent," Connors elaborated. "They didn't just say, 'Here's the latest one, shoot it.' They worked it out, scene by scene. Their caring was what made each script work. But everybody pitched in and did their best for the show. There was a real esprit de corps there and I think that showed."

Mannix revived the brain-dead genre by, of all things, caring. No one gloated over the victims' deaths because Joe would always be there, his face filled with concern. Just as he had at Intertect, he took the dark horses, the no-win cases, the lost causes. He was constantly challenged, but always up to it. He personified the joy of the private eye genre. He set things right because it was the right thing to do.

Not only did he put the TV P.I. back on the map, he gave him something to wear. "Well," Connors says with a smile, "Bruce Geller wanted him to wear winter materials, English materials, heavy tweeds. These materials tended to look a bit more baggy, a bit out of shape. We put patches on the coats so it would look like he's had the jacket for a hundred years. We went for plaids . . . *heavy* plaids.

"At first they were a little more subtle, but as time went on we decided he'd be a sport coat kind of guy and the patterns got louder. Finally we tried to get a lighter material because it was hell to work in those heavy tweeds all the time, but it was too late. All of a sudden, the audience picked up on the heavy plaid jacket. It became sort of a symbol. To this day, people still come up to me and say, 'You know, I've got a Mannix jacket.' "

Over eight seasons Mannix had become the top television private eye, so the Mannix jacket became de rigueur for any self-respecting dick. Here they were, trudging around sunny, hot Los Angeles in baggy plaid tweeds. Harry O wore them. Jim Rockford wore them. Even Remington Steele had one.

It seemed like *Mannix* would run forever. Sure, certain plot lines became awfully familiar. A regular viewer had to wonder about Joe's taste in women. I mean, how many ex-girlfriends can get into so much trouble? A *Mannix* fan was also forced to wonder how many psychos were after Joe and his Korean War army buddies.

But *Mannix* also set the standard for seasons to come, in both

Mike Connors tried to fill Efrem Zimbalist, Jr.'s shoes for *The New F.B.I.*

behavior and plot. Some of his classic cases have appeared on other shows repeatedly through the years. "Silent Target," for example, has Mannix discovering a hit man "pool" awaiting assignments (as they later did on *Mickey Spillane's Mike Hammer*). The show's traditions continued in their final years. "Desert Sun" has a small town covering up the death of an American Indian. "To Cage a Sea Gull" has the dying message "sea gull" and a crashed plane's gas tanks filled with popcorn. "Fly Little One" was about an emotionally disturbed child on the run from a killer.

Then there were the Mike Connors showcases. Between consistently involving mysteries, fairly authentic detecting, and thundering action, there were episodes which challenged Connors from an acting and physical standpoint. In 1972 there was "Death in the Fifth Gear," wherein Joe is gripped by paranoid hallucinations (Connors' second Emmy nomination). In 1974, he went undercover as a heroin addict in "The Ragged Edge," and struggled triumphantly through "The Dark Hours" after being shot with his own gun (third nomination).

"In our last year, we had a thirty-four share average," Connors remembered. That was extremely high, but like *Tightrope*, Joe Mannix was finally brought down by network-studio politics. Paramount Pictures, for whom Desilu was making its shows, was using deficit financing on Bruce Geller's series. That is, they were spending a million a week on *Mission: Impossible* and almost as much on *Mannix* with supposedly no chance of making a profit until the series went into syndication.

Mission was already in syndication, so Paramount hit upon a great idea for *Mannix*. "Apparently they went to CBS," Connors related, "and said, 'We'll go another year on *Mannix* but we want to put the show into late-night syndication at the same time.' That was unheard of then. And CBS said, 'No way, you're crazy. You'll kill the show.' Paramount replied, 'Look, we're millions of dollars in the hole. We can get profits in syndication after eight years of deficit spending.' CBS said, 'We won't renew you if you do that.'

"Paramount put us on at 11:30 at night on ABC, and CBS cancelled even though they found it didn't hurt the prime time summer reruns at all. But they had already called the whole thing off."

Still, *Mannix* went out on a first. It established the late-night syndication precedent of series still in production, a practice that is common today. They also went out a winner. The stories remained high quality, a trick very few series can claim.

In the final year there was "A Word Called Courage," where a former Korean War friend uses the same interrogation torture on Joe that he himself had cracked under. "Quartet for Blunt Instruments" was the evocative title of another hard-hitting case. Then there was the two-part "Birds of Prey," based on both Victor Canning's 1951 novel of the same name (and the 1953 movie *The Assassin*).

Mannix's last case was "A Small Favor for an Old Friend," in which a low-grade hood asks Joe to grant a last request—solve his murder. Joe was in there to the end, plugging away with the same consideration and brute strength he always had. It was what kept his fans watching through the weaker episodes amongst the almost two hundred produced.

After such a successful career, it's surprising Mannix hasn't returned—while less popular TV detectives have. "It seems like a natural," Connors admitted. "In fact, Bruce Geller called me and asked if I would be interested in a two-hour made-for-television *Mannix* movie.

I said of course. He said he was working on it and he'd get back to me. He was killed in a plane crash a few months later."

Ivan Goff and Ben Roberts continued, but never with the same mix of begrudging critical and clear financial success. They helped launch *Charlie's Angels* (1976–81), then mounted the short-lived *Nero Wolfe* (January–August 1981) series. As for Mike Connors, he kept busy with some television appearances, a short-lived new series (*Today's F.B.I.*,

The cast of *The New F.B.I.* only got to pose and point for a few weeks before cancellation.

1981–82), a few low-budget movies, and commercials. But it was clear his most famous character is closest to his heart.

"Mannix is still working," Mike Connors mused. "Just a little slower." He thought about the character for a moment. "There was a decency and a dignity about the man . . . ."

CHAPTER

The Death Head Grin

"Book him, Dan-o."

—Steve McGarrett
Hawaii Five-O (1968)

THIS IS THE LONGEST CONTINUALLY RUNNING MYSTERY-DETECTIVE SHOW in the history of television. *Dragnet* ran longer if one includes the radio and resurrected versions, but that doesn't really count. Other programs may be better respected, more beloved, and more fondly remembered, but no other show lasted longer.

There has to be a better reason for that besides the obvious and oft-repeated one—that the beauty of the location scenery made people tune in. In fact, while Hawaii is undeniably beautiful, *Hawaii Five-O* almost always downplayed its splendor. In truth, there were two reasons the series held on for so long.

One was a man who instinctively knew how to create viewer involvement (i.e. tension) with both the concept and the stories. Second, and ultimately more important, was an actor who knew how to clamp down on an obsessive, passionate character, and hold on like a pit bull.

Every gigantic entertainment success has reasons for its popularity beyond popular opinion. Every movie which has made over $100 million delivers more to the audience than superficial thrills or laughs. There is always a spine, a heart, and a brain at work. The spine is the film's theme, the heart is its message, and the brain is its story structure.

Television series take shape over a longer period of time. Audiences' memories for films differ from their recollection of television. Scenes and stories are remembered from movies. Concepts and characters are TV memories. *Hawaii Five-O* had the least obvious, but most powerful foundation of all. It started with Leonard Freeman.

Freeman is virtually unknown to the public. If mentioned at all in show business reference works, it is usually just as creator and executive producer of *Hawaii Five-O*. His other television show, *Storefront Lawyers* (1970–71), lasted only one season on CBS. My personal opinion of it is as low as almost every other critic's.

"Three young members of a prestigious law firm set up a free legal-aid service for the needy," the network publicity release read. "Their first case is a sensational murder." Well, of course it is! Doesn't every nonprofit law firm get a headline-grabbing homicide right off the bat? The problem with the program was already apparent. They wanted to have their cake (relevance, realism) and eat it too (action, thrills).

Things were not improved when the format changed a hundred and eighty degrees four months into the TV season. Gone was the cake, and back the noble, intrepid lawyers went to the huge legal firm they had left to open the storefront. No one likes a fink, and certainly not ones with their tails between their legs. Viewers tuned out in droves.

It's hard to believe that Freeman had anything to do with the production of that show at all after his work on *Hawaii Five-O*. It may have been a happy accident, but his entire career culminated with the cop show. He had only been recognized by the Academy of Television Arts and Sciences once: for writing "The Answer," performed on the *Four Star Playhouse* in 1954. It was also nominated for best editing, best art direction, best director (Roy Kellino), and best actor (David Niven). None won. *Dragnet* walked away with most of the genre Emmys that year.

Freeman continued to toil in the industry, sharpening his writing skills and making a bridge toward production, where the real television power was. He also continued to investigate the tensions that could be created inside a story—how a subject could be composed of two opposing forces.

In 1965, he came up with what would turn out to be his pièce de résistance. He mixed intrinsic opposites, beauty and ugliness, and came up with a winner. The only thing left to do was convince a studio and network of it.

"It has taken me three years to convince CBS to put up the money for this series," he told *The New York Daily News*. "I waited because I was determined to get off a studio lot and bring a new look to television."

Freeman was fascinated with storytelling and with the Pacific. He had discovered Hawaii and the incredible diversity (and tension) of the teeming Asian life there. While the Chinese have historically hated the Japanese, who have hated the Vietnamese, who have hated them back —in Hawaii, these three races, along with Polynesians, Malaysians, Filipinos, and many others, have lived in peace. But the tension between them and the "haoles" (as they called Caucasians) was always there.

Leonard Freeman felt it, and he saw how nature's beauty could clash with human violence. That was what *Hawaii Five-O* was all about. It was the ultimate confrontation between good and evil in the world's most beautiful place. No namby-pamby, minor cop melodrama for Freeman. Lieutenants, nor captains, nor even chiefs were good enough. His leading man would be a police power unto himself.

"He takes orders only from the governor," a character said of that man in the pilot. "Or God. And sometimes even they have trouble."

He was Steve McGarrett. No prefix, no set place in the police hierarchy. If he were called anything, it was "detective" or "sir." He was the penultimate legal power in Hawaii. He ran an elite, understaffed unit, ostensibly attached to the Hawaiian State Police. Of course, he could supplement his team with the entire force if necessary, but his main job was a cerebral one. He was the ultimate good mastermind set in place against ultimate evil masterminds.

The Five-O group was named for the state itself, the fiftieth state in the union, and it was their job to go after the worst the islands had to offer. Although stationed in Oahu, they could, and often did, go anywhere in Hawaii to get their man—or woman. There were no petty sexual distinctions for McGarrett. To him, you were either a law-abiding citizen—or in big trouble.

The network readily agreed the idea was exciting; especially in light of the fact that on 1967 television, the cop genre was all but dead. There were the half-hour *Felony Squad* (1966–69), *N.Y.P.D.* (1967–69), *Dragnet*, the hour *Ironside* (1967–75), and that was it. The genre needed an infusion of new blood, and since *Hawaii Five-O* also incorporated many of the pleasures to be found in the still successful James Bond films, it seemed a good idea to finance.

The big problem was Freeman's insistence that it be filmed on location. *Hawaiian Eye* had not been, nor had any of the few others which had supposedly taken place in the tropics. All they had were a few establishing shots of palm trees, and the rest was done on the back lot or on California beaches. The network argued that the logistic problems would be nightmarish. They were right, but Freeman put his feet down and let them take root. It was either Hawaii or no Five-O.

The only things which swayed, and finally persuaded, the network to give the show a try were the quality of Freeman's work, and the fact that press junkets and executive visits to the set would be very popular. *Hawaii Five-O* could be a CBS showcase. It could gain them very good press indeed.

The show was budgeted, and Leonard Freeman got a go-ahead. Then he faced his second problem. He had an extreme character. He needed an extreme actor. To the audience's delight and almost everyone else's chagrin, he got one.

Enter John Joseph Patrick Ryan, an artistic man with a huge passion for the arts—and many said an ego to match. That was all right. McGarrett had to be larger than life. So was the actor who played him.

Freeman had started looking for his McGarrett with Gregory Peck in mind. Although Peck had never done television, that didn't stop Freeman from asking. "Who knows?" the producer rightfully said. "Maybe today he'll say yes."

He did not. Freeman continued down the line until he came to a forty-year-old actor who had been the first replacement for the pivotal part of Brick in the original Broadway production of *Cat on a Hot Tin Roof*.

The reviewers had been kind to the actor, who had burned with intensity even then. Freeman knew him better as a performer in a variety of middling movies and television shows. Of the hardly notable dramas, westerns, and action films he had been in, his best-known achievement was playing Felix Leiter (James Bond's CIA friend) in the first 007 movie, *Dr. No* (1962).

That made him somewhat bankable and led to the title role of *Stoney*

Jack Lord as C.I.A. agent Felix Leiter is just about the only one to get the drop on James Bond (Sean Connery) in *Dr. No.*

Burke (1962–63) on ABC television. He played a modern-day cowboy, a rodeo rider whose work got him involved in scrapes of every nature on the road to the highest award for bronco busters—the Golden Buckle.

The show lasted only one season, but J.J.P. Ryan made out fairly well. His limited fame led to a profitable pastime of touring state fairs and real rodeos to show off just two of his many unexpected talents: horse-riding and singing.

"I'm ironing shirts today," he said metaphorically. "Tomorrow I'll buy the laundry." By then he was already fairly well known by his new stage name—Jack Lord.

Ambition and assurance. Those were but two ingredients within his personality. They had led him to write articles for *Variety* magazine about the travails of a young actor, when he was being typecast as a villain because of his dark features and craggy good looks. Interestingly, he got his first big television break on *Man Against Crime*. There followed parts in live television and Broadway. What every actor and director remembered about him was how driven he was. He seemed to be possessed by the parts he played.

He even got into Stoney, modeling the character on Gary Cooper. But once that series was over, he locked his mind on to other things. According to him, he was offered a great many parts which he turned down. Over the years, Lord contended that he refused to play the leading role in *Wagon Train*, *Ben Casey*, *Shenandoah*, *The Outsider*, and even *The Man From U.N.C.L.E.*

"I can't stand an atmosphere of human misery," he was reputed to have said. Meanwhile, however, he was appearing in movies like *The Ride to Hangman's Tree* (1967), *The Counterfeit Killer*, and *The Name of the Game Is Kill*! (both 1968).

"My degree is for teaching art at the college level," he said. "I got sidetracked as an actor, during the [Korean] war, in a unit that turned out training films. That's how John Joseph Patrick Ryan became Jack Lord. First there was Stoney Burke. Then they wanted to make me a marshal on the Santa Fe trail." That was a series called *Cutter's Trail*, which was all set for production the year CBS was originally planning to cancel *Gunsmoke*, the seminal western series starring James Arness. Instead, *Gunsmoke* was renewed for a record-breaking twentieth season, and *Cutter's Trail* was closed.

"Then they wanted to make me a race car driver," Lord recalled. It was another show that stalled. "Then *Hawaii Five-O* came along and that, for me, was it."

Halfway through reading the script he reportedly turned to his wife and asked if she'd like to live in Hawaii. Legend has it that the very next day the deal was made, which included a piece of the action for the actor. Leonard Freeman and Jack Lord were off to Hawaii with a two-hour script and $800,000.

The pilot movie was fairly incredible in every sense of the word. McGarrett goes up against a team of enemy secret agents, who stick him in a gaudy yellow scuba suit and a giant, clear sensory deprivation tank. They try to brainwash him, but neither McGarrett nor his mind would have any of it. He dragged himself out of the thing and beat them to a pulp. Hawaii's top cop had a will of iron.

The pilot was popular, but Freeman felt the entertainment mixture was still a bit off. Lord was exactly right, but his office staff was not perfect. Tim O'Kelly had played McGarrett's closest associate, Detective Danny Williams, but he was a little too ruddy. Freeman remembered an earnest, normal-looking young man he had worked with in the movie *Hang 'Em High* (1968), starring Clint Eastwood. He was James MacArthur, the son of actress Helen Hayes and playwright Charles MacArthur. And he was quite anxious to get out of his parents' shadows.

"CBS thought I was crazy for casting Jim as a detective," Freeman said. Up until then, MacArthur was best known for roles in *Swiss Family Robinson* (1960), *Spencer's Mountain* (1963), and *The Bedford Incident* (1965). " 'You're out of your mind,' they said. 'He's too ethereal.' But I think he has helped give the show an air of authenticity."

Freeman thought that MacArthur was the normal Joe's idea of what an honest cop looked like. He also had an air of naturalness—an edge of amateurism—which gave the impression that he was a real cop who had been drafted as an actor by the production.

Lew Ayres, the star of *All Quiet on the Western Front* (1930), *Holiday* (1938), *Johnny Belinda* (1948), *Advise and Consent* (1962), and *The Carpetbaggers* (1964), played the governor of Hawaii in the pilot. When he was unwilling to move to the islands for the series, he was replaced by Richard Denning—another inspired choice.

The blond, handsome, stern, erect Denning not only looked like someone McGarrett would take orders from, he complemented Jack Lord in appearance. He was also a very popular actor with the cult film and television crowd, having starred in *Creature from the Black Lagoon* (1954), *Target Earth* (1954), *Creature with the Atom Brain* (1955), *The Black Scorpion* (1957), the *Mr. and Mrs. North* (1952–54) TV series, and the *Michael Shayne* (1960–61) show.

The rest of the Five-O team remained the same. Freeman also showed his mettle by casting Chinese actor Kam Fong as Detective Chin Ho Kelly and Hawaiian entertainer Zulu as Detective Kono. The traditional television approach would be to hire handsome Hollywood performers. Zulu was burly while Fong was short and chunky. They were also not wildly convincing actors. But they seemed real, and they reflected Hawaii's racial mix.

Five-O's office was in the Iolani Palace, which had once been the seat of the Hawaiian Legislature but was now a museum. The series made

James MacArthur as Danny Williams, doing what Dan-o did best . . . staying out of McGarrett's way.

the building famous once again, since the exterior establishing shot of McGarrett's corner office was one of the show's most repeated visuals. The most famous sequence was the entire *Hawaii Five-O* opening.

Morton Stevens wrote a suitably pounding, pulsating theme song (as well as orchestrating the show's soundtracks for years) around which veteran director Reza Badiyi created a mosaic of Hawaiian sights. It was then cunningly edited to the beat, utilizing a variety of lab and lens tricks. The central image was that of a gigantic ocean wave, from which the title appears. Then there's the wonderful shot in which the camera seems to fly right at McGarrett as he stands on the balcony of a skyscraper.

Freeman also decided that the show couldn't sustain a season of espionage plots and futuristic hardware. Instead, he demanded that the

Richard Denning played TV's Mike Shayne before becoming the governor of Hawaii and McGarrett's superior.

stories focus on the nastiest criminals possible, so the powerful McGarrett would have suitable antagonists. While other series have featured really heinous villains (most notably *The Untouchables* and *M Squad*) Freeman and company introduced the tube's first true "crime slime."

The audience was ready for *Hawaii Five-O*, and it was ready for them. The initial episode had the sizzling, gritty flavor the series would become known for. Kevin McCarthy played a "love 'em, leave 'em, rob 'em, deep-six 'em" lothario. After he had killed ten lovesick old ladies, Five-O was set on him.

The New York Post was enthusiastic. "Fast paced, sharply produced. If the rest of the shows are as good as the first one, the series should be a shoo-in."

Variety was less impressed. "Although a strong contender, it's doubtful *Hawaii Five-O* will break NBC's streak. It is a handsomely produced cop meller, enhanced by first-rate thesping and visuals, but it is still too much in the mainstream to pull loyalists away from NBC's *Daniel Boone* and *Ironside*."

CBS seemed to agree. Four of the series' first nine shows were preempted for specials or other network events. Their first twelve shows ran $810,000 over budget—the cost of the pilot film. Everything had to be shipped twenty-five hundred miles from Los Angeles to Hawaii.

"A production line that long is a constant battle," said Freeman. "If you don't whip it, it'll whip you."

They seemed to be losing. They had little support from the network and no studio to work in. They were forced to use a navy warehouse out past Pearl Harbor and through some sugar cane fields. It was the only thing they could find. A mix of experienced Hollywood technicians and naive local help begrudgingly turned it into a makeshift sound stage.

"At night the rats would come in and chew up the furniture," James MacArthur told *TV Guide*. "In the daytime, directors would have to fire a gun before we did a scene. That was to stop the lizards from squeaking and to scare off the mongooses. They'd stampede across the tin roof or run right in front of the camera. So we called the place Mongoose Manor."

Hawaii Five-O did not look long for this world. But at Christmas time, CBS switched the show's time slot, and got behind it with all their considerable enthusiasm. Suddenly the show was a top-twenty hit, eating up its competition.

Freeman had done his work: juxtaposing the stunning beauty of Hawaii with the ugliest crime imaginable. Although the Five-O unit was outside traditional authority, they were always inside the law. Their extreme position meant they always worked in extreme circumstances—the stuff of great action television.

Lord had done his duty: creating his part with equal amounts of intensity, conviction, and dedication. The problem with many actors is that they are forced to fake world-weary experience. Lord didn't have to play larger-than-life. He *was* larger than life. He had traveled all over the world as a teenage merchant seaman. He had played college football, he got a solo pilot's license, and he had organized his own art school. He had prints made of his artwork, then sent them to his favorite museums.

CBS had done their part as well: after spending almost $6 million on the series, they weren't going to let it collapse without a fight. If the audience wouldn't come to it, they would bring it to the audience anywhere it worked.

The series was finally on solid ground and everyone wanted to make sure it took root. Freeman and company continued to wrestle with production problems. Their weekly budget was the then lordly sum of almost $300,000—a full ten percent of which was for transport, housing, and sending the film back and forth from L.A. to Hawaii.

"The logistics are staggering," Lord said. "We use as many as twenty locations for a one-hour episode. In one day, we can move as many as three different times, which usually means a loss of at least two hours."

To maintain the series' tension, Freeman also invoked a realism rule. No one was to gussy up the islands. There was to be no concentration on the glamorous aspects of Hawaii. Five-O was dealing with the scum of the earth, and their environs were sometimes just as scummy. The local press began to complain about the mingling of natural beauty and unnatural death, as well as the fact that none of the standard cops and robbers plots came from island life.

Just about the only person who saw value in the series was then Governor John A. Burns. He was proven right, when more and more tourists came, even though the show gave the impression that Hawaii was awash in psycho killers. But there was always McGarret to set things right. Psycho killers didn't have a chance when McGarrett got on their trail.

No one else had much of a chance when the actor playing McGarrett got going, either. Once the new year, 1969, and success started, Lord's demands became grist for the press mill. The most famous involved the contention that there was only one star of *Hawaii Five-O*. There were no co-stars. There was only him, Jack Lord. The rest were to be called featured players.

"I had a deal with the network going in," said Lord to the Associated Press, "that called for star billing. I don't know where the criticism began. It's mostly about Jimmy MacArthur. But he wasn't even in our pilot. I congratulated him when he was hired. He's a marvelous actor but I don't see why any actor who has nothing to do with the pilot or selling it on Madison Avenue should be handed star billing. Stardom is something you earn."

Of course it was one thing to be the star. It was another to demand that everyone call you and only you the star. Respect was also something a person was supposed to earn. It appeared as if the press subsequently set out to teach Lord humility. From then on, it was open season. Newspapers and magazine writers seemed to delight in taking the actor on.

They called him "the Lord." *TV Guide* ran several scathing pieces, the worst being the account of a publicist who was fired by Lord before he had even met him. They called him a "Sandy Koufax who thinks he can pitch without an outfield." They made fun of the way he grit his teeth and clapped his hands with increasing frenzy in order to build energy for a scene. They said he personally inflated his own biography.

"If you are ninety-eight percent for him," said Dave Donnelly of *The Honolulu Star*, "he somehow feels you are against him."

They concluded that "those who know him, hate him."

For his part, Lord made such statements as "Anyone who's spoken about is spoken against" and "Knowledge is knowing that fire burns and wisdom is remembering the blisters." He kept working. Hard. In those first seasons, he seemed happy to put in eighty-hour weeks.

"Something happens to an actor on location," he said. "The smell of reality does something to a guy. I think it transmits itself to the screen—the smell of reality. . . ."

It was also the look of reality. One of the most memorable things about the show was its bright, bleached-out images of a too hot world. It enhanced the mood of the confrontation between equally obsessive good and bad. As the series continued, the supporting cast became less and less central to the theme of jousting knights—one in shining armor (a severe blue suit) and one in black (gauche Hawaiian shirts).

"The light on the islands is ten thousand kelvin," Lord told Kay Gardella of *The New York Daily News*, "compared with Los Angeles, which is thirty-five hundred kelvin. The hot light burns into the film and gives it a different look."

By the beginning of the second season, things were humming along. McGarrett continued to bash down heinous evildoers in no uncertain terms. Freeman and the staff continued to create frightening plots, while the viewers were soothed by Five-O's unrelenting desire to set things right. The first episode of the new season had a corrupt army sergeant using dead Vietnam vets in an insurance scam.

Then there was "Speedkill," about a seventeen-year-old hooked on drugs, which was cited by a teen viewer for having saved her from a similar fate. The most powerful episode was "I Want Some Candy and a Gun That Shoots," about a young man who goes to the top of Diamond Head to snipe at passing cops for no apparent reason. *Hawaii Five-O* was just as goofy as *Dragnet 1970* when it came to picturing the younger generation, but the former show far surpassed the latter in the skill of its presentation.

Finally, there was "Three Dead Cows," the finale of the second season, wherein a conscience-stricken scientist tries to alert the public to the dangers of chemical warfare by destroying a Chinese farmer's cattle. The network used that as an example of the series' conscience, but critics used it as an example of the program's bloodlust. It was the first of many attacks against the show's violence.

One watchdog group counted forty-three weapons during one hour, with an average of 20.3 an episode. Their episode high for mayhem was seven deaths and three injuries. But while Senator John Pastore condemned them for spilling too much blood, John J. Gunther of the U.S. Conference of Mayors attacked them for too little.

He felt the use of weapons on the show was "uncomfortably antiseptic. The severity of the results is ignored. This represents a distortion of a most serious nature. Viewers must be made aware that pain, suffering, and trauma result from a bullet or stab wound. Weapons seem to be used simply as props to advance the drama rather than as the instruments of deadly force that they truly are."

Lord's reaction was apt. "There are levels to a violent television act. What you see on the surface, and the statement it's making." *Hawaii Five-O*'s statement was always very clear. McGarrett had his line of death. You don't cross it and stay healthy. The entire brunt of his mental acuity and the collected armament of the Hawaiian police will fall on you like a ton of guano.

Freeman and Lord had collaborated for the show's greatest tension of all: first McGarrett thought; then he moved. Each action pushed against the other. McGarrett may have been a fanatic, but he was a brilliant one. The episodes were much more than a battle of weapons; they were a battle of wits. With McGarrett in the lead, the best ones were also battles of will.

The scenes inside the Iolani office, with the collected staff and chalk-covered blackboard, were often as exciting in their own way as the fights and chases. McGarrett and Five-O would figure it out. Steve, like Sherlock, would stalk back and forth behind his desk like a caged animal, piecing the mystery together.

His Watsons would comment and then the light would go on over his head like an erupting volcano. The game was afoot and they would race from the building and into their cars. Tires always squealing, they would race to the scene and do whatever had to be done. It would range from taking the villains down personally to surrounding the place with more firepower than in the last Israeli War.

By 1970, almost everybody was hooked on Freeman's pulp vision. *Variety* called him "the master of the slick actioner. He whips it together with style and so tautly as to muffle the creakiness of the plotline. It's, of course, nothing more than action for the passive viewer, but the most refreshing thing about it in a year that finds the networks straining for relevance is that it is so unabashedly irrelevant."

They also reserved some nice words for Jack Lord, saying his "good looks, brashness, and fierce dedication to duty are the dominant characteristics of the character he plays."

The new season also saw the first appearance of Wo Fat, McGarrett's Moriarty, played by Khigh Dhiegh. Fat was an Asian criminal mastermind who occasionally worked for the Red Chinese, and occasionally pursued his own evil goals. His first assignment was to prevent the recovery of a wounded secret agent. He tried to accomplish this by kidnapping the daughter of the only brain surgeon who could save the operative. Her ransom was the death of the injured spy. As always, however, McGarrett saved the day. This espionage-laden episode was a throwback to the pilot film, but the rest of the year featured the more standard tension-filled scripts which made Five-O famous.

The inner tensions on the set were another matter. Zulu had created the most friction, so he was the first out. He had long complained that his natural humor and full abilities had never been utilized. His nightclub act was well known on the island, where he was considered a Hawaiian Zero Mostel.

The culmination of his dissatisfaction came when Lord supposedly forbade him to accept an honorary membership to the U.S. coast guard. The press suggested that Lord was jealous and wanted the honor for himself, but nothing written about Lord from that point on could be

The (Jack) Lord—
Steve McGarrett.

taken at face value or completely believed. Whatever the reason, Detective Kono was out and Detective Ben Kokua (Al Harrington) was in.

The audience didn't seem to care one way or the other. For them, the show began and ended, often quite literally, with McGarrett. Each program finished with a preview of the next episode, narrated by McGarrett himself. It, in turn, always ended with the line, "Be there . . . aloha." Although not exactly a "Just the facts ma'am," McGarrett also had his own "names have been changed to protect the innocent."

It came at the end of many episodes, when the cop had taken on another wily miscreant, then beat him at his own game—all while staying inside the law. As a very perceptive article in (of all places) *Playgirl* magazine noted: "McGarrett represents menace and ominous danger. He is a paragon of cunning paranoia even more devious than they [the villains]."

This reality made McGarrett's triumph in defeating his enemy all the greater, since he did it on his own strict terms. Then, with the cringing criminal finally cornered, McGarrett would smile that death head grin of his and say, "Book him, Dan-o. Murder one."

Instant catharsis. The line between Lord and his character was gone. The audience loved it. They loved him. Steve McGarrett was not just interesting anymore. He was magnificent. He was a deity of law enforcement. He made all his viewers feel safe and protected. Heaven help the criminal with McGarrett on our side.

As the years went on, more and more program characters, on both sides of the law, offered McGarrett shortcuts to justice—which he would never take. Sometimes he would thank them, sometimes he would threaten/promise them a comeuppance, but he always walked the Constitutional razor's edge. Again, it was the art of *Hawaii Five-O*'s inner tension which glued eyes to it. It was also the art of Freeman's vision and the skill of his writing staff.

Magazine critics, who weren't jaded by a constant barrage of television, were so perplexed by their enjoyment of the show that they occasionally waxed philosophic. Their unanimous conclusion was that while the series' scripts consisted of purple prose, it was the absolute best purple prose possible. Late in the show's run, *Cue* magazine stated that the scripts "flout credibility so cunningly that they are hard to resist."

One script from the sixth season, said *Newsweek*, showed "how and why stocks and bonds are negotiable and untraceable. We learned how the Hawaiian stock market operates. The criminal mastermind was undone by a surprising, yet completely plausible detail that he had neglected, but was significant in light of what the audience had learned about the market, stocks, and bonds."

Both articles concluded that *Hawaii Five-O*'s writing was the best their genre had to offer. It was the best violent mystery trash on television.

"Ours is a classic dramatic form," Lord told United Press International. "In the first act, a major crime is committed. After that we concentrate on action. There is a head-on conflict between a very strong antagonist, a powerful villain, and the protagonist McGarrett. The triumph of good over evil is never boring." Certainly not the way *Hawaii Five-O* did it at its height.

The audience was on their side, the network was behind them, and even the critics gave them grudging respect. The only thing which slowed the program down was the sudden death of its creator and guiding light, Leonard Freeman, in 1973. Until then, the show had been going through producers like Kleenex. They changed every year, like clockwork. Joseph Gantman was the producer of the first season, Leonard Katzman was in the second, Robert Stambler and Stanley Kallis shared the third.

Finally Robert Sweeney and William Finnegan mastered the process in the fourth. They made it through the fifth and sixth season, when Freeman died. By then they had the system down to a science. "This whole company is based on good planning," said Finnegan, who was on set in Hawaii, while Sweeney was manning the fort in California.

"Bob prepares the script and does the casting—we usually have two or three actors from the mainland," Finnegan told a trade journal. "I follow through on the production here. Our biggest problem is the twenty-five-hundred-mile communication gap. We try to solve it by phone, running up bills like a couple of gossiping old women. But we need to talk for many reasons, including the dailies which he sees five days after they're shot. If anything goes seriously wrong, we need to act fast."

That acting fast usually took place on the spot, immediately, so the team could stay on schedule. Most regular problems were not with the crew, but the scripts and the actors.

"Most of the mainland scripters are writing in terms of New York basements and Los Angeles swimming pools," explained veteran Five-O director Paul Stanley in the same trade journal. "We have to take the material and adapt it to Hawaii. For instance, one script called for a scene at a daytime baseball game. The writer didn't know that they play only night games in Hawaii." (It's too hot otherwise.)

What a lot of the viewers didn't know was that ninety-five percent of the series' actors were non-professionals. The production made it a habit of using local help for all the small roles, like waiters, waitresses, hostages, doctors, nurses, murder victims, store owners, hotel clerks, maids, innocent bystanders, etc. It maintained a freshness Freeman always wanted, but it grated on the professionals.

"Try working with an amateur," Lord once suggested. "I'm best on a second or third take. When an untrained performer is in a scene, it can take eight or ten takes." The crew regularly filmed more footage than necessary, so the Los Angeles editors could cut around a bad performance and still bring the episode in at the proper length.

"The average shooting time is seven days, but the shows can run anywhere from five to ten," said Finnegan, "with budgets averaging $265,000, although there have been some which went as high as $300,000 and others which went as low as $210,000. There's a great advantage to elasticity."

Because of the problems, the show developed a close-knit staff. The regular writers included Jerome Coopersmith and Ken Pettus, while the most used directors were Paul Stanley, Charles Dubin, and Michael O'Herlihy (who, together, worked on more than a hundred episodes). They all deserved purple hearts.

"The climate's no help," said O'Herlihy to his union publication. "You don't notice the heat because of the constant trade winds. But by the middle of the afternoon, it begins to weigh on your shoulders and you find the edge beginning to go off your acuteness."

"We'd like to try new directors," said Finnegan, "but we can't take the chance. If one segment starts to fall apart, it can be a total disaster. Directors often stay an extra day just to recover."

During Sweeney and Finnegan's reign, the series surged forward in the image of Leonard Freeman. McGarrett traced down the legendary Peking Man, the oldest skeleton in history. Then he tracked the murderer of two people, whose corpses were discovered a decade after the crime. Then he went after high-tech drug dealers who used sky divers and minisubs. And on and on and on, week after week, one sharply designed episode after another—each featuring the burned-out photography and driving intensity the series had become known for.

"The staff has made fast-paced action a standard ingredient," *Variety* wrote in 1973. The mixing of beautiful scenery, stark settings, abominable wickedness, amateur feature players, and McGarrett's barely contained power kept the series at the top.

In 1974, the foundation finally cracked. The network had been dreading a production confrontation with Lord since Freeman's death. It came during the fourteenth episode of the seventh season.

"Jack has the worst press of anybody I know of," Finnegan said shortly before the blowup. "He is reputed to be difficult, but I can tell you that he has never had any problems with directors. He is as close to the perfect leading man in a series as you could find—a total professional. You can plan for a six A.M. call and be damn sure that he will be there and prepared."

A perfect leading man, certainly, but perhaps not the perfect gentleman. It was reported that Lord became incensed over the presence of a visiting navy man on the set during shooting. He demanded that the visitor leave. Finnegan, the on-line producer, said no. Lord fired Finnegan. The network vetoed the firing. Lord walked out. The network threatened to fire the actor. Lord returned.

Four months later, Sweeney and Finnegan started their own production company. Philip Leacock was brought in as *Hawaii Five-O*'s new producer. The series had been operating without an executive producer since Freeman's death.

"Yes, I'm tough," Lord later told the Associated Press. "That's the only way to survive in a series. I would prefer to say I was firm. You can't be wishy-washy in this business. They go for the jugular. Show one small weakness and they'll destroy you. I know. I've got the scars to prove it. Since Lenny died, I've run the show and I've done the chores that he would have done. When we have problems, I sit down with CBS and we resolve them like gentlemen."

Translated, all this meant that as McGarrett was the undisputed head of the Five-O unit, Jack Lord was now the undisputed leader of the production unit. "I try to create an atmosphere of harmony under which we all can work," he said. Work was the operative word there. Lord was a workaholic and expected everyone to live up to his example. Another ironic inner tension came with the juxtaposition of the island's lulling atmosphere and the production's frantic schedule.

"There's no buddy system here," Lord stressed. "Everyone must pull his own load. Unlike other operations in Hollywood, you won't find any relatives on this show—no nepotism." This edict certainly must have put Lord in further disfavor with some.

"If you're ready to work," said guest star Jack Albertson (of *Chico and the Man*, 1974–78, fame), "and know your lines, you have a wonderful time. But if you're expecting a vacation, forget it."

The difference between Jack Lord and his closest television contemporary, Jack Webb, was that Lord knew what he wanted when he saw it and didn't feel the need to prove himself outside that one successful character. Lord was already respected as an artist, and took great consolation in his previous achievements. Jack Webb seemed to want to show the world that he was more than Joe Friday. What Jack Lord wanted to do was retire.

"They'll have to take me off this island in a box," he said repeatedly. "I've bought my last house. My ambition is to live on the beach for the rest of my life. When a man finds paradise, that's where he should stay." But first he was going to take McGarrett to the edge of the envelope. He was going to push Five-O to the max.

He gloated when the series forced its competition into cancellation. He complained bitterly when the network rescheduled him in unsuccessful time slots. Finally, in 1976, Philip Leacock was made the new executive producer, Douglas Greene was named producer, and CBS itself took over the production—giving a piece of the action to Freeman's widow. That freed up Lord to do what he did best.

The Death Head Grin.

"In an age of compromise, McGarrett is a totally truthful, honest, open man," said Lord. "He says what's on his mind. He's never neutral. We share that trait in common. He steadfastly refuses to back away from his ideals. He never backslides into evil."

That was *Hawaii Five-O*'s final contribution to the art of good script writing. It brought into focus the point that you cannot pursue good to an evil extreme. To McGarrett, "backsliding into evil" meant that the ends justified the means. It meant going outside the law to uphold the law. McGarrett simply would not do that, which created the tightest internal energy and tension of all.

Which also meant that the release of that tension was all the greater when the McGarrett Decree was spoken. "Book him, Dan-o."

Hawaii Five-O made waves even in its ninth season. Wo Fat reappeared, planning nothing less than the conquest of the world. *Variety* showed preposterous callousness in its review of this episode by saying the show "works better when it follows its standard formula—in search of a psychopath who rapes and kills stewardesses, for example." The review was wisely unsigned.

The new staff had more on its mind than the *Variety* reviewer. Their most famous and controversial episode of the season involved criminals building a nuclear bomb for sale to terrorists. The Atomic Industrial Forum cried foul, practically begging CBS to run the episode after the impending national elections. "It is antifactual and highly emotional," a spokesman said, although they had not seen the segment or read the script. "It plays into the hands of the opponents of nuclear power." They also complained that it made the stealing of plutonium and the construction of a working device seem absurdly easy. The network reaped the publicity rewards and ran it on schedule, before the elections.

By that time, *Hawaii Five-O* was an island institution and industry. The weekly budget was up to a half million dollars and they needed about a hundred and fifty people a day to fill the crew requirements. Over their many years on the air, they had used more than twenty thousand residents as extras. It added up to prosperity for all concerned.

"Another reason for our longevity," Lord said in a U.P.I. interview, "is that I'm wary of using stories seen on other cop shows that have been changed to a Hawaiian setting. Then there's our use of the rainbow of multiracial faces and folklore. We use Hawaiians whenever possible and we base many of our episodes on their legends. We provide new things for people to look at."

But there's just so much a show can say in a decade. The series continued to deliver, but the law of diminishing returns was going into effect. The audience and critics were beginning to take the show for granted. There were just so many times Dan-o could book them before it got redundant.

CBS switched the top staff, promoting Douglas Greene to executive producer and installing Bill Sadefur, Jim Heinz, and Fred Baum as supervising producer, Hollywood-based producer, and Hawaiian-based producer, respectively. But there was little spin they could put on the well-worn program. They had licked most of the logistics problems, but the production was tired.

The *Variety* review of the tenth-season premiere episode was only two pararaphs long, concluding that the "talky episode was hardly worth all the verbosity." By the end of the season, things were strained at best, desperate at worst. The ratings were slumping, and the segments were increasingly lifeless. To try renewing audience interest, Chin Ho Kelly was killed by a mad-dog murderer played by Steven Keats. Steve McGarrett ran him to ground at the base of a palm tree on the beach and stuck a gun in his face. Even so, he managed to resist the impulse to become a cold-blooded executioner. As always, he had Dan-o book Chin Ho's executioner . . . murder one.

After that, McGarrett seemed to reassess life. The following season, the eleventh, found him slightly less rigid. He would occasionally get out of his severe blue suit and wear Hawaiian shirts and Panama hats. It was a surprising and not altogether pleasant sight.

"We get letters from people wanting to see something of McGarrett's personal life," Lord explained. "I think the mystery piques people. I think it also annoys them." The revelation that McGarrett was human was not satisfying. Solace from the villainy the program presented would not be achieved with a human protagonist. The character only worked as a demon of good.

At least one actor saw the writing on the wall. "After eleven years I decided it was enough," said James MacArthur to *TV Guide*. "I wanted to do other things. I didn't quit for any one thing in particular. I haven't spoken to Jack. I was out of the country and I told my agent to call the producers with my decision. I didn't think it was necessary to tell Jack. I suppose it will be hard to imagine *Hawaii Five-O* without Danny . . . but that's the way it goes."

MacArthur's apathy must've stung. Little wonder that Williams' replacement was so totally different from Dan-o. There was still Duke Lukela, played by Herman Wedemeyer, who had been on the show since 1972 (taking up the slack for a departing Ben Kokua in 1974), but he wasn't enough. Filling the offices were now Truck Kealoha, played by Moe Keale, policewoman Lori Wilson, played by Sharon Farrell, and most astonishingly, James "Kimo" Carew, played by hulking, battered William Smith.

Smith was ostensibly MacArthur's replacement, and a weirder choice could hardly have been made. Smith was a stuntman and B-movie veteran, well known to the cult crowd for a series of classic psycho roles in such infamous films as *Darker Than Amber* (1970), *Grave of the Vampire*

Strange new paradise: *Hawaii Five-O*, final season—Jack Lord, Sharon Farrell (Lori Wilson), William Smith ("Kimo" Carew), Herman Wedemeyer (Duke Lukela), and Moe Keale (Truck Kealoha).

(1973), and *Rich Man, Poor Man* (1976). To see him brutalizing Rod Taylor (as Travis McGee), wiping the walls with Michael Pataki as his vampire father, or threatening Susan Blakely as the wife of the Rich Man, was what good bad-guy acting is all about. But seeing him in *Hawaii Five-O*—not as the worst creep McGarrett had ever caught, but as Dan-o . . . I mean, Kimo—made audiences think they had fallen into the Twilight Zone.

In retrospect, the best theory I can come up with is that CBS and/or Lord visualized the craggy, memorably tough actor as a younger, latter-day McGarrett, ready to take up the gauntlet when Lord finally called it quits. But nothing worked in this twelfth season—the acting, writing, or direction. The production had lost touch with its audience. The stories ranged from mediocre to laughable.

"Working on the show has become like serving a stretch on Devil's Island," said one unnamed production assistant. Smelling blood, some critics became particularly condescending and sarcastic in their coverage. Lord and the company finally accepted the all too obvious. The Five-O team was no more. Location scenery would not save them now. McGarrett would have to clean out his desk.

But not before he did one thing. He had sworn he would bring Wo Fat to justice if it was the last thing he did. It was.

"Woe to Wo Fat" was the final episode, and clearly representative of everything that was wrong with the last season. "A rather simplistic stanza," said *Variety*, "in which McGarrett masqueraded as an aging scientist, with makeup that hardly disguised him at all, to infiltrate a doomsday weapon project, headed by Wo Fat, who has slowly become Fu Manchu over the years. If anything, the final stanza rather accurately illustrated that *Five-O* had indeed reached the point where it should sensibly fold up its tent."

The final episode: McGarett puts Wo Fat (Khigh Dhiegh) away.

The last episode probably would have embarrassed Leonard Freeman. There was no tension. There was hardly any logic. Wo Fat was put behind bars, but they couldn't resist a "humorous" final moment when the mastermind pulls a hidden file from his prison slipper. The episode owed more to *Get Smart* (1965–70) than it did to the glory days of *Hawaii Five-O*.

After 284 hours, it was over. The grandest epic in the history of television detection was finished. It went out with a whimper, but it had more than its share of bang in its first landmark decade. Other shows would follow it—Lord's own *M Station Hawaii* (1980) and the abysmal *Hawaiian Heat* (1984–85)—but only the series made in its image, *Magnum, P.I.*, would succeed because it broke many of the clichés McGarrett had established. Tom Selleck and company were wise. There was only one—there could only be one—Steve McGarrett.

One of Jack Lord's favorite quotes comes from James Russell Lowell. "Not failure, but low aim, is crime." *Hawaii Five-O* aimed high and pretty much hit the mark. Thomas Magnum would often invoke McGarrett's name. McGarrett would often be the source of respectful wit everywhere from the top-rated NBC comedy *Night Court* to the cable music channel MTV.

But even with all the lasting devotion of his fans, Jack Lord stayed in his island paradise, refusing all offers to return—several of them from Selleck (who repeatedly requested McGarrett as a guest star). But Lord had nothing to prove to anybody.

"Most TV has about a one and a half octave range," he once said. "Sometimes we hit a two and a half octave."

No matter what anyone thought or said about him, Jack Lord was Steve McGarrett. And Steve McGarrett was the greatest television cop of all time.

Smile and Jiggle

"Where's the best place to shop?"

—Charlie's Angels (Cheryl Ladd, Jacklyn Smith, Tanya Roberts—spoken in unison—last line, last season's first episode

IT IS TIME TO SPEAK OF UGLY THINGS. HOLLYWOOD IS NOT ONLY RACIST, it is sexist. Though much lip service is given to the contrary, and more and more inroads are created for both minorities and women on television, one has only to work in the entertainment capital for a short time before the truth becomes abundantly apparent.

Minorities are simply invisible. If they do not match a current stereotype, it is an awful uphill battle to be recognized as anything—be it doctor, lawyer, cop, or businessman. Even parts which are written by minority members for minority members are all too often changed in the name of "not upsetting the viewer."

Seemingly the depiction of Asians as dictum-spouting wise men with an unsure grip on grammar is not upsetting. The depiction of Puerto Ricans as car thieves and blacks as hookers or pimps is not upsetting. The depiction of the Orientals, Hispanics, and blacks as just people (be they secretaries or private eyes or partners in espionage) must be terribly threatening to some.

The usual cry is that the audience will not accept it. In truth, if there's one thing television has repeatedly proven, it's that audiences will accept anything that's well written, produced, directed, and performed. How many great shows would have died if this still oft-quoted dictum were true? Still, it is a great excuse for not doing something a producer doesn't want to do.

For women in Hollywood, the problem is reversed. If anything, they are all too visible. A woman's role in Hollywood is to be seen—and one can never be too rich or too thin. Since the television camera gives the impression of added weight, the working actresses in Hollywood are extremely thin. The weather is always good and the women are always in their summer dresses. Hollywood women are selling themselves—not as actors, but as human packages.

Unlike most of the men, television women are on display as objects. That is the nature of the business. Only the most attractive survive, and, unless the woman is in comedy, she can expect a much shorter TV career than her male counterpart.

This can lead to defensiveness on the part of actresses, and an overwhelming thankfulness when they are finally cast in a major role. Since new, young, attractive talent is pouring into the city all the time, actresses are less apt to rock the boat by making demands. You know, little things: believable motivations, non-humiliating situations, plots which display more sensitivity than skin.

Things have gotten better. In 1984, Levinson, Link, and Peter Fischer created *Murder, She Wrote*. "There had almost never been a successful television crime drama with a female lead," said Richard Levinson. "Other than *Police Woman* (1974–78), where she showed her legs a lot, *The Bionic Woman* (1976–78), which was a spinoff, *Wonder Woman* (1976–79), which was a comicbook, and *Cagney & Lacey* (1982–88). But Jessica Fletcher was a woman of a 'certain age' who wears glasses.

"What we're proudest of is that you finally have a woman who doesn't have to display parts of her anatomy. The show's all talk, there's almost no action, it's slow, it has what we call 'Aaron Spelling lighting,' the music is 'melodic-conventional,' it successfully follows *60 Minutes* where the last three shows in that time slot failed, it features 'mature' performers (read: old), and it's a whodunit! The smart money in town didn't give it a prayer. Even we were astonished by its success."

It wasn't always this way. Back in the mid-sixties, Levinson and Link were working on another whodunit about a multimillionaire police homicide inspector who liked to create adages. He was Amos Burke and his sayings were *Burke's Law* (1963–66). "We were doing the series for Aaron Spelling," Levinson recalled, "and he flew us out to California to do a pilot for a show called *Honey West* (1965–66). We didn't create the character (Gloria and Forrest Fickling did, under the pseudonym G.G. Fickling), but we wrote the half-hour pilot and three segments. It was one of the first dramatic series with a female lead, but the problem was they always stuck a man in there to save her at the last minute. There

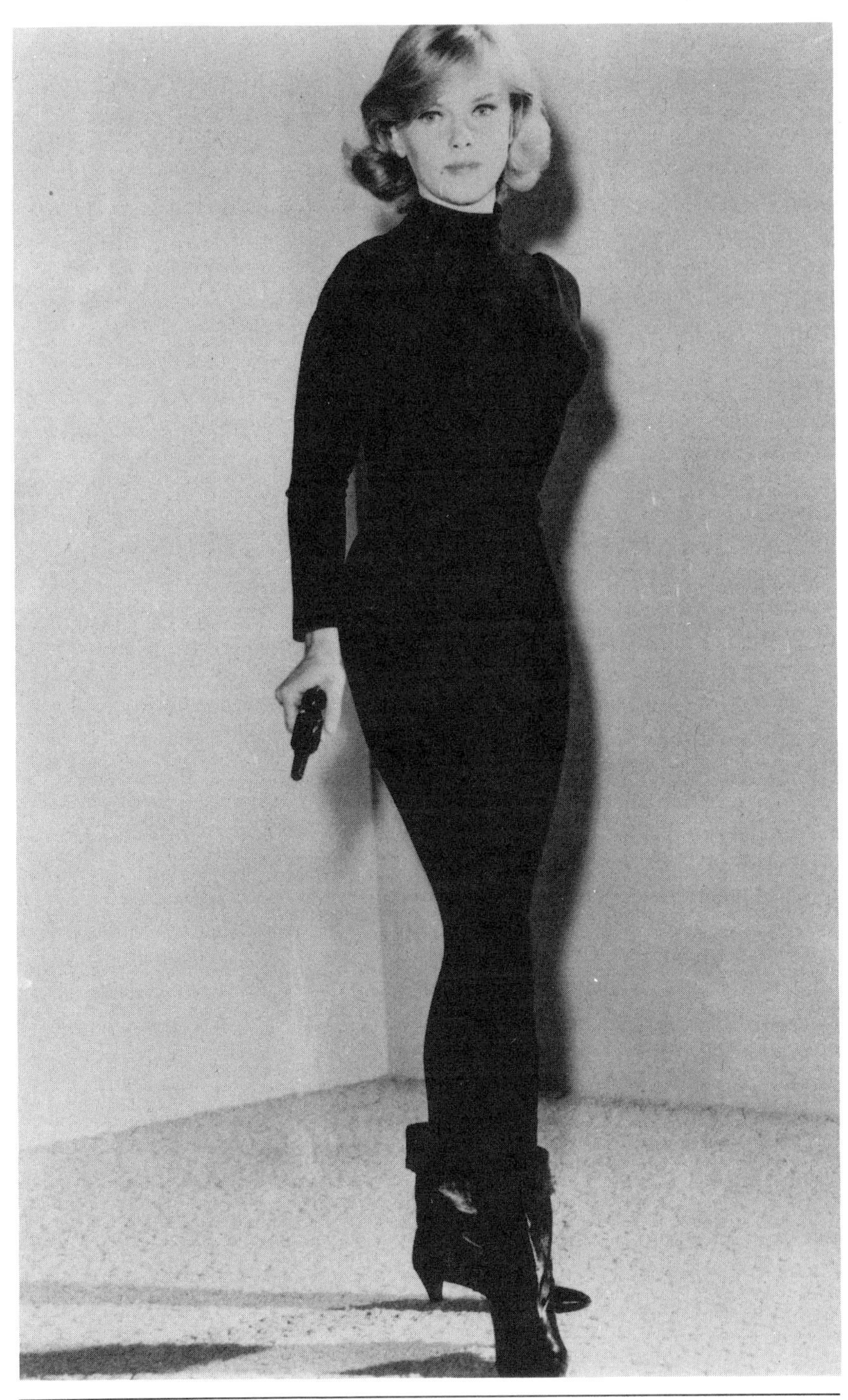

Anne Francis as *Honey West*—James Bond without portfolio, Mannix with breasts.

have been a lot of successful comedies with female leads, but very few dramatic ones. They always have her bailed out by a man in the last act!"

Anne Francis had introduced the character of Honey on an episode of *Burke's Law*. To the producers, she was an inspired choice. Not because of her eighteen-year acting career, which peaked in the mid-fifties with *Rogue Cop* (1954), *Bad Day at Black Rock* (1954), *Battle Cry* (1955), *The Blackboard Jungle* (1955), and *Forbidden Planet* (1956), but because she looked like Honor Blackman.

Blackman had played Catherine Gale, John Steed's first partner in *The Avengers* (U.S.: 1966–69)—the cult favorite which didn't premiere in America until after Mrs. Gale was replaced by Mrs. Peel (Diana Rigg). More importantly, Blackman's *Avengers* work got her the role of Pussy Galore in the wildly successful third James Bond movie, *Goldfinger* (1964). The television executives couldn't get Blackman for Honey, so Francis was signed. They wanted their Honey to remind viewers of Pussy since they were planning to do a 007 on the series.

Bonditis had gripped television in the mid-sixties. It had led to *The Man From U.N.C.L.E.* (1964–68) and *The Wild Wild West* (1965–70) before infecting the stylish, entertaining *Burke's Law*, warping it into *Amos Burke—Secret Agent* for its last, sorrowful season. That incident did not bode well for *Honey West*. When her half-hour series reached the air, it was laden with gadgets and inanities.

It barely lasted the season and set an unfortunate precedent which Hollywood has still not completely shaken. The tragic reality of most television actresses is that if the executives can't make them men with breasts, they'll turn them into jokes. This goes far beyond the desire of viewers to look at a pretty girl. This extends to how women are treated on screen and what they have to do to their bodies and minds just to get a job.

The path to pablum is riddled with good intentions. The monetary success and artistic failure of *Charlie's Angels* (1976–81) seems to reside with its Svengali, Aaron Spelling. Spelling, although partnered with Leonard Goldberg on this production, takes the rap on circumstantial evidence: he was the most visual and vocal of the two executive producers. He was the most quoted and the most publicized man on the project. And no matter how many people complained, including the press and his stars, he laughed all the way to the bank.

"I am convinced that Spelling thinks he's doing good stuff," said Robert Shayne, a writer on *Charlie's Angels*. "I have found that everyone I work with in TV thinks what they are doing is good. I have never worked with anyone whose attitude was, 'Well, this shit is good enough for garbage.'

"But," Shayne continued, "I think Aaron Spelling has the most amazing mind in TV because of his track record. Of everything he's serious about, about seventy-five percent became hits. And a normal track record is about ten percent. I'm very impressed with him . . . I can't watch any show he's ever made, but I am impressed with his ability to be in touch with the public."

That touch started in 1953 when Spelling went from being an actor to a scriptwriter to a producer on *Dick Powell's Zane Grey Theatre* (1956–62). Following that was the aforementioned *Burke's Law*, which had just the right mix of fantasy wish-fulfillment and wit. Gene Barry played the millionaire homicide inspector who solved all the murders from his chauffered limousine or his sumptuous mansion. Thankfully, in addition to being urbane, Amos Burke was brilliant and had a great sense of humor. The only bad thing was its subsequent perversion into a lame spy show.

From there came *Honey West*, which didn't work, then *The Mod Squad* (1968–73), which did. He followed that with the ultra-militaristic *S.W.A.T.* (1975–76), which was reportedly cancelled by the network in reaction to anti-violence pressure groups, even though it garnered good ratings. In this case, the self-appointed watchdogs might have had a point. There was far too little insight in this glorification of the Special Weapons and Tactics police division. The series gave the impression that these brainless, over-armored yahoos would shoot anything that grew.

A violent pattern seemed to be emerging in Spelling's career, but he broke the mold with the warm, domestic drama *Family* (1976–80). Pigeonholing was not the wisest idea with this man. Even so, the saga of *Charlie's Angels* made a legend of the already justly famous producer.

"He calls himself a Jew from Texas," said Shayne, "which is very important because he felt like an outsider there. This allowed him to observe, from the outside, the likes and tastes of the people he grew up with—because he didn't feel he was one of them."

Spelling could see one thing clearly whether he was in Texas, New York, or California: everybody liked looking at beautiful women. In 1975 he and Leonard Goldberg took that reality and shaped it into a concept called *Alley Cats*. They sold the idea to Fred Silverman, then the head of programming at ABC. It was a fairly demeaning concept, although it portrayed several woman troubleshooters making it in a man's world. Silverman suggested it was too rough in its initial form.

The producers brought in Ivan Goff and Ben Roberts to develop the idea into a series. True to their origins, the team made the single best episode—the pilot, in which three female police dropouts become the operatives of an unseen male private eye named Charles Townsend. In the pilot, the women foiled the villains with their brains rather than dazzling them with their breasts. The Alley Cats had become Charlie's Angels.

Goff and Roberts had found exactly the right mix of reality and fantasy. They had the three attractive female stars, but also an interesting plot (the Angels go undercover at a race track to solve the murder of a female doctor), a colorful environment, and decent dialogue. The women were smart as well as beautiful, and acted that way.

There was Sabrina Duncan, the multilingual brains of the bunch, played by Kate Jackson. Jackson had appeared on another Spelling-Goldberg project, *The Rookies* (1972–76), and therefore was ostensibly the star of the show. The producers had reportedly built the show around her and she was paid twice as much as her co-stars.

Next, there was Kelly Garrett, an ex-showgirl. As originally conceived, she had the toughest life before working with Charlie. There was even talk that she had been a prostitute for a short time. Jaclyn Smith, the elegant Texan who played her, was the granddaughter of a Methodist minister. She demanded all references to Garrett's sordid past be stricken from the scripts. Kelly's tough life was all but forgotten the way the refined Smith played her.

Finally there was the blonde, athletic Jill Munroe. Originally that was all she was; the producers figured they needed a blonde to sell Sil-

High concept Angels—Kate Jackson as the smart one, Farrah Fawcett as the blond one, Jaclyn Smith as the third one.

verman on the idea. The blonde they chose was Farrah Fawcett (-Majors), then wife of Lee Majors and a veteran of several Spelling-Goldberg television movie projects.

So far, so good. The complicating factors arose in the form of producers' changes. Instead of handling the series 77 *Sunset Strip* style, with one Angel starring in each segment, they wanted all three in every episode. And instead of concentrating on their savvy, the producers wanted to concentrate on their skin. The word they used to describe it was "action."

Like every word in Hollywood, action has several meanings. To some, it's a cover for the word "violence." For others, it may mean movement, without necessarily involving confrontation. Here it meant living pinups. The producers didn't want reality. They didn't even want the sort of brutal fantasy pictured on other private eye series like *Mannix*. They wanted mock peril and pseudo-danger, in the form of drawn guns, squealing tires, and foot races. Anything, in other words, which got the Angels jiggling. Goff and Roberts wisely (and unfortunately) stepped aside.

In stepped Rick Husky and the farce got underway. Please understand, however, that farce is eminently watchable and vastly entertaining. As long as the writers and directors cared about the balancing act they were doing, *Charlie's Angels* was engaging. There was a tension created in the audience to see whether anything would actually happen or whether it was all just a tease.

Everyone spent years trying to explain the success of the show. It took years because everyone was careful not to actually touch on the subjects which accounted for its success. With reporters labeling the program sexist and the Angels sex objects, it is a shame the producers couldn't simply say "true" and get on with it. Instead, words like "fantasy" and "fun" were bandied about by the publicity department.

The truth was that this was a combination of a video girlie magazine and a movie serial. People watched because they wanted to see what happened to these women. They wanted to see what predicaments the Angels would get in, and how little they would wear. On some college campuses, there were beer-drinking games: whoever guessed the Angel wearing the most clothing paid for the next round. Viewers wanted to see legs, faces, stomachs, rears, and cleavage. *Charlie's Angels* soon became a skin show. ABC's public relations was wise, however, to concentrate on the actresses' hair and wardrobe. The scripts and acting were certainly nothing to write home about.

The producers were spending a quarter of a million per episode at first. It quickly rose to more than a half million, but that was still pretty light for this kind of glossy hour. The press made much of the fact that hairdressing for the trio cost eighty thousand a year. This was the beginning of the inordinate pressure exerted on the show by reporters who professed to hating the series but loved to write about it. There were more articles and features on *Charlie's Angels* than any other genre show of its decade.

They talked about the hair, they talked about the clothes, they talked about the shoes, they talked about the stars' pets, they even talked about the lack of bras—a fact ABC supposedly went along with because, according to someone on the set, "the girls are so lovely"!

What was really lovely to ABC were the ratings. The tales of these dropouts from a sexist police force who went to work for the Townsend Investigations Agency were an immediate success. Townsend was the Angels' version of Richard Diamond's Sam—only heard and never completely seen. In the first season, parts of him were visible (mostly the back of his head). In later years, he was just a disembodied voice on a speaker-phone. John Forsythe said Charlie's words.

The visible male was John Bosley, the Angels' aide-de-camp, played by David Doyle (rumor has it that the character's name was an in-joke, based on actor Tom Bosley of *Happy Days*, who the producers originally wanted for the role, and whom Doyle resembled). He and Charlie's voice remained the same as the Angels raged around them.

The trouble with the series was immediately apparent: the producers had created a frustrating fantasy. The Angels lived in a flat, artificial world. The fact that they were extraordinarily beautiful was underplayed and overplayed at the same time. The good guys never noticed and the bad guys always did. Neither of them ever did anything about it. But everybody on this show became such ciphers so quickly, one could hardly attribute any recognizable life to them at all.

All the actors were handsome, all the sets were colorful, and all the drama was superficial. The look of everything became so important that little things like plot and character were soon completely swallowed up. But in that first season, some of Goff and Roberts' strength held on. Angel standards were set in the very first month on the air.

In the second episode, they go undercover as a teacher (the smart one), a stewardess (the blonde), and a swimmer (bikinis!) to break up a dope ring. This established the Barbie programs, where the Angels dress up to fight crime. Episode three established the most unsettling tradition: the woman-killer programs, where the staff manufactures the most perverse fantasy, then downplays it for an hour. Beautiful women are killed by a one-dimensional motiveless serial killer who is finally brought to justice by chance. This first example had a psycho using rag dolls to strangle fashion models.

The killers had to be motiveless or else the series would have had to address the reason why women are the main victims of fictional psychos. In addition, the Angels' investigations had to be subdued or else the show would have had to face their inherent sexism. *Charlie's Angels* was always an exercise in how to offend the least amount of viewers.

Episode four, "Chained Angels," is considered the best. The private eyes go undercover on a chain gang to investigate the disappearance of a Louisiana convict. The climax has the Angels chained together as "desperate ones," trying to escape from their homicidal female wardens. The filmmakers did their best juggling act on this one. The story was exciting without being degrading or particularly obvious.

It's a shame there weren't more episodes created with as much thought and care. As the weeks ground on, the staff increasingly depended upon the irrational psycho or kneejerk sexist. When the mass murderer wasn't strangling, stabbing, or shooting, the chauvinists would be persecuting all-female businesses. Even so, *Charlie's Angels* was an interesting, moderately entertaining show in its first season. Then something horrible happened: the Farrah phenomenon.

No one can explain it to this day. The girl with the mussed mane, the Cinerama smile, and the protruding nipples became an object of obsession all over the world. The feeding frenzy was astonishing. Within six months, Farrah Fawcett was one of the world's biggest stars . . . for no particular reason. It was a classic case of too much, too soon.

The actress may have been smarter, in retrospect, to stay with the show and learn more about her craft before navigating the shark-filled waters of moviemaking, but it soon became clear that no one could've learned her craft on *Charlie's Angels*. They had scripts which would have felled Sarah Bernhardt in her prime.

At any rate, Farrah Fawcett announced that she would not return to the series the second season. This, no doubt, didn't ingratiate her with her co-stars, who were already smarting in her inflated shadow. It made it even tougher for her replacement.

Cheryl Ladd had worked with Spelling-Goldberg in their "high concept" television movie *Satan's School for Girls* (1973) under her original name Cheryl Jean Stoppelmoor. She then just missed getting a major role on *Family* (losing out to Elayne Heilveil in the pilot, and Meredith Baxter-Birney in the subsequent series), leaving her depressed and insecure. The more Spelling and Goldberg wanted her as Fawcett's replacement, the less she wanted to do it. That just made them want her all the more.

Finally, they cast her without a screen test and the second season was under way. She portrayed Kris Munroe, Jill's little sister, another police force deserter. The scripts were still just holding water, but instead of concentrating on that, the press analyzed Ladd as if she were a lab animal. That, and her co-stars' resentment, was murder. The program responded by showing more of Cheryl's body. The ratings held, so the series continued under standard operating procedures.

The first two episodes of the new season were two-hour television movies. Not a two-part episode, but a single two-hour episode, giving the cast and crew a month's work in the first two weeks of the second

Trouble in paradise—Cheryl Ladd joins the cast.

season. Quality suffered and boredom ensued as the Angels tried to ransom a kidnapped Charlie in Hawaii (bikinis!), then went undercover at an ice show to save the abducted stars (micro-miniskirts!).

More and more gimmicks appeared in the following weeks, as did stories recycled from other shows. Sammy Davis, Jr. played himself and his look-alike, who are stalked by kidnappers. A stewardess is terrorized. A sensitivity trainer at a mountain spa is murdered. The Angels go to a dude ranch. The Angels break up a baby-selling ring.

By now, all perspective on the show was gone. It wasn't a piece of fluff entertainment anymore; it was a battle of the network stars. The fan press wanted a cat fight and they'd create one if they had to. Sadly, Hollywood's sexism had been perfectly encapsulated on the show. The girls had to look great at all costs. They had to fight crime in high heels and subdue villains without breaking a nail. That constant battle took an additional toll on the stories.

Kate Jackson had been crying for better scripts throughout. As attractive as she was, she couldn't stand up against the classic beauty of Smith and the bombshell status of Ladd. What good was being the smart one on a show that didn't require it? Occasionally the writers would attempt a strong, hard-hitting story, but interjecting reality into a fantasy like this only serves to trivialize it. In such an unreal environment, the inclusion of rape, drug addiction, and bullet wounds (all *Angels* episode fodder) seemed jarringly unnatural, ugly, useless, and mercenary.

The program was further rocked by lawsuits. First by the production company against Fawcett for walking out of her contract. That was settled out of court when Farrah agreed to appear in three episodes a season until her contract ran out (her price per episode was reported to be between $25,000 and $50,000). The second lawsuit was far more serious.

Jennifer Martin, an ABC lawyer, reported allegations that hundreds of thousands of dollars paid by ABC to Spelling-Goldberg for "exclusivity" were actually hidden revenues from *Charlie's Angels* used to defraud profit participants in the show (who included Goff and Roberts as well as actors Robert Wagner and Natalie Wood). The investigation into this situation had Hollywood preparing for a brutal blast against the common practice of so-called creative bookkeeping.

Instead, the Los Angeles County District Attorney John Van De Kamp decided that "there are insufficient grounds to institute criminal charges." The result was that Jennifer Martin was fired from ABC for "unfinished and sloppy work" while Spelling-Goldberg tried to soothe their suspicious associates. At any rate, *Charlie's Angels* continued its downward course.

An all-girl football team is persecuted by bikers. There's a sandcastle killer at a beach community (bikinis!). An apartment house for hookers is terrorized by a killer of blondes. The Miss Chrysanthemum beauty pageant is sabotaged. A Broadway star is terrorized. A female golf pro is terrorized. The Angels go on a south sea cruise (bikinis!). Angel look-alikes (that's right, Angel look-alikes) rob banks. Three disco queens are murdered. There's a strangler loose at an all-girls school.

And, in the series' most numbingly obtuse episode, religious zealots kidnap scantily clad cheerleaders to show them the error of their stimulating ways. Not only is their brainwashing incredibly civilized, but absolutely no one comments on the episode's real theme. The fanatics were wrong to kidnap the girls, of course, but word one isn't spoken about exploiting women's bodies for profit.

Then came the nadir of the series, episode sixty-five, "Running Angels." Two female marathon runners are abducted and held captive in the back of a van for fifty minutes so villains can substitute two ringers in an all-girl marathon. Their plan is to kidnap an Arab princess who is participating. Not only was this episode dumb to begin with, it was dreadfully padded with slow-moving dialogue and ridiculous subplots. It was also rife with technical mistakes.

Kate Jackson had had enough. When her initial three-year contract ran out (the same three years Farrah Fawcett had to make good on), she left the show. The series had done worse than hurt her credibility; it had hurt her career. She had been offered the Meryl Streep role opposite Dustin Hoffman in *Kramer vs. Kramer* (1979), but the *Angels* producers wouldn't let her do it.

Fawcett also declined to make any more appearances beyond her contracted ones. The search for a new Angel was on, seemingly an occasion for celebration. A media circus followed, with the heavily publicized auditions of a hundred and fifty aspirants. It became the in thing for starlets to report that they had been offered the part . . . and turned it down.

Shelley Hack did not turn it down. She played Tiffany Welles, a well-bred daughter of a Connecticut police chief. Hack herself had been a fashion model for years and, ironically, was getting a lot of airplay on Revlon's commercials for their perfume Charlie. She was the Charlie girl and now, much to her future dismay, she was a Charlie's Angel.

During all the furor finding Hack, no one seemed to be paying any attention to the scripts. Form had entirely taken over substance. The producers apparently thought by getting just the right pretty face they could surmount anything. Either that, or they thought their audience consisted of fools who deserved dross.

The fourth season's work was surprisingly shoddy, even in light of the previous work. Some blame this on a change of time slot to an earlier hour where women in clingy clothes were frowned on. Production sources said they were returning to elegance; what they were actually turning to was ennui. There was no excuse for the poor writing, but all the blame seemed to be placed on Hack's shoulders. The misplaced pressure on her was ridiculous. She was essentially condemned for the continuing erosion of the ratings when the Sirens of Ulysses couldn't have helped the nearly unwatchable junk.

Everything about the characters was forgotten. Their personalities had nothing to do with the stories, creating a soulless, vapid series. The very first new case had the Angels searching for stolen art on the Love Boat. Yes, the Love Boat of the 1977–86 series. Then there was the sabotaged all-girl trucking company, the kidnapped roller disco queen, the white slavery ring at the college sorority house, and all the familiar rest.

It was a numbing, almost frightening experience to watch the series at this juncture. Everyone seemed to be walking on eggs. Everyone seemed to be made of eggs! The Angels' faces were frozen in some sort of high-fashion rictus. It looked like the show had been taken over by emotionless pod people from *Invasion of the Body Snatchers* (1956) or animatrons from Disneyland. The height of sad absurdity came in an episode where a plastic surgeon is persecuted. The subplot concerns an attractive young girl who finds true nirvana under the knife.

"You're beautiful!" breathes Tiffany as the girl stares in awe at her "new, improved" self. Yes, true happiness is achieved through superficial beauty. Not a word is spoken about the beauty of the soul. The show had taken on a new dimension. Watching it held the same pleasure as watching really awful movies, like *Plan Nine from Outer Space* (1959). There is something comforting in the truly abysmal. It can get a viewer to relax in ways great entertainment cannot. It was fun to look at the skin and to see just how bad the series could get. Believe it or not, the worst was yet to come.

At the end of the season, Hack was out. She had been sorely used by the production which was beginning to eat its young. All along she had been blamed for the continually declining ratings. But the trumpets came out again, blaring the announcement of a new search for yet another Angel. At first it appeared that the production might have had a change of heart, for they cast Tanya Roberts. They promoted her as a funny, earthy new addition, which ran counter to their previous formula of slim intelligence, blonde bombshell, and elegant brunette.

Roberts played Julie Rogers, a sexy, troubled redhead working undercover for a vice cop played by Vic Morrow. The young actress was a veteran of exploitation movies, both on TV and in theaters. In the Aaron Spelling television movie *Waikiki* (1980), she was abducted, terrorized, raped, and murdered. In *Tourist Trap* (1979), she was merely held captive, tortured, then knifed in the back of the head. What *Charlie's Angels* had in store was just a little better.

In the press, the producers promised a sharper, stronger, wittier effort. After an extended delay, a three-hour premiere was telecast on November 30, 1980. It was, in a word, embarrassing. The plot involved an old man with thick glasses (Jack Albertson) who takes pictures and then kills photographer's models. When he is finally caught in the second hour, his spoken motive is, and I quote: "I had to do it. I don't know, I don't know."

Charlie's Angels' titillation had become pathetic, and its use of serial killers as mere plot devices had become despicable. Were the writers using the story as a subtle attack on the show itself? After all, the dirty

Night of the living Angels—Tanya Roberts was no help when the scripts didn't improve.

old man killed women after taking their pictures because they excited him. There should have been a plot where heroines killed producers for debasing them.

But the episode wasn't over yet. In the third hour, Kris was kidnapped by a psycho for no reason and held captive in his Hawaiian farmhouse. The scripters used this as an opportunity to have Bosley ride around in a convertible with Kelly and Julie sitting in the back seat. The finest bit of witty repartee came at one of the high points of the long, pointless convertible trip and is reprinted here in its entirety:

JULIE: "Thanks."

KELLY: "For what?"

JULIE: "For caring."

KELLY: "It's all right."

JULIE: "Yeah."

This episode boggled the mind. There wasn't any further down they could go. They kept putting the girls in bathing suits and revealing dresses, but that didn't work anymore. The series was cancelled by March of 1981.

Besides the huge amount of money the series made, and the launching of several actresses' careers, the only benefit of the show was that it so horrified other producers that *Murder, She Wrote* and *Cagney & Lacey* were created to take away some of the curse.

It was with those two dramas that women came to be viewed as human beings who cared about the victims around them. *Charlie's Angels* only said they cared. They weren't believable for a moment. Watching these cardboard cutouts disguised as people try to administer justice was scary.

In the first season, before the desire to look good replaced completely the desire to *be* good, *Charlie's Angels* had merit and promise. For the rest of the run, it could be enjoyed as a chauvinist's dream—three squealing, shallow fashion plates, controlled by two men, pretending to be detectives. But it could also be viewed as a societal warning. In the transparent attempt to supposedly respect women, the series degraded, debased, and killed more women characters than any other in television history.

CHAPTER

Fat and Old

"Bigger than life. That's William Conrad. As private eye CANNON. Big excitement every week."

—ad copy, September 1971

QUINN MARTIN WAS A VERY SUCCESSFUL PRODUCER. FROM WRITING FOR Dick Powell's *Four Star Playhouse* he graduated to producing for Desilu Productions. His first big hit was *The Untouchables* (1959–63), which set the stage for his subsequent career. Crime was his specialty, and he worked hard to give his networks, advertisers, and audience something to depend on.

If a television series is a package, then Martin's packages were all wrapped the same. There was always an announcer reading the name of the show, then immediately intoning "A Quinn Martin Production." The stars would be announced, then the guest stars, and then the title. After an interrupting commercial, each episode's segments would be labeled Act I, Act II, Act III, Act IV, and then Epilog.

All these affectations made for an involving show. Not only did they serve the producer's ego, they gave viewers something to look forward to. The music was always stirring, the announcer's tone was always somewhere between sonorous and satiric, and each story grew in tension through the acts. And as each episode of each of his major successes proved consistently entertaining, the gimmicks became marks of distinction; like a brand name buyers had come to trust. Buying and/or viewing A Quinn Martin Production was almost like buying an item with the *Good Housekeeping* seal. Everyone knew and wanted what they were getting.

Robert Sack as Eliot Ness had an answer to anything. He's holding it in his right hand.

After the controversial demise of *The Untouchables* (nipped in the bud by anti-violence decrees and pressure from Italian-American organizations), Martin perfectly encapsulated the country's mood with *The Fugitive* (1963–67). Within two months of its premiere, President John F. Kennedy was assassinated. The need of the nation was escape; the public wanted to run away from a reality which was getting increasingly upsetting.

More and more corruption came to light, making audiences yearn for a simpler time when good guys wore white and bad guys wore black. Martin responded with *The F.B.I.* (1965–74), starring Efrem Zimbalist, Jr. The huge success of both these shows put Martin in the catbird seat—a seat he was unable to occupy while controlling his two runaway hits.

Martin was generally regarded as a "big daddy" sort of producer; one who wanted to feel he was in control of the entire operation. Those who flourished under that sort of paternalistic control had a long-time home with QM Productions. Those whose own egos didn't approve of someone always looking over their shoulder moved on. But, like Aaron Spelling, Martin had extraordinary instincts.

He looked at his two shows, which had handsome heroes. Then he looked at *Ironside* (1967–75), with a hero who was not only grumpy, not only overweight, but crippled to boot. He knew it was time for engaging detectives with handicaps. Nothing so extreme as a wheelchair or blindness (as in *Longstreet*, which only lasted the 1971 season). His new heroes would be regular Joes, with everyday afflictions normal people would be sensitive to.

Like obesity. Martin also remembered the man who had played Marshal Dillon on the radio *Gunsmoke* for eleven years. When it came time for the western series to go to television, the five foot nine, over two-hundred-pound William Conrad was considered "nonvisual." James Arness got the role and the TV show ran for twenty years (1955–75).

This was the same William Conrad who had co-starred in many memorable movies, including *The Killers* (1946), *Body and Soul* (1947), *Sorry, Wrong Number* (1948), *East Side, West Side* (1949), *Dial 1119* (1950), *Cry Danger* (1951), and *The Naked Jungle* (1954). This was the same William Conrad, who, when Arness got the *Gunsmoke* role, went into television and movie production. He produced the aforementioned sixth season of *77 Sunset Strip* and the entire one-season run of *Klondike* (1960–61). He directed episodes of *Bat Masterson*, *Naked City*, *Route 66*, and even *Gunsmoke*. To top it all off, he was a voice-over expert—best loved for narrating the popular *Rocky and Bullwinkle* cartoons. Conrad was a powerhouse who was virtually unknown to the public.

Quinn Martin wanted to change all that. He was sure a solid show could be built around the solid man, and lured Conrad back to acting after a hiatus of nearly twenty years. Being a producer with three gigantic successes behind him, Martin could, and did, sell a show on the concept of "a private eye who solves cases." *Cannon* was an overweight *Mannix*.

Conrad played Frank Cannon, a policeman who left the force after the seemingly accidental death of his wife and young son in a car crash (the first episode of the last season revealed it to be murder).

"The gimmick with *Cannon*," Conrad said at the time, "is that there is no gimmick." That would seem true to Conrad, who certainly didn't think of himself as fat. Not only was there no gimmick, but there was no secretary, no girlfriend, no stool pigeon, no friend on the force, nothing. William Conrad was the one and only star of *Cannon*. Him and the big Lincoln Continental he drove.

At first there was some reluctance on the part of the CBS network to give the big guy a chance after the pilot was produced. "Salinas Jackpot" was about hit men disguised as rodeo clowns. It was an interesting com-

William Conrad as Frank Cannon—Mannix with fat.

bination of the macabre and traditional, all filmed on location in sunny Southern California.

There was no question that Conrad was commanding, but the network doubted the public would accept an overweight action hero. They were afraid the actor would look foolish. The show itself had a love-hate affair with Cannon's weight. While he ignored it, almost everything else in the series revolved around it.

The writers made him a gourmet and gourmand. He would occasionally ask for rare wine or a fine meal as payment. They didn't let his girth slow him down, however. When the fists and lead started flying, Cannon was always in the thick of it. In retrospect, it was a clever ploy: there was always an unspoken fear that Cannon wouldn't be able to escape danger because he was too short and dumpy. Even though no direct attention is brought to it, Conrad's weight created an immediate, subconscious suspense.

His weight also made him likable. The show's villains shared the network's opinion of their adversary, which put viewers on Cannon's side. It was hard not to to be insulted when the detective is called fat—even when it wasn't to his face. It served to make the bad guy seem nastier and Cannon more heroic. Although the character was obviously respected by his contemporaries and peers, he became an underdog just because he was overweight.

The network gave its reluctant blessing to what appeared to be a risky experiment because of Quinn Martin's track record. When *Cannon* first hit the air in 1971, the network's worst fears seemed to be realized. Although the press largely applauded the idea of a fat private eye, the ratings points weren't big enough fast enough.

The production company took a long look at the series. Frank Cannon was only getting involved in large-scale, complex cases like "Death Chain," in which his client is married to a bank executive who had an affair with the victim of a serial killer. He was asking for high fees. His concern for his stomach seemed to be directing him. He ate all the time. He rhapsodized about the flavor of beer. He was not a wildly attractive guy to begin with, and the character's blunt, brusque manner was rubbing the network the wrong way.

"I got called in to produce it," said Harold Gast. "Nobody was happy with it. The network wasn't happy, the ratings were rotten, and they needed some help. The principal problem, as far as I was concerned, was the scripts. William Conrad was fine but he wasn't being given scripts which would enable him to be all he could be. All I had to do was start making my kind of story and it went very well from there."

Gast's kind of story, as he tells it, was simple. He had written for *The Defenders* (1961–65), *Armstrong Circle Theatre* (1950–63), and *The U.S. Steel Hour* (1953–63). He was not a private eye show writer so he had no private eye preconceptions. He pared down the big-case mentality, concentrating on the importance of the individual and Cannon's moral strength and conscience. He instituted his three rules of scriptwriting.

"First, it has to make sense," he said. That, he found, is not as easy as it sounds in TV biz. "Secondly, it has to have some sort of interesting 'spine,' not too cliché. Thirdly it has to have some relationship to life and not to old television shows. That's been my concept all along and it worked with *Cannon.*"

Gast had tended to the scripts, but he knew television series lived or died on the strength of their leading character. He had to find a comfortable compromise between Conrad's girth and the action the network wanted to see. "I developed the idea of making him human and fallible, but vulnerable in that he is a fat man and he's struggling against it.

"You see, I had him always on a diet. I developed the idea that he is a gourmet cook, but cannot eat his own cooking because he's always on a diet. Before, they had the guy sitting in his car driving after thieves and eating candy bars, which was kind of disgusting. I put him on the opposite track. He would have all sorts of people up to his apartment and feed them the things he couldn't eat himself."

That taken care of, Gast also had to quickly relieve the network's concerns in other areas. The initial reaction to the show's poor ratings was that Conrad was not personable enough and a younger co-star had to be introduced. Gast had to put his foot down quickly.

"The other guy, the secretary, the fan, what have you, is invariably brought up because it is such a standard thing to do," he explained. "People in the networks who don't have brains to say anything else will say that. I'm not kidding. Everybody knows to say that.

"It had not been part of the original concept and when I got on it I wouldn't even consider it because I think it's a bad thing. It's a 'hedging your bet' thing when the executives say, 'Okay, your star is middle-aged so let's have a younger person to appeal to the younger people.' I say screw that because it's somebody else to write a role for who doesn't have a role. It's a fifth wheel to shoehorn in.

"The story is how Cannon helps somebody who is in big trouble. Now what has that got to do with a second banana?"

Still, there was some concern that other than being overweight, Frank Cannon was no different than any other TV private eye. "I have to tell you I don't look at it that way," Gast disagreed. "I don't look at it in terms of what can I do to make him different. I look at it in terms of what can I do to make him a human being that I will like and, therefore, that other people will like. That was really basic to the thing; that he become an enormously likable person.

"And William Conrad himself is a likable person. He wasn't portrayed that way before. He was portrayed as a crusty, gruff man. The kind you couldn't get past the outside shell. That was a one-dimensional concept and it did not attract an audience. Once we got him to be a rounded person—no pun intended—then his own personality came through. Although he liked to pretend that he was a mean son of a bitch, he came off as an extremely nice, warm, loving person."

Harold Gast's changes seemed to do the trick, because *Cannon* became one of TV's top twenty shows in 1972. No more plots like "No Pockets in a Shroud," where Cannon investigates a hermit millionaire and his missing heir. It was figured that the audience would have no sympathy for a millionaire. And certainly no more episodes like the one where Cannon faces fists, guns, and has to go underwater to clear a framed Vietnam vet. Too strenuous, and therefore too unbelievable.

Instead there were shows like "Blood on the Vine," where Frank makes a pilgrimage to grape country to protect an aged wine maker. There he could rhapsodize about good food as well as protect someone the audience's sympathies could be with. With the pressure to succeed off, the producers started playing with audience sympathy. Quinn Martin had a soft spot for classic hard-boiled fiction, where the only one readers could relate to is the hero.

Martin experimented with that sort of storytelling on *Cannon*. The first great example was the "To Kill a Guinea Pig" episode. There, a lady doctor is caught in a moral and legal quandary when she's forced to murder a convict during a prison visit. Quinn Martin loved that sort of suspense-building, no-win scenario where the audience's preconceptions are routinely juggled.

The key was to have a moral hero who followed the trail of clues until the murderer was brought to light—no matter what the cost. Court justice always occurred after the final fade-out. This way the viewer could be stirred, not shaken, and there could be a satisfactory conclusion without taking any kind of real stand. I mean, who are you supposed to side with? The lady doctor murdered someone and then tried to cover up. The convict was killed, but was already a hardened criminal. Neither are that attractive, so you side with the fat detective. Right?

It worked for years. *Cannon* broke into the top ten for 1973. The network did studies to figure out why and the results were clear. Men, women, and children enjoyed *Cannon* because he looked like somebody they could have, would have, and sometimes did have as a friend. He was dependable, familiar, and almost totally unthreatening.

In any event, the new and improved *Cannon* worked, but Gast was quick to point out that he shouldn't get all the credit. "It was a smoother show to produce than some others that I've been involved with, for several reasons. First, the Quinn Martin Production Company was very well organized and not cheap . . . not chintzy . . . with money. I mean, you could spend money where money needed to be spent. So there wasn't that kind of hostility that you might get in other studios.

"Secondly, William Conrad was good to work with. Oh, he would carry on and holler a bit once in a while, but he was a nice man and we always had a very cordial relationship. And, you know, the way a star behaves in a series is very important, believe me. I have had both extremes, but Bill was very nice to work with, and we had a good company. They didn't mind hard work if we were going to get something decent out of it. It was a nice series to produce."

Gast left after two successful seasons. In that time, he established a variety of precedents. It was established that Cannon was a very smart man and almost everybody knew it. His old police pals were constantly calling him in for consultation on their more difficult investigations. Clients were constantly telling him that they called because he was the best. Second, Cannon had fewer personal cases than most television detectives. More often than not his friends and family had nothing to do with the episodes. Quinn Martin and Harold Gast wanted the fat man to be a classic hard-boiled dick—smart, tough, and virtuous.

By 1974, *Cannon* was an established success and could run on its reputation. The staff gave Cannon not one, but two look-alikes. The first, in "The Hit Man," was the title character. The second, in "The Setup," was a lawyer stalked by killers. They made Cannon a dupe more often. Although still respected, several lying clients tried to arrange a frame or a fall for the big man.

There was "Coffin Corner," where Cannon's client says her husband's out to get her, when, in reality, she's out to get him. "Search and Destroy" has a lady hiring Frank to find her niece . . . so she can kill the young girl. Try as the bad guys might, however, Cannon was never fooled for long. Meanwhile, of course, the audience gets to enjoy the suspense of "will he find out in time?" and "what will he do about it?"

That was another joy of the *Cannon* show. Conrad looked and sounded like a bear, and he growled when he was crossed. Since his fatness made him vulnerable, it was fun and cathartic for a viewer to cry, "Go get 'em, big guy!" Quinn Martin and William Conrad rarely disappointed. The central strength of the series was the actor's skill. Conrad played the part so strong and so straight that his fans never doubted Cannon's actions.

Cannon was not a whodunit. It was more a "watch-em-do-it." The most involving episodes pushed the audience into truly heinous plots by amoral villains against innocent dupes. Any and all hope was pinned on the detective—who, in this case, was fat. Since he wasn't the muscular pretty boy, it was hard not to be concerned. So when Cannon saved the day, the release of tension was all the greater.

The beginning of the end came with the 1975 "Nightmare" episode,

William Conrad and Harry Townes in the fateful "Nightmare" episode, where Cannon puts his demons to rest.

Conrad post *Cannon,* playing the justly popular *Nero Wolfe* (with Lee Horsley as Archie Goodwin).

in which a dying hit man confesses to murdering Frank's wife and infant son. Conrad's performance of the grieving, vengeful detective was powerful (the killer's client commits suicide rather than face Cannon's wrath), but there was nowhere else for the character to go after that.

The very next week, "The Deadly Conspiracy, Part One" introduced another Quinn Martin character who would have even more success and influence than the round man in the big car. "The Deadly Conspiracy, Part Two," was telecast on the premiering *Barnaby Jones* program one week later.

Although Harold Gast was contacted by Quinn Martin to return for *Cannon*'s sixth season, that season never materialized. William Conrad had been quoted several times saying that he was looking forward to a five-season run. He said that if the show went five years, he'd be quite well off. The fifth season ended with "Mad Man," in which Cannon investigates medically induced hysteria which gripped a scientist on a top-secret project. After that, Conrad called it quits.

Although he returned to the role in a 1980 made-for-television movie, *The Return of Frank Cannon*, he left his audience wanting more. The key to the series' success was Quinn Martin's love of hard-hitting detective stories, William Conrad's talent, and Frank Cannon's loneliness. The character's innate sadness over the death of his family—the only thing he ever loved—created an invisible bond between him and his viewers.

The tragedy of Cannon's wife and child explained his eating and his devotion to people in trouble. The unspoken undercurrent to the program was that people like Cannon never get a second chance at love. At the end of the 1980 TV movie, Frank Cannon has been rejected a last time, by the widow of the man whose murder Cannon was investigating. He is left staring into a lamp, his face etched in sorrow and strength. It was the only challenging moment in the revival . . . and the most truthful.

Not for *Cannon* the glories of the pure Quinn Martin show. That was perfected in, and personified by, Barnaby Jones.

> ***"It's like playing the guitar by ear. You just keep plucking the strings until you hit the right notes."***
>
> ***—Barnaby Jones***

Death had come into the living room. At the start, the murders had happened on the street, in the world of the hard-boiled dick and the tough cop. Audiences didn't know the people who were gunned down. Not for the real lives of viewers the likes of smoky nightclubs or fetid alleyways or miserable flophouses. That was what television was for. All the guilty pleasures and none of the pain.

With the success of the medium came sophisticated technology, which took audiences everywhere. It told the audience what was happening in the real world, but gave it heroes worthy enough to handle it. It was still a fantasy that was being played out and everyone knew that the dead bodies weren't real. The stories may have been true, but the names had been changed to protect the innocent. They may have been real once, but not by the time they reached our eyes.

Then came November of 1963. It wasn't so much that President John F. Kennedy was assassinated and the world knew through television. It was the live, unrehearsed murder of his alleged assassin, Lee Harvey Oswald, which changed everything. The medium would never be the

The turning point, Quinn Martin style—Cannon meets Barnaby Jones.

same again. It would no longer take the audience to anywhere. It would take anywhere and drop it into the audience's homes.

Death had come into the living room. The challenge for television drama producers was to protect their audience from trauma. Levinson and Link's *Columbo* (1971–77, shown once a month) handled it by placing the hound-dog, seemingly absentminded homicide detective into the realm of the rich, who are not like us.

Barnaby Jones, on the other hand, invaded the world of the middle class. These weren't the mobsters and losers Mannix tangled with—these were our next-door neighbors. These were nicely dressed, seemingly civilized folks who were actually amoral monsters.

So while *Columbo* was first and rightfully more acclaimed, *Barnaby Jones* (which was initially patterned after *Columbo*) was one of the most underrated and misunderstood shows in the genre. Its accomplishments were quiet but amazing nonetheless.

This is another of those series which audiences embraced, but critics had a tough time explaining. No one seemed able to figure out why it lasted almost eight years. There was a lot of guessing—how it was so low-key and so easy-going—but those theories missed the point. As a matter of fact, they were dead wrong. *Barnaby Jones* excelled for two reasons: one, Barnaby was one of the best private eyes in the business, and two, the program's plots were the most perverted in television history.

But first, some background. There are three vital names when considering most of the 1970's TV detectives. Two are Aaron Spelling and Quinn Martin. The third is Fred Silverman. He became the head of the CBS program department in 1970 at the age of thirty-two. After a decade of perceptive analysis on the television game, Silverman started to be more and more intuitive. When an hour of comedies failed on Sunday night in 1972 (*Anna and the King* and *The New Dick Van Dyke Show*), Silverman decided they needed another mystery adventure in the lineup.

To almost everyone else it appeared like they needed another investigator like they needed another wart. *Mannix* was still the cream of the P.I. crop, leading a pack which included *Cool Million*, *Banacek*, *Banyon*, and *Jigsaw*. Elsewhere on the airwaves were the likes of *The F.B.I.*, *Columbo*, *McCloud*, *McMillan and Wife*, *Hec Ramsey*, *Madigan*, *The Rookies*, *Hawaii Five-O*, *Cannon*, *Adam 12*, *Search*, *The Mod Squad*, *Assignment Vienna*, *The Delphi Bureau*, *Ironside*, *Mission: Impossible*, and Quinn Martin's other hit, *The Streets of San Francisco*. Who needed another detective?

The market was saturated, Silverman was told. He didn't seem to care. He explained that the new series was just going to be a temporary stopgap, a mid-season replacement to tide the network over until the fall 1973 season. Silverman decided the new show was going to be about a private eye, and so he called Quinn Martin.

They were two minds thinking as one. Both had toyed with the idea of, as they called it, a mature detective. According to Richard Levinson, Silverman was interested in an elderly *Columbo*. Silverman had the character doing 'schtick.' You know, drinking milk and things like that."

Other reports told of Silverman's desire to have the character be a foxy grandpa type. The single most important consideration was that the program had to be produced fast. It was the autumn of 1972 and Silverman wanted it on the air by January of 1973. But both the network head and the producer agreed on two things: the character would be named Barnaby Jones and Buddy Ebsen should play him.

It was a natural choice. After a fifty-year roller-coaster career in vaudeville and movies, Ebsen had hit pay dirt ("Black gold, Texas tea, oil, that is") as Jed Clampett, the leader of *The Beverly Hillbillies*. The Paul Henning comedy had been a surprise (make that stunned) hit which ran on CBS from 1962 to 1971. Ebsen was now at liberty, doing guest shots. In fact, he had one lined up for *Cannon*.

"Well," said Ebsen in that relaxed, comfortable drawl of his, "I was minding my own business, doing a *Movie of the Week*, when my agent came to me and said, 'Don't tell anybody but there's been a change of plans. An hour of time has fallen out on CBS and they need a show in a hurry. So instead of you being a guest on *Cannon*, he will be a guest—with the same script—on your first show.' "

That script told of an ex–private eye—the best in the business—coming out of retirement to avenge the murder of his son, Hal. All the writer had to do was change the ending slightly. Instead of returning to retirement, the old man keeps the agency he handed down to his late son—with the help of his son's young widow, Betty.

That was just fine with Ebsen. He and his agent, Jimmy McHugh, worked out a nice deal with the producers and prepared to get started. "McHugh said, 'Don't tell a soul,' " Ebsen recounted, "So I didn't tell a soul, not even my wife. So the next morning I'm on my way to work and I turn on the radio and it says, 'Guess who's going to have their own series next week?' And he tells the whole world the whole thing I was keeping deadly secret."

The result of that disclosure was not exactly pandemonium. Actually, it was cause for widespread indifference, if not wholesale derision. The press saw it as exactly what it appeared to be: a CBS cork in the video cask.

"They gave it two weeks, tops," Ebsen said with a laugh.

The actor was unconcerned by the nay-sayers. The same pronouncements of doom had been directed at *The Beverly Hillbillies*. Quinn Martin ignored the negative reports as well, bringing in Gene Levitt (who had worked on *Combat*, 1962–67) to whip things into shape. For the first few episodes, they went the easy route on Jones' character, making him a natural extension of Jed Clampett. He was cornpone to the point of irritation.

Yet there was still something underneath the rather facile exterior. Like William Conrad, Buddy Ebsen was a commanding presence—although neither appeared to be. Still, when they said something it was believed. Frank Cannon would say it strongly, with that deep, powerful voice. Jones said it softly; it rolled off his tongue like honey. But there was no doubt he knew exactly what he was doing.

That was the beginning of a winning formula. People had been trying to figure out variations on *Columbo* for years. Talents no less than Jimmy Stewart had tried it (*Hawkins*, 1973–74) but failed. *Barnaby Jones* succeeded because it was that rare, perhaps unique, situation where the natural needs of the star served the show's end.

It's like this; even at his very best, the sixty-five-year-old Ebsen couldn't be in almost every scene, like Mannix or Cannon. Especially since Quinn Martin insisted that most of the filming be done on location. Ebsen was well known for wanting four-day weekends and stopping work on the spot at six. So the writers developed stories where the machinations of the villains ran parallel to, and were just as important as, Jones' investigation.

On *Columbo*, the villain spends the first third of the episode planning and executing the murder, then the detective spends the last two thirds finding the necessary proof to convict. *Barnaby Jones* was similar only in that the audience knows 'whodunit'; otherwise, the criminal's dirty deeds and efforts to cover his tracks take up about sixty percent of the show. Jones only appears in integral joints to nonchalantly punch holes in the villain's plan.

Although Barnaby was initially conceived as an "old Columbo" (both detectives were unassuming and seemed less capable than they were), by the time Philip Saltzman became the new producer, Jones had changed. Now there was no doubting his sagacity. Barnaby was so good at his job that the bad guys became increasingly frustrated by the detective's clear-headed ability.

Thankfully the character didn't do this by punching or shooting or brilliant deductions. He did it by pure and simple detective work. It made for a refreshing change. Barnaby Jones was an actual detective who did what actual detectives did. He checked up on suspects' alibis—usually on the payroll of the California Meridian Insurance Company. While the murderers would be racing around frantically tying up loose ends, Jones would be casually checking stories, interviewing witnesses, doing library research, going over evidence in his office lab, discussing theories with Betty, and communicating with law enforcement officials.

In short, Barnaby Jones was the Droopy Dog of the TV private eye—with a little bit of the Roadrunner thrown in. While the various Wile E. Coyotes scrambled all over the place doing unbelievable things to avoid the inevitable, they'd always turn around and there droopy old Barnaby would be. Watching an episode of *Barnaby Jones* held the same perverse pleasure as watching a classic cartoon.

While the bad guys were racing to motels to empty ashtrays, Barnaby would be interviewing the room maids. While they would be bribing waiters (who would no doubt blackmail them in return) Barnaby would be interviewing the busboys. While they were lying to their wives, Barnaby would be talking to their mistresses—who would later mention that Barnaby planned to check the wastepaper can in the motel bathroom.

"The wastepaper can in the motel bathroom!" the villain would scream, tearing out his hair. Then off he'd race to cover up that forgotten clue. He'd usually arrive just in time for Barnaby to get the drop on him.

The series was just as warped as Bugs Bunny's perspective. In order to keep their villains' stories afloat, the writers came up with twisting and twisted tales of double-crosses, triple-crosses, revenge, psychosis, angst, guilt, paranoia, terror, and sometimes downright evil incarnate.

After solving his son's murder, Barnaby went up against a sportsman

What you see is not what you get: Buddy Ebsen as *Barnaby Jones*, a deceptive, perverse series.

who wanted a new life and would do anything to get it. "To Catch a Dead Man" began Barnaby's long association with obsessive adversaries. Two weeks later (after Barnaby solves a hit-and-run in "Murder Go Round"), he makes his first acquaintance with guest star Gary Lockwood, who would come to represent Quinn Martin's idea of the perfect Everyman villain. Lockwood guest-starred as the bad guy in a half dozen *Barnaby Jones* episodes, as well as many other QM Productions.

Lockwood's episodes were also prime examples of the series' labyrinthine puzzles. One had him as a double-crossed, left-for-dead partner of a bank robbery gang who returns to demand his split and his lover back. Another had him as a kidnapper who gets out of jail after a decade only to find out his partner still has the captive.

"He was a low-down skunk in every one of them!" Ebsen remembered. "Every time I saw him, I'd say, 'Didn't I put you in jail once?' "

After Lockwood's first appearance, the classic "QM-episode" took form. In "The Murdering Class," two prep-schoolers turn an accidental death into a homicide frame-up just to get back at somebody they didn't like. Week after week, year after year, the cast and crew would exult in stories like that. In otherwise totally normal surroundings, one or two seemingly ordinary people would be closet sociopaths. They would latch on to some sort of obscene idea, usually with a completely innocent fall guy in mind, and carry it through with lip-smacking tenacity.

Producer Saltzman went on the record, saying, "We're never nasty." Don't you believe it. *TV Guide* reported that the program didn't even have "any villains bad enough to make you mad" when, in fact, this series had the most heinous creeps on record. There were men who use shell-shocked best friends as murder dupes ("A Simple Case of Terror"), killers who terrorize handicapped children ("Run to Death"), girls who decide to off their teachers for the heck of it ("Academy of Evil") — then start torturing each other when nerves stretch. Perhaps what fooled glancing critics was that these villians did not look like the stereotypical bad guys on other shows. These horrendous beasts looked normal.

Not nasty? *Barnaby Jones* was deliciously nasty. Delicious, because, throughout, there would be solid, dependable, trustworthy, polite, soft-spoken Barnaby, inexorably tracking the monsters down with good old-fashioned dogged detective work. The writers could include the most horrible situations because good old Barnaby would be there to save us.

All this was apparent under the placid, traditional QM surface. *Barnaby Jones* was superficially set up just like *Cannon*: an excellent theme song by Jerry Goldsmith with an effective flute solo, the same sort of narration, naming guest stars and special guest stars that most people had never heard of, four acts, an epilog, and some of the most melodramatic titles since the pulp magazine days.

"See Some Evil, Do Some Evil" was about a pianist faking blindness

Barnaby and daughter-in-law Betty (Lee Meriwether) seek to calm another persecuted victim in a long line of terrorized clients.

as a cover to his blackmailing and murder schemes. "Day of the Viper" was about the seemingly accidental death of a rancher from snake bite. "Divorce, Murder Style," had the killer blackmailed by greedy friends of the victim. The titles wouldn't have been out of place on melodramatic radio programs. "Death on Deposit," "Image of Evil," "Fantasy of Fear," "The Price of Terror," "A Taste for Murder" . . . .

Out of 175 episodes, *Barnaby Jones* had twenty-eight with "Dead" or "Death" in the title, eight with "Terror," twelve with "Murder," and plenty more with the catchwords "Fear," "Killer," "Evil," and "Blood." In the last season, they even resorted to titles like "Uninvited Peril," and "Design for Madness." They tried everything but "Room of Doom."

It would not have been out of place. As time went on, the writers became more and more daring with the outlandish villainy. David Wayne and Eileen Heckart co-starred in "Dark Legacy" as two of the sweetest serial murderers you've ever seen. In "Circle of Treachery," two hopeful country-western singers go on a robbery and murder spree to finance a Nashville demo record. These two crazies proved so popular that they escaped from jail and continued on the bloody road to Musictown in "Runaway to Terror."

The writers continued investigating the lengths they could go to for desperation and dementia. A man kills his wife's lover at the start of

"Stand In for Death"—only he soon finds out that the victim wasn't his wife's lover. In "Wipeout," a surfer accidentally kills a beach bunny when she makes fun of his impotence. In "Dead Heat," an ambitious father tries to sabotage his son's competitors in a swimming meet by putting pep pills in the opposition's water . . . except that one boy has an allergic reaction and dies.

In each case, the guilt-wracked killer tries to cover up, but the ever faithful, ever dogged, ever intrepid investigator for the insurance company, slowly, relentlessly uncovers the truth. These episodes rose in an increasingly hysterical crescendo as the desolate murderers become more frenzied in their attempts to escape truth, justice, and the American way.

Then there were the *really* sick episodes, like "The Inside Man," where a particularly loathsome rapist-murderer does the former to Betty's friend and threatens the latter to Betty. "Terror on a Quiet Afternoon" has a spoiled heir sadistically persecuting the girl who spurned him. In "The Eyes of Terror" a town nearly lynches a retarded stutterer at the scene of the latest in a series of rapes.

Sweet stuff, but effective stuff since the audience's tensions are professionally built, then released by a detective character everyone liked, trusted, and felt strongly about. The uglier the crime, the calmer Barnaby Jones seemed to be. The torment could be enjoyed without guilt because it was so certain Barnaby would make things right.

And all along Ebsen's need to relax fed right into the show's strength. "I just tried to make everything work," the actor said. "At first they would write it like radio—with these long lines of dialogue. I just said, 'You don't need all these words.' I would just cut out some of the unnecessary talk.

"But I'm a writer myself so I respect a writer's work. I tried to make whatever they wrote work under the supposition that maybe they see some values in there that I don't. I tried to do it their way if at all possible and if it doesn't work, then I make suggestions."

Barnaby was slow walking and slow talking, which also added to his attraction. "What a nice old man," the audience might say, and harbor secret fears that he wouldn't be up to collaring the clearly odious nut cases he was constantly up against. In "Death Leap," a faked suicide attempt is just a diversion for a jewel robbery, but, in true *Barnaby Jones* fashion, everything goes wrong and the three villains fall all over themselves trying to cover up, not kill each other, not get killed by one another, and still escape from the relaxed, purposeful detective.

The set was notorious for its lack of ego and its smooth schedule. Ebsen was a gentleman and his good manners influenced the entire crew. He called his co-star, Lee Meriwether, "a darling lady," and didn't even huff when the producers brought in a young assistant at the start of the fourth season without consulting him. Now this was the sort of patent attempt to attract a younger audience Harold Gast had been so set against on *Cannon*.

"I was a little ambivalent at first," Ebsen admitted, "because we were doing well, but I recognized the fact that I was carrying a heavy load." Since the actors and producers didn't mind, the studio and network figured a little pandering wouldn't hurt the top-twenty-five show.

The assistant was Jedediah Romano (J.R.) Jones, a law student nephew of Barnaby's, who first joined the firm to track the murderer of his father. He was played by Mark Shera, who had just come off the canceled *S.W.A.T.* The young actor was slightly intimidated when he joined the cast.

"But he immediately proved he was a good actor," Ebsen contended. "He was just fine and he went along with Lee in affording me a four- or five-day weekend. They would do, oh, let's say twenty-two shows a season, and write me heavy for twelve, light for eight. Then Lee and Mark would share the other two so I had a lot of time off."

Even so, Shera's inclusion threw off the show's synergy. The producers might have been wiser to find someone who was less the classic young pretty boy, since everyone but a young audience wouldn't have much sympathy or interest in J.R. Jones. And even at its most successful, *Barnaby Jones* wasn't a wildly popular show with the teenage crowd.

Making matters worse was that the writers simply wedged Jedediah into the stories without creating a believable relationship between the wise old hound and the supposedly headstrong young pup. Outside of the pleasant way Ebsen said the name Jedediah, there seemed to be little or no spark between the characters. Betty's presence was necessary to create a damsel-in-distress or an attractive, mature female to whom Barnaby could give instructions, but J.R. was that fifth wheel Harold Gast had been talking about.

The series' weakest episodes were the ones featuring a solo J.R., starting with 1977's "The Mercenaries," wherein he infiltrates a vigilante militaristic group. Although he had played Officer Dominic Luca on *S.W.A.T.*, he was too slim to be convincing as a he-man, and too young to balance the mature *Barnaby Jones* story structure. After "Gang War," in which J.R. is kidnapped by street punks to find out who murdered their leader, the writers integrated Jedediah in more traditional stories—rather than trying to script youth-oriented plots.

Meanwhile, the other networks were doing everything they could to slow the show down. The most famous line came from an executive at another channel, who allegedly said, "You can't kill that thing with a stick!"

"In the meantime," Ebsen reported, "Freddie Silverman went from CBS over to ABC at double or triple the salary [in 1975]. And he professed that his first job was to create something that could knock off *Barnaby*

Enter Mark Shera as J. R. Jones, an obvious attempt to gain younger viewers for *Barnaby Jones*.

Jones. And he never did. He threw everything out over there but never outdid us in the ratings. So he finally wound up by taking credit for us in all his future relations."

Indeed, nothing seemed to dent *Barnaby Jones'* imperturbability. The program seemed all set to head into a ninth season, becoming the longest-running private eye show, when it was cancelled—much to the surprise of its stars. The official reason was "declining rating shares." Buddy Ebsen cites another reason which may have had some influence.

"They had a funny notion about the show at the very start. Because it was a replacement, you see, for an hour that fell out. So when the people of that executive echelon get an idea in their heads it sort of takes root and stays there. And they always had the notion it was a temporary show."

If that was the case, then it was a stopgap whose time only came seven years later. "What happened," Ebsen went on to explain, "was that they got a very big surprise when we first started. Quinn called me off the set—we were shooting the third episode—and said, 'Hey, did you see the numbers?' I said no. He said, 'We knocked off *Lawrence of Arabia*!' They showed this big blockbuster on ABC and the score was Lawrence 17, Barnaby 37.

"So when we kept bouncing around, ratings-wise, that year, they were afraid to cancel it. The second year the same thing happened. The third year I was at the Beverly Hills Hotel and my superboss Freddie Silverman invited me to sit down and have a drink. So I did. And he said, 'Enjoy this year.' So I figured that could only mean one thing—it would definitely get cancelled the end of the year.

"So I enjoyed the third year . . . and the fourth year, and the fifth year, and the sixth year, and the seventh year, and the eighth year!" Buddy Ebsen laughed.

He had good reason to. He had beaten the odds again. While the networks and studios had raced frantically about, trying to make something that would destroy him, there good old *Barnaby Jones* was, calmly giving the audience something it wanted and needed—release from the tensions of an all too perverse world.

CHAPTER

The Jello Wall

"That's a fairly astute observation for somebody without any brains. You know?"

—Harry Orwell

THE ATTRACTION OF THE HARD-BOILED PRIVATE EYE IS A POWERFUL ONE to writers. Although the television P.I. is almost totally a media-created fantasy, it is returned to time and again. While there have been realistic series about doctors (*Ben Casey*, 1961–66, *St. Elsewhere*, 1982–88), lawyers (*The Defenders*, 1961–69, *L.A. Law*), reporters (*Lou Grant*, 1977–82), and cops (*Police Story*, 1973–77), there has never been, and may never be, a successful realistic program about a private detective. It would be too boring.

So television writers return to the icon: the troubled, impoverished, illegitimate son of Humphrey Bogart with his hat brim down, his trench-coat collar up, and the weight of a corrupt world on his shoulders. It is a well-worn stereotype, but always interesting because ethics and morality still mean something to these detectives. The writers can script passion plays where honor is more important than reality.

Both screenwriters and novelists have followed in Raymond Chandler's footsteps. The most artistically successful television character made in the mold of Philip Marlowe was Harry Orwell. The series about him, *Harry O*, was the best video noir program since *Peter Gunn*. But while *Gunn*'s noir aspects were mostly in its style of presentation, *Harry O*'s noir was in its content. It is one of the best and most popular shows of the type, but only stayed on the air for two seasons.

It is also one of the best examples of how a successful series is created and destroyed. It stumbled and died, but not for clearly apparent reasons. The story of *Harry O* is a quintessential television tale of backstage politics, front office ego, and Hollywood hysteria. It is an excellent example of murder on the air.

The show's conception was fittingly outlandish. "My understanding," said Howard Rodman, the man the studio signed to create the series, "was that Warners really wanted to take off on the *Dirty Harry* movies, which is why he's called Harry Orwell. But it had nothing to do with Dirty Harry as far as I was concerned."

It had nothing to do with Dirty Harry as far as the executive in charge of Warner Brothers programs was concerned either. "The truth is that it wasn't originally written for David Janssen," Harvey Frand revealed. "It was written for someone else who turned it down because he wasn't going to do television. He had a feature career in Europe at the time and he did that until he came back to do *Kojak*."

That's right. Telly Savalas was originally going to be . . . not Harry . . . but Nick Orwell.

"Once it wasn't going to be Telly Savalas," Frand continues, "the name Nick was changed." See? It's that simple to create a television show. Just add *Kojak* to *Dirty Harry* and you get *Harry O*.

"I'll tell you where Harry O derives from," said Rodman. "Nathanael West. In his novel *The Day of the Locust*, there is a page or two describing this guy walking up Sweetzer—that slope between Santa Monica and Sunset Boulevard—on a very, very hot day. He's a door-to-door salesman going through bungalow courts and he's got his jacket off, his thumb through the hanger loop holding it over his back, and his shirt is all wet. I believe I remember that. That was the image I used to create Harry O. I mean that literally. That's where I started."

Rodman then rejected all vestiges of Dirty Harry Callahan. He detested the character's big gun, the San Francisco locale, and the squealing car chases. "I hate car chases," he said flatly. "I hate chases of any sort. So I thought I was going to fuck the networks and not give them a goddamn chance to screw up my work. So he had no car and he used the bus. And he had a bad back so he couldn't run. That was interesting in and of itself, but what I was really trying to do was fuck the networks so they couldn't squeal another tire in my stories."

As the man credited with selling more TV pilots than anyone else in the Writers Guild, Rodman had the clout and the ability to make the studio see the light. His Harry Orwell was a former San Diego policeman who retired on a disability pension after being shot. The bullet is lodged too close to his spine for surgery and is always threatening to move—either paralyzing or killing him. That gave the character an innate sensitivity and vulnerability. But his mind was too active to let his body stay inert. He became a private eye, working out of his beachfront shack. In the era of *Mannix*, this concept was a challenging one.

"The network thought that no dramatic series could survive without 'hard action,' " explained Rodman. "I've been working in TV since 1946 and the frustration back then was that five or six shows in a dramatic series would disappoint the audience because it wasn't as good as the very best ones. So we had a sneaking suspicion that the producers were deliberately lowering their sights so there wouldn't be this constant frustration on the part of the audience.

"There was a tendency to level off at banality because true creativity was very hard to achieve. Ultimately this led to a system which doesn't want innovation. It wants stability. And stability is achieved only through stereotyping. I'm not sure all this is true; I'm simply sure I believe it."

Rodman's pilot was titled "Such Stuff as Dreams Are Made Of" (paraphrased from *The Maltese Falcon*). It was produced and directed by Jerry Thorpe. He also carried considerable weight with the ABC network, having been executive producer for *The Untouchables* and *Kung Fu* (1972–75).

This initial work told of Harlan Garrison, the man who shot Harry in the first place, asking the detective to find his missing girlfriend. Orwell does it, uncovering a nasty plot which involves drugs and the Vietnam War. "When that got to ABC in New York," said Rodman, "they liked it and they didn't like it."

On the one hand, they appreciated Rodman's and Thorpe's abilities. On the other, they would have been more comfortable with a car, a gun, and no bullet in Harry Orwell's back. This balking is what is known in the business as "the jello wall." They "loved" the pilot, but they didn't trust it to succeed because it wasn't like everything else.

"One of the executives called," Rodman remembered, "and said, 'Can you get us some kind of small memo to give the network head in two days?'

"I gave them a thirty-page tutorial," Rodman said. "For years, I had been trying to explain to them what it is I try to do in a script and this was a good opportunity. They were very upset seeing how long it was, but they were so pressed for time they couldn't shorten it. I find the network guys are not uncreative—they're not dumb—they just don't think in the same terms I do. They start from different premises. So they gave their bosses the whole memo and it worked."

The memo brought the network through the entire creative process. Rodman started by delineating what the writer wanted as opposed to what was required by the studio and network. "The trouble with designing a series," he wrote, "is that you always have to worry about more than one thing at the same time. You have to come to your series from different directions simultaneously, fitting the disparate into a single, integral machine for entertainment."

He went on to the series' precepts. "In this case, what was 'given' was a requirement for a private eye series, and it had to be a guy who was totally honest. The sort of guy who would listen to you and then say calmly, 'That's bullshit. Because . . .'—whatever the reality of 'because' happened to be. I liked that. God only knows what it set off in my mind, but I liked it at once. Thinking back, I liked it because it was reassuring. One of the qualities of the world I live in is that nothing is fixed and steadfast anymore. Everything changes so fast from day to day I have to learn new rules. . . . Even changing against change is change. What verities remain then? Well, certain ways we like people to behave, like a man who says, 'Bullshit is bullshit.' "

Rodman also liked that Harry O was once a cop, because a cop represented authority in the world. But he also acknowledged that authority could have a negative effect on the viewers.

"Now, at the same time, a cop has a drawback for a series which requires audience empathy. Because almost as much as an audience wants stability and effectiveness, it rejects too much stability and effectiveness, because that makes the audience feel the guy is arrogant, or too perfect. 'Too perfect' is a serious charge against a hero in fiction, since individuals in an audience, including thee and me, aren't perfect at all. 'Too perfect' is somebody you can't identify with.

"It's a very careful balance, because you want somebody to identify with who has the power to remain alive and the ability to overcome the problems in this changing and impossible world we all live in; and, at the same time, if he does either or both too well, then not being us, it is useless for us as a reassurance. So I watched that."

Then came Harry Orwell himself, who was a mix of both Rodman's conception and David Janssen's interpretation. The writer thought this particular actor perfect for the role which required a sadness, toughness, tiredness, and sweetness.

"Harry O is a man who has to have compassion; he has to have feeling. Again, it is a matter of balance. For on the one hand, he must seem to be cool, self-contained, and invulnerable. What must open to the audience, what the audience must be able to discover for itself, is a secret that none of the bad guys will ever uncover—that Harry is vulnerable and caring and has pity and compassion."

Harry O also had violence. He was created from violence. He has a bullet lodged in his back. Rodman had a reason for that, too, as well as thoughts on the nature of television action.

"It is not violence which offends me," he wrote, "although I may be offended by certain types of violence which are in and of themselves a representation of sadism rather than a release of tension. Release of tension is what violence is for, and that is a useful function. It helps people. What bothers me most often is that in our lives we have, ideally, a tripartite system of justice: the police apprehend the criminal, the courts and juries try him, and the prisons serve out his sentence.

David Meyer, the twenty-fifth actor to audition for the part of *Richard Diamond*. Producer Dick Powell was to change the actor's name to Janssen.

"But when you get the split-second framed pieces of time which confine the TV presentation, you want to keep everything going until the very last second, so that your climax comes as close to the final commercial as possible; with the commercial, itself, and the tiny epilogue serving as the denouement. To meet the requirements of this dynamic, more often than not the good guy becomes a good-guy-with-a-gun, who serves as cop, judge, jury, and executioner with the same bullet. Within my means, and within the parameters afforded by the particular kind of story I chose, I tried not to let this happen."

He also asked the network not to let it happen either. But he knew that he had to give them something to replace the gun fights and car chases with. "Almost always, when I'm writing, I find that the really hard questions I must ask myself, and that others ask of me, contain the answers to what to write next. If it must be established that Harry is someone you can trust, then that is the direction in which to go for a while in order to find stories for the man. I would pick out stories in which he does things that are helpful to other people, choose for him actions which are altruistic—even though, at the same time, I would have Harry deny that altruism if he were faced with it."

Rodman's idea of good action was a hero who would do what had to be done, without thinking that shooting the problem was the solution. The scripter also felt that action worked best in contrast to something equal and opposite . . . something he had even forgotten in the rush to write *Harry O*.

"There are no 'frozen moments' in the pilot," he told them. "I hadn't built any in. There are no moments when Harry does nothing. When he goes out to the beach with a beer can in his hand and sits there and regrets something, or feels sad about something, or realizes he has done something wrong. One, maybe two moments like that, would be all it would take. Because without it, you leave your audience without a depth of caring. And it's so damn easy to make such scenes, and since they are truly wanted by the structure and character and audience, too, it is so damned easy to make such scenes work."

He concluded his memo/tutorial with a suitably stirring sentiment. "Sometimes I hate the disregard and callous disrespect of a script and I want to take my name off it. But this time I have a pride, which is why this extraordinarily long exposition was written. Because, I think, with that vision which is still nonintellectual and nonverbal, that if you put this on the air as a series there would be a growing and, finally, I think, a remarkable fusion between story and character. Ideally, of course. But then, most of the things I see don't really permit the possibility to begin with. This one, from where I sit, ought to be born. Good luck one and all."

The memo seemed to do the trick, since ABC ordered a second

pilot, but it was possible the network was equally interested in seeing how David Janssen would flourish in a script which was written specifically for him—not altered from a script meant for Clint Eastwood or Telly Savalas. Janssen was one of the great television actors, ever since his rough start as Richard Diamond.

His original name was David Meyer and he was the twenty-fourth actor to audition for Dick Powell. The highpoints of his bumpy career had been playing Johnny Weissmuller's kid brother in 1946's *Swamp Water*, a detective on the *Alcoa-Goodyear Theater* (1955–57), and a sullen cowpoke in a March 1957 episode of *Dick Powell's Zane Grey Theater*. Well-meaning producers had changed his hairline and glued his ears back. He was still smarting from a pole vaulting accident in high school, an injury which would haunt him with pain throughout his career.

Finally, at the age of twenty-eight, he was cast as Richard Diamond. After that came scores of guest roles and *The Fugitive*. In 1974 Rodman wrote "Smile, Jenny, You're Dead," the second, two-hour *Harry O* pilot (excerpts from "Such Stuff as Dreams Are Made Of" were adapted by Howard Rodman into a future episode of the series).

This pleased everyone, including the weary Janssen. He had recently racked up his worst television experience, and his worst series, *O'Hara, U.S. Treasury* (1971–72), produced by Jack Webb for CBS. Reportedly, the actor was glad to do a new series where the leading character couldn't exert himself and was amused that the name Harry O was basically O'Hara backwards. He also liked the concept Rodman had of his character.

"Harry O was a romantic in the same way Philip Marlowe was," the writer said. "An honest fellow, a compassionate man. And somewhere, in the back of my mind, on that long hot summer day walking up that slope, that salesman and Harry went on forever. The image was stopped in time and Harry never really went anywhere. He had no goal except possibly living well, with self-respect. People could beat him up, but he couldn't run after anybody. He was simply a man with some self-respect. And that's all he needed."

But while the scripter and star were happy, everything else was going to hell in a handbasket.

"On the opening day of the show's production," Harvey Frand related, "I went down to San Diego, where we were shooting, as the representative of the studio to welcome everybody. I suddenly found myself staying for four months as executive in charge of production because the shit hit the fan. The day we started the actor playing Harry's police contact quit."

Frand thought it best to mention no names. "He was an actor who was unhappy," he related. "There was some friction between him and the producer. He was later replaced by Henry Darrow (as Lieutenant Manuel Quinlan)." This turned out to be the least of Frand's worries.

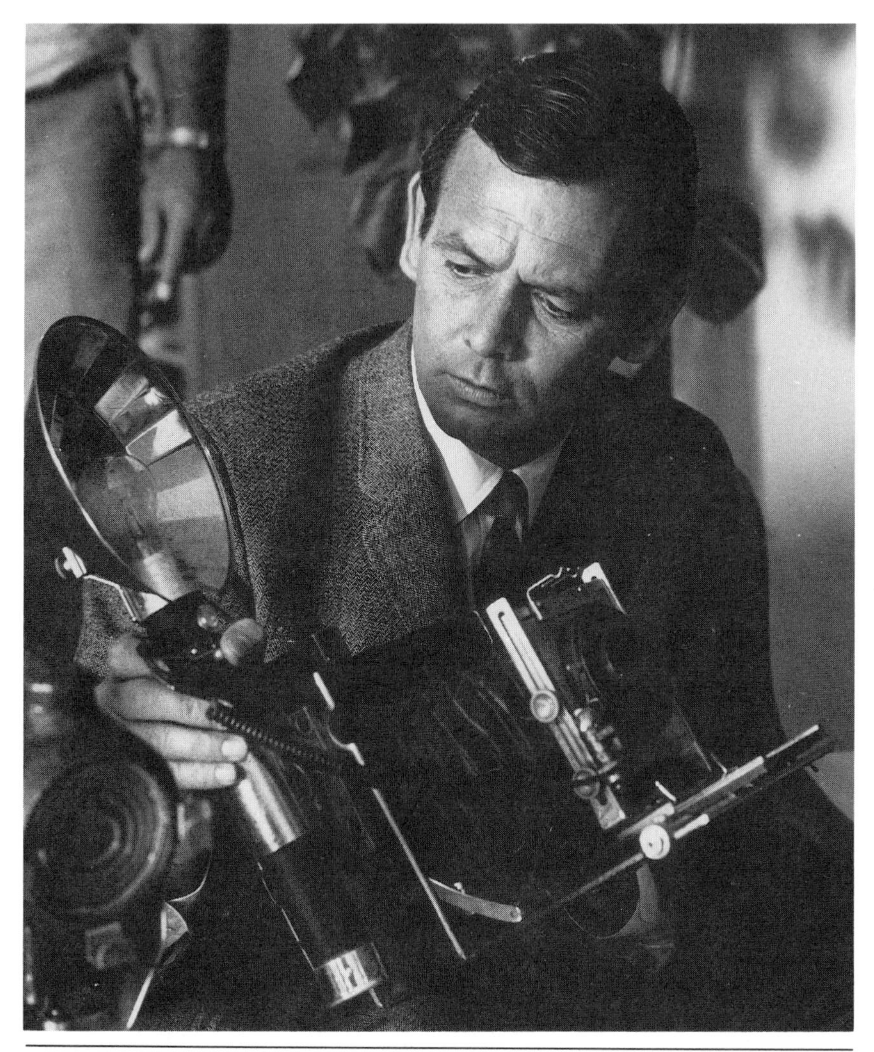

David Janssen, as Richard Diamond, gets the picture.

"On the second day, the actor who was playing the major guest star in the first episode started talking in tongues. Quite literally in tongues. And so he had to be recast and the whole first two days filming had to be completely reshot. It seemed like the thing was never going to get off the ground."

The *Harry O* production, and curse, continued. It soon became apparent that the network had never given up the hope that Orwell would get a gun, get a car, and start chasing suspects. "Harvey said, 'You must have a car,' " Rodman remembered. 'He must have a car.' We said why? Harvey replied, and I believed then and I believe now that he was simply echoing the network's position. That position was, 'There's no fucking way we're going to pass up the possibility of a General Motors commercial!' "

"In the pilots, he only rode the bus," Frand related, "but ABC would not let us get away with that. So we finally conceived of giving him this beat-up old Austin MG that was always in the shop. It became a part of his life, going to the mechanic." In fact, the mechanic was going to be a regular role until further shake-ups occurred.

The next adjustment was sartorial. Although Janssen had personally picked out Orwell's wardrobe of a tweed Mannix jacket and khaki pants, ABC wanted him to have more clothes. Frand confessed that they finally budged by getting Harry a dark suit which was almost indistinguishable from his sport coat. With each compromise, the relationship between the studio and the network got worse.

ABC always had to fight these battles on *Harry O*'s territory—on location in San Diego. It made it tough for their convictions to have any strength after the long commute from Hollywood. So another ultimatum came down: Harry was moving to Los Angeles.

"San Diego is not really more visually interesting than L.A.," Frand conceded, "and it is a lot more expensive. You have to bring your cast and crew from Los Angeles and there were other financial reasons not to be there." Hollywood was geared to television production while their southern neighbor was not. Since it made sense to Frand, the production packed their bags and moved to Los Angeles.

The writers responded by making Harry's life miserable. Although the series looked like every other action series, it didn't play like one. Everything Harry had come to depend upon began to be destroyed. His mechanic was crushed to death under a car ("Sound of Trumpets"). Lieutenant Manny Quinlan died, killed while trying to protect his drug-addicted niece ("Elegy for a Cop"). Even Harry's boat disappeared.

The boat was an unfinished yacht in Harry's yard named *The Answer*. In his memo, Rodman talked about it. "It means that Harry, like everyone else, has an unfulfilled, inchoate hunger. A boat like that takes you away (my homage to Clifford Odets, whose irrelevant third acts always took his protagonists to that far place). Even though, no matter how long the series would continue, the boat would never be finished. Because, like everyone else, Harry has answers which never come to reality; has dreams which remain dreams.

"The boat is simply a statement about what he's after," he told me. "Both in the specific, of a detective's work, and in general, a human being trying to find out what kind of world he's living in. And that answer is never finished because it's always in the making. It's always under construction."

In any event, the first eighteen episodes (twelve in San Diego, and the eighteenth, where Quinlan dies) became the finest sustained work of

David Janssen, as Harry Orwell, always seeks The Answer.

video noir the tube has been able to do. It was tougher and more challenging to the character and his audience than anything else in the TV P.I. canon.

"A lot of it was intentional," Frand maintains. "A lot of it had to do with playing to the man's strength—making him a loner and vulnerable."

Orwell's on-screen persecution mirrored the chaos behind the cameras. The superficial result was that Harry spent one episode in Lancaster, California ("The Last Heir" was his most inconsistent story; Harry solves a gothic Agatha Christie type of murder mystery in a haunted house), then two episodes in a Los Angeles apartment house (including one, "Eyewitness," about a rape victim who made an inaccurate identification, which was precisely the same as a *Mannix* episode), before the crew's location managers could find him a suitably bohemian beach house—where *The Answer* was finally returned.

"If you're away from home," said Harry in a voice-over speech, "you have to have a place to live. I like to live near the ocean. In Los Angeles the ocean is in Santa Monica. So I rented an apartment in Santa Monica. The waves are nice, and the girls dress differently at the beach. That's nice too."

Harry's new next-door neighbors were a bevy of stewardesses, the most visual being Sue, played by Farrah Fawcett. "The two of them really liked each other," said Frand, "and it showed. At the time Farrah was not the most experienced actress in the world, but they were so good together that we found ourselves waiting for them [to get it right], which was nice. The stuff with her and David was wonderful."

Orwell's new police contact was Lieutenant K.C. Trench, played by Anthony Zerbe. "Trench was not an invention of mine," Rodman relayed. "Jerry Thorpe was convinced that every private eye had to have a hook into the police department. I don't think that's a handicap, but I really deplore it. It has become part of the conventional wisdom of television private eyes, and I think it's horseshit."

Rodman's reservations aside, the new addition to the cast was both a large blessing and a small curse. While Rodman was correct that the Harry-Trench relationship did detract from Harry's standing as loner hero, it was the acting sparks of David Janssen and Anthony Zerbe which kept the show artistically afloat during its hard times.

"The best stuff in the show was when those two were together," Harvey Frand maintained. "It was Jerry's idea that the character be a real hard-nose. I mean the name 'Trench' kind of says it. And I think it was also Jerry's idea that Anthony Zerbe should play it. I don't think we interviewed anyone else. It had to be Anthony Zerbe, who was wonderful."

It was more fire in the tradition of Mannix and Lou Wickersham—two men with different loyalties who sniped at each other while sharing a deep, abiding brotherhood. The same thing happened off-stage as well. Not only did David Janssen have an acting rapport with Zerbe, but he had a distinctly Trench-Harry relationship with Jerry Thorpe.

With the move to L.A., the balance of power shifted to the network. Robert Dozier came in as producer, forcing Howard Rodman to step aside. Dozier liked what Rodman didn't and disliked what Rodman did.

"He hated the voice-over narration," the writer contended, "and if you notice, after a while it becomes more and more cursory. Bob just didn't approve of narration. I liked it because it attached the show to its own past history and its own genre. That's what the hell private eyes are; they talk to you that way."

Dozier also seemed to side with the network on the question of car chases and gunfights. "ABC would have preferred seeing Harry in a Mercedes Sport 50 SL," Frand joked. "They didn't see how a man could have a bullet in his back and still be a hero. But I think, in fact, that ABC was right to some degree that we did too many character pieces in the first season. Because we were so caught up with the people, we lost some of the traditional action viewers expect in detective shows."

"In came car chases and guns," Rodman translated. "One of the things Jerry, Bob [Dozier], and the network held against David is that he didn't want to use the gun. They felt you couldn't be macho without it. In the end, as I understand it, Bob first and then Jerry came to be very hostile toward David. I don't know what the details were, but I saw it in the scripts."

As script consultant, Rodman always made his feelings known. In his comments for what was to become the series' twenty-fourth episode, "Anatomy of a Frame," Rodman wrote "By now all the stories are similar to other stories used on our own and other series in the past. There has to be an exceptional effort made to discover and use fresh details."

Rodman was well aware that there are just so many plots a certain kind of series can do. He was also aware that these familiar stories could be given new life through a fresh character. But it took a staff willing to trust that new character and write for him—rather than trying to make him like all the others.

"This is what I think I know," Rodman mused. "Janssen had been drinking himself into a stupor on *O'Hara*. He was bored with it. *Harry O* seemed to have some life and vitality for him. He came to it, I thought, eagerly. For a while he didn't drink as heavily. But as the show went on . . . I don't know whether it was the grind or whether it was the terrible wear and tear . . . but I think they became hostile because he annoyed them. Maybe he wasn't on the set when he should've been. Maybe he was bored when they wanted him not to be."

At this point, press reports began to appear about accidents and delays on the *Harry O* stage. Janssen appeared to be in greater and greater discomfort because of his injuries—most especially his damaged knee. His need for more recuperation time might have further eroded his relationship with the producers.

A result was the introduction of a new character who had about as much in common with Harry Orwell as Jerry Lewis would have with Gary Cooper. Les Lannom played an overanxious, overzealous, self-absorbed criminology student named Lester Hodges. In the episodes "Les-

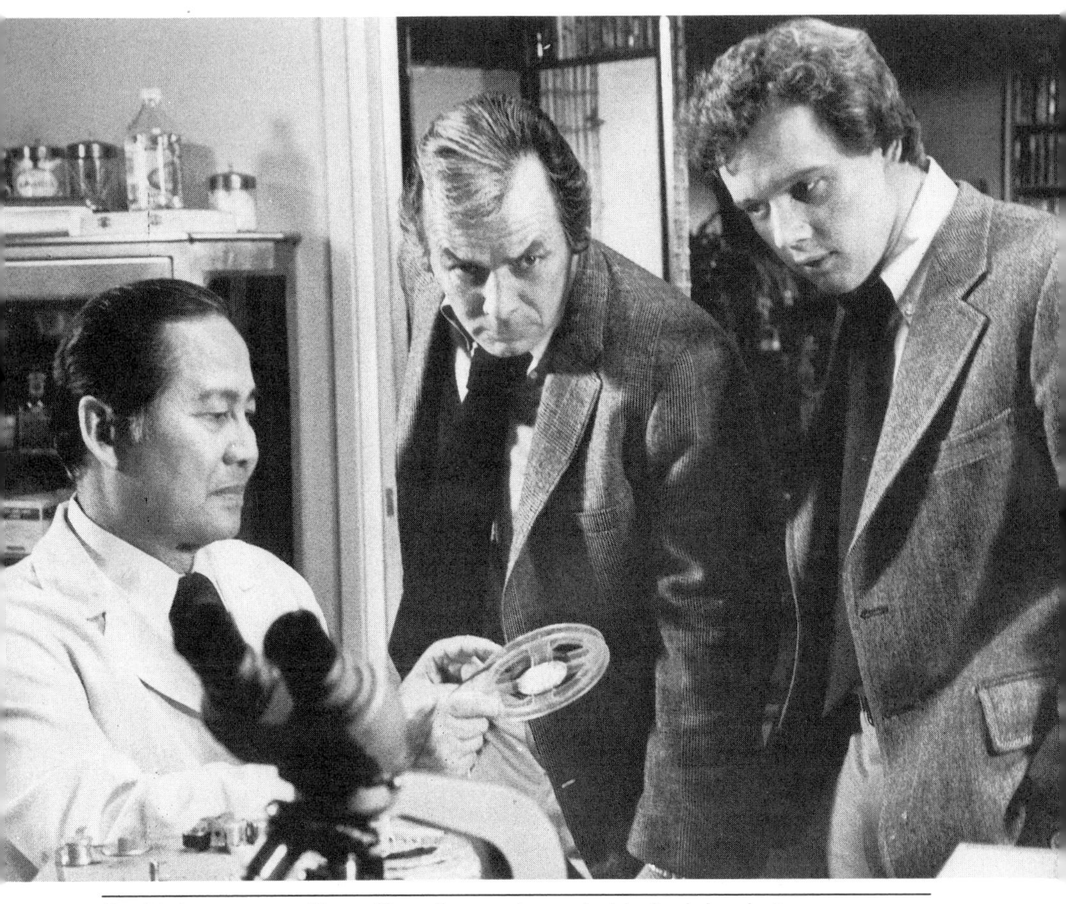

David Janssen, as Harry Orwell, wonders what he's doing between Dr. Fong (Keye Luke) and Lester (Les Lannom).

ter," "Lester Two," and "Mister Five and Dime" he caused endless headaches for Orwell with his well-meaning stupidity.

Even though he was obviously out of place, the producers tried to spin off the character. In *Harry O*'s second-to-last episode, "The Mysterious Case of Lester and Dr. Fong," they tried to pair Hodges with a Charlie Chan–like criminology professor played by Keye Luke. It was a most unbecoming and unnatural attempt.

Thankfully, many of the other episodes ran truer to form. One of the most memorable and ironic was "Group Terror," in which Harry poses as an alcoholic to infiltrate a therapy group where murder had struck. Ironic, for a famous Hollywood rumor said that every bar on the Sunset Strip closed for an hour in memorial the day after Janssen's untimely death.

Whether or not that was true, the producers' alleged hostility toward

Janssen during production couldn't match that of Fred Silverman. The programming wunderkind jumped from CBS to ABC in 1975, the year of *Harry O*'s second season. Anthony Zerbe first told me that Silverman was directly responsible for the series cancellation. Harvey Frand subsequently corroborated the co-star's story.

"One of the reasons I left the show was that it was clear Silverman bore a grudge against the series and I think it had to do with the fact that Janssen hadn't been successful for him over at CBS." That was a nice way of saying that *O'Hara* had been a deeply troubled show and there was bad blood between the star and the network head.

"He was putting unbearable pressure on *Harry O*," Frand continued.

David Janssen as Harry Orwell—tired, wounded, hurting, sensitive, vulnerable, tough (the "Shadows at Noon" episode).

"The pressure was to make it something it wasn't. There was no way the show was going to be renewed. The show had a thirty-six share, it was in the top twenty, and you just don't cancel a show like that! So Zerbe was right. And I think there was something personal going on between Silverman and Janssen."

True to the rumors, *Harry O* was cancelled after its second season, the year Anthony Zerbe won an Emmy for his performance. The final episode was "Death Certificate," in which Harry investigated possible medical malpractice. It was a fitting end for a series which died way before its time. Fred Silverman went on to a disastrous job at NBC, and David Janssen went on to several television movies before his abrupt death on February 13, 1980. His obituaries acknowledged that he was one of the form's great actors—a nearly perfect example of the television action hero.

"I've always felt that nothing good is ever easy," Harvey Frand stated, remembering his *Harry O* years in 1985. "But the experience was wonderful because we had a good crew, and because of David. Who he was shaped what the series was about."

Harry O continues in syndication, which is surprising since it only ran for two years. It is rare for a show with that few episodes to be rerun constantly. Just about the only other action series which can make the same claim is *Star Trek*. This abortive private eye program remains fresh because of the star and his well-suited role. David Janssen always looked tired, but he always fought on. It was fitting that *Harry O* be his last show, and that the detective exists in a never-ending loop of the same cases.

"Orwell's still walking up that street," said Rodman. "He's still in that one moment of time that never stopped and has no beginning and no end. *Harry O* was a pair of khaki pants, a tweed sport coat, a shirt without a tie. It was a way of life that didn't have the Answer. . . ."

CHAPTER

Throwing the Curve

"This is Jim Rockford. At the tone,
leave your name and message;
I'll get back to you.

—James Scott Rockford

THERE WERE FEW SURPRISES IN 1974. TELEVISION HAD SETTLED INTO A routine. It was a high-class routine of shows like *Kojak* (1973–78), *Gunsmoke* (1955–75), *Happy Days* (1974–84), *Little House on the Prairie* (1974–83), *The Odd Couple* (1970–75), *M*A*S*H* (1972–83), *The Mary Tyler Moore Show* (1970–77), *All in the Family* (1971–83), *Adam 12* (1968–75), and programs we've aleady examined, like *Mannix*, *Cannon*, *Barnaby Jones*, *Hawaii Five-O*, and *Harry O*. It made for an entertaining schedule.

The true inspiration and experimentation was occurring in the comedies, which were getting more dramatic. Perhaps it was about time that the dramas became more comedic. It was also about time for a detective hero whose life didn't begin and end with his job. It was time for a character with a little more character. It was time to throw a curve into a genre formula that was getting staid.

Jim Rockford was a man who knew his limitations. That was part of what made him the best-loved private eye of the medium. This was an era when production technology matched writing ability; where producing exceptional weekly fare wasn't the impossibility it once seemed. *The Rockford Files* took things one step further. It combined terrific scripting, filming, and acting to make magic.

Don't get me wrong. The show itself was hardly spectacular. It wasn't

The Jack Benny of private eyes, Jim Rockford.

flashy, unique, or original. Sometimes, it was downright derivative. The key to its success was its star. James Scott Bumgarner was James Scott Garner was James Scott Rockford, and while he wasn't the strongest, smartest, or most realistic private eye, he was certainly the cleverest. He was, in short, the most enjoyable to watch.

That was fortunate, because the series survived on his strength alone. Without Garner, there was no way the program could have survived. Garner's mother died when he was five. Garner started working for a living by the time he was ten. At thirteen, he was a janitor at the University of Oklahoma. He cleaned from 3:30 to 7:30 in the morning, then went to school. When he was sixteen, he worked in the oil fields of Texas. When he was seventeen, he was clearing trees for Bell Telephone.

All along, he was collecting injuries. He ground up his knees playing football for Oklahoma U. He compressed his back in a car accident. He was shot and burned by friendly fire—our own shells—in the Korean War. Only by meeting up with an old friend he had known before the war was Garner introduced to acting.

Producer Paul Gregory had him feeding lines to Lloyd Nolan in the original Broadway production of *The Caine Mutiny Court-martial.* As the show toured, Garner became more and more enamored of the theater. His big break came in 1955 when Warner Brothers signed him to a seven-year contract. He had to get through fodder like *Shoot-Out at Medicine Bend* (1957) before Roy Huggins made him *Maverick.*

Warners paid him $500 a week the first season, and $600 the next. They more than doubled that salary as *Maverick*'s success continued, but it was still a ludicrously small amount considering the popularity of the show and how much money the studio and network were raking in.

So Garner walked off the set in 1960 and sued to get out of his contract. His friends and business associates told him he was nuts, and more than one power-that-be intoned, "You'll never work in this town again!" At the very least, they were sure he'd never win the court case. But he did, and James Garner became a free agent.

The quality level of his film roles went up almost immediately. There was a demand for his sort of amiable personality, and starting with *The Children's Hour* (1962), Garner racked up success after success—both critically and financially. Audiences loved *The Great Escape* (1963) while critics loved *The Americanization of Emily* (1964). He became second to Rock Hudson in Doris Day's heart with *The Thrill of It All* and *Move Over, Darling* (both 1963).

As the decade continued, Garner shifted with seeming effortlessness from domestic comedy to hard drama. 1964 had *36 Hours* and 1965 *The Art of Love.* 1966 had *Duel at Diablo, A Man Could Get Killed, Mr. Buddwing*, and *Grand Prix.* He reinjured his back and broke two ribs during the production of the latter racing film. That didn't stop him from doing *How Sweet It Is!* and *The Pink Jungle* in 1968, however.

Jim Rockford started to take form in his 1969 movies. First Garner tried his hand at Raymond Chandler, starring in *Marlowe*, an adaptation of *The Little Sister* (1949). Although it was largely disliked at the time, retrospective reviews give Garner higher marks for his savvy, amiable performance. While it is an entertaining picture (featuring a show-stopping scene with Bruce Lee), it cannot compare to Dick Powell's or Humphrey Bogart's incarnations of the detective.

Later that same year came *Support Your Local Sheriff*, an extremely amusing and witty western satire that made audiences wistful for Maverick. Perhaps in response to this, Garner went to Europe to make the violent, grimy Italian western, *A Man Called Sledge* (1970).

Even so, the following year saw the release of two more Garner western comedies. *Support Your Local Gunfighter* (1971) was cut from the same mold as *Sheriff*, though less amusing. Considerably more amusing that year was the unjustly underrated *Skin Game*, a wonderful film co-starring Louis Gossett, Jr. and directed by Paul Bogart (who also helmed *Marlowe*). These movie roles went a long way in developing the persona which was to become Jim Rockford.

They portrayed a clever, versatile man who sought excitement, but didn't want trouble. But when it invariably came, he tried to deal with it as practically as possible. If talking didn't help, he'd run away. He'd only stand and fight if there was no other way. He was a man of limited, very specific patience, who would never take adversity stoically. Above all else, he was a likable man. Sometimes a rascal, sometimes a con artist, but always a well-meaning hero.

By the early seventies, Garner was ready to return to television. The vehicle was the unfortunate NBC western comedy, *Nichols* (1971–72). Garner reportedly loved this show and is still smarting over its quick cancellation. He played a man with no first name, Nichols, who returned to his family's town (Nichols, Arizona) in 1913 only to find it taken over by the Ketcham family of varmits. It was a strange show which tried to embody the charm of his latest film successes.

When it became clear that his original concept of a cowardly, ultimately ineffectual hero was not working, No-first-name Nichols was shot down at the beginning of the last episode of the season. He was replaced by his twin brother, Jim Nichols (also played by Garner), who was a more traditional western hero. This was part of Garner's plan to make the second season more dynamic, but NBC pulled the plug.

Garner angrily went back to movies, only to find them less receptive. He made one more detective effort, *They Only Kill Their Masters* (1972), and two Disney westerns, *One Little Indian* (1973) and *The Castaway Cowboy* (1974). This was quite a step down for the man who had nearly been in the same leading-man league as Paul Newman and Steve McQueen. He soon put the word out that he was willing to do television again, even for Warners or Universal.

"I may have asked him if he wanted to do some television," Roy Huggins explained, "and he said, 'No, I won't work with Universal after my bad experience with *Nichols*.' But then I got news through a film partner that he would be willing to work with them, which was another way for Jim to say, 'Roy, if you want to come up with a TV show for me, I'll do it.' "

In the interim between *Maverick* (1957–62) and *Rockford*, Huggins had created *77 Sunset Strip* (1958–64), *The Fugitive* (1963–67), and *The Outsider* (1968–69). He had been executive producer for *Run for Your Life* (1966–68), *The Bold Ones: The Lawyers* (1969–72), *Alias Smith and Jones* (1971–73), *Toma* (1973–74), and *Baretta* (1975–78), among others. Although his first love was the western, he kept returning to the mystery genre. For his new James Garner show, he would find a way to mix both.

"I immediately came up with *The Rockford Files*," he said. "But this was not going to be a classic private eye. I wanted to do *Maverick* as a private eye. I wanted to do a private eye who was kind of cowardly, kind of reluctant about putting himself in danger, and not too serious about the world he lived in."

"And he doesn't love trouble!" Huggins added triumphantly. "He really hates trouble!"

He teamed with *Toma* producer and *Baretta* creator Steven J. Cannell to round out the character. He gave Cannell ten days to write a ninety-minute script. Cannell took five days, saying he laughed as he sat at the typewriter, breaking all the TV P.I. rules and incorporating all his own wrinkles and fantasies. What Cannell kept foremost in his mind was that Rockford would be the "Jack Benny of private eyes."

He didn't have a gorgeous secretary. Instead, he had a salt-of-the-earth father, Joseph "Rocky" Rockford (Noah Beery, Jr.) who lived on Willowcrest Drive and was slightly embarrassed by what his son did (although the love they had for each other was always apparent). Jim didn't live on the Sunset Strip, he lived in a mobile home on the beach (first 2354 Pacific Coast Highway and then 29 Cove Road in the Paradise Cove Trailer Park).

"It's cheap," Rockford said, "tax deductible, earthquake proof, and when I get a case out of town, I take it with me."

He wasn't an Ivy Leaguer, he was an ex-con wrongfully jailed for a robbery he didn't commit. Although he was pardoned, his jail buddies kept popping up to ruin his day—most especially Angel Martin (Stuart Margolin, who also co-starred in *Nichols*), who went from stir to working in a newspaper morgue and lived in the Hotel Edison. And unlike his noble TV predecessors, Jim demanded a fee: $200 a day plus expenses (although he was often hard-pressed to collect it).

The Jack Benny allusion was apt. Benny surrounded himself with all sorts of characters to play off of, as Cannell did to Rockford. The creators didn't fight the need for a police contact, only they didn't make him a high-ranking lieutenant. All the lieutenants on the show disliked Rockford. His L.A.P.D. pal was a working stiff, Detective Dennis Becker (Joe Santos), who could get into serious trouble helping Jim. They also added Beth Davenport (Gretchen Corbett), a lawyer who, in the words of Becker, "collects lost causes like old coins."

They had everything but the title. Roy Huggins came up with that final piece himself. "In order to make the network feel that they were getting something other than just another private eye show, I said to them, 'This one is different. He only takes closed cases. He will not work on a case that's open because he doesn't want to get the cops mad at him. He's afraid of the cops. He doesn't want trouble with the cops. He doesn't want trouble with anybody! If you come to him with a case the police are still working on, he will say go away.'

"Although this was all similar to *Maverick*," Huggins said, "it also happens to be very realistic. Private eyes don't work on cases the cops are working on, as a rule. The truth is they just don't. But I used it as a sales device. So 'The Rockford Files' were closed files."

The project seemed blessed. Universal funded the pilot in which Robert Donley played Jim's father because Beery was working on another series (*Doc Elliot*, January 1974–August 1974). The plot was a clever, charming, exciting adventure with Garner at the top of his affable form. The only problem was that NBC wouldn't touch it with a ten-foot pole.

"They had no interest," Huggins recalled, "because they had been burned with *Nichols*." Luckily for everyone concerned, a ninety-minute slot opened on the network and NBC filled the emergency with *The Rockford Files* pilot.

"The needle went all the way over to the right and disappeared, the ratings were so high," Huggins contended. "NBC decided to buy it, although until that point they had been negative as hell. Maybe they sensed that at last Garner had a series that he loved."

Even so, *The Rockford Files* was born of bile and that bad taste in the network's mouth would not diminish, no matter how well *The Rockford Files* did. The networks, like elephants, never forget. Meanwhile Garner surrounded himself with a hand-picked crew, chosen both for their professional skill and their easygoing personalities. The program was made under the aegis of Cherokee Productions, Garner's own company, created in partnership with his long-time managing agent, Meta Rosenberg.

"Well," Huggins remembered, "Jim had made a promise that if he went into television again, Meta would be the executive producer." She had filled that post on *Nichols*, in fact. "So he said to me, 'Roy, we may have a problem.' And I said, 'Jim, I once did a very successful series with no credit at all [*Kraft Suspense Theater*, 1963–65]. No problem, she can have producer credits. But it has to say 'A Roy Huggins Production' so the network won't be worried.'

" 'I will give you the credit,' I said, 'but Meta is not going to produce the show, not the first year.' Now Jim knows that I never stay with a show more than two years, not even *Maverick*. I walked away from that. Jim knew it. Anyway, *The Rockford Files* is a hit, number twelve in the ratings. But at the end of the year, Jim came to me and said, 'Roy, Meta is very unhappy. You gave her the credit but she doesn't do anything. She is accusing me of having lied to her. I really want her to do this show.'

"And I said, 'Jim, Meta can't do the show. She isn't capable of doing the show.' He said, 'How do you know?' I said, 'I know because I saw *Nichols*!' Well, that did it. He went up to the black tower [Universal's executive office building] and said, 'I don't want Roy Huggins to do the show.' Frank Price got me off the series. He said, 'Garner went insane about *Nichols* and all I could think of was how do I get out of his trailer alive.' Anyway, he got me off the show. Fortunately I had made Steve Cannell the producer."

Huggins maintained that the series was never as good as it was in the first season. Indeed, many of the continuing Rockford staples were established in that initial year. First of all, the episodes mixed traditional private eye action with a dry wit which only became more pronounced as time went on. Jim would always be available for cases brought over the transom, but many Rockford capers were instigated by his associates. When Rocky wasn't stumbling over murders which looked like suicides ("Exit Prentiss Carr"), Beth was wheedling Jim to help an impoverished woman beat a murder rap ("The Dark and Bloody Ground").

When his father and lawyer weren't getting him into trouble, his girlfriends and ex–jail buddies were. In "Claire," the greatest love of his life, Claire Prescott (Linda Evans), returns to use him as a dupe. Two weeks later, the first of Jim's former cellmates comes by to use him as a sap ("Charlie Harris at Large"). It seemed everybody loved using Rockford as a fall guy, no matter how well he continually exonerated himself.

Even without Huggins, each of the subsequent seasons was of a consistently high quality, but of a slowly dropping ratings share. The diminishing viewership could have been the result of NBC's perpetual juggling of the program. In its six seasons, the time slot was changed seven times and the day it was telecast was changed five times. Just as its audience was finding it, the network moved it—sometimes with little or no fanfare.

In addition, both Steve Cannell and Meta Rosenberg spoke of the pressures NBC exerted on them to change the show. During the second season, the network mounted a campaign to eliminate Rockford's whimsy and make him a straight shooting, dour P.I. of the *Mannix* mold. It was

Eternal fall guy, continually exasperated Rockford, has to deal with an irascible mobile home park neighbor played by Joseph Cotton.

not successful, as episodes like "The Aaron Ironwood School of Success" (another "pal" of Jim's sets him up), and "The Real Easy Red Dog" (an evasive client wants her sister's supposed suicide investigated) showed.

At least they didn't have to argue about whether he should have a car. Rockford (and Garner) loved to drive, and tooled around in a gold Pontiac Firebird. Despite his racing-related injuries, the actor insisted on doing most of his own driving, and probably advocated the use of car chases in the scripts. Every fan of the series remembered Rockford's elan behind the wheel—and the business card printer he kept in the back seat to take on new identities when needed.

Garner and company fought off the network's attempt to empty the series of humor, but that was just the beginning of the problems between NBC, Universal, and Cherokee. There were little things, like Universal refusing to upgrade the crew's quality of coffee (Garner personally paid for a better brand). And there were big things, like the lawsuit between Cherokee and Universal for distribution of profits (a fight Garner took to the CBS news magazine show, *60 Minutes*).

Just about the only thing that kept *The Rockford Files* going was Garner. Although Supervising Producer Cannell, producer-writer David Chase, and Executive Story Consultant Juanita Bartlett contributed some terrific scripts, they only worked because Garner was in them. Curiously, there were also two episodes which were adapted, plot twist by plot twist, from other shows. "Sleight of Hand," in which Jim's date disappears between his car and her front door, was taken from *Jigsaw* (1972–73), and a tale of a sedated Jim in a hospital witnessing a possible murder ("The Deuce") had been used on *McMillan and Wife* (1971–77).

Aside from those two fillers, the series continued on its ingratiating way. The second season introduced more recurring plotlines and characters. "The Farnsworth Stratagem" had Rockford setting up the first of many scam stings to get revenge on con artists who had bilked his friends (in this case, Detective Becker). In "The Great Blue Lake Land and Development Company," Jim's car breaks down in the first of several small towns which are hiding a deep, dark, ugly secret. And in "Chicken Little's a Little Chicken," that lovable weasel Angel gets Jim into his first major trouble with the big boys.

After establishing a storyline, the staff seemed unashamed about re-scripting it until they had squeezed every possibility out. A month after Jim's car broke down in the first small town, "Pastoria Prime Pick" had the car break down in another small town—only this time the plot is a minor masterpiece of mistaken identities, misunderstandings, and homicidal mania. Rockford's second sting came in "Joey Blue Eyes," where he cons corporate swindlers. Cannell had the detective constantly at odds with big corporations, another thing which endeared him to viewers. It also mirrored the production's own problems with their studio and network.

Cannell and crew not only stole from themselves, they wrote homages to other great detectives. "The Italian Bird Fiasco" was Rockford's Maltese Falcon story, with Jim running afoul of shady art dealers. What set the familiar programs apart was Rockford's individual way of handling problems. He used his brain and was almost always surprising. The way he'd get his dander up and force barking cops and threatening feds into their own corners when you expected him to back down. The way he would get around suspects when you thought he'd give up. The way he'd defeat muscular enemies when you thought he'd get the tar stomped out of him.

The creative team helped by writing for Garner's strengths and fighting against stereotypical characterization. One of the reasons the familiar stories worked on *Rockford* was the way Cannell and company embraced and flaunted tradition at the same time. One of the series' best examples was "Feeding Frenzy." It was about an elderly con who wants to return a half million dollars he stole years before. He comes to Rockford for help when other crooks kidnap his daughter. They use the stolen money for ransom. Rockford traps the kidnappers and returns the cash. Even though the old man returns to his waterfront shack penniless, his daughter is safe and he's happy. That's when the IRS arrives and slaps him with a tax bill for the missing money. The episode ends with a freeze frame of the aged crook going crazy on the beach.

Every week couldn't be this odd. By the third season, the *Rockford* machine was oiled and rolling. Angel continues to involve Jim in daffy and deadly deals like "Drought at Indianhead River," where he loses a mob-financed real estate fortune, and "Rattler's Class of '63," where he tries to extort money from a mob-run garbage collection agency. Gandy Fitch, another jail associate, reappears after twenty years in stir to force the man he calls "Rockfish" to clear his name ("The Hammer of C Block"). He finally calls Jim by his right name after they team up to find Gandy's kidnapped ex-wife in "The Second Chance."

Dennis Becker gets into more trouble, as do Beth, her clients, her boyfriends, and her relatives. Old army buddies and more jail pals were also introduced. In the episode that sets the record for longest title, "Sticks and Stones May Break My Bones But Waterbury Will Bury You," several of Jim's fellow private investigators (played by Simon Oakland, Cleavon Little, and James Whitmore, Jr.) hire him to find out who is destroying their practices. The writers mounted more episodes about these losers, starting with "Beamer's Last Case"—in which the nerdy P.I. played by Whitmore impersonates Rockford to gain respect.

The series was fun for everyone but the network, which was worrying about the ratings. They rarely reached the top twenty, but the show continued to survive for several reasons. First, because *CBS Late Night* started rebroadcasting earlier episodes. That gave Universal more money and more impetus to keep the show going. Second, because Garner got great publicity with a series of pleasant Polaroid commercials with Mariette Hartley. They were so good together that some thought they might actually be married and a *Rockford* script was written for the actress ("Trouble in Paradise Cove").

The last two years of the show had some of the best and the worst episodes. The writers had perfected pure Rockford episodes by then, in which the detective would cross paths with some of life's great losers. "Quickie Nirvana" was a beautiful, sad episode in which Jim helps Sky Aquarian, a lost soul desperate for any kind of self-help, to retrieve $30,000 from another of her many false gurus. The Rockford curve was at the end, when Sky had still not discovered her own self-worth—as she would have on any other show. Rockford meets her on the street sometime after the case where she tries to sell him a flower.

Serving as subtexts to the pure episodes were the "ninety-nine and forty-four one-hundredth percent" pure episodes which hinged on incredible coincidences (made barely believable by the writing and acting).

"The Queen of Peru" had Jim's barbeque grill stolen by tourists, while, unbeknownst to both, a million-dollar diamond is hidden in its ashes. "The Competitive Edge" has the F.B.I., in a case of mistaken identity, dragging Rockford down to Mexico to break up a scam.

Then there were the many episodes about the regulars. Angel, Becker, and Beth were still around, but now added was Richie Brockelman, a young, clean-cut college student who becomes a private eye (and had a short-lived regular series of his own for three months in 1978), John Cooper (Bo Hopkins), a disgraced lawyer who can only do law research, Megan Dougherty (Kathryn Harrold), a blind psychologist with whom Rockford falls in love and gets his heart firmly broken, Rita Capkovic (Rita Moreno), a hooker with a heart of gold, a brain of zinc, and a mouth of copper; and finally, the fabulous Lance White.

Introduced on an episode called "White on White and Nearly Perfect," he was a satire of the pretty-boy private eye who is never wrong. And no matter how he messes up and Rockford cleans up, Lance always winds up on his feet and Jim is always neck deep in yogurt. He was played by Tom Selleck.

The Rockford Files' final year was a blur of familiar faces and clever titles ("A Good Clean Bust With Sequel Rights," "A Three Day Affair with Thirty Day Escrow," "Local Man Eaten by Newspaper," and "With the French Heel Back Can the Nehru Jacket Be Far Behind?"). It also fluctuated wildly in tone and approach.

Megan is terrorized ("Guilt") and then marries another man ("A Different Drummer"). Beth is terrorized by her own guilty client because he wants a mistrial ("Deadlock in Parma"). John Cooper seeks revenge after his sister is raped and Rockford is beaten by a motorcycle gang ("The Return of the Black Shadow"). Rita wants to stop being a hooker but a sadistic pimp wants her to continue ("The No Fault Affair"). All of Jim's private eye "pals," including Lance White, try to solve a murder at a private eye award dinner ("Nice Guys Finish Dead"). Angel blabs Jim's hide-out to a crazed hit man ("The Man Who Saw Alligators") and then poses as a killer to take large advances for murders he has no intention of committing ("A Material Difference").

The staff went spin-off crazy in the last year. They seemed to want at least one character who would carry on after Rockford retired. None of it worked. As capable as all the actors were, none of them was a James Garner. The final episode, "Just a Couple of Guys," didn't even have Rockford in it. It's about two hapless hoods and their laughable attempts to break into the mob. Rockford's final appearance was in "The Big Cheese," the fairly pure second-to-last episode in which he is caught between two rival gangs while on a fishing trip.

No one seems quite sure whether *The Rockford Files* was cancelled or Cherokee called it quits on account of injury (Garner's back and knees were getting worse). Whatever the cause, the series went off with its fans wanting more. Rockford had something that no other private detective had. And James Garner could play that better than anyone else this side of Jack Benny. That something was exasperation.

"That was part of his character," Roy Huggins stressed. "That was what the others couldn't do. They couldn't be fed up with it, like Rockford

James Garner returned to the part that made him famous—*Maverick*.

could. He was human. He had weaknesses. And only Jim could do that to perfection. There is no one else in the world who can do what he does. He's unique. He doesn't get the credit he deserves as an actor. He did Rockford in a way that no one else could do it."

Even when Rockford was in the middle of a very familiar case, and even when he's victimized by his lying jail buddies and sleazy fellow P.I.'s, it was always rich entertainment to see him handle it. He would complain. He would wheedle. He would argue. But he was never annoying. Quite the opposite, in fact.

Rockford was, at heart, a fairly normal guy. In fact, he was a little lower than normal. He was a little paunchy. He lived in a mobile home. His dad was always on his case to get married or find a better living. He liked beer. He liked to fish. He never had a romantic relationship which lasted, but he didn't seem to mind all that much.

He was a great man and a good detective. He was sharp but realistic, wily but sentimental, tough but a soft touch. He was comforting because he was a lot like us, and he liked it that way. He never apologized for who he was or how he lived. He was a sane, trustworthy, believable human being in a world of cheats and wackos. He could get the audience right where they lived—in the heart.

In the final analysis, *The Rockford Files* wasn't revolutionary. It was just a curve in a world of fast balls. What made it memorable and special came from an amazing synthesis of star and actor which the audience got to share over six seasons. Thanks to the leading man, it was more than a television show. It was a friendship with a terrific talent who was never better anywhere else.

"I say Jim is one of the most underestimated actors in the business," Huggins concluded. "He doesn't get credited for creating a role the like of which will never be seen again. That's Jim Garner. That's it."

CHAPTER

Breaking the Cliché

"He's a wisecracking, fun-loving, freeloading freelance private eye. He's a hell-raiser in paradise! Meet Tom Magnum, ex-navy officer turned Hawaiian private eye. He's a good-looking, laid-back charmer in a loud shirt who loves fast cars and slow blondes. And frankly, hates to get hurt. He gets his man, sometimes he also gets the girl. You're gonna love the guy!"

—ad copy

IT IS 1980 AND TELEVISION HAS BECOME THE PREDOMINANT MEDIA FORCE in the world. While the fictional series had a little something to do with it, the news media had forced itself into people's homes. In the name of keeping the public informed, there were news programs at the beginning of the day, late morning, midday, late afternoon, early evening, mid-evening, late evening, and all night. They even had capsulations of the news between shows, and interrupted the entertainment whenever they saw fit. All without admitting they had any sort of effect or influence.

The fictional series were in shock. A minor civil war was going on. While some shows appeared to be advocating sophistication and intelligence, many stridently insisted that the audience was as stupid as ever. On one side there were *Charlie's Angels, Chips, That's Incredible!, Three's Company, B.J. and the Bear, Vegas, The Dukes of Hazzard, Fantasy*

A Hawaiian shirt, a Ferrari, a mustache, and a smile: Tom Selleck as Thomas Sullivan Magnum, Private Investigator.

Island, *The Love Boat*, and *The Misadventures of Sheriff Lobo*. On the other were *60 Minutes*, *20/20*, *M*A*S*H*, *Lou Grant*, *Little House on the Prairie*, *White Shadow*, *Barney Miller*, and *Hill Street Blues*. Straddling the fence was *Magnum, P.I.*

The blessing and curse of *Magnum, P.I.* was that the way it was perceived was opposed to the way it was developed. The publicity copy at the beginning of the chapter is true as far as it goes. What made the series a success is the depth the filmmakers achieved with the hackneyed material. This identity crisis has dogged the show from its schizophrenic creation through its success to its awkward anticlimax.

It started when Jack Lord told CBS that *Hawaii Five-O* was not going to continue after its twelfth season. Until then it had been a mainstay of CBS' Thursday nights. The natural inclination was to give the audience more of the same, so it became known that the network wanted to have their cake and eat it too.

Meanwhile Tom Selleck had finally made it to a position of relative respect, after more than ten years doing commercials (he was the Chaz man while Shelley Hack was the Charlie girl), movie cameos (*Coma*, 1978, where he played a corpse), soap operas (a year and a half on *The Young and the Restless*), and failed pilots.

But his performances as Lance White on *The Rockford Files* were so enjoyed that Universal, to whom he was contracted, wanted to create a show around him. Enter producer Glen Larson, who had recently been responsible for two boneheaded science fiction series—*Buck Rogers in the 25th Century* (1979–81) and *Battlestar Galactica* (1978–80). Larson had also produced *McCloud* (1970–77) and *Switch* (1975–78), however, so his contributions were solicited by CBS. He offered them a script called *Magnum*.

"It was very much a James Bond private eye," said producer Donald Bellisario. "An ex-C.I.A. agent who lived on the private estate of an author named Robin Masters. Magnum lived in the guest house all by himself except for his killer Doberman and a roomful of fantastic radio-wrist watches, hang glider equipment, special machine guns, and all that kind of stuff."

Selleck was finally in a position where he could take more control of his career, and he exercised that power by nixing Larson's conception.

"Tom said he didn't want to do that kind of story," Bellisario continued. "Glen had other fish to fry and it was getting to the point that the whole project was going to fall through." That was when Larson called Bellisario, with whom he had worked on *Battlestar Galactica*.

"He asked if I would direct the pilot and 'do a little polish on the script,' " Bellisario said with a grin. "So I met with Glen and said, 'Tell you what. I'll take this and run with it. You collect the money, we'll share the credit, but it'll be my show.' And it was from the moment I walked out of that office. I never discussed it or consulted with Glen after that."

The first order of business was to sit down with CBS. "I asked them what they liked about the original project and they said they liked Tom Selleck as a private eye in Hawaii."

The next order of business was to sit down with Tom Selleck. With the success of such shows as *All in the Family* and *Columbo* attributed to their stars, leading actors had justifiably claimed more and more power on the sets. It was now a given that producers would negotiate, then collaborate, with their stars—especially if they were tailoring a project to them.

"I asked him what he didn't like about the original project," Bellisario continued, "and he said that it was basically the same old clichéd stuff. 'I know I have a certain look,' he said. 'I want to play against that. I really want to play somebody who doesn't have to get the girl. I don't always want to play the hero. I want to be able to make mistakes, to be human.' "

It couldn't have worked out better for Donald Bellisario. "I had a project I had been trying to sell the network called *H.H. Flynn,*" he revealed, "who was a private eye on Rodeo Drive who drove a Ferrari and had an office above a flower shop. It was a real plush office and he dressed real well but at night he drove to the Beverly Hills estate of the man who owned the flower shop, got into some Levi's, jumped into a beat-up old Jeep and drove to San Pedro where some friends from Vietnam ran a bar.

"So I thought I'll just transplant that to Hawaii. I made it a combination of the two scripts; three guys who had been in the war together added to the Robin Masters estate angle because it fit with what I had in Beverly Hills, and just went from there."

Bellisario changed H.H. Flynn to Thomas Sullivan Magnum, then developed the characters of the Vietnam buddies. When he finished there was still something missing. He needed a conflict beyond the weekly bad guys. And he hated the cop angle, almost as much as Howard Rodman did.

"It was very deliberate that I wasn't going to have a cop on the show. In fact, one of the writers introduced a cop [Lieutenant Tanaka, played by Kwan Hi Lim] but I never liked him. Finally I just said no, stop it. It bothered me. Here we were dealing with cops just like any other detective show."

Bellisario wanted something special. He was right in synch with Selleck on the idea of playing against the pretty-boy cliché as well as the hard-boiled TV private eye cliché, but neither wanted life to be easy for T.S. Magnum.

"I had just seen a movie called *Guns at Batasi* (1964) starring Richard Attenborough," Bellisario said. "It was about a very tough little sergeant major in Africa at a time when the country was in transition. At the end, although he had done the right thing, the people he saved were not the ones who won, and, to save face, the British chastised him and sent him away.

"And I wondered: whatever happened to that little guy? So he became my Higgins." Jonathan Quale Higgins III, to be exact, the majordomo of bestselling author Robin Masters' Hawaiian estate. "I said, okay, he left the British Service and went to work for Robin. So here I had the sloppy, ex-military man Magnum, who couldn't care less, and I had this very proper, very stern, British majordomo." He also had the Doberman.

Whatever happened to the majordomo character in *Guns at Batasi*?

"I gave it to Higgins and added a second dog. What that basically did was put a lot of humor and humanity in." The dogs were subsequently named Zeus and Apollo and, along with Higgins, were the bane of Magnum's existence.

Bellisario also managed to include the Ferrari, making it Masters' loan-out to Magnum and another bone of contention between the private detective (who was ostensibly allowed to live on the estate as security man) and Higgins.

"I remembered John Hillerman from *Ellery Queen*," the producer explained. Hillerman had played the always theorizing, always wrong, radio personality Simon Brimmer. "I met him, we talked, and I thought he'd make the perfect Higgins, although I had a little difficulty convincing the network. But once he read for them—which was marvelous of him to do because he was beyond reading for networks at that point—they went along with it."

With Higgins set, Bellisario had to cast Magnum's war buddies. The characters had all served together, with one man flying a helicopter and the other manning the machine guns. The pilot was named T.C., short for Theodore Calvin.

"The character originally started out as a white southern crop duster in Texas!" Bellisario laughed. "In fact, we had actually all agreed that Gerald McRaney, now the co-star of *Simon & Simon* (1981–1989) was the one we all wanted to be T.C.—when Tom Selleck said, 'Gee, what if we had a black guy as part of the group?' I said, 'Why not?'

"So we started recasting, just to see, and Roger Mosley walks in. Now Roger can be very intimidating. He did a reading, left, and the director of the pilot, Roger Young, says, 'I don't think he wants this job.' I said, 'Not much. He came in wearing a baseball cap and a leather jacket to read for a pilot. I think he wants this job.' So that's how we cast him."

The third war buddy was another near miss, but of a different sort. The actor who was originally set to play him got the role, but it wasn't the same role Bellisario had envisioned. The producer had known actor Larry Manetti since the days they both worked on *Black Sheep Squadron* (1976–78). He had also co-starred on the last Lance White episode of *The Rockford Files*. Bellisario wrote a *Magnum* role just for him. It was Orville Wright, the copter gunner who got so frightened in the 'Nam that he retreated into the persona of the toughest man he knew—the Humphrey Bogart of *Casablanca*.

"Larry was going to play the manager of a club who was always doing shady deals and was mixed up with the underworld," Bellisario elaborated. "Literally, in his head, he thought he was Rick from Casablanca. But the network said, 'He's doing a terrible Bogart imitation!' I said, 'That's the point! He can't do Bogart, that's the whole idea behind the character. He's a little crazy. It's a joke.' They didn't get it. They said, 'No, no, please, please just let him run a regular place—take him out of that dark club.'

"They were probably right about the club," Bellisario admitted. "It should've been on the beach in the first place. But I wish they would've let him keep the bad Bogie. In the rush of changing the character for the series, it lost its focus. Larry's never had the character to grab, really. He was always a bit nebulous, floating around out there."

So Orville sold the dark club but kept the name Rick to run the beachfront "King Kamehameha Club" (pronounced Ka-may-ha-may-ha), which is half owned by Robin Masters.

Everything seemed ready to go on *Magnum*, until the Universal legal department called with an emergency.

"We tacked the 'P.I.' on the title because they were terrified that Clint Eastwood . . . you know, *Magnum Force*? . . . would sue us for ripping him off or something. So it became *Magnum, P.I.*, which is really funny because in Hawaii P.I. means Philippines. So everybody on the islands was saying, 'What is this show? *Magnum Philippina*?' "

Again, everything seemed ready to go. Just then another emergency threatened to halt telecast. Steven Spielberg was coming to town.

"He asked to see the *Magnum* pilot," Bellisario said, "then he came

The man who would have been a southern cropduster, Roger E. Mosley as T.C.; and the man who would be Bogie, Larry Manetti as Rick.

to see the studio and the network to ask if we would delay launching the series so he could use Tom as Indiana Jones in *Raiders of the Lost Ark* (1981). It was basically Universal's decision because Tom's contract was with them, but CBS said no."

The real tragedy was that a subsequent actors' strike delayed the series' launch and Selleck could have done the movie after all—in a perfect world. Industry legend has it that in Selleck's first major movie, *High Road to China* (1983), all the special effects heads on spears were molded to look like the executive who denied Selleck leave.

The *Magnum, P.I.* pilot finally premiered, the ratings were good, and the series started on December 11, 1980. It was, for all intents and purposes, a midseason replacement (on the same day and in the same time slot) for *Hawaii Five-O*. The big visual difference between the two programs was that Bellisario sought the romanticism Leonard Freeman had rejected.

"I wanted the look of the show to be 'Hawaii 1940,' " Bellisario remembered. "I gave orders that they were never to film beaches with highrises in the background, that they were never to show telephone wires along roads, and they were to avoid superhighways. I wanted two-lane roads with tropical trees hanging over and white, sandy beaches. I wanted to create an environment which was really lush and mysterious.

"If we were in downtown Waikiki, we'd show downtown Waikiki, we wouldn't try to hide it. But when we were out, I wanted that 1940's feeling. That's why we had three different locations for the King Kamehameha Club and Robin Masters' estate. The estate sits among other buildings and homes that you never see. It's always to get that feeling that you're out on 7,500 acres."

The show, much to the cast's chagrin, was not an immediate success. "We went against the formulas too much," Bellisario felt. "We had a good opening ("Don't Eat the Snow in Hawaii," where Magnum clears a navy friend who died with ten bags of cocaine in his stomach), but the following shows ("Never Play With a China Doll," where Magnum protects an Oriental vase from an Asian sect, and "Thank Heaven for Little Girls and Big Ones Too," where Magnum gets mixed up with a gang of school kids, their teacher, and a priceless painting) posted a ratings drop.

These shows mixed moments of steel-eyed toughness with a great deal of whimsy. Everyone started worrying that the audience couldn't accept Selleck making fun, then gunning down awful antagonists in washrooms ("Snow") and graveyards ("China").

"John Hillerman called me," reported Bellisario, "saying, 'Change the format of the show! Change everything! I've been on too many shows which have gone down the tubes. I gotta have a hit!' I told him, 'Give it time, relax, take it easy.' "

The pressure to change the show not only came from the actors, but the network. They were used to, and initially wanted, Jack Lord's patented *Five-O* snarling, righteous, puritanical justice. Bellisario and Selleck refused to give in to them.

"I wouldn't do seamy-side stories about Hawaii," the producer said. "I wanted to stay away from that. Besides, *Hawaii Five-O* had done that so well." And for so long. Bellisario took a wait-and-watch posture, certain that the ratings would pick up after the Christmas and New Year holidays. Even though the network believed in the project, the production was subject to pressure. Selleck was a gorgeous hunk, so the network wanted him to act the way they thought gorgeous hunks should.

"Now, when you're talking about CBS," Bellisario reminded me, "you're talking about a lot of people. Some people understood what we were trying to do right away, while others didn't. It was never an insurmountable problem at CBS. It was always something I could work out. Originally they didn't want me to do Vietnam stories, they didn't want me to do flashbacks, they didn't want Tom to look at the camera, they didn't want mystery stories, they didn't want twist endings. So there were a lot of things they ultimately allowed me to do. They didn't have to; they could've rejected them."

Bellisario's instincts paid off. *Magnum, P.I.*'s ratings grew throughout 1981. People began to respond to Selleck's capricious brand of machismo. He was always self-deprecating, but was never reluctant to deal with cold-blooded killers. After a period in which anti-violence decrees had mutated action shows into immoral exercises where killers got away with motiveless mass murders, Thomas Magnum was allowed to mete out vigilante justice.

In the seventies, TV heroes had not been allowed to kill, or even physically punish the villains in any way. The criminals, if they weren't turned over to the police, had to die by accident or by their own hand. All too often, however, their victims were murdered most foully while the murderers got to go trotting off to jail (where they were pardoned or paroled or freed on technicalities—this was common fodder for the news programs and talk shows).

Not on *Magnum, P.I.* One of the first season's most memorable moments came when Magnum purposefully executed a smug, hateful K.G.B. agent in the twentieth episode, "From Moscow to Maui."

"That was the most controversial thing I've done in television," Bellisario stated. "Sure, I had a lot of problems getting that by, and there were a lot of fights over the violence. The network said they wouldn't allow it, but Tom backed me up on every one of them. Now I have some power as creator and executive producer, but the star has the real power with the network. And Tom said 'we're standing together' on every one of those issues."

Thankfully, there were also a fair share of nonviolent episodes that first year. Some of the more effective were "The Ugliest Dog in Hawaii," wherein Magnum protects a pooch everyone wants; "The Black Orchid," in which a lonely woman hires Magnum to act out her 1940's detective fantasy, and "Beauty Knows No Pain," where a fitness instructor maneuvers Magnum into a grueling iron man endurance race.

The creators' stand paid off. "At the end of the first year it was a successful show," Bellisario stated. "But nothing spectacular. Then in the second year, it exploded. Just exploded." Suddenly *Magnum, P.I.* was one of the biggest shows, and Tom Selleck was the hottest TV star going. Although most of the publicity went out of its way to say what a nice guy Selleck was, the blast of attention was turning him and the show into something it was not.

It led to a crisis of production which came to a head when the star closed the set and flew to Hollywood for immediate negotiation. "The production offices are here," Bellisario explained. "The pre-production and post-production is here. All the casting and most of the writing is done here, while all the filming is done there. Unless you're very careful, you develop an 'us-them' mentality that telephones don't solve."

That was exactly what did happen and it was clearly reflected in the episodes. Just about the only memorable ones were the second season premiere, "Memories Are Forever," in which the Vietnamese wife Magnum thought dead returns, "Mad Buck Gibson," where Magnum guards a seriously self-destructive writer, and "One More Summer," wherein Magnum goes undercover as a football quarterback. The rest were familiar formula efforts, such as "Try to Remember" (Magnum battles amnesia) and "Double Jeopardy" (a movie star is felled by real bullets).

No one was happy with the way the second season was going, and crew members were beginning to blame different factions for the production chaos. People were siding with Selleck or Bellisario before either could say they were both on the same team. Peace was attained before the war broke out through the wonders of modern science. Bellisario set up a computer link between the Hawaiian and Hollywood production offices, then hired Charles Floyd Johnson as on-line producer. Johnson was a former member of the diplomatic corps who found a related career in Hollywood.

"Charles Johnson smoothed out the operation nicely," Bellisario praised. "He's a wonderful diplomat and a damn good producer."

This would not be the last confusion to plague the set. If ever there was a misunderstood private eye show, it was this one. Most people thought it was just another action series. Much of its own audience only remembered the car chases, fights, guns, and girls. Everyone involved in the series wanted the one thing they didn't have. Respect.

"You see," said Bellisario, "I didn't want to do a detective show.

Magnum on the set, in all his glory.

That's the one thing people don't understand. *Magnum* is very difficult to write because it 'happens' between the scene of a 'normal' detective show. A normal detective show is about a detective finding clues and interrogating suspects. Magnum, well, he might get a clue but he can't get to the Ferrari because Higgins is doing a number on him. The next thing you know, Magnum has already interrogated the desk clerk or whatever and is telling you what he found out in a voice-over. *Magnum, P.I.* falls through the cracks of a normal detective show."

True to these words, the staff had the freedom to explore all sorts of stories, investigate Magnum's personality, and delve into the characters' past. Bellisario had all this in mind when he sat down to write the "Memories Are Forever" episode. "I had these letters from all over asking why Magnum never fell in love. During the entire first season, he didn't crawl into bed with anybody. So I asked myself, 'Okay, why doesn't he?' And the answer was that he was still married. In his head."

Magnum's wife returned from the dead and CBS wanted her to go back as well. "The network naturally figured that she had to die at the end of the story," Bellisario stated. "But I said no. She goes back to Vietnam. That show was probably the best *Magnum* I've ever done. It's the show I'm the most proud of, that's for sure."

It was these little breaks with tradition that made the show consistently watchable. The series mingled satisfaction and surprise. The odd combinations the writers were encouraged to make were responsible for the press and public's schizoid attitude.

"In the first season, the critics really hated the show," Bellisario maintained. "And what they hated were all the things which made it work. Then, in the third and fourth seasons, we started getting wonderful write-ups about the things which were panned initially. It only goes to show that people don't know what they like at first. They've got to get used to it for a while.

In *Magnum, P.I.*, the quirk was king. In "Past Tense" (the forty-first episode), T.C. and Higgins are hijacked to aid in a prison break. The following week, the "Black on White" episode showed members of Higgins' Kenya Mau Mau regiment being systematically murdered. The week after that came "Flashback," where Magnum wakes in 1936 and gets involved with labor union violence.

For every episode which concentrated on Magnum, there was at least one about Rick, T.C., and, most especially, Higgins. The Higgins-Magnum relationship was central to the series, but the creators never neglected T.C. or the "lost" Rick. The fact that Magnum stood by his friends no matter what made viewers like him all the more.

Finally, even when the episode concentrated on Magnum, the staff went out of their way to make sure it wasn't the same Magnum every time. His episodes involved fantasy, flashbacks, and character studies rather than just crime and punishment.

Later in the third year came "Faith and Begorrah," which introduced a charming wrinkle. John Hillerman started playing members of the Higgins family (this time his Irish half brother, Father Paddy). More eccentric members of the clan, all played by Hillerman, would follow. But a week after the first Higgins family episode came another *Magnum* landmark.

"Home from the Sea" was a powerful broadcast which secured *Magnum, P.I.*'s reputation. It had no real action or mystery content at all. Instead, Magnum is swept out to sea and only his delirious memories of his father (played by Robert Pine) and mother (Susan Blanchard) keep him alive—until the desperate Higgins, T.C., and Rick locate him.

Both Selleck and the series played against type, and, in this case, it worked. It wouldn't always. Selleck's most obvious technique was keeping Magnum's voice high. Magnum's questions were almost always slightly whiny. It shook things up for a while, but wore thin during the fifth and sixth seasons. The press and public started to complain.

And then there was Cosby. Bill Cosby, whose *The Cosby Show* premiered in 1984, was scheduled opposite *Magnum, P.I.* The comedian was vocal in his dislike of Selleck's show (although he had never seen it). Cosby's interviews gave the impression that he thought the program was just what Selleck and Bellisario had been fighting all along—a gun and jiggle fest. Viewers were abandoning *Magnum* in droves.

Selleck and Bellisario fought back. The producer continued to lead his team on to better stories, and Selleck went on the campaign trail. He became friends with Bill Cosby. He convinced the comedy superstar that *Magnum* was not just another shoot-em-up. He won back his audience by making fun of the confusion and misunderstanding on talk shows.

Soon, there were cross-over in-jokes on both programs. Cosby's TV son had a poster of Selleck on his bedroom wall. As Magnum had mentioned McGarrett and Five-O in his early seasons, he was mentioning Cosby now. If the detective series was to go down, as everything opposite *The Cosby Show* had, then it would go down with a smile, knowing it had done a good job.

Magnum had much to be proud of. The very thing which cursed it to an eternity of misunderstanding was also responsible for some of the most touching, emotional, and affecting hours in the TV P.I. canon. "Holmes Is Where the Heart Is" has Higgins relating how he betrayed an old friend who thought he was Sherlock Holmes and Higgins was Watson. "Blind Justice" places Magnum in a moral quandary when he discovers that one murder was actually suicide, and that a freed suspect was actually a murderer. The series became expert in melding parallel stories, as in "Professor Higgins." While Magnum solves a case, Higgins tries to do a *My Fair Lady* on his punk rocker cousin.

"We take a lot of pride in the fact that you never know what you're going to see when you tune in," Bellisario stated. "You may see a farce one week and a heavy drama the next. You may see something in between. We don't hold any formulas. That's the kind of thing I think makes people want to watch. You never know what to expect."

Its resurrected audience certainly did not expect Magnum's death, but that was planned at the beginning of the seventh season. The series was being murdered in the ratings, dipping from number fifteen to as low as number fifty. The characters had been developed to death, and even Selleck was dropping weighty, tired hints that it might be best if Magnum went to that great island in the sky.

That was just what happened—but not before CBS moved the series away from *Cosby*. Suddenly the ratings bounced back. Viewers may have liked Cosby more, but they still liked Magnum. It was the age of the videotape machine, and the rating systems had no way of knowing how many people taped *Magnum* while watching *Cosby*. But numbers were numbers, and on its new day, *Magnum, P.I.* was back in the high life.

The last episode of the seventh season was telecast. Thomas Magnum was gunned down in a warehouse. He was in a coma, as his friends gathered around him. A murdered friend took Magnum's spirit on an odyssey of regret. Magnum only had one heaven-induced chance to soothe his friends' minds. As a ghost, he discovered that Higgins was actually Robin Masters, then he influenced events so his ex-wife could begin a new life.

The final image of that episode was Magnum, in his Detroit Tigers cap, Hawaiian shirt, and khaki shorts, walking into eternity.

CBS renewed the show. A flurry of negotiations were held. Bellisario and Selleck, who now co-produced the series, came back. *Magnum, P.I.* would reach eight seasons. Thomas Magnum came out of his coma only to see what Bellisario refused to let happen in the second season. Magnum's ex-wife gets killed by a terrorist bomb. That shocking, strange event cast a pall on the rest of the year. Although they tried to end the series on a triumphant note, *Magnum, P.I.*'s violent, rushed redux was not worthy of what had come before.

The final final (sic) two-hour farewell episode ended with Magnum rejoining the navy, discovering the survival of his young daughter, the marriage of Rick, the possible reconciliation of T.C. with his ex-wife, and Higgins' abrupt denial of a double life. "I was only kidding," he said about being Robin Masters. The presentation of these events was cursory and unsatisfying. The last image of Thomas Sullivan Magnum was in his navy uniform, facing his audience. Using a television remote control, he said good-bye and turned his viewers off—without so much as a "thank you" or "good luck."

This finale was surprisingly unfeeling for a series which had cared deeply about what it was doing for seven seasons. It had not been satisfied to simply be a *Hawaii Five-O* clone. It had struggled for its own identity.

Bellisario was convinced that the main reason Selleck was willing to do the eighth year at all was to be certain his co-stars would be financially secure. That was hardly a reason for the disheartening conclusion, however.

But it was 1988 and television had changed. The good guys had won. *60 Minutes* and *20/20* were still on the air, while *The Misadventures of Sheriff Lobo* and *Chips* were long gone. In addition, there were *Cagney & Lacey, St. Elsewhere, L.A. Law, A Year in the Life, thirtysomething, Moonlighting, Crime Story, Murder, She Wrote, Wiseguy,* and many excellent comedies. Even the borderline series, like, *Hunter* and *Matlock*, benefited from a more sophisticated or emotional approach. The really bad programs were all the more obvious and abortive in this light.

The cliché had been broken by *Magnum, P.I.* The same old thing just wasn't good enough anymore. Producers, studios, and networks still

First McGarrett, then Magnum. Next?

tried to foist off derivations of past successes and present movie hits, but more than ever, quality would out. In the morass of cable and video, television artists tried harder. In some cases, it led to stridency. In this case, despite year eight, Thomas Magnum emerged a good man, a likable man, a staggeringly good-looking man, and maybe even a real man with a stupid name.

Against all odds, he left the air with his head held high.

CHAPTER

Film at Eleven

"Let's be careful out there."

—Sergeant Phil Esterhaus
Hill Street Blues (1981)

TOO OFTEN, TELEVISION DEMANDS THAT PROBLEMS BE SOLVED AFTER ONLY a superficial examination. Curiously, it is not fictional television which insists on this rapid decision-making process—it is not the comedies or dramas which insist that viewers take an immediate stand on complex issues. It is the reality shows, the news and talk shows, which stridently confront the audience with "or" propositions.

Guilty or innocent? Good or bad? Right or wrong? Film at eleven.

In the ever-demeaning desire for money, reality is being packaged as fantasy by television. The facts are presented with such urgency and immediacy that the word "and" is completely lost. The reporters and hosts don't allow a question to have more than one aspect—at least not in their florid come-on commercials. Television news tries to make it easy for the viewer to take sides on complex problems which might be best solved by compromise. But rational compromise doesn't sell.

Television, for better or worse, eliminates the question of compromise in a wash of harsh words and exploitive images created to tease the audience into watching. Once the baited hook is taken, an answer is rarely given. The truth shows simply stoke the ashes to start new fires. They try to present a given problem in all its emotional complexity, then leave the viewer empty. This emptiness is forgotten as they go to the next crisis—presenting it with the same sideshow mentality.

The hypocritical nature of television is not immediately apparent in the production of *Hill Street Blues*, but nowhere can one find a better example of it. It was a drama with comedic overtones, a comedy with dramatic overtones. It was an extremely realistic fantasy which pictured a fantastic reality. It was a wholly original concept made up of derivative parts.

It was an award-winning, hard-hitting television milestone which accurately reflected the chaos of its period. As reality was being made fantasy, TV drama-makers were trying to make their fantasies more realistic. In 1980, the top ten shows were a fascinating mix of the ridiculous and the sublime. *Dallas* (1978–), a glitzy, heady, glorified soap opera parcelled out in weekly chunks, was number one. *60 Minutes* (1968–), the powerful, important news magazine, was number three.

The almost always abysmal *The Dukes of Hazzard* (1979–85) was number two, while *M*A*S*H* (1972–83) was number four. The rest of the top ten was filled with comedies which ranged from decent (*Alice*, 1976–85, *House Calls*, 1979–80) to giddy (*The Love Boat*, 1977–86, *Three's Company*, 1977–84). Meanwhile, confusion mounted out on the streets. The confrontations of the sixties had led to the reassessments of the seventies, which were having a hard time taking root in the eighties. Scabbed tensions were beginning to reopen.

Into this mess stepped Fred Silverman, then head of NBC, who seemed to think he couldn't underestimate the intelligence of the viewer. He had just come off one of the worst programming jags in the history of the medium, having been responsible for conceiving and/or scheduling such immediate critical and/or ratings disasters as *The Misadventures of Sheriff Lobo* (1979–81), *B.J. and the Bear* (1979–81), *Hello, Larry* (1979–80), *Buck Rogers in the 25th Century* (1979–81), *Kate Loves a Mystery* (aka *Mrs. Columbo*, February–December 1979), *A Man Called Sloane* (1979–80), *Prime Time Sunday* (1979–80), *Eischied* (1979–83), *Shirley* (1979–80), *The Steve Allen Comedy Hour* (1980–81), *Games People Play* (1980–81), *Marie* (1980–81), *Walking Tall* (January–June 1981), and *Speak Up, America* (August–October 1980).

Even his successes, like *Real People* (1979–84) and *Barbara Mandrell & the Mandrell Sisters* (1980–), were uninspiring. He needed something decent, quick. He looked around the channels and focused on a quiet, unassuming, but strong show. This was Danny Arnold's *Barney Miller* (1975–82), a station house police comedy which was to *Car 54, Where Are You?* (1961–63) what *The Defenders* (1961–65) was to *Perry Mason* (1957–84). Hidden amidst the regulation humor was some of the best drama and acting within the cop subgenre.

It started as *The Life and Times of Captain Barney Miller*, a one-shot comedy pilot aired on *Just for Laughs* (1974), a summer replacement series which ABC used to get some mileage out of their expensive test shows. That version was a standard sitcom about the domestic trials and

The policeman's favorite: *Barney Miller*. From the left, Hal Linden, Ron Glass, Maxwell Gail, Steve Landesberg, Ron Carey, and James Gregory.

professional tribulations of a policeman. When the show reappeared the following year, the concentration was on the "old one-two," the detective squadroom of the twelth precinct in New York City.

Eventually the captain's family was written out (except for the occasional phone call) and the series became a one-room, one-set dramatic comedy, revolving around the lives of its occupants. It was the closest thing to "The Golden Age of Television" since the fifties. The whole thing was done on a stage as a weekly one-act play. There was a laugh track, but no audience. But the actors performed as if it was Broadway.

The sternest critical complaint was that the cast seemed picked by computer. Barney (Hal Linden) was a reasonable white man. Detective Philip Fish (Abe Vigoda) was a grouchy, elderly, hound dog with intestinal problems. Detective Sergeant Chano Amenquale (Gregory Sierra) was a fast-talking Puerto Rican. Detective Ron Harris (Ron Glass) was a black with literary aspirations. Detective Nick Yemana (Jack Soo) was a subtle Japanese who made horrid coffee, and Detective Stanley "Wojo" Wojohowicz (Maxwell Gail) was a thick-headed, thick-skinned cop of Polish descent.

Fans came to know and love the characters in the seven-year run, during which time the series took on more depth than most straight dramas. Fish was retired in the program's single most powerful episode, in which he rails against the unfairness of being put out to pasture. His replacement was a sardonic know-it-all named Arthur Dietrich, played by Steve Landesberg. Amenquale left after one season and was never replaced. Jack Soo died in 1978, and he, too, was never replaced—although the cast stepped out of character for one episode to pay tribute to him.

On this series, there were continuing plots from episode to episode and the characters were changed by their experiences. Adding to the mix were Ron Carey as the diminutive, overcompensating uniformed officer Levitt, and James Gregory as the coarse, old-fashioned Inspector Frank Luger. Producer Arnold fought for his show and managed to maintain the quality, even though it drove him to a serious heart attack. He stayed on, but was helped enormously by co-producer Reinhold Weege.

Fred Silverman saw this and thought of a masterstroke. "Barney Miller outdoors." He turned to MTM Productions with that single sentence. MTM had been successful for CBS with *The Mary Tyler Moore Show* (1970–77) and *Lou Grant* (1977–82), but they had never done a cop show. They turned to two fellows who had.

Michael Kozoll and Steven Bochco had been around. Kozoll had worked on *Quincy, M.E.* (1976–83) and *Kojak* (1973–78). Bochco had worked on *Columbo* (1971–77) and *McMillan and Wife* (1971–77). Neither were wildly enamored with the idea of doing another cop show. But on the recommendation of MTM head Grant Tinker, they went to see Silverman.

"If NBC's primary concern was to protect itself from minority pressure groups, then we couldn't do the series," said Bochco. "This show had to be grim, gritty, and rude. I said, only half jokingly, that we were going to be equal opportunity offenders."

The network gave them an offer they couldn't refuse.

The team would have creative autonomy. Silverman was so desperate for a good show that with one stroke he eliminated the jello wall. He did ask them, however, for "Fort Apache." On second thought, *Barney Miller* was too tame for him. Even though it took place in Greenwich Village, it didn't have the action and passion Silverman was looking for (which was one of the reasons *Miller* rated so highly with real-life cops —a policeman's life is mostly paper, not bullets).

Fort Apache, The Bronx (1981) had Silverman's "right stuff." It was a Paul Newman movie, based on the real-life tragedies of the worst precinct in the country. The network figured that within its battered walls were enough blood and plots to keep the show going and the action-starved audience sated. The team went to work: Kozoll wanted to smash all television's barriers, while Bochco wanted to extend them.

Throughout his career, Bochco had listened to real-life policemen, who came to pitch ideas for Columbo, McMillan, or the other series he worked on, *Richie Brockelman, Private Eye* (March–August 1978). He thought the cops' ideas were uniformly terrible, but he found their personal stories fascinating.

"We had a strong belief in the cop as hero," said Bochco. "Not in the Kojak sense, but as an individual performing a thankless task under extreme physical and emotional stress with no reward to speak of—social, psychological, or financial."

Kojak had been the model for most of the cop shows which had followed it. Created by Abby Mann for a fact-based television movie, *The Marcus-Nelson Murders* (1973), Theo Kojak was a sartorially splendid detective for the thirteenth precinct in south Manhattan. The TV movie (based on the actual 1963 Wylie-Hoffert murder case) was suitably gritty, but the story of a ghetto youth unjustly accused of the killings was overshadowed by Telly Savalas' performance as the tough investigator with the bald pate and heart of tarnished gold.

The same thing happened when the series started soon afterward. Although executive producer Matthew Rapf made sure the stories and atmosphere were realistic, it was Savalas who controlled the program's fate. Here was a character actor with a leading man inside waiting to burst out. Savalas had been highly respected for his portrayal of villains in movies like *Birdman of Alcatraz* (1962), *The Dirty Dozen* (1967), *The Scalphunters* (1968), *The Assassination Bureau*, and *On Her Majesty's Secret Service* (both 1969). It was only his performance in *Kelly's Heroes* (1970) that convinced anyone he could play a hero.

After turning down what would become *Harry-O* and suffering a setback in his film career (resulting in awful Spanish, Italian, French, British, and Mexican movies), Savalas decided to grab *Kojak* and hold on for all he was worth. He was worth plenty and his multifaceted, ingratiating performance of the tough, amusing, lollipop-licking cop made the show a success. Without Savalas, however, there was no telling what would have become of the character.

Kozoll and Bochco didn't want a star-driven vehicle. They wanted a program where the show itself was the star. They sat down to write a script which resisted every formula. It was not always successful. What was finished in two weeks was an interesting mix of the old and the new, the borrowed and the Hill Street blue. They had the Job-like Captain Frank Furillo leading the hard-hit squad—a man having a secret affair with a public defender named Joyce Davenport while trying to satisfy the alimony demands of his strident, increasingly neurotic ex-wife.

Furillo was wise and fair and strong and so astonishingly patient that even Joe Friday would have smiled on him. What was downplayed and almost forgotten was that he and his ex-wife had broken up over his alcoholism as well as her neuroses.

Kozoll and Bochco had another tower of strength in their roll-call

Who loves ya, baby? Telly Savalas as Kojak.

sergeant, Phil Esterhaus, a multisyllabic, sweet-tempered giant of a man with a seemingly insatiable sexual appetite but an overtly romantic soul. Next came Mick Belker, a mean, messy, Yorkshire terrier of an undercover detective who borrowed the look of the photographer Animal from the *Lou Grant* show and the manners of the Animal character from *The Muppet Show*. When he wasn't biting felons, he was calling them all manner of non-profane names (mostly "hairball").

The most overtly borrowed character was Lieutenant Howard Hunter of the Hill's S.W.A.T. team, here called the "EATers" (Emergency Action Team). He was essentially the Frank Burns character from *M*A*S*H*—all snob, stupidity, and racism. Then there was Johnny "J.D." LaRue, who had exactly the same name and sleazeball manner as a character played by John Candy on *SCTV* (1981–85), a landmark Canadian comedy series. The rest of the main cast was from Barney Miller by way of Ed McBain's "87th Precinct" series of police novels.

Sergeant Henry Goldblume was so sensitive that he had his heart on his sleeve, along with the rest of his internal organs. Lieutenant Ray Calletano was, essentially, and sadly, the token Hispanic. Detective Neal Washington was LaRue's street-smart, matchstick-sucking black partner. Officer Lucy Bates was the token woman. Then there was the all but forgotten Lieutenant Alf Chesley, who served almost no purpose at all.

That was the front line. Serving on the backline were Officer Joe Coffey (they needed a partner for Bates), and Officers Robert Hill and Andrew Renko. They were the designated expendables of the first episode—two cops slated to die in a slum massacre at the end of the pilot. All in all, Kozoll and Bochco had decided on nine regulars. When the time came to cast, that total would grow.

Daniel J. Travanti, an actor who had hit bottom and was staging a comeback, was the first male to audition, and Veronica Hamel, a strikingly beautiful ex-model, was the last female to read. They got the two leading roles of Furillo and Davenport. In between them came all manner of actors—not one a bankable star.

"We found actors to fit the parts," said Bochco, "rather than building the show around actors."

They did, however, have certain people in mind for certain roles. Michael Conrad, the vet of the group, having done theater, television, and movies for decades, was always slated for Esterhaus. The others were fellow class members of Bochco's alma mater, Carnegie-Mellon. James B. Sikking was asked to read for Hunter. They wanted Bruce Weitz for Belker, but he had to prove himself to a doubtful Grant Tinker. Weitz came in growling, leaped up on the desk and started tearing the place apart.

"I'm not going to tell him he doesn't have the job," Tinker reportedly said.

Hunter (James B. Sikking), Furillo (Daniel J. Travanti), and Goldblume (Joe Spano) discuss ways to deal with a hostage crisis.

The last person written specifically for was Bochco's wife, Barbara Bosson. "Well, I knew I'd be buying tons of tsouris trying to put my wife in a running role," Bochco told *Playboy* magazine in its seminal "Hill Street Blues Interview."

Curiously, he gave her the least-liked role—that of Fay Furillo, Frank's annoying ex-wife (interestingly, he continued to give her very unlikable parts. In his subsequent series, *Hooperman*, she plays John Ritter's strident, uptight, neurotic, female police captain. He must take all his aggressions out on her in the scripts because she has maintained that their marriage would have sunk if not for the series).

Joe Spano originally read for the part of Renko, a cowboy in the Wojo manner, but was offered the part of Goldblume. Charles Haid, another Carnegie-Mellon graduate, became Renko. Haid was a burly presence who stood out in TV shows like *Delvecchio* (1976–77) and movies like *Altered States* (1980). His partner, Bobby Hill, was played by Michael Warren, a former basketball star who wanted to prove his worth as an actor.

Rene Enriquez, vet of shows like *Charlie's Angels* and *Baretta*, became Ray Calletano. Taurean Blacque, who changed his name from Herbert Middleton when working with the Negro Ensemble Company in New York, became Neal Washington. Kiel Martin, who was originally signed by Universal and played his first role on *Dragnet 1968*, was LaRue, and Barbara Babcock was cast as Grace Gardner, Esterhaus' paramour. She was originally conceived as a lead.

According to the *Playboy* interview, former football star Ed Marinaro

A baker's half-dozen Hill Streeters: Veronica Hamel, Taurean Blacque, Travanti, Rene Enriquez, Michael Warren, Kiel Martin, and Michael Conrad.

was chosen as Coffey because Barbara Bosson wanted him. "I said, 'Come on, Steven, let me have a nice Italian cute guy on the show.' "

All went to work producing *Hill Street Station*, the pilot episode. Jumping onto the wagon at that point were producer Gregory Hoblit and director Robert Butler. Both had their work cut out for them. At first Kozoll considered doing the entire episode with hand-held sixteen millimeter cameras to further heighten the realism. He found a tempered, seasoned, and amenable voice in the director.

Influenced by a PBS documentary called *The Police Tapes*, Butler started by filming with thirty-five millimeter hand-held cameras, but the edited, final result was too confusing even for Kozoll. They decided to use hand-held only when they needed "heightened emotion." Instead, the word went out to the camera crew: "Make it messy." Television people were used to making everything look as flat and even as possible. But here Butler wanted the grit and shadows. He didn't want perfectly aligned framing.

The mood was partly *Peter Gunn*, but the images certainly weren't. While Gunn toiled in an empty world—just him and his adversary—the *Hill Street Station* set teemed with life. "Twelve people standing around looks like the Acropolis," Butler told *American Film* magazine. "People should be on the move; scenes should flow into one another."

In addition to the regulars, they also had twenty extras, whose job it was to get in the picture. Butler had the nameless, almost faceless background characters jockey for position—sometimes right in front of the conversing principals. After twenty years directing such widely diverse subjects as *Hogan's Heroes*, *The Fugitive*, *Batman*, *Star Trek*, *Gunsmoke*, and *Columbo*, Butler reveled in his new found freedom.

The unit filmed the Maxwell Street precinct house in Chicago to serve as the exterior of the Hill Street precinct house. Then, for the most part, eliminated the concept of the establishing shot. Things just happened on *Hill Street*. If they were set up at all, they were set up verbally and quickly. The camera would follow one character and suddenly latch on to another crossing in the other direction. It was all fairly experimental and revolutionary, but it all reflected the voice of the script.

That voice was the cop show at its most extreme: funny, sad, pathetic, and majestic. It was *Barney Miller* with the gloves off. It was anything goes on the Hill, reflected by the climax of the pilot—Renko and Hill are gunned down in the doorway of a tenement. The network was shocked when they saw the finished piece. They found it too violent, too sexy, and too grim. Fred Silverman, however, liked it, and gave the production safe passage to series.

Grant Tinker, whose son was a cop, saw the pilot and said, "My faith was justified."

The network previewed the pilot to a selected audience. "Boy, were they pissed off!" Bochco remembered in *Playboy*. "They didn't have a clue as to what the hell it was." Keeping a stiff upper lip and trying to force it into the TV cookie cutter, the network suggested changing the show's name to *The Blue Zoo*. "Which, as my thirteen-year-old would say, barfed us out," said Bochco.

The one place the production crew bent to network wishes was in the violence department—in a manner of speaking. While the show was given the big question mark by its test audiences, the characters of Renko and Hill scored so well that the selected viewers were outraged by their slaughter. The producers liked the chemistry of Haid and Warren, and saw plenty of dramatic opportunity in their characters, so they changed their D.O.A. status to seriously wounded and started negotiating for lead parts.

Warren was happy to sign on. Meanwhile, in deference to Haid's previous experience, he was given the all-important "and Charles Haid as Renko" credit second-to-last in the opening (Veronica Hamel got the final spot and a double full-name "Veronica Hamel as Joyce Davenport" credit). This jockeying for position was the first instance where Kozoll felt his influence slipping. It would not be the last.

Hill Street Blues was unleashed on the world January 15, 1981, after the actors' strike delayed all network premieres. The reaction of the major critics was somewhat bemused. *TV Guide* said it was "an odd mixture of comedy, police procedure, and domestic melodrama."

Time asked if it was "too good for television?"

The New York Times hated it from the very start. "Needs help very badly. It veers back and forth between comic situations that aren't funny and a romance that is merely silly. The sense of gritty reality further confuses an already choppy script."

The other critics, however, waxed ecstatic. Most of the magazines, newspapers, and reviewers on TV went several shades of the rainbow to praise the work. By the end of the month, every member of the critical community wanted to see the show, but had a hard time finding it. NBC moved the series five times (on four different nights) during its first year. This was called Fred Silverman's "panic button programming style."

"With the best of intentions," Bochco told *Playboy*, "he kept screwing us deeper and deeper into the ground." Silverman wasn't just trying to find an audience. He was throwing the program after them. The public was ducking.

In its first season, *Hill Street Blues* was ranked eighty-seventh out of ninety-six shows. They were not helped by what seemed to be a continuing vendetta on the part of New York newspapers. Even *The Village Voice* went after it with a vengeance—attacking the critical reaction to the show rather than the show itself.

"Is it worth all the hoopla?" they asked. "Alas, no." They then cited the broad comedy relief clashing with the violent realism. They also bemoaned the bustling backgrounds, bobbing cameras, patchy lighting, and grit-seamed surfaces. Over the years, their assaults on the series became almost laughable in their use of pseudo-intellectual jargon. At first they called it "American liberal, middle-class ideology turned on itself." Later they tried to explain it as "an experiment in radical narrative which became a yuppie marketing tool."

The attacks came from abroad as well. *The Observer* (London) drily observed: "In the middle of a nightmare is a precinct station full of more wisdom than Periclean Athens ever knew, more kindness than ever obtained in the ambience of St. Assisi or Vincent de Paul. All the policemen are philosophers. The Captain is a Schopenhauer who has seen too much of war. The female attorney looks like a fashion model."

The network was not happy. Reviews they could ignore. The public's apathy they could not. All that technical prowess and all those actors were costing $600,000 a week. It took four episodes to resolve at least a half dozen story lines. There was a main plot, a main subplot and as many weaving minor subplots as the cramming of characters would allow. Veronica Hamel maintained that most of her fan mail asked for plot explanations, not autographs.

It looked bad. Silverman's staff was telling him that people didn't like to really "watch" television. They just liked to have it on and not have to pay undue attention to it—which *Hill Street* demanded. They also weren't used to series which had a cumulative rather than an immediate effect.

"The show has no real spine," Ben Roberts, the producer of *Mannix* and *Nero Wolfe* (January–August 1981), told the press. "It's a collection of brilliant middles. It puts character above plot. Dramatic structure demands a beginning, middle, and end, and this you don't find. There is no cleansing catharsis."

There was, actually; it just didn't come nicely tucked into a single episode. The series was infuriating many, but it was still most critics' darling. There were hundreds of press clippings from all over the nation, telling NBC executives how wonderful the show was. When renewal time came around, *Hill Street Blues* got the green light.

"We were the lowest-rated prime-time show ever to be renewed," said Greg Hoblit.

But with renewal came some compromises. The network asked that at least one major plot would be introduced and resolved within a single episode. More exterior scenes would be mounted to make things less claustrophobic. They wanted more action and less talk. The producers considered their options, then agreed. Michael Kozoll was less satisfied than ever before.

"I wanted it to be irreverent, funny, and always changing," he said. "I didn't want fourteen regular characters. I wanted them to do six shows, eight shows, and then die or disappear." Kozoll was especially upset when Joe Coffey was scripted to die in the first season's final episode, but was saved at the last minute. "The show went from being quasipolitical to a psychosexual encounter group. It became a little more shrill and more comfortable with psychotherapy than sociology."

A writers' strike forced the production to start late and the network to run repeats of the first season. That didn't make it any easier for the staff. The scriptwriting was done entirely in-house: each scripter took one of the four acts in four different episodes. Then they still needed two and a half weeks for each finished script, since Bochco always did a complete final rewrite. Meanwhile, the technical crew needed a full week to prepare for a full week of shooting. They all got so far behind that the production had to close down twice the second season.

Then came the Emmys. *Hill Street Blues* won best sound editing, best cinematography, best director (Butler), best writing (Kozoll and Bochco), best supporting actor (Conrad), best actress (Babcock), best actor (Travanti), and best drama series. You would have thought the Red Sea had parted the way the Emmy stage was mobbed by *Hill Street* celebrants. When accepting the best series award, Bochco blessed the now ousted head of the network by saying, "Thank you, Fred Silverman, wherever you are."

Hill Street Blues' future was suddenly secure. Donald Mohr of the Compton Advertising firm explained the complexities of the new ratings age. "No one expected *Hill Street* to deliver as it has. The Emmy program had a thirty-seven ratings share. *TV Guide* did a big piece on the show itself. The baseball strike delayed NBC's play-off coverage, allowing more advertising of the series closer to its second season premiere. The Dodgers then went on to win the world series in six, so the *Hill Street* preem didn't play opposite the seventh game on ABC. And . . . Grant Tinker [ex-head of MTM] is now the head of NBC." He was Silverman's replacement.

The audience was properly inspired and watched the show in ever increasing numbers. They were thankful for the reruns so they could catch up on their favorite characters. They were charmed by Esterhaus' toughness and gentleness, so they forgave his interruption of a hostage crisis to discuss decorating patterns with Frank. They were fascinated by Belker's ugly manners on the street and patience during the daily calls to and from his mother.

And they were most fascinated by Furillo and Davenport. He was a rock at home and at work because he was always afraid of falling off the wagon. The only sign of his control was the way his words became clipped when he was angry. Davenport was an ice queen in court but warmed up during her subtle flirting with Furillo. She called him "pizza man" (thanks to a local L.A. pizza chain with the motto "Pizza Man—he delivers").

Bochco had always been sickened by what passed for adult relationships on television. He was tired of the awful titillation which was *The Love Boat*'s and *Three's Company*'s (1977–84) stock in trade. Although the networks felt that titillation was safer, he wanted to portray two people with a serious commitment to each other. He succeeded admirably with Frank and Joyce. Theirs was a loving, playful, and honest relationship which gave the series a much needed anchor in affection and hope.

Elsewhere, things were not so rosy. With about a baker's dozen actors to worry about, the tensions on the set always ran high. The pressure to get the work done weighed heavily on everyone. The subject matter and the gruesome surroundings in which they worked didn't help. Although reviewers have guessed that Hill Street was everywhere from San Francisco to New York, it was actually set in a mythical city.

Theirs was not a true reality—it was what Donald E. Westlake called an "Arthur Hailey reality." *Hill Street Blues* existed in a condensed, heightened reality where everything that ever happened in every station house everywhere in the country happened to them all at once. Given that truth, the series could hardly be called lifelike. It may have been more authentic to certain inner-city locales and sensibilities, but ultimately it was no more true to life than *Barney Miller* or *Kojak*.

In fact, as the novelty of the series wore off, it was being accepted

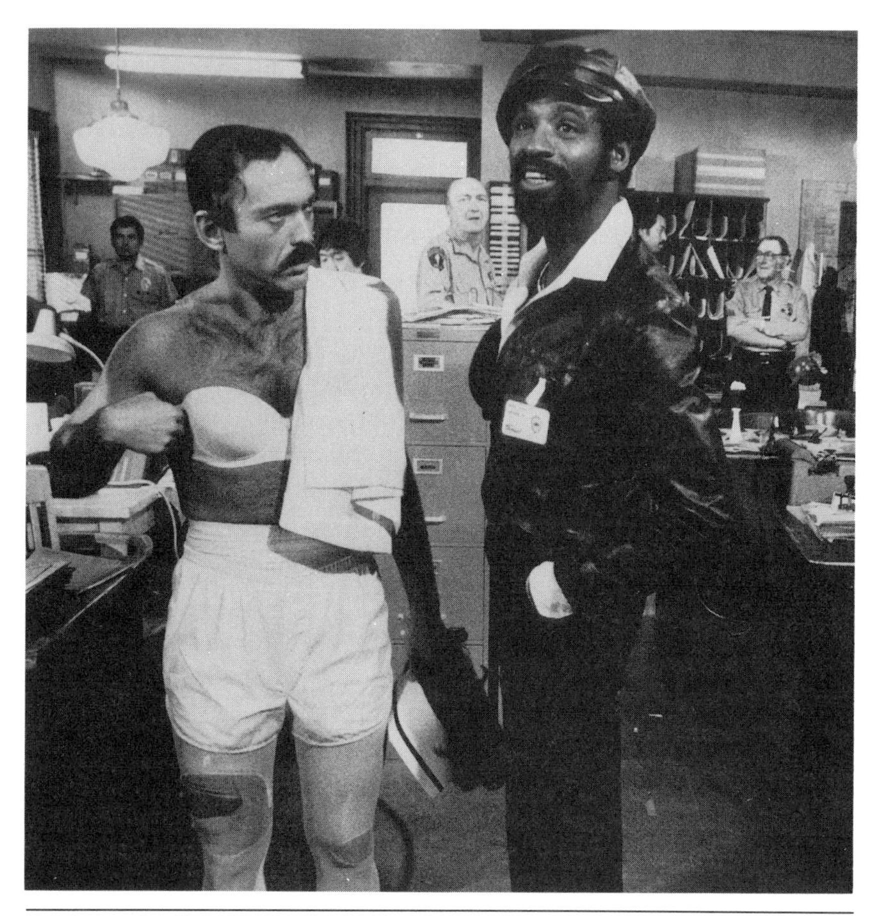

Belker (Bruce Weitz) with his own "hair-ball" problems.

the way *Police Story* (1973–77) and *Naked City* (1958–63) had been. "The reality of network television is that you can't surprise," Bochco told *Playboy*. "We never started out to surprise people. We simply were, I guess, surprising."

Kozoll might disagree with that estimate. He and Bochco disagreed on an increasing number of things as the second season came to a close. The result was that the co-creator and co-executive producer agreed to quit. "I was never going to stay," he contended. "I did the pilot as a favor to Grant Tinker. Writing *Hill Street* was a collaborative effort and I didn't find that very satisfying."

Coming in his stead were two Yale classmates, Jeffrey Lewis and David Milch, who were to be vital in the series' future. Because, with Kozoll gone, this was now officially and totally Bochco's baby. In its first two seasons, *Hill Street Blues* won fourteen Emmys and set the standard for what could be accomplished in a weekly hour show. Bochco set out to prove that we hadn't seen nothin' yet.

In the third season, there was a sort of streamlined chaos. The precedent had been set. The crew knew what they were dealing with. But they still needed seven days to prep, and the casting people still needed to fill twenty to thirty new parts every episode—everyone from guest stars to extras.

"Recording the show is an exercise in very, very controlled insanity," said a sound director. There were as many as ten sound people, all holding microphones on fish poles out of camera range. The dialogue was recorded on set, but the background station house sounds were dubbed in afterward. The background extras were instructed to mime speech.

The camera crew had rules to follow as well. About twenty-five percent of each show was filmed with hand-held cameras, and all the footage was made to look slightly grainy. Rather than flatten the lighting, they actively sought to create shadows. Rather than create clear sightlines, they cluttered the shot with people. They also didn't care whether main characters were entirely in frame. That would just heighten the realism.

The set design crew also had their work cut out for them. To open the space so the picture wouldn't be unbearably claustrophobic, they added glass partitions to the station house set. The writers delighted in destroying at least one of the partitions per episode. It soon became a trademark incident on the show. Usually a felon would make a break for it and get shot or shoved; or someone like Belker would hurl a hairball through one.

Two or three days of the week were set aside for location shooting in downtown Los Angeles. The location crew would find suitably grungy places without palm trees poking into the shot. The set dressers would then clean out the alleys and streets of potentially harmful real garbage, and replace it with "clean dirt." That was their mix of newspapers, boxes, mattresses, and sugar glass.

Back at the costume department, they had to clothe an average of seventy-five people an episode, and usually in pretty grungy outfits. The staff would use electric sanders and chemicals to attain the required look. The head costumer, Bob Harris, Jr., described his job. "Wear it down, put in holes, tear it, rip it, patch it, and rerip it. It was many hours of boredom punctuated by a few minutes of sheer terror just before filming started."

After the week of shooting on street and set, it took the editors ten to eighteen days to complete the work. The result was a weekly price tag of $925,000, making *Hill Street Blues* the most expensive show on television (*Dynasty* cost $900,000 at the time). The network blamed much of the expense on Bochco. His credo seemed to be "Why have two people talking when you can have six?" All those guest stars and all that preparation was adding up.

In spite of the studio executives' dissatisfaction, *Hill Street Blues* was in nirvana. The press couldn't get enough of them. Although rarely sneaking into the top ten, its demographics (the wide range of age groups who watched) were great. They were a legitimate hit—but would only make money for their producers if they reached the hundredth episode. In the wacky world of television, a hundred shows is the generally accepted number to go into syndication, where the big money is.

In 1983, Bochco was increasingly concerned with his new series about a minor-league baseball team, *The Bay City Blues*. That left the bulk of *Hill Street* in the capable hands of Hoblit, Milch, and Lewis. They only stumbled once, when E.A.T. chief Howard Hunter's minor corruption of many years prior was revealed. He tried to commit suicide at the end of the episode with a .357 Magnum revolver. Unbeknownst to him, LaRue had loaded it with blanks.

Hunter was back the following week with a bandage on his forehead, embarrassed but unbowed. But John Erik-Hexum, a young actor on another show called *Cover up* (1984) had done exactly the same thing in real life, as a joke, and died as a result. Even a blank can put enough pressure on the skull to break it. Nothing was said of this unfortunate oversight on *Hill Street*.

A far more serious setback was the death of Michael Conrad, from cancer. A Thanksgiving day episode was telecast concerning the death of Esterhaus, reportedly from his heart giving out while having sex with Grace Gardner. Heart specialists criticized the story for inaccuracy, but the core of the script was the Hill Street Blues' reactions to his death. It was an extremely affecting show. The cast and crew had no idea how much his absence would affect them.

The most serious event happened in the production offices. Arthur Price, the new head of MTM, was convinced that a cap had to be put on the production's budget. MTM suggested that the cast be trimmed (both main and guest) and that the location work be lessened. Bochco reportedly said that they could do that over his prone body. Price's reaction was basically, "Okay, lie down." Bochco stood his ground and MTM backed off—for the moment.

The crew had a cure for almost any malady—write it to a pulp. The ongoing vitality of *Hill Street* was proving that good writing could conquer all. Whenever there was an inaccuracy or a plot oversight, Bochco and company would structure a beautifully scripted scene about it, the cast would perform it beautifully, and all was almost always forgiven.

"Writing a wonderful character is everything," Bochco said. "We can try startling things because we're not bound by formulas. Sometimes they work and sometimes they don't, but the sum is greater than the parts."

The destiny of the show was changed in 1984. First, *The Bay City Blues* failed big—yanked off the air after only four episodes (October–November 1983). The network and studio had paid big money for Bochco's services, the construction of a minor league ball park, and all the extras to fill the stands. They were not pleased.

Next, instead of trimming the cast, Bochco added more characters, several of them holdovers from *The Bay City Blues*. Ken Olin had played baseballer Rocky Padillo. He was now Detective Garibaldi, the troubled partner of beautiful Detective Patricia Mayo, played by Mimi Kuzyk (who was originally introduced as a new love interest for Furillo). Then there was Dennis Franz, who had played sleazy coach Angelo Carbone. Now he was Bad Sal Benadetto, a bad cop in a precinct which prided itself on good cops (indeed, Bad Sal left in a blaze of glory—blowing his brains out after five episodes).

Finally, in came Robert Prosky, chosen out of four hundred to replace Michael Conrad. The short, round, aged actor who had been well known for award-winning performances on Broadway and in movies, played Sergeant Stanislaus Jablonski. Stan was a veteran of the force, but his similarity to Esterhaus ended there. The writers tried to make him flawed, but they hadn't taken into account Esterhaus' balancing persona. The Hill didn't need another loony. They needed a shoulder to cry on. It would be months before they realized this. It was only Prosky's skill which kept the character's head above water.

Esterhaus was best known for ending all his roll call assignments with "Let's be careful out there." They gave Jablonski "let's do it to them before they do it to us." The National Association of Chiefs of Police called a quick halt to that since it "sends a false message that cops persecute indiscriminately." This situation showed how much the series had changed in four years.

In the beginning, Bochco's attitude was liberal. Howard Hunter was a big joke and the writers seemed to side with the attempts Furillo and Goldblume made to bridge the gap between the good guys and bad guys. "I come out of the sixties generation that saw the police as the enemy," Bochco admitted to *Playboy*. "I find myself no longer thinking about cops generically. I find myself thinking about them individually."

What Bochco and company seemed to realize was that "those poor, misunderstood victims of society" had guns too, and no laws governing their actions. It was now the police who were the misunderstood victims, although all weren't squeaky clean. In fact, pretty much everyone but Furillo was bent in one way or another and it took all of the captain's considerable willpower to stay on the straight and narrow.

Goldblume was made to pay for his liberalism in no uncertain terms (he was increasingly shamed as the series progressed), while Howard was broadened and deepened (though never quite straightened). Calletano, after an early moment of glory—reacting to an embarrassing department dinner in his honor with a thought-provoking speech on racism—was all but written out. The scripters made his zealousness negative and transferred him to another precinct where he "wore the brown helmet" (alienated his men).

The scripting situation was becoming so shaky that even the press noticed. "Davenport hasn't had an emotion for eight months," one critic complained. "The writers have gone rape crazy." It did seem that they were responding to every feminist issue with a sexual assault. They were also killing off every character Belker became friends with. Bochco thought it was time to spin Belker off into his own show, in any case. MTM wasn't interested in any more of Bochco's ideas.

The final straw came shortly after the completion of the magical one-hundredth episode. Steven Bochco was invited to quit. His R.S.V.P. was in the affirmative. Gregory Hoblit followed him a week later.

"The problem with the show," said a source close to production, "is that they can't tell stories as fully as they would like because they have too many stories to tell."

What remained was a $3,200,000 deficit for the first three years, mostly attributed to cast and crew salary raises. MTM pointed to the number of times Bochco had seventeen or eighteen characters speaking in the space of three script pages. It really wasn't so much that the cast was gigantic; it was that so many of them were crammed into the same scenes. The bottom line was that any show regularly rating under the top twenty shouldn't cost this much.

The *Hill Street* set was of two minds at the beginning of the fifth season. Milch and Lewis were in control. That made some people happy: the cast would be trimmed and there would be more concentration on the survivors. That made some people unhappy: they loved and trusted Bochco. Suddenly it was every blue for himself.

The varying pay scales became known. Hamill and Travanti were in the A scale. Haid and Weitz were in the B. Everyone else was at C. The general idea was that everyone in their scale got a raise at once. Then someone leaked that Betty Thomas got a raise. That made the other C's very unhappy. The B's wanted more as well. Suddenly all the actors got "Blue Flu."

This time the production was halted by the cast. Negotiations were held. Everybody who was anybody was made happy. Fay Furillo was written out. Joyce and Frank got back together. That didn't leave much use for Mayo and Garibaldi. They got rid of the latter by making him another bad cop on the take who got knifed for his trouble. They got rid of the former with the "Calletano maneuver."

She was transferred out, later returning as a sexual discrimination victim of the oily but well-dressed Chief Fletcher P. Daniels (Jon Cypher). But what really shook the tree was the return of Dennis Franz.

Milch and Lewis had looked around at all the good cop characters—Steven Bochco's good cop characters—and decided they couldn't do much with them. Changing Hill and Washington and Coffey and Bates into creeps wouldn't ring true. They reacted to Belker by improving him with a wife. They even went so far as killing off his mother at the beginning of the season. That never made sense to Weitz, who knew a great acting opportunity when he saw one. Why not milk the death for an end-of-the-season climax?

Instead, the new producers continued to load pain on Renko and LaRue and Hunter and Goldblume, but that wasn't enough. They decided they wanted something that would really rattle the rocks. What they came up with was Norman Buntz. Buntz was a much transferred sleazeball in loud sport coats who may or may not be seriously bent. He was Bad Sal on the side of the angels, and the show's fans howled at such an obvious maneuver—at first.

What was initially created to be an inspiration to the other characters turned out to be their conscience. He was supposed to cause Frank problems but became the id to Furillo's superego—the Fool to Frank's Lear. After five years of the blues' tensions building (only responded to by the endless, frustrating patience of Furillo), it was cathartic to have a character who would shoot first and manufacture the probable cause later. All the audience's sympathies were with the knight in tarnished polyester as he sought to stem the rising tide of street violence.

More and more major plot lines—even whole episodes—concentrated on Buntz. It was he who ran Furillo's assailant to the ground after the captain was shot by a maniac. It was he who spent an entire hour tied to a chair by a vengeful con, only to throw the guy out a window. It was he who racked up more kills in the series' final two seasons than the rest of the cast put together. They even wrote an episode about that, in which Buntz tries *not* to kill someone for the entire shift.

It was he who got the best situations, the best lines ("Do you know

The knight in shining polyester, Norm Buntz (Dennis Franz, *right*), with his sunglassed snitch, Sid (Peter Jurasik).

what life is? It's when you're alive."), and the best fan reaction. That did not sit well with the rest of the cast, especially since the show was further battered by the premiere of *Miami Vice* (1984–). Here was a new wave series that was all style. Although ostensibly a cop show, it was actually a fashion show, a fantasy show, and a war series.

Executive producer Michael Mann and creator Anthony Yerkovich had envisioned a hopelessly hip squad of Florida undercover cops, who spent more time in D.E.A. territory than in strip joints or hooker haunts. Their world was one of fancy clothes and expensive toys. They had cars and boats and houses up the wazoo—as well as a tormented, self-conscious "aw, what's the use?" attitude which wore out its welcome real quick.

It also turned into an unbearably self-important series before too long. But in its first season it was the hottest thing going. It glided into the top ten (something *Hill Street* had never done), and star Don Johnson was on every magazine cover. Travanti was lucky to get on a few by himself (*Hill Street* was always a gang publicity machine—with at least three characters featured at a time).

Suddenly television became the site of a minor war of the meaningful series versus the expensive series. *Hill Street* had relevance and realism dripping all over it while *Miami Vice* was strictly sci-fi-ville, complete with designer guns and roaring shootouts every half hour. Problem was, the latter series wanted to be important but had painted itself into a pastel corner.

Like *Charlie's Angels* before it, the *Vice* staff started to think that a change of look would mean a rise in ratings. *Miami Vice* faltered quickly, but not before others saw gold in them thar skills. Both types of programs had others created in their image. *Hill Street* begat *St. Elsewhere*, while *Miami Vice* begat *Crime Story* and *Private Eye* (1987)—the latter usurping *The Bay City Blues*' distinction of being the most expensive flop in TV history.

Crime Story (1986–88) survived on a heady mixture of glittering visuals and tough pulp scripting, while *St. Elsewhere* (1982–88), created by MTM as "*Hill Street* in a hospital," joined its predecessor as one of the TV's most honored. Steven Bochco, however, hit the top again by co-creating (with Terry Louise Fisher) and being executive producer of *L.A. Law* (1987–)—which was a little *Miami Vice* in its style, and a lot *Hill Street Blues* in its approach to the legal profession in Southern California.

Meanwhile the precedent-setting instigator of the form went along its unmerry way. In its sixth season, the characters and situations became more extreme, leading real-life cops to cry foul. *Hill Street* now had a lecherous, two-faced chief, a transvestite judge (Jeffrey Tambor), and a female undercover operative willing to bare all for her job (Megan Gallagher).

They also had a very unsatisfied actor in Ed Marinaro, who had been doing less and less as the season wore on. He finally gave them an ultimatum straight out of his football days. "Play me or trade me." The result was a script entitled "Iced Coffey." Coffey's first-season fate was not cancelled . . . only delayed. He was gunned down in a cigar store after accidentally stumbling into a robbery.

He was replaced by Milch and Lewis' own nice-guy cop, played by Robert Clohessy. By this time, critics had dubbed the show "Hill Street Lite" and everyone knew what was coming. Most of the main actors had signed seven-year contracts. The next season would be the seventh year, and their renegotiations would break the program's back.

"I think it's a shame when shows, in effect, limp off," said Grant Tinker, "rather than leaving them laughing."

Major uncool, lady. *Miami Vice*'s Philip Michael Thomas as Ricardo Tubbs and Don Johnson as Sonny Crockett. You got a problem with that, pal?

David Milch was more pragmatic. "There was no financial reason to go on," he said. "And aesthetically we had nothing left to prove." Both producers swore, however, that the final season would not be a retreat, organized or otherwise. They would continue the *Hill Street* tradition of beating the audience back with great writing.

The highlights of the seventh and final season were episodes by Robert Woodward, the Watergate reporter, and Pulitzer Prize–winning playwright David Mamet. Woodward's episode was the lightest, with Buntz checking on Joyce just to make sure she wasn't cheating on Frank, and LaRue going cockroach hunting. Mamet's "A Wasted Weekend" was the deepest.

In it, Jablonski, who had suffered the same forced retirement fate as *Barney Miller*'s Fish, went deer hunting with Hill and Renko. Buntz became a father figure and confessor to a shaken female cop (played by Mamet's wife, Lindsay Crouse) who had just killed her first alleged perpetrator. And poor, persecuted Goldblume was kidnapped by a psycho, made to dig his own grave, and then left terrified but alive.

As usual, the trotting out of plot lines doesn't do the writing or acting or direction justice. *Hill Street Blues* was excellent in the viewing, not in the telling. Its accomplishment is all the more impressive because the show's format was just as rigid as *Dragnet*'s. Each episode told the story of a single shift, starting with the roll call and ending with the characters at home.

It was only at the end that Milch and Lewis changed this approach, most notably in the "Blues in the Night" episode—which took place after work. The fact that this strict frame was not apparent makes the cast and crew's achievement even greater.

The final episode was "It Ain't Over Till It's Over." By then, Goldblume, like *Barney Miller*'s Harris before him, had written a story about his associates (essentially a story which was true; only the names were changed to protect the innocent). The episode's most apt line was reserved for Belker. After everyone else was perplexed by Goldblume's honest depiction of them, the hairball-biting undercover operative approached his friend quietly.

"It was funny," he said of the story. "It was sad. It was a lot like life."

A lot like *Hill Street Blues*.

But, as usual, the best moment belonged to Buntz. When the chief finally maneuvers him into an impossible situation, Norm quits, but not before he slugs his double-dealing, back-stabbing superior. It is Buntz who is one of the last characters on screen: shoving a piece of gum in his mouth and walking off the Hill (into his own short-lived spinoff, *Beverly Hills Buntz*).

"It's time for *Hill Street* to get off," said Grant Tinker. "It's a wonderful body of work. It's a much better memory than if it had run out of gas."

His second in command, Brandon Tartikoff, the head of programming, gave the show a fitting epitaph. "It signalled a new NBC," he said. "Its talented team consistently hit and bettered the standard of excellence the series established for dramatic television."

It also ushered in a new age of television. An age where the line between fantasy and reality almost doesn't exist. Between the fictional series trying to be realistic, and the fact programs trying to be entertaining, the audience psyche is being increasingly flattened.

As James Sikking said, "In the Aztec days, they had human sacrifice. Today, we have television."

Will there come a time when it is impossible to distinguish truth from media hype? Television: entertainment or danger? Film at eleven.

The Fine Line

"Let's dig deeper into the evidence.
This case is not as simple
as it seems."

—Jessica Beatrice Fletcher

WHY DO PEOPLE HAVE TO DIE? IT'S A DUMB QUESTION BECAUSE IT CANNOT be answered (outside of dry biological explanations). It's a fact of life which cannot be avoided. Better we should ask ourselves questions which *can* be answered—like why are we so fascinated with the murder mystery? Why is the form which deals with that unavoidable dread so popular?

The men with the answers we've already met. Their names have been peppered throughout this work as creators and writers of such esteemed fare as *Burke's Law*, *Mannix*, and *Ellery Queen* (the 1974 version). But their most beloved work has yet to be considered.

Richard Levinson and William Link have won the Mystery Writers of America's Edgar award for their trilogy of whodunit telefilms, *Murder by Natural Causes* (1979), *Rehearsal for Murder* (1982), and *Guilty Conscience* (1985)—each a labyrinthine murder puzzle with an all-star cast (Hal Holbrook, Robert Preston, Anthony Hopkins) and exemplary direction by David Greene. But those are not their greatest contribution to the canon.

They also wrote and produced such ground-breaking television movies as *My Sweet Charlie* (Emmy winner for 1970), *That Certain Summer* (Golden Globe award winner for 1972), and *The Execution of Private Slovik* (1974). But even those are not what they are best known for.

"The critics kept saying to us, 'How come you guys always do

Both Hal Holbrook and Katharine Ross are planning *Murder by Natural Causes*.

dramas?' " Richard Levinson told me. "And we said, 'Fellas, on our tombstones, it's going to say 'Creators of *Columbo*.' "

That internationally famous, rumpled, seemingly absentminded police lieutenant would have been enough to secure their lasting fame, but they also created *Murder, She Wrote* with collaborator Peter Fischer. Those cherished characters are on everyone's list of the genre's best. They are also the finest examples of the kind of gratification audiences get from the art, stripped down to their most basic.

Neither *Columbo* nor *Murder, She Wrote* came with Levinson and Link's award-winning trappings of relevance and controversy. While their most critically successful efforts were about racism, homosexuality, moral corruption, violence in fiction (1977's *The Storyteller*), in the streets (1974's *The Gun*), and in our schools (1981's *Crisis at Central High*)—their most financially successful series were pure entertainment without a whiff of polemics.

"We've been lucky enough," said Levinson, "to carve out this little niche for ourselves where the networks say, 'Let's indulge them in these social dramas because maybe they'll give us another sensational series.' "

The team met on the first day of junior high school and collaborated throughout their school years. They sold their first story during their freshman year at college, which coincided with "The Golden Age of Television." Equally interested with televised dramas and literature, they pursued their goals by writing books and plays for six months in New York and scripts for six months in Los Angeles.

"You could do it in those days," said William Link. "It wasn't like the twelve-month siege you have in Hollywood now. It was 1960 and we were under contract at Four Star Television, which was the largest television supplier in the world. We were story editors on *Michael Shayne* [1960–61] while working on *The DuPont Show with June Allyson* [1959–61] and potboilers like *Black Saddle* [1959–60] and *Johnny Ringo* [1959–60]. Then there was, God help us, a writers' strike."

Although the Writers Guild strike of 1988 had almost crippled television production during its five months, the 1960 strike went on for two weeks longer. Four Star told the novice scripting duo to clean out their offices, leaving them treading creative waters.

"At that time there was a clause in the Writers Guild contract that you could write for a live television show," Link continued. "And there was one live television show left, on NBC, and it was also one of the first color shows. It was a summer replacement series for Dinah Shore, called *The Chevy Mystery Show* [1960-1961]."

The pair had the outlet, now they needed the script. As always, their minds worked along original lines. "We said, 'Let's do a mystery that isn't a whodunit,' " Link remembered. " 'One where you see the murder committed. That hasn't been done on television yet. Then enter a policeman who pins it on the perpetrator.' We went back to a story called 'May I Come In' we had published in *Alfred Hitchcock's Mystery Magazine*. It had a very nice alibi in it for a psychiatrist who murdered his wife. Then we suddenly realized we didn't know who this cop was going to be.

"We had read extensively in the golden age of the mystery—John Dickson Carr, Ellery Queen, Agatha Christie—but we needed someone who was different as well as a policeman. We talked and talked, then remembered the cop Petrovich in Fyodor Dostoyevsky's *Crime and Punishment*. We remembered he was a rather subtly intimidating creature, with a whole humble act. But behind that mask was a very brilliant detective who got the suspect's defenses down, caught him off-guard, and pinned the murder on him."

Levinson and Link had their cop and they named him Lieutenant Columbo. They liked the sound of it. They called the script "Enough Rope," which was bought and produced on the mystery show. "It was embarrassing," Link said. "It was a live show and full of mistakes. It was truly coronary country to see that thing go on. I cringed as I watched it."

The most interesting thing was Columbo was played by the gruff, crusty character actor Bert Freed (who has appeared in dozens of television shows and movies, including *Paths of Glory*, 1957, *Invitation to a Gunfighter*, 1969, *Wild in the Streets*, 1968, and *Billy Jack*, 1971). "It was the exact same character as the series one," said Link, "but with a topcoat instead of a raincoat.

Bert Freed (seen here in *Billy Jack*) was the first Lieutenant Columbo.

"Years later, I'm at a party at a friend's house after the success of the *Columbo* series, and who should walk in with his wife but Bert Freed. So I start talking to him about it, trying to feel him out, and he says, 'Didn't you guys do that?' I said, 'Yeah. You realize you were the first Columbo?' He said, 'What!' He had no memory of the show. Nothing. He had played so many characters he had forgotten all about that one."

The public would have forgotten about the character as well had the team not quit Four Star and searched for freelance assignments. "We realized 'Enough Rope' would make a great play," said Link, "because it was very contained. You couldn't very well do a car chase on a live show, so the drama was only in a few locations. It had a unity of time and place which would work fine for the stage."

They sublet the New York apartment of director Stuart Rosenberg (*Cool Hand Luke*, 1967, *The Laughing Policeman*, 1973, *The Amityville Horror*, 1979) and set to work. Within three days of returning to Los Angeles, one of the most powerful producers in the theater industry wanted to do it. "Paul Gregory," said Link. "He had produced *The Caine Mutiny Court Martial*, *John Brown's Body*, and had a huge hit with *Don Juan in Hell*. The game plan was to tour our play all over the U.S. and Canada, then bring it to Broadway."

As the pre-production rehearsals started, the title was changed to *Prescription: Murder*. Joseph Cotten was cast as the psychiatrist, Agnes Moorehead as his shrewish wife, Patricia Medina as his mistress, and Thomas Mitchell, who had played Scarlett O'Hara's father in *Gone with the Wind* (1939) and won the Oscar as the drunk doctor in *Stagecoach* (1939), was Columbo.

"I'll never forget it," said Link. "Our first day, these two vulnerable guys from Philadelphia, in our early twenties, with our first play, and Thomas Mitchell says, 'Listen. In *my* theater, writers sit in the last row!' We couldn't believe it."

Prescription Murder toured for six months, becoming the second-highest grossing play in the country (after the Pulitzer Prize–winning *A Man for All Seasons*). It didn't, however, open on Broadway. "Dick and I used to consider Broadway a shrine," explained Link. "We really looked up to it as a place where only excellence was allowed. But Paul Gregory virtually froze the script after its first performance. We wanted to get the kinks out of our play. It *needed* changes. They wouldn't let us do it, so we didn't allow them to take it to Broadway."

Lieutenant Columbo went back on the shelf while his creators went back to Hollywood. They wrote for *The Alfred Hitchcock Hour* (1962–65), the TV version of *The Third Man* (1959–62), and *The Fugitive* before realizing the character was too good to keep down. "What probably triggered it was that the two-hour *Movie of the Week* was conceived," Link decided. "Agents were saying, 'Do you have anything that could be adapted to this format?'

"Our agent took *Prescription: Murder* to Universal, where we met with Don Siegel. He was going to produce and direct it as a 'World Premiere Movie,' but then the call came through from Warner Brothers that they had green-lighted *Dirty Harry*. Clint Eastwood was a dear friend of his, so he said, 'Guys, this is a prior commitment, it's activated, I have to leave.' Richard Irving, a long-time Universal contracted director/producer, took over."

Columbo was back in action. Gene Barry, the star of *Burke's Law*, was cast as the killer psychiatrist. Nina Foch played his wife, and Katherine Justice played his mistress. All they needed was the cop. "We wanted Bing Crosby," Link admitted. "That's how silly we were. But Crosby was in semiretirement. He said, 'I like the screenplay, but I really just want to play golf.'

"We also liked Lee J. Cobb (whose last role was the Columbo-like cop in *The Exorcist* 1973), but I don't know if the studio ever offered it to him. Then Peter Falk called. We had known Peter when he was a struggling actor in New York. We used to have breakfast with him. We always liked him and his work. His agent had gotten him a copy of the script and he said, 'Listen. I'd kill to play this cop. I've got to play this guy Columbo.' He came in, he read, and he got it. It was a marriage made in television heaven."

Prescription: Murder was broadcast in 1968. The ever-inquisitive, ever-apologetic, ever-digressing homicide detective went after Dr. Ray Fleming, whose perfect alibi had him out of the country when his "dear" wife died (for more on every twist and turn of every episode, see Mark Dawidziak's study, *The Columbo Phile*). Falk, who had been impressing audiences since 1957 in movies like *Murder, Inc.* (1960), *Pocketful of Miracles* (1961), *It's a Mad, Mad, Mad, Mad World* (1963), *Robin and the Seven Hoods* (1964), *The Great Race* (1965), and television shows like *Studio One*, *The Untouchables*, and *The Twilight Zone*, was tremendous as the hunched, cigar-waving detective. The ratings were equally terrific (number one show of that week). It made no difference.

"NBC naturally said, 'Let's do this as a weekly hour show,' " said Link. "Dick and I said no. It's impossible. The format is too constricting." So the network went to Falk. He also said no. "He had done *The Trials of O'Brien* (1965–66) and it was so time-consuming he never saw his family. He said, 'I can't do another twenty-six-episode series.' So it went back on the shelf."

Once again, the creation of a new format signaled the return of the prodigal lieutenant. NBC created the "mystery wheel." Instead of a weekly hour program with the same character, three characters would be spokes on a ninety-minute revolving wheel. They would take turns being featured under the blanket title of *The NBC Mystery Movie*. The network already had Rock Hudson in *McMillan and Wife* and Glen Larson's *McCloud* starring Dennis Weaver.

After the first television movie was aired, the score was Columbo: one . . . Murderers: nothing.

"They remembered the little detective in the raincoat," Link said. "So Dean Hargrove produced and wrote the screenplay of *Ransom for a Dead Man* from our story. The rest, as they say, is history." *Columbo* ran for six seasons, becoming increasingly popular every time it appeared. It soon overshadowed its companions and Falk's salary grew until he was the highest-paid actor on television. The series also maintained its quality of content under the guidance of Dean Hargrove, Steven Bochco, and Richard Alan Simmons.

Columbo faced murderer after murderer, often played by the same actors. Patrick McGoohan, Robert Culp, and Robert Vaughn were the most visible villains, returning time and again as different characters in different situations trying to pull off different perfect crimes. But no matter how precise their alibi, no matter how complete their planning, no matter

Peter Falk as the formative, and formidable, Columbo of *Prescription: Murder*.

Robert Culp tried to get away with murder several times on *Columbo*.

how they squirmed and lied and cheated, the unassuming, messy, overly polite but incessantly questioning policeman would be there.

Both *Columbo* and *Barnaby Jones* used Droopy Dog's technique from the Tex Avery–directed MGM cartoons of the 1940's. The Wolf would always attempt to elude the hero, but always found him directly behind, his placid face and manner unchanging. But while Barnaby's villains were wolflike in their desperation to escape Jones' justice, Columbo was dogged in his pursuit of his ever-unctious, always wealthy and influential foes. Part of the series' success came from thrusting the hound-dog sleuth into incongruous upscale environments. *Columbo* was not only involving, it was funny.

"I recently saw *Ransom for a Dead Man* again with a big crowd," said Link. "I was amazed by how funny it was. Some scenes got belly laughs. I never realized the full extent of the humor that ran through the show. It was a real eye-opener."

It was another testament to the talents of Falk that he maintained audience sympathy and empathy with such an obsessed, grungy character. He got a full range of reactions out of what seemed to be a limited man. Columbo was always the same, but Falk played him differently, so the viewer could be delighted and surprised by the least little details. When the rare show of emotion or anger did come, it had all the more power for it. When the star decided the scripts couldn't be adequately maintained, he called it quits.

"NBC and Universal always wanted to resurrect the show," Link said, "but Peter wasn't interested. I don't think they ever even negotiated. We certainly didn't develop any more *Columbo* scripts." But a funny thing happened on the way to 1988. Falk's film career was slowly regaining momentum after stalling in 1979 (he had made *Murder by Death*, 1976, *The Cheap Detective*, 1976, *The Brink's Job*, 1978, and *The In-Laws*, 1979). He had done an amusing, but small role in *The Princess Bride* (1987), then appeared to be confronting his lasting fame as Columbo in the impressionistic German film, *Wings of Desire* (1988), written and directed by Wim Wenders.

In it, Peter Falk plays Peter Falk, an actor playing a detective in wartime Berlin for a modern-day German movie. During production, he discovers the existence of guardian angels throughout the city, but that is not the part that concerns us. Wherever Falk goes in Berlin, he is greeted by pedestrians as "Lieutenant." The funniest scene has Falk passing a gang of youths who all do double takes and go, "Was that Columbo?" He had not shaken (or even stirred) the role for more than a decade.

So Falk went home and wrote his own *Columbo* script. "It was unlike the others in that it's almost a love story," said Link. But the script wasn't as important to the studio as the star. Universal let it be known that *Columbo* was back. The ABC network bought him. "I think the time was right in Peter's life to come back to it," Link continued. "The mystery wheel had returned so he can spend six months doing television and six months doing movies." ABC's wheel had Burt Reynolds and Louis Gossett, Jr. as all-new characters on the other spokes.

Although delayed by the 1988 writers' strike, ABC, Link, and returning executive producer Richard Alan Simmons were constantly negotiating. The network wanted to know how the detective was going to be updated. "I said, 'We're not in the business of curing a hit,' " answered Link. "We can't make the character any smarter. He still has the dog and is still married."

But to whom? One of the only ignoble things about the original *Columbo* was Fred Silverman's decision to mount a spin-off stolidly titled *Mrs. Columbo* (1979). Instead of taking Levinson and Link's suggestion to cast Maureen Stapleton, he signed the attractive twenty-four-year-old Kate Mulgrew to play Kate Columbo (although the lieutenant's wife was actually named Rose). The series was a disaster which went through several title changes (*Kate the Detective* and *Kate Loves a Mystery*) after Silverman had the character divorce the lieutenant and reclaim her maiden name of Callahan. The program was put out of our misery after six months.

A raincoat, a cigar, a squint, and a digression. "Pardon me, sir, am I boddering you . . . ?"

"We were thinking of doing an inside joke," Link revealed. "In one of the new episodes, we were going to have Columbo say, 'You know, a couple of years ago there was a woman impersonating my wife—using my credit cards and everything. What a tragedy. I had to put her away.' We would have loved to do that, but decided against it."

Instead, Levinson, Link, and *Ellery Queen* co-creator and executive producer Peter Fischer reunited to conceive a real "Mrs. Columbo"—a natural extension of all the lieutenant's skills and charm.

"The way it worked," Peter Fischer explained, "was that CBS had said to Universal—where Dick and Bill were consultants and I was under contract as an executive producer—that they would be interested in a mystery show under the auspices of Levinson, Link, and Fischer. Did we have any ideas?"

Fischer was included because of his associates' consistent praise, as well as his own credits. He made it to Hollywood on the strength of a science-fiction "Movie of the Week" script he wrote "on my dining room table back in New York . . . the way you're not supposed to get into the business." *The Last Child* was made in 1971, starring Michael Cole (of *The Mod Squad*) and Janet Margolin as 1994 parents in a nation which forbids more than one child per family.

"So I came out here," said Fischer, "and they said, 'Oh yeah, he's a science-fiction writer.' So I lived with that label for about six months. Then I got a job with *Marcus Welby, M.D.* [1969–76], so I became a 'medical writer.' That led to a job on *Owen Marshall, Counselor at Law* [produced by the same people from 1971–74], where I became a lawyer writer. Finally I did a *Columbo* script, on spec, which got me in with Hargrove, [Roland] Kibbee, and Bochco. Then I met Dick and Bill, and became a mystery writer."

Levinson and Link were immediately impressed by Fischer. "We had latched on to Peter as soon as he got a contract at Universal," said Link. "We thought he was definitely a rising star and had one of the best mystery minds around." They asked if he would like to work on their *Ellery Queen* program.

"I said, 'Whoa. I don't even know if I can write this kind of thing,' " Fischer replied. "So they handed me a book of short stories (1934's *The Adventures of Ellery Queen*) and said, 'See if there's anything in there you like.' I found 'The Adventure of the Mad Tea Party' and went to town. One of the joys of my life was writing that script. My mind just seems to work in puzzles. I love puzzles."

The new puzzle was figuring out what CBS wanted and giving it to them. The trio had been working apart for four years until they had hit upon the idea for a show called *Blacke's Magic*. "We had been over at NBC and twice had gotten very close to a buy," said Fischer. "But we had a conceptual problem. We didn't want a magician running around the country with a nightclub act. They had tried that once with Bill

Bixby (*The Magician*, 1973–74) and it didn't work. We felt it should be a retired magician who was an armchair detective. But what they wanted was a thirty-five-year-old guy, and were talking about sex symbols like Armand Assante. It sounded great, but it wasn't our concept. It wasn't what we wanted to do. We kept saying, 'Wait a minute, what is he doing retiring at thirty-five?'

"So we went over to CBS and pitched it. They looked at us and said, 'That's sounds very interesting. . . . And then Carla Singer said—and this was the first time we had heard it—'You know, what we really want is a female lead.' And the three of us looked at each other, feeling like we had just swallowed a cyanide pill. Because, in those days, a female lead in a mystery show was death. I mean, it had never worked."

But if anyone could make it work, it would be these three. Although *Blacke's Magic* (January–May 1985) would ultimately sell to NBC for one season, they went back to Universal and started batting CBS ideas around. "I had seen Helen Hayes playing Miss Marple in a TV Movie that weekend [A *Caribbean Mystery*, 1983, adapted by Sue Grafton and Steve Humphries]," Fischer recalled. "It was scheduled opposite *The Love Boat*, and they did respectfully in the ratings. So we decided to combine *The Love Boat* and an Agatha Christie–type murder mystery."

Fischer had always loved the Love Boat idea of star-studded guest casts, even back in their *Ellery Queen* days. He figured if they had to have a half-dozen suspects, why not make them recognizable names from television hits and the movies' golden age? Levinson and Link liked the idea of a mature leading lady, rather than the blonde bombshells who had always been featured before (*Honey West*, *Charlie's Angels*, *Police Woman*, etc.).

They devised a suitably intriguing title. *Murder, She Wrote*. "We Americanized it, naturally," Fischer continued. "The networks have a terrible prejudice against anyone with an English accent. So we made her a bestselling mystery writer from Cabot Cove, Maine. We had initially decided that she was just going to use her initials, like P.D. James. We came up with J.B. Fletcher, then got something to go with it. Jessica Beatrice.

"Then I said to Dick, 'Look, we're going to learn from our mistakes. We're going to use the lessons we learned on *Ellery Queen*. First, no matter what we do with this lady, she is going to be a dynamo and drive this story. I mean, she isn't going to run around like a private eye, but even though she's fifty-plus, she's going to have a high energy level."

Levinson and Link agreed with their partner, remembering the unfortunate fate of their previous labor of love. "Jim Hutton was a very sweet, very cooperative guy," Link related, "who used to take pride in how easy he was to work with. In fact, we used to say to him, 'Jim . . . less cooperation and more charisma!' "

"Jim was told to play a laid-back, Jimmy Stewart sort of absentminded

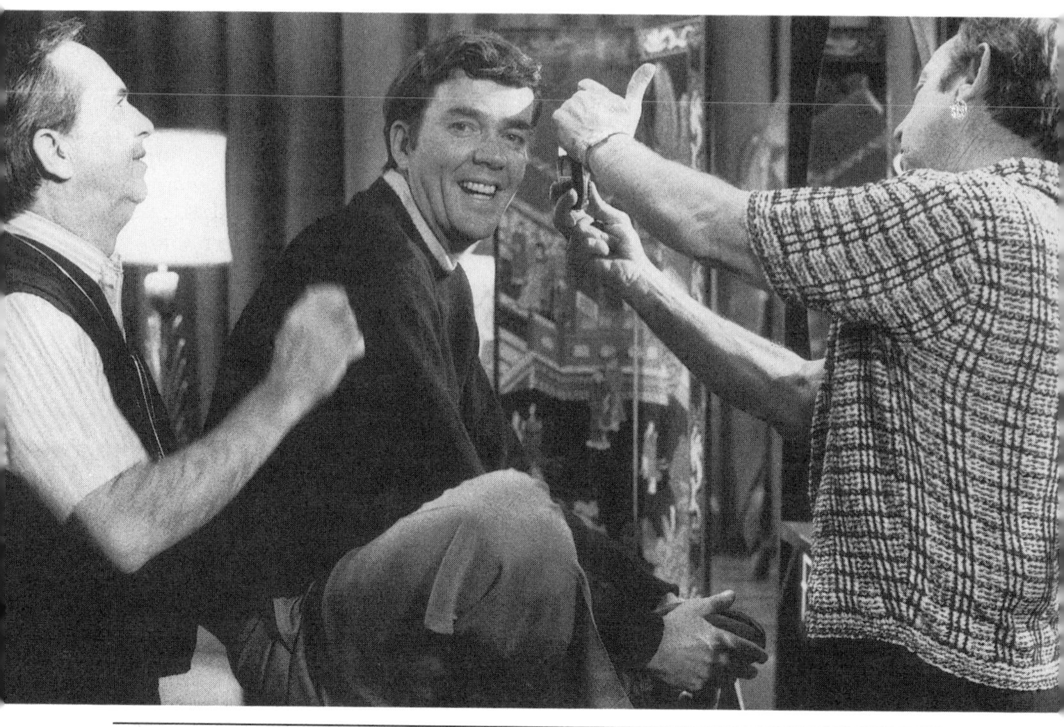

"Less cooperation . . . more charisma!" The engine without an engineer—*Ellery Queen*.

professor," added Fischer, "and that's what he did. As likable as he was, there was no engine driving the show there. We were going to have one here."

The producer-writers remembered more hard-learned lessons. "Sometimes in *Ellery Queen*, the solutions to the mysteries were so damn obscure, convoluted, and difficult that even Dick only understood them halfway," Fischer complained. "People would get frustrated and turn off. We decided to let some air in, and let the audience feel proud of themselves for having figured it out. Then, once in a while, we could throw a tough one in."

Jessica Beatrice Fletcher was born, but for the life of them, the team couldn't figure out who to play her. "Who will the audience tune in to see?" Fischer had wondered. "Who can you get that's fifty-plus, in television, and has a following? The only one we could think of was Jean Stapleton." Stapleton had just come off the huge success of *All in the Family* (1971–83) and was shopping for a new series.

"We met and sold her on the idea," said Link, "but she said she'd have to see a script. Dick, Peter, and I conceived the pilot story, 'Who

Killed Sherlock Holmes?' and Peter wrote the teleplay." In it, Jessica Fletcher finds murder at a high society costume ball, where an obnoxious hard-boiled writer dressed in deerstalker and cape is eliminated. It was an impressive mix of solid sleuthing and light romance.

"The least likely suspect turned out to be Jessica's publisher," Link disclosed, "with whom the audience thought she was going to begin a love affair. So you have a very nice bittersweet ending and a real surprise."

They sent the script to Ms. Stapleton. "She was very confused by it," Link continued. "I think the murder mystery was just not her cup of film. The genre did not go down well with her. We were very surprised and saddened, because with her wonderful success we would have had it on the air, few questions asked."

Jean Stapleton would later play "Ariadne Oliver," the mystery writer Agatha Christie based on herself in the later Hercule Poirot novels for one of the CBS movies starring Peter Ustinov as the Belgian detective. Back in 1983, however, the head of CBS programming, Harvey Shepherd, came running to the trio's rescue.

"He said, 'We don't need Jean Stapleton for this,' " Link recalled. " 'You've got to get this around to other actresses.' We didn't want to let this bone out of our mouths. Then we discovered that Angela Lansbury was shopping for a series."

Although her name was rarely recognized by the general public, she was a big star in the industry, known for her versatility and vitality. She received an Oscar nomination for her very first screen role (1944's *Gaslight*) and had proven herself in comedies (*The Court Jester*, 1956), musicals (*The Harvey Girls*, 1945), and dramas alike (a spellbinding performance in *The Manchurian Candidate*, 1962).

Her greatest fame came on the New York stage. While she was a noted supporting actress in Hollywood, she was a show-stopping star on Broadway, having won raves and Tony awards for her bravura performances in *Mame* and *Sweeney Todd*. In addition, she had recently played Miss Marple in the 1980 movie version of *The Mirror Crack'd*.

"We never thought Harvey Shepherd would allow us to cast Angela," said Link. "Although she was a big Broadway star, she was relatively unknown on television. So we were stunned when Harvey Shepherd turned out to be a big Angela Lansbury fan! I'll never forget; he said, 'You go get her.' "

The actress was seriously considering an offer from Norman Lear, producer of *All in the Family*, to co-star in a situation comedy with Charles Durning. The trio despaired about their chances. "We figured she was going to take it," said Link. "It was a natural. She said she would read our script over the weekend and give us an answer on Monday. The answer was yes."

"It was one of those happy coincidences," said Fischer with a laugh.

Passion, compassion, energy, and skill—Angela Lansbury as Jessica Beatrice Fletcher.

"Everything happened at the same time. We were ready with our script. She was sort of, half ready to do television, if she could find the right property. So we got in each other's way. Thank God."

Although they were all delighted by her wit and savvy, their first few production meetings were disconcerting. "She said, 'Now, darlings, we have to talk about my wigs,' " Fischer remembered. "I looked at her and said, 'What wigs?' She said, 'I've got to get this character down.' I think her original concept was a little pillow-stuffing here and a crazy wig there, like her role as Mrs. Lovett in *Sweeney Todd*. I said, 'Angela, what we're going to do is have you play Angela Lansbury.'

"She looked like she had been hit in the head with a wet fish. She said, 'I can't do that. I've never played myself. I don't know how.' I said, 'Yes, you can. You're going to find it's the key to survival. When you're working five days a week, twelve hours a day, this character will become you and you are going to become her. It's the only way it'll work.' I think she said okay reluctantly and I still feel that she thinks she's not really acting. It's not the same challenge she was used to.

"But then Peter Falk said to her a year or so ago: 'You know, Angie, we got the same problem. This is very hard because you and I are doing the toughest thing in the world. We're playing ourselves.' And it is tough. They're very exposed out there. When you're an actor hiding behind a bizarre character, it's safer. But when you're playing yourself, it's your charm and sense of fun which has to come through. It's your intelligence which has to come across. That's what comes right out of that tube."

Lansbury skillfully adapted her prodigious skills to the small screen. Watching her in action was seeing an artist at work. She controlled Jessica Fletcher's emotions and reactions so that the audience was convinced only they knew what she was feeling or thinking. She pulled off the most delicate of performing challenges by underplaying her overacting!

"I think she does it very nicely," Fischer judged. "She does it with a look. She does it with a tone of voice. She plays it straight. That's one reason I think the show works. She's terrific."

The pilot was finished with Brian Keith as Sherlock and Richard Anderson as Jessica's publisher. "We got the usual network slathering of 'isn't it lovely' and 'just terrific,' " said Fischer, "but three or four of the key people over at CBS had privately said, 'Yeah, it's a nice, quaint, old-fashioned little show that's going to last six episodes.' "

"Here's a woman of a 'certain age' who wears glasses," Richard Levinson described. "She isn't bailed out by a man in the last five minutes and she doesn't display parts of her anatomy. The show's all talk, there's no action, it's slow, it deliberately has what we call 'Aaron Spelling lighting,' the music is 'melodic-conventional,' it features 'mature' performers, and it's a whodunit! The smart money in town didn't give it a prayer."

"Our money!" Link announced. "Even we thought six and out. It *couldn't* survive!"

Then came what the team perceived as the final nail in their coffin. Shepherd scheduled them after *60 Minutes* on Sunday nights. "We said 'Harvey, don't do this to us!' " Fischer cried. " 'Don't you know what's happened to every show behind *60 Minutes*? *Goodnight, Beantown*? *The Sally Struthers Show*? You're going to kill us!' He said, 'Don't worry about it. You're going to be a massive hit.' Well, last laughs do come.

Harvey Shepherd got his and we got ours. He's the man who made sure it all happened and we're eternally grateful."

"The pilot went on, and the ratings went through the roof," said Link. "The show never stopped going through the roof. It's broken a lot of roofs."

In hindsight, the scheduling was brilliant. The escapist whodunit fare was a breath of relief after the doom and gloom of the news magazine. *Murder, She Wrote* basically became the antidote for *60 Minutes*. The comedies CBS had been scheduling were too jarring a change in tone. The mystery series contained a similar ominous atmosphere, but featured a pleasant heroine who solved all the problems.

What remained was a sticky situation. There had only been one previous long-running televison whodunit. *Perry Mason* had lasted nine seasons. The best anyone else could do was three (*Burke's Law*). The team tried out their newly learned lessons and they worked. "It's drawing that fine line," said Fischer. "You know how difficult it is. If you're writing novels, like Miss Christie did, you write two a year. Over a forty-year career, you still end up with only eighty novels. When you have to put out twenty-two of these a year, they're coming on one a week, and you're trying to make them different, it's hard . . . and it's getting harder."

At first, it was all they could do to introduce the suspects, kill the victim, and solve the crime. "We tried to open it up a bit," said Fischer, "give her different locales, different kinds of characters, and different situations to play against. It's an invisible high-wire act. If it works, no one should see the effort. If you watch the show and don't notice any effort at all, it's perfect. This is what I've been telling the network and studio executives for years. This is the reason we rewrite the scripts eight times. When it reads like butter and plays like the simplest thing in the world, I say, 'Fellas, you got it right.' "

During the first season, all aspects of the winning formula were shaken down. Jessica Fletcher started as a mild, slightly dowdy eccentric, but became more polished and professional as the weeks wore on. She also became more elegant as she realized Fischer's pre-production dictums were true. During the costume ball sequences of the pilot, she wanted to be Madame DeFarge. He wanted her to be Cinderella.

"I wanted her to knock everybody on their ass when she came down those stairs," he said. "I wanted her to look absolutely gorgeous." Angela Lansbury soon saw the light and accentuated Jessica Fletcher's natural attractiveness. Her wardrobe and makeup became a lot cleaner and more stylish. Even so, she quickly vetoed deep emotional relationships for her alter ego. "Angela said, 'My God, please, not the romance-of-the-week,' " Fischer explained.

She was right. Even the likes of *Hill Street Blues* looks stupid when a character's relationships are dashed on the rocks every seven days.

Marriages and long-term love affairs rarely work for television heroes—although they are often and unsuccessfully used as a last-ditch effort to boost sagging ratings. *Murder, She Wrote* had no such problem and didn't require occasional affairs. Besides, it wouldn't be proper. One of the show's strongest ties to audience sympathy is the obvious love Jessica had for her late husband, Frank. To betray that love would be foolish.

Testing that bond during the first season was a Cabot Cove fisherman played by Claude Akins. "We had no intention of developing that relationship into a romance," Fischer maintained. "We needed a male presence in the town besides Tom Bosley (who played Sheriff Amos Tupper). His purpose on the show was to be a rough and tough buddy, but I don't think Claude liked the idea of being an occasional second

The Murder Capital of the East Coast: Cabot Cove, Maine, and three of its leading citizens—fisherman Ethan Cragg (Claude Akins), best-selling mystery author Jessica Fletcher, and Sheriff Amos Tupper (Tom Bosley).

banana. He made it clear he was unhappy. We took him at his word and wrote him out of the show."

"That's when we brought along William Windom as Dr. Seth Hazlitt. We could do more with him, because he was more Jessica's age and temperament. He was also the town doctor, which made it easy to get him into the show. When you're finding bodies, you need both a sheriff and a doctor." And heaven knows Jessica was finding bodies. She found one, sometimes two, a week, in every town and almost every locale.

"We avoid any subject which smacks of grim reality," Fischer states. "We're not going to have her skulking around in slums, looking for drug addicts." But as a bestselling author, Fletcher travels constantly and stays in the very best hotels.

"We spent a lot of money on production values," said Fischer. "One of the things I remembered about *Perry Mason* in its final seasons was that there was a lot of talking in offices. Since they were in black and white and they didn't use big-name guest stars, the shows all began to look alike. We try to avoid that at all costs. It's a very warm, rich, and colorful show in its own way."

In order to maintain the quality, Fischer has developed a story system. "Everybody says, 'How many nieces can this woman have?' " he relates. "We did have a bunch of relatives in trouble during the first season. We still occasionally do that, but not as much as people think. If we do that three times a year, it's a lot. She has a regular nephew, Grady [Michael Horton], who we use twice a year. We do five Cabot Cove shows a season—no more and no less. The rest of the time she's on the road."

Pinpointing her environment is just one of the ways Fischer and company develop a script. "Sometimes we start with a clue. We say this idea will work and then we go backwards to get a story. Or we'll see how she'll react to a certain group of characters. Or we'll try to find someone out of her past so she can play all the shadings, because at some point she'll have to face that her friend might be the murderer. Those are the basic ways we attack the scripts; but there are only so much of those you can do before you start repeating yourself."

Levinson, Link, and especially Fischer (as executive producer) had to keep walking that fine line between familiarity and contempt. Every show in the series had to be similar—they use the same mystery ingredients—but they couldn't be repetitive. "Even though we're stuck with the artificial conventions," said Fischer, "the corpse, the six suspects, and the valid clue, we have to strive for the 'reality of the fantasy.' You have to keep saying, 'But it's real, folks.' You have to, sort of, take it seriously. Otherwise there's no credibility at all."

That's why there will never be a *Murder, She Wrote* about a murder mystery game vacation. "It's been pitched to us a hundred times and I will not do it," Fischer declared. "I say, look. You've got to understand that the murder mystery weekend is an artificial convention in which people play at murder. *Murder, She Wrote* is a show in which people play at murder. All you'd be doing is compounding the felony and underlining what is basically the weakness of our show. Which is its artificiality. In effect, you'd be spoofing the genre and I won't do it."

Instead, the crew work at making the commonplace special with top-notch guest stars, opulent production values, and a superior leading performance that is canny and compassionate. "For our show, the number-one key to success is Angela Lansbury," says Fischer. "Her persona is so ingratiating and so delightful that people tune in to watch. People will tune in to see performers they regard as friends."

On the basis of *Murder, She Wrote*'s ratings, Angela Lansbury is one of the public's best friends. But again, excellent acting and scripting

Angela Lansbury underplaying her overacting again.

Elegance and intelligence—TV's finest female sleuth.

cannot be the only reasons for the format's long-term success. The answer to the mystery of *Murder on the Air* has to go deeper.

"Satisfaction," said Fischer. "That's what they get out of it. It's a nonthreatening show, which is a pretty incredible thing to say, considering that we have a murder a week. We try not to make things too predictable, but overall it's a predictable show, which makes it comfortable. People tune in because they know what they're going to see. And they're going to be able to participate to whatever degree they want to. There are people who don't care whodunit, and there are others who make a real game out of figuring out the murderer's identity before the denouement. We ask you to participate where most other shows don't, and I think that's the big key."

To use the brain. To think. Rational thought distinguishes humans from animals, and it is the reason the mystery form is a perennial one. It allows the reader or viewer to consider the most daunting situation he will ever face, without being unduly upset or threatened. Death is a mystery we will all get to solve, but the great television mystery series allow us to do it with friends.

Afterword

"People who are capable of aberrant behavior on the basis of stimulation will be stimulated by the six o'clock news, which, in many ways, is far more irresponsible in the depiction of violence."

—Steven Bochco

THANKS. I NEEDED THAT.

Having spent more than fifteen years researching television, it's apparent that the form is always improving. Modern series are both more mature and more sophisticated than their predecessors. While many remember the highlights of the "Golden Age," they forget the amazing amount of dross. The dross-to-quality quotient today must make the seventies and eighties the "Platinum Age" of television.

Furthermore, it's continually gratifying to praise overlooked and underrated artists. As I said in the Foreword, television is the most forgettable art form, and these creators' efforts deserve to be acknowledged. It was invigorating to remind myself of the mistake-laden pleasures of the live shows, put Jack Webb and *Dragnet* in perspective, give credit on *Hawaii Five-O*, and champion the likes of *Mannix*.

It was also satisfying to clarify the allure of shows which eluded casual praise. Series like *Barnaby Jones* were easy. All I had to do was watch it to understand the perverse method. My biggest problem was with *Charlie's Angels*. I will admit I was predisposed to liking it—I was trying to approach it in a positive manner—to surprise readers with its affirmative aspects. I failed miserably. Viewing the entire run of that show was like seeing George Romero's trilogy of "Living Dead" movies. I watched the characters die and come back as zombies.

Even after all these fictional deaths, what I'm left with is a feeling of optimism. I was impressed by the conviction and dedication of television's filmmakers. These were not low-regarded creators, struggling to force quality onto the medium—these were the top-line, highest-grossing, most respected artists, whose visions are competed for. The cream does rise on TV and continues to rise.

Having studied the entire history of the industry, it becomes clear that, for the most part, good shows succeed and bad shows fail. Of course there are exceptions (the Angels being one), but they are not the norm. The only thing which concerns me about television is not the fiction, but the way it handles fact.

Thirty years after witnessing my first television murder, there's only one that sticks in my mind. Of all the hundreds of people I've seen killed, I can only remember one of their names. Lee Harvey Oswald.

I find that amazing. What I also find amazing is that since his death in 1963, I can remember only the names of the murderers. I remember because, of the victim and murderer, that is who television wants me to remember. That is who television glorifies and glamorizes.

In order to prevent a further deadening of our culture, television must distinguish between entertainment and news. In an effort to make the latter profitable, TV has rendered the fact shows untrustworthy. The hype has taken over the hope. This is extremely dangerous, as a new generation will find it harder and harder to distinguish between reality and fantasy. What's worse is the feeling of frustration and futility this causes. The new generation is putting faith in nothing—not even itself.

It's a shame that television needs to wallow in agony as well as to observe it. It's too bad it seeks to pander as well as inform. The rationale is that the news and talk shows are only giving the public what they want, but that is a denial of their responsibility to society. If they must cater to the audience's basest desires, it's a pity that producers don't exploit the dead, rather than the deadly. Instead of finding the killer so fascinating, why don't fact shows expatiate on the victim?

Better yet, why not leave the pandering and wallowing to fiction, which is what it's for. Report facts and leave the opinions to the comedies and dramas. This is a vain hope, of course, but it is the one area which cries out for repair. Thankfully, there are other names I can remember besides the real-life serial killers. They are Kane, Barnett, Queen, Friday, Gunn, Bailey, Mannix, McGarrett, Jones, Cannon, Orwell, Rockford, Magnum, Furillo, Kojak, Miller, Columbo, and Fletcher.

These are the heroes who continue to save me. You may have others—Holmes, Ness, Mason, Steed, Peel, or Solo. If you're wondering why they aren't in the book, I can only plead temporary insanity. I attempted to tell the history of television through its most important and influential mystery series. I wanted to share the pleasures and put into context all the great sleuths in this immediate medium. I wanted to illuminate, inform, and entertain. I wanted to do for them what they did for me.

Just the facts, ma'am. Book 'em, Dan-o. Let's be careful out there. Who loves ya, baby?

LA—NY—CT: 5/75–8/88

INDEX